THE CAPTIVES

DON WRIGHT

TOR

A TOM DOHERTY ASSOCIATES BOOK

This is a work of fiction. All the characters and events portrayed in this book are fictitious, and any resemblance to real people or events is purely coincidental.

THE CAPTIVES

Copyright © 1987 by Don Wright

All rights reserved, including the right to reproduce this book, or portions thereof, in any form.

A Tor Book
Published by Tom Doherty Associates, Inc.
175 Fifth Avenue
New York, N.Y. 10010

Tor® is a registered trademark of Tom Doherty Associates, Inc.

ISBN: 0-812-58991-2
Library of Congress Catalog Card Number: 86-51496

First edition: April 1987
First mass market edition: January 1988

Printed in the United States of America

0 9 8 7 6 5 4 3 2

To my Mom and Dad, Joe and Hallie Wright, who, in their own special way, opened new frontiers for my brothers, Joe, David, and me.

Many Thanks To

Tony Burlson who went out of his way to take the time and effort to gather documented maps and records on Bird's invasion of Kentucky. Tony's assistance was invaluable to the historic value of my story.

And to my friend June White—how many times did you type this, June? Eight—nine?

SPECIAL DEDICATION

When one thinks of pioneers, the mind has a natural tendency to transgress a two-hundred-year time span and focus on buckskin-clad men and women who heroically faced the perils of the "Great Unknown Wilderness," with stouthearted, unflinching bravery.

That unselfish willingness to give one's life to open new frontiers is indeed an undisputable element that has helped to make America what it is today—and will continue to do so—for, as we all witnessed on January 28, 1986, that brave pioneer quality is as prevalent now as it was when this nation was aught but an unexplored wilderness.

It is with great admiration and respect that I dedicate this book to the memory of those seven heroic frontiersmen who faced the "Great Unknown Wilderness of space," so that we, the less brave, might someday travel safely and comfortably in their footsteps.

Gregory Jarvis, Sharon Christa McAuliffe, Ronald E. McNair, Ellison S. Onizuka, Judy Resnik, Francis R. Scholee, and Mike Smith, who gave their lives aboard the space shuttle, *Challenger*, January, 28, 1986.

"For they, like the Americans in this story, were true pioneers."

D.K.W.

Scale of Miles
10 20 40 60 80 100

A MAP
Showing the Routes of
Captain Bird's Invasion
into Kentucke & Return to
Detroit with the Captives
in 1780.

Fort Detroit

CANADA

LAKE ERIE

Maumee River

Au Glaize R.

Indian Village
St. Mary's R.
Grand Lake
Hut
Lorimer's Store
Pickawillany Creek

The Portage
Indian Lake

Standing Stone
Wyandot Village
Great Miami River

Piqua Town
Chillicothe
Little Miami River

Falls of
The Ohio

Licking River
Bird's Cannon

N.th Fork

Ruddles Fort
Martins

Patterson's Cabin

OHIO RIVER

Clark's Fort

Salt R.

Harrods

Boonesboro

Kentucky River

Green River

Fort Jefferson

Cumberland River

Mississippi River

Tennessee River

PROLOGUE

WHEN PONTIAC, chief of the Ottawa tribe of the Algonquin nation, surrendered to the British in the year of our Lord 1763, the French and Indian War was brought to a bloody close. It would be the last foreign war ever fought on American soil. Eight long years had passed since General Edward Braddock and his thirteen hundred British troops had set out to capture Fort Duquesne from the French, eight long years since Braddock's inglorious defeat at what historians refer to as the Battle of the Wilderness, eight long years of death and destruction—but it was finally over.

Men who had fought that war trickled homeward to Pennsylvania, to Virginia, to New York; to Massachusetts, Vermont, Rhode Island, New Jersey, glad that it was finished; glad they were still alive.

Morgan Patterson rode slouched in the saddle, bone-weary, as he guided his horse through the streets of Williamsburg, Virginia. The village had changed little since the last time he was home. Home. He had no home. He had left his wife, Susan, in the care of her parents while he went off to war. And on his infrequent visits to Rosemont, the residence of Susan's mother and father, there had been little time to consider building a place of their own.

All that would change now. He was free. He and Susan could pick up the pieces of their war-shattered lives and start over. No, he thought, not start over, start anew. For, in reality, in seven years of marriage they had never been granted the privilege of even sharing a dream together, unless the very fact that they looked forward to that simple pleasure could be considered "sharing a dream."

Patterson had had his fill of killing and violence, and he had had his fill of people. He longed for nothing more than peace and happiness, and the solace of Susan's company—for a life that had thus far been denied them.

As he turned his horse up the lane to Rosemont, his mind drifted to a land he had not seen since childhood, a land of unparalleled beauty—Kentucky. He could smell the bluegrass blowing gently in the breeze, could see the rolling hills of virgin timber, trees fifteen feet in diameter, could taste the clear bubbling streams and rivers. He and Susan could recapture their lost years there; he was sure of it.

Patterson had been at Rosemont for less than a month when Susan woke him in the middle of the night, kissing his lips tenderly. "I was dreaming of Kentucky, Morgan," she whispered, snuggling her cheek against his shoulder, "and in my dreams it was real. I was seeing it as you see it. Go there, darling, find us the most beautiful spot in the world for we will be there a long, long time . . . a lifetime."

Patterson rolled onto his stomach and pushed himself up with his elbows. "I will find you God's own Eden," he promised, gazing down into her young and pretty face, made even more beautiful by the love that shone there. In silence he added, Lord knows, there has been little beauty in your life thus far.

Morgan Patterson went alone, crossing the rugged Appalachian Mountains through the Cumberland Gap, into a country where few white men had ever trod: Kenta-Key, a land of tall cane, of rolling blue grass plains, of majestic forests, a wilderness the Indians called "the dark and bloody grounds." He chose their homesite carefully, selecting a spot on the main branch of the Licking River some twenty miles east of what would later be called the Blue Licks Salt Springs, a spot he knew Susan would love.

He spent the summer exploring eastern Kentucky, hunting, fishing, and girdling timber so it would cure by the time he returned with Susan to begin building their cabin. He carried stone for a chimney, he hacked out a garden plot, and he stretched out at night and dreamed of their life together—and it was good, that dream.

He went back over the mountains in late fall, crossing the Gap just as the trees had taken on their brilliant reds and oranges, yellows and browns, and he longed for the day when Susan could see the magnificence of it. But he didn't ride east toward Virginia. For at the last moment something compelled him, drew him south, across the eastern tip of Tennessee into North Carolina and up the Yadkin River Valley.

That trip to Kentucky, and especially the almost supernatural force that urged him to see the Yadkin, would change his and Susan's lives forever.

In 1764, when Morgan Patterson brought Susan Spencer Patterson—and what belongings they could pack on ten sturdy horses—through the Gap for Susan's first view of her new homeland, not only did Susan's wide, awestruck eyes travel the length and breadth of Kentucky as far as she could see, but so did those of the six-month-old child, Bitsy, who rode in a small, woven cane basket attached to the pommel arch of Susan's saddle.

Patterson rode close and caught Susan's hand.

"A fine land to be bringing up a lass in, don't you think?"

"'Tis truly beautiful, Morgan," she breathed, unable to tear her gaze from the rolling hills and valleys that stretched to the horizons.

She turned at last, leaned from the saddle, and kissed him full on the mouth.

"Thank you for bringing me here. . . . I love Kentucky already."

"And I love you," he returned softly.

They built their cabin together and turned the soil and planted their crops. They laughed and played and sang, and for the first time since they had met, they found peace and tranquillity—and time to truly discover each other, time that war, and threats of war, had denied them.

The Indians knew they were there. But they tolerated the white family's presence in their private hunting grounds because Black Fish, chief of the Shawnee nation, had so ordered it.

But it wasn't until the spring of 1765 that Black Fish made an appearance. Carrying two wild turkeys, he cautiously approached Patterson's cabin. The Indian and the white man stood at arm's length studying one another, each afraid to make the first gesture of recognition—or of the father-son relationship they had once cherished.

It was Susan who broke the ice. Gathering Bitsy in her arms, she walked to Black Fish and held the child up to him. "Tell Black Fish to behold his granddaughter, Morgan."

And eighteen-month-old Bitsy reached out and grabbed a tiny fistful of the Indian's stiff-roached hair and pulled herself toward him. Black Fish's stonelike face shattered into a broad smile and, dropping the turkeys, he took the child into his arms. With Bitsy on his knee, Black Fish squatted and motioned for Patterson to do the same. The two men talked then of the days some twenty years before when Morgan Patterson had lived with the Shawnee as Black Fish's adopted son.

"Ho, Patterson," said the Indian, grinning, "I knew you could never be satisfied in the white man's cities. I knew you would come back to the forest someday."

Patterson grinned, too. "We have come to raise our daughter close to God, Black Fish. We only desire peace and happiness here in Kenta-Key."

The old Indian nodded in agreement. "I will do what I can, Patterson."

From that day forth, although Shawnee frequently approached the Patterson cabin, never was there a hostile look or warlike gesture. Black Fish had given his word.

Still, there were threats and occasionally even a pitched battle in which Susan, and later Bitsy, would stand beside Patterson and defend their small world against the Cherokee, the Creek, and other tribes who ventured into Kentucky to hunt, tribes who were enemies to the Shawnee. But for the most part, the years passed quickly for the trio—quickly and happily, until Black Fish's untimely death during an assault by Colonel John Bowman on Chillicothe, Ohio, in 1779.

And up until that moment, until Black Fish's death, Kentucky was indeed a fine land to bring up a lass in. Bitsy spent her days in the wilderness, hunting and exploring with her father. She spent her evenings at the fireside with Susan, learning to read and write and do womanly chores. She had the best of two worlds and loved them both.

But nothing, no matter how beautiful or fine, could last forever—not even the Eden in Kentucky. In 1774, Morgan, Susan, and Bitsy Patterson watched with mixed emotions as the first settlers filtered into Kentucky. The dawn of progress had begun, and a way of life had ended.

In truth, Susan was elated that they would, after ten years, have white neighbors only forty miles away. So she watched with pleasure as James Harrod, Daniel Boone, Benjamin Logan, and a host of others brought their families into Kentucky and built their fortified strongholds.

To Patterson, however, the westward movement of the pioneers meant trouble, for he knew that wherever white men gathered, confusion and turmoil were not far behind. He was quite correct. Indian problems arose immediately, followed by the inevitable disputes over property rights, then arguments over boundary lines, and finally the heated controversy over who actually had the right to deed property in Kentucky in the first place—the Commonwealth of Virginia or the British Crown.

That argument came to a head two years later when America went to war against Britain. It was then that the Pattersons, along with their fellow Kentuckians, made their choice. They were, and always had been, Americans.

CHAPTER
· 1 ·

Detroit—April 3, 1780

CHARD IS THE handsomest officer in the Eighth Regiment, decided the pretty barwench as she admired the tall, well-built young man who had just entered the tavern. And indeed, Ensign Richard Morgan Southhampton, with his dark hair, pale blue eyes, and chiseled, aquiline features would turn any woman's head—and he knew it.

"You are wasting your time making moon eyes over Chard Southhampton, Marge," said a lieutenant at a near-by table. "He's up to his arse in preparations to evacuate Detroit. Bloody hell, but he's anxious to get to Kentucky and do battle with George Rogers Clark and his rag-tag Militia."

He was up to his arse in something else three nights ago, thought the girl. But all she said was "War is all you soldiers ever think about." She knew she had made a mistake even before the words were out of her mouth.

"Some of us think about other things." His hand groped at her waist to draw her onto his lap. "But you never give us a tumble. Leastways, not when Chard's around, and he don't give a damn about you, or any of these local lasses who swoon at his feet."

"Go cry in your ale," she said, moving out of his reach. "I'll fancy who I please."

But she knew the lieutenant was right. Chard was obsessed with the idea of honorable warfare, of leading his troops across the open battlefield amid the roll of drums, the high-pitched whine of musket fire, the roar of cannon. It was all he talked about, except when they made love, which

6

was too infrequently to suit her. Indeed, he had hardly been around at all since the troops had been ordered to prepare their field gear for an extended march on Kentucky.

Margaret was not aware of, nor would she have understood, the passion with which Chard viewed the coming campaign. He saw it as a thrilling crusade that would offer him the opportunity to excel as an officer and a gentleman. He had purchased his commission in the British Royal Army for one purpose: to prove to his father, Major James Southhampton, that he was worthy of the man's love and respect. And he could think of no better way to accomplish that goal than by demonstrating his skill and courage on the battlefield. After all, that was where his father had gained his rank and position during the French and Indian War.

"Hello, love," called the girl as she ducked around the lieutenant's table and hastened up to Chard. "Decided to pay us a visit, did you? What will you have?"

Chard did not miss the open invitation in her voice or the burning desire in her eyes, though she tried to conceal both. But at that moment he was too preoccupied with his own yearnings to be bothered by her needs.

"A cup of ale, lass, and a bit of privacy," he said, seating himself by the door.

"My, aren't you the surly one," she laughed, not at all offended by his rebuff. In truth, she considered herself quite fortunate to have been granted upon occasion the honor of his company—an honor that nearly every female in Detroit secretly coveted.

"Will you be coming up later?" she whispered, setting a full mug before him.

Chard looked at her over the rim of the cup. "I told you, Marge, I've got more important things to consider."

"Another woman?" She raised her eyebrows.

Chard frowned. He resented possessiveness and would tolerate it in no one, except his mother. " 'Tis none of your business, but no, I'm not meeting another woman."

"You are a poor liar," she said, smiling saucily. "You should learn to mask your emotions. Who is she? . . . C'mon, lad, who's the lucky trollop?"

Chard's face darkened thunderously, and he rose slow-

7

ly off the bench. "Just because I pleasure your body, Marge, you have no right to assume that you are aught but a bedmate . . . a circumstance which I can change immediately if you insist upon sticking your face in my personal business."

Margaret took a quick step backwards. She had never seen Chard angry, and the look in his eyes frightened her. What had she said to trigger such fury? In the past they had joked many times about his conquests.

"I'm sorry, love," she whispered. "I didn't mean a word of it, really I didn't."

A clamor for more ale from the far side of the room broke the tension, and Chard slumped down on the bench. Margaret hurried a tray of mugs to the table and without ceremony banged them down in front of the patrons. She resented their intrusion, for she wanted to get back to Chard and smooth things out. She had no false impression of what she meant to him. He was a titled blueblood; and she was much too realistic to foolishly entertain the idea that she could ever be anything more than his sleeping partner. But that was enough. For, even though he was arrogant and on occasion a bit cruel, Chard could make the lowliest woman feel as though she were indeed a grand lady. "Aye," Margaret sighed, as she turned toward his table. "I love you for that, Chard . . . for being different from the others."

But he was gone.

Chard stood in the drizzling rain and strained to see what was transpiring in the darkness beneath the parapet of Fort Detroit's West Palisade.

He thought about what he had told Margaret. He had not lied when he said he was not meeting another woman. What he had failed to admit, however, was that he intended to spy on one. But the woman was not a trollop; she was Lady Judith Ann Cornwallace Southhampton. His mother. And it was not the first time he had secretly observed her. He had followed her twice in the past week and a half.

It had been by accident that first time. Slipping out of

Margaret's room at midnight, he had chanced upon Judith cautiously returning to the building that housed several high-ranking officers and their wives. He had wondered about it, but then dismissed it. Less than a week ago, however, he had again encountered his mother slipping down a dark alley. The incidents were so out of character that he could not help puzzling over her strange comings and goings. So, feeling guilty for spying, but determined to satisfy his mounting curiosity, he had watched her house for four nights in a row. His patience had finally paid off.

"Does your husband suspect anything?" asked Abraham Chapline, captured major of the Continental Army of the United States.

Judith pushed a lock of silver-gold hair off her forehead, tucking it under the edge of the dark hood that all but hid her small, aristocratic face.

"No. He suspects nothing."

"Ma'am," said Chapline, leaning close so he could see her face, "are you certain you want to go through with this?"

"I'm sure." She lied, refusing to meet his eyes. The truth was, she detested her decision to help Chapline escape. She was a British noblewoman, cousin to the first Marquis Charles Cornwallis, who at that very instant was directing the British campaign against the American general, Nathanael Greene, in North Carolina. She was wife to Major James Southhampton, the aide to Captain Henry Bird of His Majesty's Royal Eighth Regiment. And she was mother to Ensign Richard Morgan Southhampton, who was in charge of artillery in that same regiment.

No, she was not at all sure she wanted to go through with her decision to aid the enemy, even though it had been her scheme from the very beginning, ever since she had heard that Britain intended to invade Kentucky.

Invade Kentucky? Judith knew that was not the entire reason. Actually, she had reached the decision when voices awakened her in the middle of the night some three weeks ago and she found her husband deep in conversation with Simon and George Girty, the most notorious white renegades under British employ. She had paled at the enormity of what her eavesdropping revealed: Hundreds upon hundreds of savage Indians would join the British Army, using the army's superior weaponry and military expertise to accomplish a feat that, try as they might, had thus far been denied them: to capture and destroy the American forts in Kentucky.

"If they catch you," continued Chapline, "they'll try you as a spy. 'Tis not too late to change your mind, ma'am."

It was too late that first day I sought you out, she thought bitterly. You, an American prisoner of war who has given his word of honor that he will not attempt to escape, and I, a trusted officer's wife who is believed to be above suspicion. She raised her eyes to his, and her voice was angry. "There's no need in discussing it, Major Chapline. We have flung aside our integrity and self-respect. I just pray we are doing the right thing."

"I know we are, ma'am. But I would sure hate to see a fine lady like you, one who is Christian and humane, wind up on the wrong end of the gallows."

Christian and humane? She almost laughed outright. Nothing about her was Christian or humane. Her decision to help Chapline was purely selfish.

She nearly blurted out that her only reason for sending him off to warn the Kentucky settlements of the bloodbath her husband and the Girtys were planning was to alert one man of the danger that was brewing, a man she had been in love with twenty-five years before. A man she was still in love with. Instead, she removed a coil of rope from beneath her cloak and handed it to Chapline.

"I hid a musket and shot pouch in a hollow chestnut tree where the road enters the forest."

"I know the place," he said, drawing the rope through his large hands, testing its strength. Then, as though reluctant to suggest such a possibility but too concerned for her well-being not to, he said, "You could come with me, ma'am. I'd feel better knowing you were safely away from Detroit." As if to punctuate his words, an eerie light

10

flickered momentarily as a blast of lightning lit up the area under the parapet, bringing Judith into bold relief for all the world to see. But the only witness to the conspiracy was Chard, who was stricken by the revelation.

"That is out of the question," snapped Judith. "Besides, I can help your cause more by continuing to work from the inside. I will do my best to slow the army, though as of this minute, I have no idea how I might accomplish such a thing."

"You've already done enough, ma'am. If I get back to Kentucky, I'll make it plain what you have done—"

"Never!" she cried, forgetting the danger she placed them in by raising her voice. "You tell General Clark everything I have told you. If for some reason you can't reach Clark, then, and only then, pass the intelligence on to . . . Morgan Patterson. But under no circumstances are you to reveal my name. Do you under—"

Chapline clamped his hand over her mouth and drew her close. Fearfully, she followed his eyes to the parapet above, where the footfalls of the night guard could be felt more than heard, for a strong wind had sprung up, pushing the turbulent clouds together with such force that the sky belched forth its angry protest with tremendous crashes of thunder and lightning, drowning out all other sound.

"If he heard you, we're dead," whispered Chapline. His eyes moved slowly along the bottom of the overhead walkway as though he could see through the rough planking to the guard, whose steps had become suspiciously stilted.

Judith could taste the nervous sweat of Chapline's palm as he forced his hand even more tightly over her mouth. She knew her thoughtless outcry could mean the ruin of their well-laid plans, and she could joyfully have bitten her tongue. But she would rather have abandoned the venture than have Morgan Patterson know that it was she who had alerted Kentucky. She had no doubt that should he learn of her part in Chapline's escape, he would not believe anything the man reported.

"He heard us!" breathed Chapline, gripping Judith's shoulders with such force that she winced. "Quick, now! Keep to the shadows under the walkway and run for your life!"

Above the sound of the wind, Judith could hear the guard's pounding feet as he raced for the ladder that ascended the parapet. Dropping her shoulder, she slammed into the startled Kentuckian, propelling him deeper into the shadows under the overhang, and, before he could stop her, bolted into the unprotected area of the common grounds.

Then, as if the elements had been waiting for an opportunity to betray her, a tremendous bolt of lightning lit the skies with such clarity that the entire area was illuminated as bright as day.

Chapline groaned deep in his throat as the guard shouted for Judith to halt. Then his breath caught as Judith faltered, for it appeared that she did indeed have every intention of stopping. He opened his mouth to urge her on, but she had already gathered her skirts above her ankles and, glancing fearfully over her shoulder, fled down a dark alleyway.

Chapline eased farther under the parapet as the guard raced down the ladder and sprinted to the spot where Judith had disappeared. He prayed that she had gotten safely away, but he didn't dwell on it. She was giving him his one chance to escape, and by God, he would take it. He caught the edge of the overhead planks and swung himself aloft. Quickly fashioning a loop in Judith's rope, he slipped it over a pointed stake in the palisade and flipped himself over the side. Had he glanced toward the alley where Judith had run, he might very well have climbed back into the fort, for just as the guard raced into the dark avenue a figure stepped from the shadows and smashed the hilt of a small pearl-handled dagger into the tender spot behind the man's ear. The guard dropped as though poleaxed.

Chard eyed the fallen man carefully to be sure he was unconscious. His fingers gripped the dagger handle nervously. He was well aware that for his mother's sake he should permanently close the guard's mouth. But when he bent to slash the blade across the man's throat, his hand trembled so that he cut the soldier's chin instead. The sickening truth was he did not have the courage to murder a man, even to guarantee his own mother's safety. Detesting himself, he searched for an excuse that would justify his

12

hesitancy. Again and again, he mentally gauged the distance from the parapet to the alley, finally persuading himself that on such a dark night there was no chance that the guard could have recognized Judith. He gritted his teeth, refusing to consider the consequences should he be mistaken.

The simple fact was, he had never killed a man. And he did not intend to—not in cold blood. He would serve the king and Britain dutifully, without question, and would gladly give his life to defend the Union Jack against those who would throw it over for the pretense of freedom. But he would never murder a fellow Englishman, a soldier in his own regiment. It was unthinkable. Yet, the young ensign was bitterly aware that this was but an excuse. He was indeed the coward his father thought him.

Chard would probably have stood there until the guard regained consciousness had not the drizzling rain finally given way to a full-fledged downpour, forcing him to seek shelter. Gauging the distance from the soldier to the parapet one last time, he struck off in a fast walk toward Margaret's small room over the tavern. He needed her.

Judith slipped into her dark bedchamber, easing the door shut with the greatest of care. Silently, she sped to the oversized wardrobe and hung her dripping cloak on a rear peg. Only then did she glance at the huge, finely carved canopy bed where her husband lay. She took a deep breath and slowly released it; he was asleep. Had the room not been dark, she would have seen the almost insane flash of hatred that filled James Southhampton's slitted eyes as he took in her wet, disheveled appearance.

Judith stepped out of her damp dress and smallclothes, and quickly pulled her nightgown over her head. As quietly as possible, she tiptoed across the room, her eyes on her husband's bulky outline beneath the heavy quilt. She shuddered to think what would happen should he awaken. Not a half-dozen times in the twenty-four years of their marriage had he demanded his rights as a husband, and not once had she given herself freely. Yet, since arriving at Detroit, and especially of late, it seemed that he made

13

a point of taking her against her will. So it was with mounting fear and anxiety that she stealthily slipped between the sheets. After several long moments of rigid suspense in which her husband did not stir, she allowed herself another relieved sigh.

Slowly the tension of the past few weeks began to abate. Perhaps now that Chapline was safely on his way to Kentucky, the strain would lessen and she would sleep peacefully for the first time since she had deliberately sought him out and presented her plan of escape. She smiled demurely; midnight rendezvous were for young lovers, not for ladies in their early forties.

Judith, however, neither looked nor felt forty-three. Indeed, she could very easily have been mistaken for someone ten years younger. But at the moment, she felt old beyond her years.

To her husband, James Southhampton, who lay wide awake beside her, his smoldering anger fanning into a raging fire, Judith was the perfect picture of the unfaithful wife. He was aware of her midnight meetings, he had even attempted to follow, but that had proved too difficult, so he contented himself with taking her by force whenever he assumed she had been with her lover.

Southhampton could feel his pulse quickening, pounding at his temples. He hated Judith with an all-consuming passion that could only be quenched by hurting her physically and emotionally. Without warning, he flung his body over hers and ground his mouth harshly against the softness of her full lips, his teeth raking the delicate flesh until it split.

Southhampton wound his fist so tightly in her long silver-gold hair that she cried out, the sound muffled by the pressure of his unyielding mouth over hers. His free hand slipped beneath her nightgown and plunged between her thighs, which she immediately crossed, imprisoning his searching fingers as neatly as if they had been locked in a vise.

In a rage, Southhampton tore the flimsy shift from her body, his eyes probing her nakedness, searching for signs of a recent sexual encounter, and of course he found what he was looking for. That the scratches and bruises that marred her skin were the same ones he had inflicted three nights ago meant nothing.

Judith clenched her teeth in anticipation of what was to come and prayed that it would be over quickly. But the humiliation of opening her legs to him birthed an anger in her so acute that, against all common sense, Judith twisted her hips away, preventing entry. She was sick of being debased by a man who used a piece of worthless paper called a marriage contract as a lever to exploit her. Husbandly rights? Did he have the right to rape her whenever he pleased? Then, as if in answer to her question, Southhampton spoke: "You spread your legs wide for whoever it is you go to meet, but you would deny the same privilege to your lawful husband?" His face turned even more cruel. "Like bloody hell you will. I'll take what is mine; 'tis my right!"

His hand raked between her thighs and dug deep into the delicate tissue below her pubic hair. Then, slowly, he exerted every ounce of pressure he was capable of in what Judith was sure was a genuine attempt to twist the soft mound completely free of her body.

She fully intended to scream at him, to defy his belief that she was his to do with as he pleased. But when she did speak, all that came out was a long agonized wail, begging him to take her, to do anything he desired, just so long as he stopped hurting her.

When it was over, she just wanted to lie there and tell herself over and over again that helping Major Chapline to escape was worth the hell she had just endured. But she wasn't allowed even that luxury, for Southhampton used those precious moments to attack her in the one place he had yet to despoil.

"Someday," he said, rolling off her sweat-drenched body, "I will tell the boy about you—about your past." Then he laughed as her stomach convulsed and she hung her head limply over the edge of the bed and vomited.

WITH A CRITICAL eye, Colonel Morgan Patterson watched the progress of the fort he was building at the confluence of the Ohio and Mississippi rivers, but he could find little fault with the job the men were doing. Fort Jefferson was taking shape in spite of the rain that some silly romantic had labeled April showers which, in fact, were torrential downpours that had lasted well beyond their normal span, for the month of May was just a week away.

Two workmen, shouldering a sharply pointed log that was to become part of the stockade wall, sloshed past Patterson in the slippery mud.

"If this blasted rain keeps up, Colonel, we'll jest float these goddamn logs into place."

"Might just do that," returned Patterson, his deeply lined face breaking into a boyish grin.

The men chuckled and trudged on toward the palisade, which needed several more of the pointed stakes before Patterson could mark it off his list as completed. Patterson's satisfied gaze roved slowly across the area; the blockhouses were finished, and most of the perimeter buildings were in the final stages of completion. The parapets were being built almost as quickly as the palisades were in place. Yes, the fort was coming along nicely, and Patterson knew a moment of pride for a job well done. General Clark would be more than pleased when he returned from St. Louis.

Patterson drew his rain-soaked deerskin hunting frock closer about his throat and splashed toward the long, low cabin that served as a tavern, dining hall, hospital, and meeting place. The building was nearly deserted, except for a scattering of men who lay on straw-stuffed pallets. One or two of them, Patterson was sure, were not sick at all, but were momentarily shirking their duties for the attention of the shapely French lasses from Kaskaskia who served as nurses, cooks, maids, and, of course, the inevitable "companions."

Patterson avoided glancing at the men as he pulled the

heavy oaken door shut. He could hardly blame them for feigning illness to be near the women, for most of them had come with Clark from Kentucky and, like him, had seen neither friends nor family for months.

Patterson also refused to look toward the hearth where a large black iron cauldron bubbled and hissed, giving off a mouth-watering aroma of venison stew, for he knew that the girl who served the meals would be watching him with warm, intense black eyes. She was Señorita Consetta Delmira, the daughter of a Spanish nobleman who was the officer in charge of the garrison at St. Louis. Conte Philippe Delmira had asked for and received permission to observe the construction of the wilderness fortification.

On their arrival, Delmira and his daughter had set up quarters in a cabin adjacent to Patterson's. Although a lady of quality, Consetta Delmira had insisted on working in the crude dining hall, doing her part to assist in the building of a fort that would "help keep St. Louis safe." Of late, however, when Patterson took his meals, she openly and with obvious admiration took great pains to serve him personally. No matter how innocent, the attention spawned a certain amount of malicious gossip that neither Patterson, as officer and leader of the men of Fort Jefferson, nor Consetta, as a single lady of high standing, could well afford.

Patterson crossed the room and joined two junior officers who were warming their insides with tankards of hot rum.

"Fort's lookin' good, Morgan," said Captain John Slaughter. "She'll be flyin' the colors before summer if this rain'll let up."

Patterson shook the water from his tricorne and hung it on a peg.

"With a little luck," he said, signaling the commissary agent for a hot mug before slumping down on a half-log bench, "we'll be flyin' the colors by the middle of May."

From across the room, Consetta Delmira tried to appear engrossed in the conversation of the young man standing next to her, but her eyes kept sliding to Morgan Patterson. She did not understand the reasons for the fluttering in her breast when she was near the American

17

colonel. It was there, it was real, and that was all that mattered. Unaware of her rudeness, she left the young man in midsentence and hastened to the bar where the agent was pouring Patterson's drink.

"I will take it to the colonel, señor," she said, avoiding the man's eyes.

"Well, I don't know, Miss Consetta." The agent flushed. "Your father would not appreciate his daughter—"

"I will handle my father, señor," she returned coolly. "The rum, if you please."

She took the steaming mug and, oblivious to the stares of those around her, moved gracefully to Patterson's table.

Patterson was startled, embarrassed, then angered by Consetta's sudden appearance. Ladies of quality did not lower themselves to the position of barmaid—not for any reason.

Rising abruptly, he walked quickly from the room.

Patterson wasn't really surprised when he answered the soft knock on his office door late that same night, but as he raised the latch he tried to tell himself that he was. Consetta's words—"I apologize for upsetting you this afternoon, Señor Colonel"—were nothing more than a formality. He knew why she was there.

Patterson framed himself in the doorway and studied the girl's sodden appearance. It was obvious that she had stood for some time in the downpour before summoning the courage to knock.

"Miss Delmira," he said with a touch of guilt, "it isn't fitting for a young lady of your station to be here this time of night."

"I . . . I could not sleep, knowing that I had angered you."

The girl bowed her head against the driving rain, which forced her to look up at Patterson through her long wet lashes. The look was not wasted. Patterson wondered how women, no matter their age, knew exactly how to emphasize and play upon their best features and wasted no time in using them to their advantage.

"You didn't anger me, Miss Delmira, so there's no need in your losing sleep . . . go on home."

He would have shut the door in her face had Consetta not darted past him. Before Patterson could stop her, she shed her cloak and moved to the hearth where a cheerful fire blazed. Extending her hands toward the warmth, she murmured, "The rain still has the chill of winter in it, even though it is spring."

"Damn cold rain," agreed Patterson, for lack of anything better to say, knowing how foolish he appeared holding the door open to the elements.

"I truly am sorry for embarrassing you," said Consetta, cocking her head sweetly and thrusting out her lower lip. "But I thought you would be pleased when I served your rum. It is said that your wife was a barmaid before you were married—and it is also said that she is very beautiful, and that I bear a most striking resemblance to her."

Patterson slammed the door.

"Who in hell have you been talking to?"

"Why, señor," said the girl, her eyes big with innocence, "friends of yours who have known you for years. They say you are a legend in Kentucky, and that everyone knows all about you."

Patterson crossed the room in two strides and caught Consetta by her shoulders. "I'll have no mere slip of a girl, who is barely older than my daughter, belittling a woman as fine as my wife."

Consetta's eyes widened, and anger flashed deep in their dark pupils.

"Look at me, Señor Patterson," she demanded. "I am not your daughter, and I would die before I would say aught against your wife. I was only trying to be like her, because I thought you would—" The girl spun free and turned her back to Patterson, and he was sure she was crying.

But a moment later when she again faced him, he was startled to find her laughing.

"You are not angry because you think I have slighted your wife. Oh, no! You are angry because you have just this minute realized why you are drawn to me."

"Let's get one thing straight," said Patterson, studying the girl long and hard. "You do remind me of my wife when

19

she was your age. But I'm not drawn to you, nor would I ever be." He took her cloak and wrapped it about her slim shoulders, then turned her toward the door.

Consetta spun toward Patterson, her face a mixture of anger and disbelief. "But you have been in the Illinois country for two years. And it is said that not once have you taken a woman."

Patterson exhaled through his teeth, then took a deep breath.

"I know this will sound old-fashioned, Miss Delmira, but I am in love with my wife."

In the ensuing silence, Patterson watched the young woman intently. She did indeed remind him of Susan—so much so that a great ache spread through his loins. But as he gazed into Consetta's upturned face, he knew there was much more involved than his need for a woman's body. He wished for the girl's sake that he could tell her how he felt about his wife. But Patterson seldom if ever exposed his true self to anyone, friend or foe. He couldn't begin to explain to Consetta that should he, even once, prove unfaithful to Susan, he would shatter the trust and purity of his and Susan's relationship, which could never be recaptured. Something beautiful, perhaps the intimacy of knowing that they had never belonged to another, would be gone forever. Patterson's silence struck the young woman like an open-handed blow.

The girl's eyes blazed. "You make me ashamed of my feelings, señor; the beautiful dreams that fill me with longing, the thoughts that leave me weak with hunger for you, the tenderness that is in me—they are not cheap. I will not let you make them so."

Consetta brushed past him and hastened toward the door.

Patterson caught her by the shoulders and turned her so that she was forced to look into his face. He was abashed by her honest admission and, whether he would admit it or not, pleased by it.

"Consetta," he said, appeasingly, "you are a beautiful girl, and I cherish your friendship—" Before he could go on, she slipped from his grasp and flung her arms about his neck, kissing him long and passionately.

Patterson was astounded by the young woman's
20

strength. He attempted to break free, but she clung to him with the desperation of one who has offered all and is terrified of rejection. Alarm made him push her roughly aside. He eyed her hotly. Her advances had kindled long dormant desires that he had subdued at great cost, and he was angry at her, at the situation, and at himself for responding.

"Would you have me dishonor my wife and, by so doing, dishonor myself?" he flung at the girl.

She stepped back, her full red lips trembling with bitter resentment. Then, slowly, great tears welled in her eyes.

"Señor," she said softly, "I came here tonight to dishonor myself for you—and it is obvious that I have done so."

Patterson made no move to stop her as she ran blindly into the driving rain. She slipped and fell, then stumbled on, until finally she was lost in a prison of a million thin silver bars that splashed noisily just outside the door. After she was gone, he felt not merely alone as he had been for the past two years, but lonely. It was the emptiness that filled a healthy human being who had been without affection for much too long.

He walked slump-shouldered to the table that served as desk, eating place, and catchall, and dropped heavily into a rough hand-hewn chair. After a time, he forced himself to study the plans of Fort Jefferson, plans that he had memorized weeks before. But his thoughts kept returning to the lovely young woman and her soft lips and yielding body.

And he was honest enough with himself to know that he had used his entire supply of honor and self-control that evening. With a deep sigh, he prayed that Clark would hurry his business in St. Louis, because Morgan Patterson needed to go home.

Ruddle's Fort, Kentucky—May 8, 1780

THE HOME MORGAN PATTERSON thought about was over three hundred miles east of Fort Jefferson. The same driving rain that pelted the Michigan and Illinois country seemed to pick up tempo when it reached Kentucky.

The lowlands quickly turned to quagmires and bogs, treacherous to travel; rivers rose alarmingly, their currents too swift to navigate in a birchbark or dugout; and creeks that were normally ankle deep became raging torrents impossible to cross. Throughout the spring, the Kentuckians had been forced to sit by their fires and twiddle their thumbs in a frustrated idleness that threatened to drive the inhabitants of the overcrowded forts and stations completely out of their minds with cabin fever.

Susan Patterson and her sixteen-year-old daughter, Bitsy, were no exception as they knelt beside the large hearth in the one-room cabin they shared with two other families, and attempted to coax a respectable blaze from an eternally damp supply of firewood.

"Good Lord in heaven," complained Bitsy as the small flame she was fanning flickered and died. "I'm sick to death of wet wood, wet clothing, wet everything—just sick, Mama."

Susan gathered a handful of dry tinder and laid it close. Once again, she struck flint to steel, catching a spark in a piece of charcloth, which she expertly tucked into a bird's nest of tow. She gently blew on the smoldering cloth until the tow burst into flame, and then slipped the fire beneath the dry tinder. The shavings popped and crackled, and finally they, too, erupted into a live blaze.

"Blaspheming the good Lord won't help a thing, Bitsy," said Susan, adding more sticks to the flame. "It's our own fault that we are having such a hard time with the fire. We were lazy last night and didn't bank the coals properly."

"No lectures, please, Mama." The girl moved to a small paneless window and drew aside the greased paper that did little to keep out the elements. She gazed out at the common grounds, which were cluttered with tents, lean-tos, troughs, barrels, firewood, ash hoppers, farming implements, saddles and bridles, household goods, and 'most everything else that the folk who inhabited the fort wished to keep safe from the thieving Indians. For Ruddle's

Station, like all the forts in Kentucky, was overcrowded tenfold because of frequent Indian attacks over the past two years.

"I wasn't lecturing," came Susan's dry denial, "but if I decide to, you will listen. I know it's been a long, hard winter, but that's no excuse for you to be short with me, Bitsy."

The girl sighed. "I am just tired of being cooped up here at Ruddle's Fort. I know we're fortunate to have a cabin instead of a lean-to or canvas shelter like some of the others who have come in from their homesteads, but we've been here for months, and I am sick of never having any privacy." The girl looked at her mother and frowned. "I hear them at night even when they . . . make love. Don't you hear them, Mama?"

"I hear them," answered Susan casually. But Bitsy noticed a hint of a blush on her mother's cheeks, and she wondered about it.

Susan had indeed heard the undeniable sounds of intercourse from time to time. And on those nights she would lie on her feather mattress and cover her ears with her pillow. Not because she found the sexual sounds offensive, for they were one of the givens of a cramped, fortified existence, but because they kindled in her a fiery passion for the only man she had ever known intimately, the only man she had ever desired—her husband, Morgan Patterson.

"Mama," said Bitsy seriously, "I'm near grown, and we've never talked . . ."

Susan blushed even more, the color heightening the loveliness of her face. "You are not yet grown, young lady," she said sternly, "and there will be ample time for us to talk when you are."

But she knew that wasn't true. Bitsy was a mature young woman, and her natural curiosity about life, sex, and, lately, men was surfacing quite normally. Although Susan was not prudish, her Christian teachings strictly forbade discussing such subjects or even thinking such thoughts. Still, she knew that one day soon, teachings or no teachings, she would have to have a long talk with Bitsy.

23

She added more kindling to the flames and stood up. She, too, was restless, but it was not the anxiety of youth or her cramped existence that disturbed her, for at the age of forty-two she had seen bad times and Indian scares aplenty. No, it was a mixture of things over which she had no control. The rebellion was in its fifth year, which was incredible in itself; her husband had gone with George Rogers Clark and had not yet returned; and in the two years of his absence, Bitsy had blossomed into a lovely young woman, which had significantly increased Susan's burden of responsibility. Abstractedly, she tucked a lock of thick black hair into the bun at the nape of her neck. If only Morgan would come home . . . Aye, she was fast losing control over Bitsy, and having to be both mother and father to the girl for the past two years had certainly not been easy.

Although Susan was sympathetic to the first stirrings of her daughter's emotional maturing, she was also aware that she was powerless to help or advise Bitsy. In the girl's present state of mind, everything Susan suggested was considered meddling. If she made a demand on Bitsy's time, she was being overbearing. If she commented on Bitsy's appearance, she was narrow-minded and unreasonable. All Susan could do was to pray that somehow she could quietly help guide Bitsy into womanhood as painlessly as possible—and Bitsy wasn't making it any easier with her endless accusations that Susan was trying to ruin her entire life. Yes, she wished Morgan were home. Bitsy idolized her father; perhaps she would even listen to him . . . perhaps.

"I am sick of being an orphan and you a widow," Bitsy went on, as though she had been reading Susan's mind.

"You are no orphan," snapped Susan with an unaccustomed abruptness that made Bitsy cast a startled glance in her mother's direction.

"'Twas only a figure of speech, Mama," she said, wondering what had come over Susan. "I know Papa is alive and well. I just meant that we've been alone so long I'm beginning to feel abandoned."

"I'll hear no more talk of widows, orphans, or being abandoned," said Susan with a finality that left Bitsy feeling guilty, but not knowing why. It didn't enter her mind that Susan, too, was sick to death of fort life and the concessions it forced on a lone woman with a child to raise.

Bitsy almost jumped with relief when the cabin door burst open and Captain Isaac Ruddle stuck his head in.

"Word just came from Harrodsburg," he shouted above the din of the driving rain. "Major Chapline is back. He's more dead than alive, but he brought word that the British are going to march on Kentucky this summer." He grinned at the shock on Susan's and Bitsy's faces. "Don't worry, lasses, the British can't possibly get here before late July or early August—if they get here at all. And by then, General Clark and Morgan will be back to raise an army of our own. Chapline has sent a messenger to St. Louis to fetch 'em home."

Ruddle slammed the door, and the startled women could hear him splashing through the mud to enlighten the next cabin. For a stunned instant Susan and Bitsy didn't move, didn't breathe. Then bedlam broke loose: they laughed and hugged each other close, danced and clapped their hands. The carefully controlled tension of the past months burst like a soap bubble, wiping from their minds the threat of savage Indians, the lonely days and lonelier nights, the hunger, the cold, and all the other hardships that two lone women on the frontier were forced to endure. It was as if those misfortunes had never existed: Morgan Patterson was coming home.

CHAPTER

· 2 ·

ON THE MORNING OF May 10, 1780, Major A. S. DePeyster, acting governor of Detroit, called a meeting of his subordinates who would command the long-awaited assault on Kentucky.

Among the men crowded into the small office were Captain Henry Bird, the senior officer in charge of the expedition; the well-known Tories, Alexander McGee and Matthew Elliott, whose job it was to handle the supplies and transportation; the notorious white savages, Simon and George Girty, who would recruit Indian allies and act as hunters, guides, and interpreters; and, seated in the only chair besides DePeyster's, Major James Southhampton, who, with his knowledge of the American frontier, would accompany the expedition as aide to Captain Bird and general advisor to the army.

Richard Morgan Southhampton, junior officer in charge of the six cannon that would be transported to Kentucky, leaned casually against the doorframe.

Major DePeyster sized up the men before him.

"Gentlemen, we leave for Kentucky at daybreak tomorrow." He watched their faces for the expected reaction and was rewarded with smiling hurrahs and handshakes all around. They had waited weeks to hear those words.

DePeyster waited for the congratulations to subside, then continued, "Since the scalp of the American, Chapline, has not been brought in by the Indians we sent after him, we must assume that he is on his way to the falls of the Ohio to warn the Kentuckians of our intentions."

The commandant eyed the men before him. "I need not tell you that Chapline's escape robbed us of the element of surprise . . . unless we move with extreme haste and attack Clark's Fort before it has ample time to prepare."

DePeyster rubbed his hand across his jaw. "I'd give a king's ransom to know the name of the woman who helped Major Chapline escape. I'd hang her for the traitor that she is. 'Tis a shame the guard did not see her face."

Chard felt perspiration dampen his armpits as he envisioned his mother hanging from the gallows, no longer beautiful, no longer sensitive and charming, no longer alive.

He shuddered, then glanced quickly about the room to be sure no one had noticed. His eyes locked with those of Simon Girty, and for an instant Chard panicked, for the reptilian expression glinting there gave Chard the eerie feeling that the man knew his most secret thoughts.

But then Southhampton was speaking and Girty's deadly gaze swung to him. "You cannot treat Americans honorably, Major DePeyster, for they have no honor. 'Twas folly to allow one, even a so-called officer and gentleman, freedom of the city. Chapline should have been hanged immediately. As for the woman, she is probably one of these American bitches who warm our beds while plotting ways to cut our throats."

DePeyster flushed at the veiled insult. It was he who had allowed the American officer to move freely about Detroit. But when he spoke, his words were regulated. "We are not savages, Major Southhampton. For a hundred years, we have paroled captive officers on their word of honor, and we will continue to do so in the future. It is the way of civilized warfare."

Southhampton jumped to his feet and leaned across DePeyster's desk.

"Damn civilized warfare, sir. These are not ladies and gentlemen we are fighting here in the colonies; they are peasants, the scum of the earth."

DePeyster's face turned crimson.

"Major Southhampton, your military record for service during the French and Indian War is well known. I am surprised, sir, to hear you voice such an opinion of the Americans. You, of all people, should know that they are proud and arrogant, and they hold their aristocracy in such high esteem that one cannot help but respect them for it."

Southhampton leaned forward and stared into the governor's face.

"That statement, sir, brinks on treason."

DePeyster rose slowly out of his chair, his face ashen.

"Major, it is not treason to respect your enemies. In the late French and Indian War, General Braddock held his American allies in contempt. You were there. What was his reward?"

When Southhampton didn't respond, DePeyster continued. "His army was annihilated and the general himself killed. And now, a quarter of a century later, history has shown that the only fighting that made any impression on the French and Indians was that of the American Militia." DePeyster stabbed Southhampton with a hard look, then settled back into his chair. "Furthermore, Major Southhampton, many of the men and women who have settled the American frontier are not peasants. They are as wealthy and as well educated as our own noblemen—and they consider themselves our equals."

"Piss on their considerations," said Southhampton, drawing himself to his full height. "They are traitors to the Crown and should be dealt with accordingly."

DePeyster took a deep breath. "Major Southhampton, when this war is over, whom do you think will open the western lands for the Crown? It will be those same people who are there now. And they will once again be loyal British subjects."

Captain Henry Bird, who had been studying Southhampton through narrowed eyes, spoke before the major could reply. "When we take Clark's Fort at the falls of the Ohio, Major Southhampton, the rest of the country will be subdued. They will clamor for the protection of the Union Jack."

"Let them clamor!" shouted Southhampton. "They can bloody well clamor in hell, as far as I am concerned."

George Girty crossed his arms, Indian fashion. In the dim candlelight of the windowless room, he indeed looked

28

the part of the savage. His angular face was weather-browned to the hue of boot leather, and his coal-black hair, fashionably clubbed in the back, was adorned with the tailfeather of a turkey. His buckskin hunting frock was stained and greasy, as were his leggings and breechclout. "Well said, Major," came his rasping voice. "My brother and me are in complete agreement with you. The Kentuckians will never be subdued until they are dead—all of them, every man, woman, and child."

Chard was chilled by the cold hatred in George Girty's unblinking eyes as the renegade scanned the men in the small enclosure, daring them to disagree. No one spoke.

Of all the men in the room, only Chard saw the look of conspiracy that passed between his father and the Girty brothers. And, although he had no idea what the look signified, he silently applauded DePeyster's decision to place Henry Bird in the position of command. He had no illusions about the fate of the Kentuckians should his father assume leadership of the invasion. Southhampton wouldn't stop until the frontier ran red with the blood of the defenseless as well as its defenders, and Kentucky was reduced to a smoldering pile of ashes.

"Damn you, Judith!" shouted Southhampton. Stomping about the room while his wife lay dresses, riding habits, and boots neatly inside her traveling chest. "Time is of the greatest importance, and here you are dillydallying around as though we have all the leisure in the world. Damn it, woman, do you understand what I'm saying? Clark is at St. Louis, and we've got to take his fort at the falls of the Ohio before he returns. Then, God willing, we can man the fort and ambush Clark when he runs to its defense. But time, madam, time is our enemy. Everything depends on timing."

Southhampton grimaced angrily as Judith ignored him and continued to pack. He was at his wits' end. The last thing he wanted was for his wife to be involved in the Kentucky venture. Yet, what could he do? She had gained permission from none other than DePeyster himself.

As if in answer to his thoughts, Judith spoke: "You are wasting your breath, James. I am going to Kentucky. Not even you can countermand the governor's orders."

Southhampton stopped his pacing and pointed menacingly at Judith. "And that's another thing. I resent your going to DePeyster and selling him the bill of goods that the army needs a woman present to act as mediator should we be forced to take female prisoners. 'Tis ridiculous."

Judith averted her eyes and made much of laying another dress in the chest. She was afraid he would see the panic that was squeezing the very breath from her lungs, for in truth she was terrified that he might somehow change the governor's mind and make her miss the opportunity to help save the lives of hundreds of innocent people. She didn't know what she could do to hamper the British invasion of Kentucky, but she did know that she must try. Somehow she must devise a scheme to slow the army until Clark could return to the falls of the Ohio and raise his defense.

"If you are not prepared to leave by sunup," warned Southhampton, snatching his immaculate scarlet tunic from its wall peg and storming out the door, "we will strike anchor without you!"

Judith raised her soft blue eyes and stared after him. Then she slammed down the trunk lid and pulled the binding straps tight. "I'll be on board before you are, you pompous bastard," she promised.

Judith leaned against the ship's rail and listened to the sails popping in the wind. The eighteen-mile trip down the Detroit River had been uneventful and even a bit boring after the initial excitement had worn off. But as the ship swept into the open waters of Lake Erie, Judith's mood darkened. She was reminded, as she gazed at the seemingly endless number of sailing vessels, bateaux, and birch canoes that crowded the river, that distributed throughout the flotilla were six deadly cannon consisting of four swivel guns, a three-pounder, and a wheeled brass six-pounder, instruments of destruction that the Kentuckians would neither expect nor be prepared for. And she wondered whether the frontier folk could withstand the devastating carnage cannon could produce.

Leaning leisurely against the main mast, Chard watched his mother with interest. The wind was in her hair, rustling it gently off her forehead, bringing into soft relief her finely chiseled profile.

"Her beauty is ageless," he mused. Then he frowned. "Yet, all she sees in a looking glass is that thin silver scar that runs from her hairline to her eyebrow. . . . And never has she revealed how she acquired it, only that it happened when she was in the wilderness during the French and Indian War."

He crossed the deck to stand beside her. "How does it feel, Mother, to be going back into the wild American frontier after all these years?"

Judith smiled crookedly. "A bit fearsome, I'll admit. But 'twas under entirely different circumstances twenty-five years ago . . ."

She pointed at the canoes trailing the ships. "Those Hurons were our enemy then." She almost added that they still were, but instead grinned roguishly and continued, "Those seventy green-coated Canadian Rangers who are paddling their bateaux with such vigor would have given a month's pay to have gotten a shot at your red tunic. But all that has changed in the past few years. Now we are allies—British, Canadians, Indians—marching against folk who only wish to be left alone."

"Perhaps, my dear," said Southhampton, who had joined his wife and son at the rail, "you should study the facts before you speak so openly about a subject of which you know absolutely nothing. Actually, this invasion of Kentucky is a necessary and well-planned military strategy. Our goal is not only to exterminate those ridiculous frontier forts but also to force the king's western boundaries back to the Allegheny Mountains."

"Then why," retorted Judith, "did we go to war with France in 'fifty-five? I thought we were fighting to expand our frontier."

Southhampton flushed. "The king will decide when and where to expand our territories, madam. It will not be a choice made by these foolish Americans who think they can

31

slip off into the wilderness and escape their responsibilities to the Crown. Furthermore, you would be wise to keep your thoughts to yourself. One might think that you champion these bastards who call themselves the Sons of Liberty."

Chard straightened from the rail, his aquiline features the color of the dingy gray sails whipping overhead. Did his father suspect something? Was he aware of Judith's part in Chapline's escape?

"Really, Father," he said, forcing a smile, "Mother was voicing her opinion in the strict confidence of family. We have always spoken our minds freely to one another."

"I am an officer of the king's army," said South-hampton, turning to face his son, "and so are you. 'Tis a fact you would do well to remember. Furthermore, I will not tolerate one disloyal word from anyone, and most certainly not from a member of this so-called happy family. I would dislike being forced to turn my wife over to the authorities for acts of treason." Turning on his heel, he strode angrily down the deck, his dress sword jingling lightly with each haughty step.

Chard slipped his arm around Judith's waist. He was afraid for his mother, with a fear that left him nauseated, for he knew his father's threats were not just idle conversation. Tightening his embrace, Chard drew Judith farther into his arms. I will protect you, he pledged in fierce silence, wishing he could hold her thus forever. But forever proved to be of short duration, for the bile that had been churning in his stomach rose suddenly to his lips, and he made a mad dash for the ship's rail.

The morning of May 17, 1780 the flotilla crossed the western tip of Lake Erie and entered the mouth of the Maumee River.

Chard was again drawn to the ship's rail, this time by the forbidding appearance of a forest like none he had ever imagined. The trees lining the stream were so straight and tall that they put him in mind of giant palisades, and the darkness stretching endlessly beneath their leafy branches seemed to beckon to him, to draw at his very nerves with its vast depths of uncharted mysteries.

He jumped with surprise as a painted savage materialized out of the brush along the riverbank. Chard was sure he had been looking directly at the spot, and no Indian had been there the moment before. His gaze pierced farther into the dim interior of the forest. Sure enough, painted Indians were standing motionless as shadows nearly everywhere he peered, and Chard wondered how he had managed to overlook anything so obvious.

His fingers tightened on the rail, and the muscles in his jaws stood out in rigid knots; he had a lot to learn about seeing what he looked at, and not just looking at what he saw. His parents had made him realize that. After twenty-four years of just looking at them, he was actually seeing them for the first time. How could he have been so blind?

He spent the rest of the journey up the Maumee observing the quiet, eerie forest, forcing his eyes to probe deep into every gloomy shadow and study it thoroughly before passing on to the next. He was amazed to find that the silent woods were alive with people, animals, birds, and all manner of living creatures that he had failed to detect previously. He laughed with satisfaction when, out of the corner of his eye, he caught the flick of a fawn's ear and, from that tiny movement, pieced together a head, body, and small spindly legs. What he failed to notice until she moved, however, was the doe standing not five feet behind the fawn.

Chard's elation vanished. In its place rose that ever-present nausea, that constant reminder that he could not, for his mother's sake, overlook so much as one solitary thing.

As they neared the conjunction of the Maumee and Auglaize rivers, Judith reappeared on deck carrying a lovely polished-walnut case.

"I've been waiting for the right moment to give you these," she said with a secret smile as she presented the box to Chard.

The young ensign took the case and caressed its smooth polished surface. "Open it!" cried Judith. "I had them specially made for you in London."

Chard flipped back the lid to reveal a beautifully engraved matched pair of heavy-caliber dueling pistols. His breath caught in his throat.

Judith laughed with satisfaction. "They are so finely tuned that if you breathe on the hair trigger, you had best be pointing the barrels at whatever you intend to shoot."

"Ma'am," whispered Chard, "'tis the finest pair of pistols I've ever seen. . . . How can I ever thank you?"

"If they keep you safe on this trip into Kentucky, it will be thanks enough, Chard."

"They will!" he cried with enthusiasm. "How can I miss with such weapons?"

He threw his arms around Judith and kissed her. "I feel like a child with a new toy."

Judith frowned uncertainly. "Be careful, Chard. These are instruments of death. Respect them as such."

Chard sobered, then grinned broadly. "After the newness wears off, I will be my old somber, realistic self again, Mother. I promise I will."

Judith smiled affectionately. Her son seemed so young and immature at times. Her smile faded and her eyes became distant as her lips slowly whispered the words, "I pray he doesn't come out of this wilderness venture older than his years . . . as I did." She remembered a beautiful, virginal eighteen-year-old who had ventured naively into the American frontier, a girl whose unspoiled mind and body had been forced to undergo such harsh tortures and horrible realities that when she did emerge from the wilderness, she was no longer beautiful, no longer a girl . . . and most definitely no longer a virgin. No, she was a woman, an ugly woman with a scar that would forever mar what beauty she might otherwise have possessed, an ancient woman in a girl's body. No, not even a girl's body, for it was already beginning to swell and distort from the boy child that grew in her womb. She was an eighteen-year-old crone who had left her youth and innocence in the savage wilderness forever.

"Chard," she said hesitantly, looking deep into his eyes, "this trip is not going to be what you expect. You will see, hear, and experience things that will go against all that you believe in."

Chard laughed and hugged his mother close. "Fear not,

34

ma'am," he said with pride. "I am a man and an officer of His Majesty's Royal Army. War is thrilling, and I assure you I can face up to whatever it is that you are concerned with. So worry your pretty head no more."

Judith smiled at Chard, but her eyes were sad with a knowledge of the senseless barbarity of war, the reality of which her son was still unaware.

Judith was appalled by the size of the Indian camp at the mouth of the Auglaize River. Over three hundred painted savages, greased bodies glistening in the sun, lined the bank to watch the seamen row the pirogues carrying the British officers and Judith to the shore.

George and Simon Girty broke away from the Indians they had been addressing and walked proudly down the muddy incline to the water's edge. George offered his hand to Captain Bird, who was assisting Judith out of the light craft and trying, without success, to hide his astonishment at the vast horde of red men who stood solemnly on the bank.

"Well, Captain"—Girty grinned, indicating the Indians with a wave of his hand—"never thought you'd see such a turnout, did you, sir?"

Bird's eyes traveled the long line of Delawares, Hurons, Mingoes, Ottawas, Tawas, and Chippewas. Merciful God in heaven, he thought with a surge of misgivings, and we haven't even treated with the Shawnee yet.

His voice was pleasant, however, without a trace of the anxiety he felt, when he replied with a forced smile: "When I sent you ahead, Mr. Girty, to procure enough pack animals to make the portage, I had horses in mind, sir, not Indians."

George Girty laughed heartily. "We have horses, Captain, and cattle, too. These red devils are here to join your army. Why, by the time we reach Kentucky, we'll have a thousand Indians with us."

"You've done excellently, Girty, excellently indeed!" announced Southhampton who had moved to Bird's side and was marveling at the imposing sight on the riverbank. "I couldn't have done better myself, sir," he assured Bird. "Girty should be commended."

35

Without waiting for Bird to reply, Southhampton turned to the Indians, raised his hand in a salute, and strutted haughtily up the incline.

"Friends," he cried, smiling grandly, "'tis good to see you."

Upon reaching the red men, he turned abruptly and marched back the way he had come.

"Jesus Christ, Girty," he said, rolling his eyes toward the Indians. "They stink to high heaven."

Girty's smile vanished, replaced by a contemptuous smirk that hovered at the corner of his thin lips.

"'Tis the bear oil they grease their bodies with, Major. It turns rancid and smells pretty bad till you get used to it."

"Tell the truth, Major," said Simon Girty, "you had to walk clear up to the top of the bank to smell them, when the fact is, they caught wind of your boats before you reached the shallows there." He pointed at the beached pirogues. "Indians say that white people stink worse than shit, sir, and they can smell 'em a mile away."

Judith, who had heard the exchange, laughed openly at Southhampton's squeamishness.

"You will just have to pinch your delicate nose, James," she jeered, "until you get used to the stench . . . and believe me, you will get used to it."

"You should know, my dear," countered South-hampton with a smile that extended only to his lips. "I've often wondered about your captivity with the Indians. Did you have your belly greased by some warrior's stinking body?"

Judith's face turned ashen and her lips trembled to form a denial, but Simon Girty spoke first. "If you're through with me and George, Captain, we need be checking the supplies." Ignoring Southhampton, he nodded to Judith and walked quickly toward the bateaux that were being unloaded by red-coated soldiers standing knee deep in the swift-flowing Auglaize.

George Girty, however, took a long, inquisitive look at Judith; a look filled with interest and speculation. Then, turning abruptly, he followed his brother.

Captain Bird eyed Southhampton with disgust, thinking what an insensitive ass the man was. But Bird was forced by protocol to be civil to the major, because even

36

though he was in charge of the expedition, Southhampton outranked him in time and service. That Southhampton was a major and he a captain bothered Bird not in the least, for he knew that Southhampton had gained his promotion through services rendered during the French and Indian War and had not been promoted since. That did not speak at all well for the major, for it was natural to assume that in nearly twenty-five years a major would earn a colonelcy at the very least. But Southhampton had not.

Bird straightened his sword, flicked a bit of debris from his tunic, and stepped toward the embankment.

"Would the major care to join me while I greet our allies?" he asked over his shoulder.

Southhampton scowled and sniffed the wind. "No, thank you, Captain, I believe 'tis your duty to welcome our guests. I'll not interfere."

I didn't think you would, thought Bird, as he climbed the bank toward the waiting Indians.

Judith was becoming more nervous by the minute. It was the twenty-first of May and they had already reached the fifteen-mile overland portage that separated the Auglaize and Great Miami rivers.

If she intended to slow the army, she had to do it immediately. Once across the portage, the Ohio River was less than a hundred miles away. And once they reached the Ohio, it would be too late. Tiny lines marred Judith's brow as she frowned in a concentrated effort to figure a way that one lone woman could stop an entire army in its tracks. How could she put almost five hundred men out of action for one minute, let alone for a week or two? She dropped her head back, closed her eyes and sighed, wondering what had possessed her to entertain the silly notion that she might delay an army.

Then her eyes slowly opened, crinkling at the corners into tiny crow's-feet. Her lips formed a delicate smile that broadened into an even-toothed grin that burst into a tinkling of wicked laughter.

She knew how to stop an army.

CHAPTER

· 3 ·

SUSAN STOOD IN the shorter of the two lines that were always present outside the doors of Ruddle's Fort's only necessary houses. While she waited, she glanced around the interior of the small stockade. It was plain that no one seemed interested in preparing for the British assault destined for the near future. Even the hunters, who would normally be in the deep woods spying out game and Indians, were lazing around the makeshift refuges waiting for the weather to break.

Turning abruptly, she drew her skirts above the mud and marched through a conflux of pigs, chickens, and geese, making her way straight to Captain Ruddle's cabin, where the majority of the hunters and able-bodied men congregated. Upon entering, she was not disappointed. The place was packed with men of all descriptions: hunters, home-steaders, ex-soldiers still wearing the remnants of blue and buff, and others who were waiting to push on to Harrods-burg, Lexington, or Boonesboro. She found Captain Ruddle perched on a stool amid a throng of newcomers, praising the advantages of the countryside around his station in the hope that the men would decide to settle there.

"Captain Ruddle?" interrupted Susan, as she pushed her way through the bevy of eager listeners. "It seems to me, sir, that we should be preparing a defense of some sort, at least putting out a spying party or something. The British and Indians—"

"In this rain?" shouted a man who had just arrived in Kentucky not a week earlier. Several other newcomers laughed heartily and looked at Susan as though she were a bored housewife stirring up work and trouble that was better left to the menfolk.

"Mrs. Patterson," Ruddle said with a patronizing smile, "the British can't possibly get to Kentucky before the first of August. That gives us over two months to prepare our defenses, and surely by then the rain will have ceased."

Again the men laughed uproariously.

Susan turned on them with a vengeance born of a total understanding of the frontier, a knowledge that left no room for misunderstandings when it came to Indians and their peculiar—and deadly—warfare. "Gentlemen," she said through her teeth, "I came to Kentucky with my husband before there was even a hunter's cabin in this country. I've fought Indians, elements, and loneliness to help build it into what it is today. I've buried good folk whose only mistake was an unreasonable contempt for the dangers that surround us, Indian or otherwise, but especially the Indian. And I tell you that if you think you can sit on your laurels and defend this fort you are mistaken."

"Mrs. Patterson," said Ruddle, as though speaking to a child, "we appreciate what you've said. Everyone here is familiar with Morgan Patterson; after all, he is a legend. But the defense of this fort is in capable hands, I assure you. Why, Boonesboro fought off the entire Shawnee nation, including George, James, and Simon Girty in 'seventy-eight. So I feel confident that we can do the same."

"Boonesboro was lucky, Mr. Ruddle, just plain lucky."

"Luck or not, ma'am, I think you should leave such worries to those who understand warfare."

"If my husband or General Clark were here," snapped Susan, eyeing the man contemptuously, "there would be scouts out and guards on the roofs of the cabins, Captain Ruddle."

"Mrs. Patterson," returned Ruddle wearily, "I resent your insinuation that I am lax in my defense of this fort. I've said all I'm going to say on the subject. Good day, ma'am."

Susan stormed toward the door, her face ablaze. To make matters worse, she was assaulted with shouts and catcalls from the loafers and newcomers. So amused were they by what they considered "female meddling" that they failed to notice the quiet man in buckskins, one who had been in Kentucky longer than any of them save Susan Patterson, spring lightly to his feet and follow her through the door.

"Mrs. Patterson," he called, as Susan strode angrily through the mud. "May I have a word with you, ma'am?"

Susan spun about, prepared to do battle should the caller want to make further sport at her expense. Then she smiled and retraced her steps. "What can I do for you, Simon?"

"Well, ma'am," said Simon Kenton, "I'm leavin' for Lexington Station shortly. I'd be obliged, ma'am, if you and Bitsy would go with me."

Susan studied the young frontiersman for several seconds. Kenton was no novice to Kentucky. In fact, as a woodsman he was almost as much of a legend as Morgan Patterson, so Susan weighed his proposal heavily before answering. "Simon," she said finally, "Morgan expects Bitsy and me to be here when he returns."

"But, ma'am," argued Kenton, "you were right, what you told Ruddle. I was at Boonesboro in 'seventy-eight, and I know it was a freak rain that sent the Indians scurrying —and that's all that saved us. But you can't tell those fools nothin'." He indicated Ruddle's cabin with a flick of his head. "So I'm headin' for Lexington, then to Harrodsburg. You're welcome to come, ma'am."

"Thank you kindly, Simon. If I were going to travel, you would be my first choice of a companion, but I suppose Bitsy and I will wait here for Morgan."

"About Bitsy," said Kenton with a self-conscious grin that was almost comical in a man nearly twenty-five years old, "I was wonderin', could I come courtin'?"

Susan repressed an amused smile. "Simon, although you are only half my husband's age, you are one of his truest friends, as you are mine. The reason for that, sir, is that you are mentally as old as we are. One has to be to survive in the wilderness the way you, Boone, and Morgan do. But as much as I admire you, I don't want my daughter married to a woodsman. And I know in my bones, Simon, that you'll never settle permanently—not you, not Boone —maybe not even Morgan."

Kenton's grin broadened. Dropping the butt of his long

rifle to the toe of his muddy moccasin, he replied, "For a lass that's grown up to be as pretty as Bitsy, a man might change his ways."

"And he might not," finished Susan.

Kenton laughed silently and shouldered his weapon.

"Well, ma'am, tell Bitsy I was askin' after her."

Susan smiled in return. "I will, Simon. Luck to you on your trip."

She watched the frontiersman walk away, and she knew a moment of profound sadness, for she was certain that Simon Kenton would end up dead in a hollow tree, or an unmarked grave, or with his scalp drying on some Indian's willow hoop. She shook her head regretfully. What was it Daniel Boone had said when Kenton saved his life? "Simon, you are a fine fellow." And Susan agreed wholeheartedly. But she wanted more than that for her daughter —more than a fine husband who was fifty years old before he was twenty-five.

Simon Kenton's request to "come courtin'" reminded Susan again of something she had been unconsciously trying to ignore: Bitsy was no longer a child.

And as she waded across the common ground toward her overcrowded cabin, she thought again that the time had come for her to explain to her daughter about men and women. Susan blushed at the thought, for despite Bitsy's good looks and full-breasted young body, and the close living quarters of Ruddle's Fort, the girl was still naive about sex. Not sure how to approach the subject and dreading the chore, Susan took the easy way out by telling herself that it would be a shame to spoil Bitsy's innocence with such intelligence.

"Nay," Susan decided as she entered the cabin, "I'll not clutter her young mind with such stuff. There's plenty of time for me to do that before she's wed . . . plenty of time."

Little did Susan know that with each step of Bird's army, the clock was ticking on Bitsy's innocence. And that she, Susan Patterson, when both hands of that proverbial timepiece turned straight up, would have no say in the matter whatsoever.

* * *

Judith Cornwallace Southhampton had been married to an army officer far too many years not to have learned something of military strategies. She knew that if one intended to stop a fleet of ships on the high seas, one did not attempt to sink the fleet. No, all one did was sink the flagship.

So, she reasoned, if one wanted to stop the army, one would only have to incapacitate the commander. And her active mind had devised a scheme that would accomplish that feat. The army lived by rituals that seldom varied. Judith depended on that routine when, as she stepped from her tent to join her husband for the short walk to Captain Bird's marquee, she slipped a small bottle into the pocket that hung from a narrow belt she wore around her waist. She and her husband dined with Captain Bird each evening, as protocol demanded, and if nothing intervened, when the meal was finished the men would step outside to smoke and drink rum.

With nervous anxiety, Judith watched Bird fill two cups with the fiery liquid and recork the bottle. For a terrible instant she was afraid he intended to carry the bottle with him, but instead, he carefully replaced it in the wooden crate that housed several cases of the precious cargo. Judith noted the exact location of the bottle. She was almost ashamed of what she was about to do, since Bird had received the rum as a gift from none other than her own husband. Bird had also made it quite plain that he found her company agreeable.

She curtsied with forced patience while the men went through the tedious formality of bowing elegantly to her and making their apologies. But the moment they were outside, she flew to the crate and snatched out the half-empty container of rum. Then, one eye on the tent flaps, she hastily poured the contents of her vial into the bottle.

When the men returned, Judith was sitting at the table, calmly fanning herself. "Ah, madam," said Bird, smiling appreciatively, "if I may say so, you are the picture of elegance. It is a pleasure to have you accompany this expedition."

"Thank you, Captain Bird," said Judith with her most alluring smile. "It is indeed grand to be here, sir." Then she added with slow deliberation, "With you."

Judith knew that her obvious flirtation with Bird

would bring her a furious, if not brutal, reprisal from her husband, but she knew exactly what she was doing. She was insuring her position with Bird. If the man discovered that someone had tampered with his rum, she wanted to be above suspicion. And what better way to achieve that goal than to flatter his already inflated ego?

She nearly laughed outright when Bird shot her a knowing look that said her invitation had not been wasted. What a bore, she thought, rising gracefully to her feet, loathing the fact that she had had to cheapen herself. Bird's eyes automatically traveled the length of Judith, as though he were seeing the proud lift of her breasts, her tiny waist, her delicately flared hips for the very first time.

Southhampton's face turned thunderous, and he cursed himself for being a blind fool. He should have guessed that Judith's reasons for accompanying the expedition had nothing to do with Kentucky, or with one particular Kentuckian, as he had first feared. No, her motives were not nearly so complicated, nor were they spiced with intrigue. Southhampton's mouth drew into an ugly sneer. He had given her more credit than she deserved. She was even too stupid to hide her affair with Bird.

He caught his wife's elbow, his fingers digging deeply into the soft flesh. Fighting hard the impulse to fling her into Bird's arms and tell the man he was welcome to her, Southhampton pushed her toward the door. Eyeing Bird contemptuously, he kicked aside the canvas flap and stepped through. "Come, Judith," he commanded flatly.

Bird rushed quickly to the entrance and, catching Judith's free hand, touched his lips to her fingers. "If I may be so bold, madam," he said huskily, "your husband is a lucky man, a lucky man, indeed."

Judith's bubbling laughter mixed with the breeze that rustled the spring leaves. "Aye, sir, he is, isn't he?"

Judith's last conscious thought that night was a prayer for Captain Bird to have one more spot of rum before he retired. That would be the only thing that would even remotely compensate her for the vicious way South-hampton had used her after they'd returned to their quarters. Her prayers were answered. Bird didn't appear for breakfast the next morning, or for the noontime meal either. Yet, periodically throughout the day, he could be seen marching with what dignity he could muster toward the brush that surrounded the camp.

Chard shook his head to Judith's question. "No one knows what the captain's problem is. He's got a stomach disorder. He seems to be wasting away little by little. He can't eat; all he can do is trot to the bushes all day long. And meanwhile the army sits and waits. Father is beside himself. He has even suggested taking command."

Judith's hand flew to her mouth. Perhaps her scheme to put Bird out of commission had gone awry. If South-hampton assumed command of the army, her plans and efforts could well turn out to be a complete tragedy.

"It's been a week," said Judith hotly. "Why doesn't the surgeon give Captain Bird something to cure his . . . problem?"

"He's giving him rum, but it doesn't seem to help."

Oh, God, thought Judith, if they keep adding fuel to the fire, they'll kill Bird for sure.

She would have found the incident amusing had it not become an actual threat to the captain's life. The very real possibility that Southhampton might declare himself in absolute charge of the forces and march to Kentucky without Bird complicated matters even more. Judith bit her lip; under her husband's command, the Kentuckians would receive no quarter, no chance for humane treatment—if there ever had been a chance.

Somehow she had to retrieve that bottle of rum.

She was appalled by Bird's condition when she entered his marquee. The man was drawn and shriveled and almost as white as the sheet that covered him. Judith fought to keep from pinching her nostrils, so awful was the stench of soiled clothing, linens, and no telling what else. But, instead, she smiled bravely and crossed to the sick man's cot.

"I brought you hot food, Captain," she said with a touch of shame for what she had accomplished.

Bird's ashen face became even paler, and he quickly turned his head aside and squeezed his eyes shut. "I can't even stand the smell of food, much less eat any," he

44

complained weakly, waving her aside. "My God, madam, get that stuff away from me."

"You are going to eat it, Captain. So you might as well open your mouth." Judith's gaze fastened on the bottle of rum at the bedside as she placed the platter of food on the breakdown table Bird used for a field desk. Tearing her eyes away, she slipped her arm beneath his shoulders and raised him to a sitting position. "You've got to get some solid food into you, Captain. 'Tis the only way to stop . . . what ails you."

Bird moaned aloud and, gathering the sheet about him, sprang from the cot and made a feeble dash for the woods.

Judith snatched up the bottle and tucked it beneath the folds of her dress. She prayed that the bulge wouldn't show when she walked from the tent. If anyone suspected that she had been the culprit behind Bird's diarrhea, an ailment that had long since stopped being amusing and had become a serious problem, she would probably get fifty lashes and be left behind when the army evacuated to Kentucky.

Judith made her way quickly into the forest, pushing ever deeper into the wilderness until the sounds of the camp were barely audible. She came to a bluff overlooking the Auglaize and spied out the area as far as she could see. Nothing moved. She quickly withdrew the bottle and cast it far out, watching it drop into the river below. As the bottle splashed into the water, she felt a great burden lift from her shoulders, and she all but skipped along the path that led back to camp.

Chard stepped from the underbrush and ventured to the edge of the bluff where Judith had stood. His youthful brow drew into a thoughtful frown. Why would his mother throw a bottle of fine rum into the river? It just didn't make sense. Nothing made sense anymore.

He turned and followed the same path Judith had taken, but had he waited a moment longer, he would have seen George Girty wade into the fast-flowing current and fish out the half-empty bottle. Standing chest deep in the river, Girty held the amber glass up to the light. The rum looked clean. He surveyed the bluff where Judith had stood. Then with a frown that turned to a scowl, he tucked the container under his arm and waded toward the shore.

With a weak, unsteady hand, Captain Bird finally gave the signal that again launched the British toward Kentucky. Two long weeks had elapsed since the army had reached the Auglaize River; two precious weeks had been spent moving their equipment and supplies over the portage to the Great Miami River, a distance of less than fifteen miles.

"I know it is June third," Bird said apologetically, "and I assure you, Major Southhampton, I hate this loss of time as much as you. But there is nothing you or I can do about it. I must assume that the American, Major Chapline, has long since reached the falls of the Ohio, so Clark has probably been alerted at St. Louis." Bird reached up and absently brushed a deerfly off his cheek. "Still and all, I doubt seriously that Clark can get to Kentucky before the first of July. With any luck, we should be there in plenty of time to take the fort and set up a reception for the general, too."

"If this expedition isn't handled with any more finesse than it has been up until this instant, Captain," said Southhampton with sarcasm that left the pale captain blushing with the first touch of color he had shown in days, "we will be fortunate if we get to Kentucky before next winter."

Bird dropped his eyes. "That is exactly why I have decided to change course and bypass Lorimer's Store. Instead of going down Pickawillany Creek, we will follow the main branch of the Miami all the way to the Ohio. 'Tis a shorter route and with luck we will make up a few days of lost time."

Southhampton was incredulous. "Just how in bloody hell do you intend to provision the army, sir? Lorimer's is the only British trading post between Detroit and Kentucky. I strongly advise you to reconsider, Captain." Southhampton didn't mention that he had every intention of leaving Judith at the trading post—with or without her permission or Bird's.

"We will provision in Kentucky, Major. The Girty brothers assure me that there are cattle, hogs, goats, and sheep aplenty. Also, it is my intention to allow the forts to surrender peaceably."

Bird saw no reason for taking prisoners or destroying the stockades. "After we take Clark's Fort at the falls," he

46

explained, "the rest of the country will lay down their arms and take the oath of allegiance to the king. We will simply place a small detachment of soldiers at each outlying station to ensure martial law and obedience. Then we senior officers will return to Detroit."

It sounded so simple that Southhampton feared Bird might actually succeed. "Captain," he said, hiding his apprehension, "you are in command of this expedition. But let me remind you, sir, its success or failure will rest on your shoulders. Yours and yours alone."

Southhampton tossed his head effeminately and, deliberately turning his back on his commanding officer, walked down the bank of the Big Miami to where George Girty was checking the cargo of a thirty-foot birchbark canoe. The Girty brothers were known to be mean, dangerous renegades, more savage than an Indian, and George, though popular belief differed, was the worst of the lot. Southhampton approached the man cautiously.

"George," he said out of the corner of his mouth while pretending to study the wilderness on the far side of the river, "Captain Bird is a coward and a disgrace to Britain."

Girty lashed a keg of powder to the gunwale, then reached for another.

"He's a gutless fish-belly, Southhampton. Now say what you came to say."

Southhampton blanched at Girty's obvious show of disrespect. But he swallowed a fierce reprimand and, forcing a smile, told George Girty that Bird intended to allow the forts to surrender. "And if they will take the oath of allegiance," Southhampton continued slyly, "they will also be allowed to continue operating as they are now. I don't want that to happen, George, and neither do you. So what I'm suggesting is that you and Simon stir up the Indians so that when we take Kentucky, it will prove impossible for Bird to control the savages. I don't want any . . . survivors, George."

Girty looked up from under his eyebrows, his hard eyes calculating as they locked with Southhampton's.

"Kentucky has always been known as 'the dark and bloody ground,' Southhampton. Why do you want to add more bloodshed to what's already been let?"

"That's my business," said the major easily. "All I'm

47

asking, Girty, is whether you've got enough control over these savages to get it done."

Girty set another bundle in place, strapped it to the canoe, then tested the knot to be sure it was tight. Satisfied, he again turned to Southhampton. "I can handle the Indians, but why should I?"

"Because you want prisoners, scalps, and booty. Quit playing games with me, Girty. If Bird has his way, there will be nothing for any of us."

Girty shrugged his shoulders indifferently, but he was weighing Southhampton's words carefully. Neither he nor Simon nor the Indians would be satisfied if Bird allowed the forts to surrender peaceably. Still, he was hesitant to commit himself, for the truth was he did not like or trust Southhampton. "If I stir up the Indians, Bird might have me shot," he said without conviction.

Southhampton smiled thinly. Girty was his. "Bird will never suspect that we instigated the slaughter. He will be too busy wondering what the hell went wrong."

Girty eyed Southhampton long and hard. "I'll think on it, Major. We're still a long ways from Kentucky."

"You do that, Girty, you just do that!"

Southhampton retraced his steps up the bank. He was well satisfied with his conversation with Girty. In fact, he was elated. Bird might be in charge of the expedition, but the man who controlled the Indians would be the real commander. And that man would be Major James Southhampton. He smiled, feeling expansive and pleased. Even the thought that he would have to change his plans about abandoning Judith at Lorimer's Store did little to dampen his enthusiasm.

Southhampton stepped up his pace, anxious to hurry the troops in their preparation for their trip down the Great Miami to the Ohio. And Kentucky.

CHAPTER
· 4 ·

MORGAN PATTERSON HAD COME to the Illinois country with George Rogers Clark and his motley array of frontiersmen in June of 1778. It was now June of 1780. The Kentuckians had acquitted themselves with honor several times over in the space of two short years; Kaskaskia, Cahokia, and Vincennes had fallen under their guns, thus breaking the back of British rule in the Illinois country. And Clark and his men governed their newly acquired holdings with an enthusiasm that verged on jealousy. They would retain their hard-won advantage. But the honor was wearing thin, especially since Major Chapline had sent word of the impending invasion of Kentucky.

But that wasn't the real reason Patterson was dissatisfied—not entirely. He had not been able to forget the pressure of Consetta's body molded tightly against his when she had kissed him. The memory had plagued him for days afterward, bringing to the surface a longing that had cost him a succession of sleepless nights.

Impatiently, he paced the floor of his office while the newly arrived George Rogers Clark gave last-minute instructions to Captain John Slaughter who, during Patterson's absence, was to take command of Fort Jefferson and the Illinois country in and around the conjunction of the Ohio and Mississippi rivers. Clark snatched up his Pennsylvania rifle. "Morgan," he boomed, stopping Patterson in midstride, "you know this country better than any of us, so you take the lead. Harlan, Consola, and I will bring up the rear."

The four filed out of Slaughter's office and dogtrotted

through the predawn half-light toward the main gate. They were tall, muscular men, and they moved with the peculiar grace found in those who are at home in the wilderness.

In ten minutes they were out of sight of any vestiges of the civilized world. They wove their way among the trunks of trees so tall and straight that the lowest limbs were twenty feet above the ground. The sunlight that penetrated the thick spring foliage fell in vertical shafts resembling thin strips of translucent gauze. The forest floor was covered with hundreds of years of soft loam, ferns, and mayapple, so there was hardly a whisper of sound as the men ran steadily toward the Kentucky settlements more than three hundred miles away.

They used up the daylight hours of June 10 in that mile-eating trot. Not until the sun had dipped below the wood line in the west did they ease their pace and begin searching for a suitable place to camp.

Minutes before full dark, they chose a spot in a dense thicket and settled down on weary haunches to chew cold jerky and munch handfuls of parched corn. It wasn't much of a supper for the trail-worn men, but with Indian sign so prevalent, they dared risk a shot or strike a fire.

Clark caught a strip of jerky between his teeth and ripped at it with the gusto of a hungry wolf. "We'll raise a company of men at the falls and intercept Bird somewhere up the Ohio," he said, chewing vigorously.

Harlan shifted his weight to ease his cramped muscles, then relaxed on his elbows. "Damn shame we can't hit Detroit while Bird's down here, probably could walk right in and take the place without firing a shot."

"Detroit will have to wait," said Patterson softly. "Kentucky comes first."

"Aye, it does," agreed Clark. "Though 'tis God's own truth that if we could take Detroit, Kentucky would be safe from such threats as we are now facing."

"Shouldn't be no trouble raisin' an army to waylay Bird," said Consola, crunching loudly on a handful of parched corn. "Chapline's runner says there's hundreds of new folk come into Kentucky since we been gone."

Clark gnawed thoughtfully on his jerky. His mind raced ahead to the falls of the Ohio, envisioning scores of able-bodied frontiersmen clamoring to march into the

50

wilderness and do battle with the British and their Indian allies. The thought gave him heart, and pride in being an American and a Kentuckian.

Morgan Patterson was also preoccupied with thoughts of his own. He was remembering Susan, her quick, shy smile, offset by promising bold black eyes, a trait that had never ceased to speed his pulse even after more than twenty years of wedlock. He fidgeted restlessly as he envisioned her long, shapely legs and firm, full breasts. Age had only enhanced her womanly charms.

He ran his fingers through thick hair that was graying heavily at the temples and shook his head. He had been gone too long. And now that he was actually on his way to Kentucky, he could think of nothing but his beautiful, seductive wife. And every minute lost to eating or sleeping seemed an eternity wasted, and he had to force himself to be considerate of his companions and their needs. It agitated him knowing that, even though the others were as anxious to get to the falls as he, four superb woodsmen could not travel as fast or as far as one.

They had already traveled several miles in the predawn light of June 11 by the time the sun finally broke the horizon and forced an occasional ray through the lofty treetops to flash like a mirror into their squinted eyes. Then, almost before they knew it, the fiery ball had made its long, slow loop from horizon to horizon. Still, the four woodsmen panted on, rifles swinging at their sides, keeping to that steady pace without pause or comment until an hour after dusk. Then, thankfully for their weary bodies, they reached the banks of the wide Tennessee River. Without a word, they fanned out and disappeared into the heavy timber along its banks. Thirty minutes later, they were back. There had been no sign of Indians.

While Clark, Harlan, and Consola used their tomahawks to chop down trees for a raft, Patterson cut long, thin strips of hickory bark from the saplings growing near the river's edge. The green strips, used to lash the logs together, were as tough and pliable as rawhide, and would continue to be so until the bark dried out and became brittle. It was

51

all the dead-tired men could do just to bind the logs together and push the edge of the raft into the water. The crossing would have to wait until morning.

Silently, they stretched their aching bodies out on the riverbank and waited for sleep. Patterson reevaluated his thoughts of the previous evening. It was true that four men could not travel as quickly as one, but he certainly could not accuse the other three of dragging their feet: they had covered nearly seventy miles in two days.

At daybreak of June 12, 1780, while the four American frontiersmen were busy pushing their log raft into the swift current of the Tennessee River, Major James Southhampton watched Captain Henry Bird pace the inside perimeter of his marquee. They, too, had reached a river —the majestic Ohio. Over eight hundred painted warriors had been there to greet Bird, more Indians than the captain had known existed. It was not only incredible, but frightening. Bird whirled and glared at the two men he had summoned to his tent.

"Do either of you know anything about the rumor that Clark is already at the falls?" It was said without preamble and with an anger uncharacteristic of Henry Bird.

"I don't know what the hell you're talkin' about, Captain," said George Girty. He turned to his brother. "Do you know anything about it, Simon?"

"Probably ain't no rumor at all," returned Simon. "Sounds like the truth to me."

Bird's face mottled with rage.

"Clark can't be at the falls! My spies swear that he was at Cahokia in the Illinois country on the twenty-fifth of May. There's no way he can already be in Kentucky."

Bird took another turn around the inside of the tent. "The problem is," he said flatly, "these fool Indians of yours are refusing to go to the falls. They want to attack the small outlying forts and stations, and that, gentlemen, is in direct contradiction to our original plan."

George Girty's face remained placid, but his eyes narrowed angrily.

"These Indians ain't fools, Captain," he said softly.

"They know Clark for what he is, and whether you under-stand it or not, they hold him in high regard for his ability to whip his men into an army, an army that has never—I repeat, *never*—been defeated. They won't go to the falls, Captain, and nothin' me or Simon or McGee or Elliott says is going to change that."

"But we've got to take the fort at the falls!" South-hampton shouted. "If Clark is there, then so are . . . others."

Simon Girty spit a stream of tobacco juice between the tent flaps. "These Indians won't attack the falls as long as they believe Clark is already there, Major."

Southhampton's face turned livid.

"Find out who started that lie! I'll have the hide off his arse!"

Or hers, thought George Girty smugly, as he and Simon ducked out of the tent and strode haughtily toward the Indian encampment.

"Damn it," said Bird after the Girtys had gone. "This whole campaign has been plagued from the beginning. Chapline escaped and alerted Kentucky; I took sick for two weeks; and now the Indians refuse to attack the falls because of a vicious rumor. Damn it, Major, what in bloody hell is going on?"

Southhampton's eyes glittered like a copperhead's. "I know nothing more about this than you do, Captain, but 'tis beginning to appear that we have another traitor in our midst—the person who started that rumor. And when I find him, he will pay. Believe me, Captain, he will wish that he had never been born."

My God, Bird thought, shuddering under South-hampton's wild stare. The man's demented. He's worse than that. He's stark, raving mad!

Then Bird thought of Judith, and he was suddenly thankful that the opportunity to accept her seductive invi-tation had never presented itself.

Chard sat beside his wedge tent and absently stroked the blade of his pearl-handled dagger with a small whetstone. It was a habit acquired in early childhood, something he did

53

when he was troubled. Of late, the keen edge had been honed and rehoned until the phrase "razor sharp" would have been an understatement.

The Girty brothers were investigating the rumor about Clark, but as yet had not been able to trace the gossip to its source. And, although Chard couldn't be sure, he was afraid he knew who the guilty person was. In fact, he was almost certain he knew how Judith had pulled it off. He had thought it strange when, two days before, he had surprised an Indian eavesdropping beside Southhampton's tent. Yet, when Chard entered, he found Judith alone. Had she known the Indian was there? Had she staged a mock conversation, hoping the Indian would carry the rumor throughout the camp? It was an incredible possibility.

"Knife," he murmured to the delicately engraved blade, "I wish you could tell me what happened here in the wilderness twenty-five years ago that is causing my mother to take such chances with her life."

He shrugged his shoulders and sighed.

"Whatever it was, or whoever it was, must mean a great deal to her."

Morgan Patterson lay flat on the raft. He trained his long-barreled Pennsylvania gun on the war canoe that was fast closing the three-hundred-yard gap separating the two craft.

"Don't miss, Morgan," warned Clark, not taking his eyes off the canoe. "If you do, they'll be on us before the smoke clears."

"You ask a lot of a man, General," said Patterson, taking a fine bead on the lead Indian until only the man's roached scalp-lock was visible.

Consola, who, along with Harlan, had slipped into the water in an attempt to steady the raft, shook his head skeptically. "'Tis a long shot, General, even for Morgan Patterson. Maybe we should let 'em get closer."

"Closer!" cried Harlan. "They're too damned close already. And the truth is, I've pissed my pants so many times in the last five minutes that the goddamn river has risen a foot."

Patterson's breath slowly slid between his teeth, his

finger gently squeezing the trigger. A resounding boom echoed up and down the river, and for a heart-racking instant, the world stood still. Then the lead Indian clutched his lower abdomen and was slammed backwards into the startled paddlers. As if in slow motion, the twenty-six-foot canoe turned upside down in the fast-moving Tennessee River.

"Ball dropped nigh eighteen inches, Morgan," shouted Clark, rising to his knees in order to see better.

"Steady, General," warned Harlan as his head broke water after being ducked when Clark tilted the raft. "You'll tip this son of a bitch for sure."

"Sorry, boys," boomed Clark, grinning widely. "But did you ever see such a shot? Quick, now, head for shore. Those redskins are halfway there already. Push, ye hearty lads, push!"

Harlan coughed out a mouthful of water. "General, they's enough room in this river for three."

"So there is," cried Clark. He kicked off his moccasins and slipped over the edge of the raft.

Patterson rolled to his side, ran a charge down the barrel, and reprimed his rifle. He scanned the river for the capsized canoe, but it had evidently sunk. The war party, however, was easy to see because of the heavy splashing as they swam, Indian fashion, hands locked together, for shore. It was obvious they would achieve their goal long before the slow-moving raft neared the water's edge.

"Veer right, George," commanded Patterson quickly. "There's a wide stream coming into the river just ahead. Put it between us and the Indians."

He laughed silently as the raft edged toward the bank beyond the wide tributary that emptied into the Tennessee. Unless he was mistaken, he figured the Indians had had all the swimming they wanted for one day—especially since their powder was wet. Patterson was correct. When the raft bumped solidly against the shore and the four Americans sprang into the underbrush, the war party, in frustrated anger, watched gloomily from the far side of the stream.

The four men wasted no time putting miles between themselves and the Indians. They waded creeks, backtracked, ran on fallen logs, and used every trick they had ever been taught to insure against pursuit. Just after noon, as they trotted silently through the shadowed forest, they surprised a small black bear engrossed in demolishing a rotted log in search of grubs beneath the bark. Whipping up their rifles, Patterson and Clark fired as one, killing the bear instantly. Hardly breaking their stride, the men cut sizable chunks of meat, hair and all, and strung them on their belts.

When the shadows grew long, the men began searching for a suitable campsite. They found it in the form of a large sinkhole, probably where the roof of a subterranean cavern had collapsed centuries before, leaving a deep indentation in the earth's surface. They scampered down the side of the depression and wasted no time putting flint to steel; they would have a hot meal for the first time in three days.

"Well, Harlan," said Consola around a mouthful of sizzling meat. "What's the first thing you're going to do when we reach the settlements?"

Harlan wiped his greasy fingers on his leggings. "I'm going to pick my woman up, kick the cabin door off its hinges, carry her inside, and sample her charms. Then I'll set my rifle-gun in the corner."

The men guffawed. Even Patterson managed a silent chuckle before turning on his side and drifting into a dream-filled sleep of Susan standing nude before a cabin door. Or was it Consetta? No, it was Susan when she was eighteen. The dream telescoped in on a small puckered blue scar above her left breast, a scar that covered an ounce of lead that the surgeon said lay too close to her heart to remove, a scar that was the only blemish on an otherwise perfect body.

Then the dream became a nightmare. He saw the scar burst in a splatter of deep red blood and Susan clutch her breast and fall. Indians were all about her, shouting, dancing, screaming. Then he was there, gathering her into his arms and carrying her out of the forest to the waiting arms of a blonde-haired woman . . .

Patterson bolted upright. Sweat burned his eyes, and he could smell the stench of fear oozing from his pores.

He shook his head to clear his thoughts—what he had dreamed had taken place twenty-five years before, during the French and Indian War.

*   *   *

By late evening of June 13, the four frontiersmen stood on the banks of the Cumberland River. They were still two hundred miles from the falls of the Ohio. They built another raft and crossed the Cumberland at night to insure against a repeat of the day before. But they made poor time the next day, and covered even fewer miles the day following. Weariness, lack of food, and just plain hard traveling were taking their toll.

On the eighteenth of June, they crossed the Green River in central Kentucky by swimming on their sides, holding their weapons, horns, and shot pouches above their heads. They could barely drag themselves up the far bank. Exhaustion left them no choice—they had to stop and rest. Even Morgan Patterson, anxious as he was to see his wife, had to admit that the decision was justified.

Bitsy banged the pots and pans together in the dishwater. She jerked her hand out of the thin lye soapsuds and pushed a lock of unruly copper-colored hair off her forehead, leaving a trace of soap across her youthful brow.

"Don't you realize, Mama," she said over her shoulder, "that if we had gone with Simon Kenton to Harrodsburg, we would have been where Papa will undoubtedly stop first?" She rolled her large green eyes toward the ceiling and breathed a long sigh that Susan diagnosed as exaggerated irritation with a mother who had no sympathy for a girl who would have enjoyed flirting with Kenton on the sixty-mile trip to Harrodsburg.

"I understand," said Susan, paying not one bit of attention to Bitsy's surliness, "that several hundred new men have come to Harrod's place since the Ohio became navigable, and I hear, too, that they're not the caliber of men who opened this country. They're land speculators, get-rich-quick people, vagrants running from the war, and heaven knows what else."

"But, Mama," argued the girl, "surely there is one decent young man in the group."

"I'm sure there is. We will wait until your father returns and then have a look."

Bitsy groaned aloud, but she had exhausted her argument, for the moment anyway. "Mama," she said, changing

57

the subject, "are we safe here? Can this fort stand a full-fledged attack?"

"Why, yes, I think so," answered Susan, wiping the pewter dishes and stacking them on the board above the homemade washbasin. "We have two hundred guns in this fort. I should think that would be enough, at least until help could come from Martin's Station or Boonesboro or Harrodsburg. Yes, honey, I think we're safe. . . . I just wish Morgan would hurry up and get here. He and General Clark will whip these loafers into an army in no time."

Bitsy appraised her mother's profile thoughtfully, taking in the small straight nose, high cheekbones, and delicately arched eyebrows. The soft glow from the coals in the fireplace erased the fine lines around Susan's eyes, and her skin appeared smooth and soft, much the way she must have looked when she was Bitsy's age.

Oh, Mama, thought Bitsy, why couldn't I have looked you. You are so lovely.

"You really love Papa, don't you, Mama?" she blurted in an attempt to hide her feelings of inadequacy toward beauty, for she was genuinely unaware of her transformation from a gangling, big-eyed youth, to a lovely young woman who was fast earning the reputation of being the prettiest girl in Kentucky.

"Why, of course, I do, silly," answered Susan.

"Nay," said the girl seriously, "I know you love Papa. What I mean is, you *really* love Papa."

Susan stopped her drying and looked deep into her daughter's eyes. "I've been in love with your father since the first time I saw him, Bitsy. I always will be."

"Will it be like that for me, Mama? Will I know right off when I see the one for me?"

Susan dropped her head back and laughed happily; she loved her daughter's straightforwardness. "I dare say I have no way of knowing, darling. But as honest a person as you are with yourself, you will probably know before he does."

Susan put another plate on the board. "I was beginning to think your father was never going to fall in love with me. . . . In fact, I thought he was in love with a highborn English lady, a truly beautiful woman—"

"I bet she wasn't as pretty as you," interrupted Bitsy in a childish, matter-of-fact voice.

"But she was, darling," corrected Susan. "She was very probably the most beautiful woman in the colonies at that time."

Bitsy frowned. "What happened to her, Mama?"

"I don't know for sure. You see, I was ill for a long time after I was shot by Indians just outside of Fort Cumberland, Maryland." She wondered how much she should reveal to Bitsy. "Your papa was shot at the same time. . . . No," she said upon reflection, "he was shot before I was. But he was fighting so fiercely that he was not aware that he had taken a ball."

Susan's fingers moved to a small porcelain locket that nestled between her breasts. Over half of the locket was missing, shot away so many years before. The locket had been given to Morgan Patterson by a friend who had sworn it would bring him good luck. And it had done just that, deflecting a ball that would surely have killed Patterson instantly.

Morgan had fastened the locket around Susan's neck two years ago when he had joined Clark's forces and marched off to Illinois. "It has kept me safe all these years," he had told her, kissing her lips. "Now I pray that it will do the same for you."

"Why don't you ever tell me these things?" cried Bitsy, breaking into Susan's thoughts. "You never tell me anything, especially of your life before you married Papa."

Susan's eyes became luminous. "My life didn't begin till I met your papa. Anyway, when I was finally able to be up and about, Judith was gone. They said she married a British officer and returned to England. I never did know the truth of it all."

Susan's smile dimpled her cheeks. "But I can tell you this, she sure gave me a run for my money with your father. Darned near got him, too."

"Oh, she did not, Mama," scoffed Bitsy. "Papa's loved you since the beginning of time."

Susan blushed at Bitsy's unintended reference to her age. She was painfully aware that the years had taken their toll on her beauty as well as her strength. The only thing time hadn't altered was her undying devotion to Morgan Patterson.

A flame of motherly love suddenly burned in Susan's

59

breast. She wanted to reach out and hold her daughter the way she used to when Bitsy was a child, for she realized that it was only a matter of time before some young man would whisk Bitsy away, just as Morgan Patterson had done with her. And for the first time in her life, Susan felt an acute self-pity. She thought of her own mother then and wondered if she, too, had experienced such feelings when Patterson had taken her only daughter for his wife. Then Susan did take Bitsy into her arms and hold her close. It was as though she knew, that evening of June 18, 1780, that she would perform that tender gesture only a few more times in her life.

CHAPTER
· 5 ·

CAPTAIN HENRY BIRD WAS disgusted as he walked among the tents and shelters that housed his troops and supplies at the forks of the Licking River some fifty miles above Ruddle's Fort. The strategy that had been so painstakingly planned at Detroit had fallen completely apart.

Instead of turning downstream at the conjunction of the Great Miami and Ohio rivers and taking Clark's Fort at the falls, the Indians had elected to push upstream to the Licking, descend it to where it forked, and go overland to Ruddle's and Martin's Forts—and Bird was powerless to do aught but follow along. The captain was well aware of his precarious position with his allies. He and his one hundred fifty British Regulars were at the mercy of the eight or nine hundred Indians who accompanied his meager army. The plain truth was that Captain Henry Bird feared his allies a hundred times more than he did the uncounted Americans who waited at the forts.

"Damn it, Bird," raged Southhampton as he joined the captain. "We were supposed to capture the fort at the falls and use it as a base of operations. It is pure foolishness to attack these small outlying stations, pure foolishness, sir."

"I quite agree, Major," said Bird. "Perhaps you would like to impress that point on our savage allies?"

"That's your job, Captain. You're supposed to be in command here, so do what you were sent here to do!"

Bird's face became livid.

"Major Southhampton, I know what my duties are, but to be perfectly frank, sir, I will be more than pleased if I can simply prevent a complete massacre when these forts surrender."

"What happens to the Americans is of little consequence to me, Captain. The Indians can have them, as far as I'm concerned. It's the fort at the falls that I want—and the men who garrison the place."

Bird studied Southhampton for a long moment.

"Major," he said finally, "it will take every officer I've got to maintain even a semblance of order when these forts capitulate. I hope, sir, that I can depend on you as an officer and a gentleman serving the king's army to do all that is in your power to prevent such outrages as these savages are capable of."

Southhampton waved the statement away.

"Of course, I will, Captain, but I believe you have the situation well in hand. After all, sir, the Indians gave you their word they were only interested in horses and plunder."

"Do you believe they can be trusted to keep their word, Major?" asked Bird, begging for reassurance that he was still in command.

"Why, of course, I do, sir," said Southhampton, repressing a smile. "Now I'd best see how Chard is handling the artillery." He strode quickly toward the landing where over eight hundred Indians watched intently as four swivel guns were unloaded and lashed securely to backs of heavy draft horses.

Simon and George Girty had stripped down to breechclouts and leggings and had applied black and red war paint to their faces and bodies. They grinned as Southhampton approached. "They will have the wheeled gun and the three-pounder ashore in a minute, Major." George pointed toward the riverbank where Chard and several red-coated soldiers had erected a wooden crane and were wrestling a heavy four-and-a-half-foot brass barrel over the side of a bateau. "I want to see the faces of the Kentuckians when we roll that big bastard up to their gates."

Both brothers laughed heartily at the image.

Southhampton was revolted by the savage appearance of the brothers. But by the same token he envied them their ability, as renegades, to plunder and butcher at will with no more thought or reason than a bloodthirsty Indian. Perhaps, he reflected thoughtfully, before this venture is over, I, too, will know the thrill of sinking a tomahawk deep into a man's skull. Aye, I would like nothing better than to watch Morgan Patterson wallow in his own blood as the last spasms of life jerk from his body. No, he decided, it would not be the last spasms of life; it would be the first spasms of death. Southhampton smiled at the picture he had conjured, finding it both relieving and refreshing.

"I'll tell you right off, George," he said, raising his eyebrows contemptuously, "I am bloody well displeased with you and Simon."

"If you're talkin' about the fact that the Indians won't go against Clark's Fort, I damn well don't give a hoot in hell how displeased you are, Major."

Southhampton swallowed hard. He had not expected such a retort. He smiled indulgently and tried another tack. "I thought you had more influence with the savages than you obviously have."

"I can sway the Indians about some things, some I can't."

"To the Indians, it don't make no difference where they attack, Major," added Simon Girty. "Clark has a cannon at the falls, and these Indians know it. They won't go up against cannon."

"So they throw away a chance to take Kentucky, sir?" said Southhampton angrily.

"With British backing, they can take Ruddle's Station, Martin's, Bryan's, and Lexington, Major. That's more scalps, horses, and plunder than they can carry—and they can come back anytime and do it again. So why should they take a chance against Clark and his cannon?"

Southhampton wanted to scream at the man that he didn't give a damn about Clark or his cannon, that he had an old score to settle and didn't intend for a bunch of scurvy Indians to stand in his way. Had he done so, he very probably would have captured the Girty brothers' attention. As with their adopted red brothers, revenge was a way of life with them. But Southhampton had no understanding of the Indian mind. So, instead of telling the Girty brothers the truth, he merely swore at them under his breath, refusing to admit that he did not have the courage to voice those oaths aloud.

63

"I will tell you this, Major," said George Girty, eyeing Southhampton with a hard, unblinking stare that left the officer wondering if the man ever batted his eyes. "I think I know who started that rumor."

Southhampton's anger was replaced by gaping surprise. Then his blood surged in his veins, pulsing through his body until it pounded at his temples like sledgehammers. His mind was already at work, visualizing glory and fame, perhaps even his long overdue promotion. It was all hovering just beyond his fingertips. And the means toward those elusive honors stood before him, staring unblinking, like two stupid savages, without the slightest idea of the value of such information to the right person. Trying hard to hide his excitement, Southhampton cautiously felt the men out. "What do you mean you think you know who the spy is? Are you not sure?"

"We're sure," said Simon Girty.

Southhampton's heart soared. He could see himself accepting his promotion, could hear Commandant DePeyster's extravagant praise for his outstanding service to the Crown. "Who is it?" he asked bluntly.

George Girty shook his head. "We ain't got no proof yet, Major. But if my calculations are correct, there's only one more place that a smart spy could hurt us—and if he intends to try, it's got to be done pretty quick."

Southhampton's eyes narrowed, then bulged in surprised embarrassment. It was quite galling that a white savage, a woodsrunner, had anticipated a move that he and every other military officer in the expedition had overlooked.

"The cannon," he breathed. "They'll try to spike the cannon."

"That's my guess," said Girty, "and when they do, me and Simon will be there waitin'."

Southhampton smashed his fist into his open palm. "I'll put a ring of regulars—"

"Now, that would be real bright, Major," said Simon Girty dryly. "They'd know for bloody well sure that we was on to 'em." He cast a veiled glance at his brother. "Me and George will take care of the cannon."

"See that you do, Girty," warned Southhampton, "and

you'd best not make any mistakes." His eyes became thoughtful slits. "I want the culprit, Girty, and I want him alive."

"You'll have the spy alive, Major," replied the renegade, displaying a row of bad teeth in a hideously painted face.

"One other thing," said Southhampton as the brothers turned to leave, "it will be worth a purse of silver to the both of you if the traitor is brought directly to me . . . and no one else. Do you understand?"

A spy adequately versed in the intricacies of espionage would have left well enough alone. But Judith, knowing nothing of reconnoitering, felt perfectly safe as she slipped silently along the dark riverbank in search of the wheeled gun that Chard had brought ashore that afternoon.

The moon broke through the overcast sky, illuminating the area with its silver glow. Judith, taking advantage of the momentary light, quickly scanned the terrain until she located the cannon. And to her astonished pleasure, she found that Captain Bird had been so confident of his strength and position that he had negligently refrained from posting a guard.

The elation was short-lived. A long-forgotten caution fought its way up from the recesses of her mind, a caution taught to her the hard way, through trial, tribulation, error—and pain.

She was recalling something Morgan Patterson had pounded into her head: "Never go straight into a camp —always scout it first. And don't go in after scouting it if it don't feel right."

Well, it didn't feel right—not right at all.

Judith squinted into the darkness as the moon drifted behind the clouds. She was beginning to tingle with fear. Every fiber of her nerves screamed that she was walking into a trap. Repressing her instincts, she raised her skirts and sprinted to the gun. Quickly she took a forged spike from her pocket and wedged it securely into the touchhole in the top of the cannon's breech. But when she raised the small sledgehammer she'd stolen from the farrier's tent and attempted to drive the spike into place, a strong hand clasped her slender wrist with such force that she dropped the tool.

Judith spun about and stood face to face with the Girty brothers. She shuddered, hardly recognizing the men through their war paint and feathers, and wondered how they had managed to get so close without a sound.

For a brief second, no one moved. Then Judith tensed, preparing to spring past the Girtys and lose herself in the darkness.

"Don't try it," advised George Girty, tightening his grip on her wrist.

Judith winced and tried to jerk free, but Girty increased the pressure until Judith was sure the bone would snap.

Feinting quickly to the left, she vaulted to the right, but her ruse was wasted. Girty's fist exploded against her temple, sending a thousand shooting stars into the darkness that engulfed her.

When she regained her senses, Girty was kneeling beside her. She could feel the wet grass on her naked legs and buttocks where her dress had been raised above her waist. "I thought you Indians didn't rape women when you were on the warpath," she said, more calmly than she thought possible. For the truth was, fear, mixed with outrage, was causing her breath to come in short gasps.

"I'm only Indian when it serves my purpose," said Girty, fumbling with the tie knot of the waistband that held up his breechclout. "But, judging from what your husband said by the river the other day, it ought not make any difference to you. You've lain with Indians and whites."

The hard blow from such a small fist, a blow that split Girty's lip and snapped his head back, was totally unexpected, and the string of profanity that followed the onslaught was even more unladylike.

Girty's eyes narrowed to mere slits. Quite calmly, he smashed his callused palm and then the hard knuckles of the back of his hand against her face, snapping her head from side to side as though her neck were broken. Judith's senses were reeling, but she fought violently, her body arching and twisting, her legs kicking and thrashing, forcing

George Girty to grasp her shoulders with both hands in an attempt to hold her still.

"Damn it, Simon," he grated, "help me with this wench, she's a mean son of a bitch."

Simon Girty glared at his brother. "Like the lady said, George, and you damn well know it's true, I never molest women when I'm running the warrior's path. I'll kill her if it's necessary, but I won't rape her."

Simon Girty crossed his arms, Indian fashion, and stared straight ahead. If he was shocked by what his eyes met, his next words revealed nothing. "And if I was you, George," he said without emotion, "I believe I would let the lady up."

"And if he doesn't," came a soft voice out of the darkness, "I'm going to blow his ugly head off."

As he had done so many times in the past, Chard had followed Judith when she had slipped from the camp. Had he not lost her in the pitch-black woods by the river, he would have been close behind when Girty caught her, thereby preventing her brutal beating and near-rape.

The quiet that followed his statement was shattered by the nerve-racking double click of a pair of hammers locking into firing position. Even in the darkness, Simon and George Girty knew that a brace of heavy-caliber pistols was pointed directly at them.

Then, in a voice that was barely audible, Judith whispered, "Morgan, is that really you?"

"Yes, Mother," Chard answered, his hands shaking with controlled rage, "it's me, Richard Morgan."

"My God," breathed Judith, staring at her son's silhouette. "For a moment, Chard, I thought you were . . . someone else. You . . . you sounded just like . . . someone else."

But Chard wasn't listening. "Let her up, Girty," he said almost too casually.

Because George Girty had seen death too many times to be mistaken about it, he climbed carefully to his feet and crossed his arms as Simon had done. He had no doubt that one wrong move on his part would be the last he ever made.

Judith rose more slowly, biting her lip to keep from moaning. She pushed her skirts down over her legs, then

67

staggered to the nearest tree and leaned heavily against it. Closing her eyes, she pressed her cheek to the trunk, embracing the rough bark as though it were a pillow. The enormity of being caught in the act of sabotaging the king's cannon had struck her like a well-placed kick in the stomach, making her head spin and her knees turn to jelly. She would have swooned had the tree not been there to support her. The scaly bark cut into the soft skin of her face and lips, but Judith felt none of it. She realized for the first time the full impact of what she had done. She foresaw the humiliation and disgrace that would befall her innocent parents, the scandal that would cloud the grand Cornwallace name. "God help me," she whispered, raising her eyes to the darkened heavens. And in that moment of self-condemnation, Judith truly wished that George Girty had killed her.

"Mother," said Chard, not taking his eyes off the Girty brothers as he moved cautiously to Judith, "I have no choice but to place you under arrest and turn you over to Captain Bird." Then, slipping his arm around Judith to steady her, he whispered, "Why, Mother? Why in God's name did you do it?"

Judith did not have the heart to answer.

The camp came alive as the party marched up to Captain Bird's marquee. Fires were built high, illuminating the area almost as bright as day. Men watched in wide-eyed disbelief as Bird was summoned from his cot and informed that the traitor had been apprehended.

Awakened by the commotion, Southhampton sprang from his cot and snatched on his uniform. He cursed the Girtys violently, vowing to make them pay dearly for their betrayal. He was nearly running by the time he reached the crowd that surrounded Bird's tent. He pushed through the mass and came to an abrupt halt.

Southhampton's eyes moved from Judith to Chard to the Girtys, then back to Judith.

His first reaction was disbelief that quickly turned to fear, not for his wife, but for himself should her actions be misinterpreted to include him. Then came the inevitable anger, blame, and searing bitterness. Promotions, glory, praise—they were suddenly just meaningless words without substance, words that he detested.

His eyes bored into Judith with murderous fury. He willed his wife to look at him, to see his loathing, his disgust, his total renunciation of her. He wanted her to see that she would get no support from him. In fact, he would do everything in his power to ensure that she receive the full measure of British justice for her crime—quick and severe. He would exonerate himself at her expense.

But Judith did not glance at her husband. Even if she had, it is doubtful that his scalding gaze would have affected her much. What Southhampton thought or said had little meaning at that precise moment; it was Captain Bird she dreaded to confront.

Judith could hear Bird hastily donning his uniform, and she hung her head in shame, for she remembered the admiration on his handsome face not long ago. She sighed. That same face would be filled with repugnance and contempt when he learned who the spy was.

When Bird did emerge, he showed neither of the reactions Judith expected; instead she saw pity and sympathy. Judith could have accepted hatred, even embraced it. But Bird's unexpected kindness stripped her of what little pride and self-control she had retained. Although she loathed herself for succumbing, she did a most feminine thing: she broke down and cried the bitter tears of one who has hit rock bottom.

Strangely enough, it was her husband who unwittingly revived her spirits. His two words, "Hang her," stilled her tears and rallied her courage and self-reliance. With an inborn elegance, she drew herself to full height and proudly faced the mob of incredulous soldiers and stone-faced Indians who surrounded her.

"There will be no bloody hanging," said Bird angrily. "Lady Southhampton will have a fair trial when we return to Detroit." He eyed Southhampton warningly. "There will be no more talk of a hanging, sir."

"You might reconsider that decision, Captain," said George Girty. "This woman spread the lie that Clark was at the falls, and," he smiled thinly, sure his next statement would seal Judith's fate, "she tried to poison you, Captain Bird."

"I did not!" protested Judith. "I've never tried to kill anyone."

Girty withdrew a half-empty rum bottle from his hunting pouch.

"Then you won't mind drinking what's in this bottle, the bottle that you threw in the river."

His smile broadened as Judith's face turned ashen, and people in the crowd, including Bird, sucked in their breath. Girty pulled the stopper and extended the bottle.

Without hesitation, Judith took the bottle and tilted it to her lips. But before she could swallow, Southhampton slapped her hand aside and caught her by the throat, drawing her up on tiptoe. "She would drink poison just to cheat the hangman's rope."

"There'll be no hanging, Major!" exploded Bird. Then, turning to a nearby officer, he quickly instructed the man to secure Judith in one of the supply shelters and place a twenty-four-hour guard at the tent.

Southhampton was furious, but there was little he could do. Bird was in command, and, like it or not, the captain's orders would be followed. There was one avenue, however, in which Bird had no jurisdiction: the domestic rights of a husband over his wife.

"Captain Bird," he said, knowing he was on firm ground, "I demand, sir, as a husband embarrassed by an unworthy wife, my rights to have her publicly flogged—a feat which I personally will perform with the greatest of pleasure."

Bird took a deep breath and let it out slowly. He had never liked Southhampton, but until that moment, he had been unaware that he actually despised the man.

"Under the law, it is your privilege, Major," he said with slow deliberation, making no attempt to hide his scorn, "but it will have to wait until we return from attacking Ruddle's Station. The night is almost gone, and we leave at daybreak. I suggest, sir, that we get what sleep we can."

But sleep wouldn't come to Chard. He tossed and turned, hating himself for not letting the hammers fall on the Girty brothers. It would have been such a simple way out for

70

Judith. That thought, however, made him fling his arm across his eyes and moan aloud, for he knew deep down inside that he lacked the courage to take a human life, even that of such a vile excuse for humanity as the Girty brothers. Chard closed his eyes and silently cursed himself, for his own mother would pay the ultimate price for his cowardice.

Daylight came slowly to the folks at Ruddle's Station on the morning of June 24. Once again the sky had opened and dumped its overflowing reservoir of rainwater onto the Kentuckians.

Captain Bird's advance guard had used the downpour to their best advantage. When the overcast sky grew light enough to see by, a startled crowd of Americans stood shoulder to shoulder at the loopholes in the palisade of Ruddle's Fort and stared in disbelief at the British Union Jack hanging limp and sodden above a battery of earth and rails that had been raised not eighty yards away. Through the rain, the Americans could make out what appeared to be thousands of red-coated soldiers and savage Indians moving briskly about in preparation for an offensive action.

"I want every rifleman we got on these walls immediately," bellowed Captain Isaac Ruddle. "You, there!" he pointed to a huddle of women who cringed in fear under the overhang of a blockhouse, "get every iron pot you can muster and start melting lead for bullets. Hurry, now. We've not got much time."

Hearing Ruddle's order, Susan and Bitsy darted into their cabin. Moments later, they reappeared, Bitsy with a full-stocked Pennsylvania rifle and Susan with her daughter's shot pouch and powder horn slung over her shoulder. Susan grinned prettily at the astonishment on Ruddle's face when she and Bitsy climbed a ladder to the roof of their cabin. "We've probably fought more Indians than you have, Captain Ruddle," called Susan in answer to his unasked question. "You'd best get some good riflemen up on these roofs so we can shoot down on the British . . . who," she added testily, "you and your professional Indian fighters swore would never get here."

Bitsy laid her rifle barrel across the roof tree and

aligned the sights on a red-coated soldier who had raised himself halfway out of the trench in order to see better. "Well, Captain," the girl said, resting her cheek lightly against the stock, "obviously they did get here. Now what do you intend to do about it?"

Ruddle scowled at the two women, then pushed his way along the palisade, instructing several of his men to climb to the roofs of the cabins and fire at any target that presented itself.

Bitsy took a long, steady aim on the partially concealed soldier and let her breath slide through her teeth. Her rifle roared, and the man pitched face first into the mud before the trench. He did not move. Bitsy had opened the battle with a shot that would echo for more than fifteen long years, would have the bloodiest aftermath in the history of Kentucky. Throughout the morning, between the interminable drenchings, the American eagle kept the mighty British lion at bay with nothing more than the threat of their long-guns which, inconceivably, considering the number of shots fired, had killed only one British Regular and wounded one Indian.

Just before noon, Bird arrived at the breastwork and wasted no time ordering Chard to set up the three-pound cannon. To the further dismay of the British, Chard's first shot did little more than shear off a spar by the west blockhouse. The young ensign ordered the piece reloaded. When the smoke of the second charge cleared, the Indians raised a howl of displeasure. The only visible damage was to the same blockhouse; a log had been driven in about six inches.

The Kentuckians shouted and jeered at the British Army, making Bird's face flush with anger.

"They think the three-pounder's a swivel-gun, Captain," said Chard, smiling with embarrassment. "It don't seem to be making much of a bloody impression at all."

"Then we'll bring out something that will." Bird wheeled his mount and galloped through the mud toward the tree line where the six-pound cannon stood hitched to a team of four heavy draft horses.

"You men!" he roared to the waiting gunners and teamsters, "get that damned cannon on the line. And be quick about it!"

The horses lunged into motion, straining at their collars and breeching. Trace chains snapped tight, and double trees groaned as the massive wheels slowly turned.

"Jesus Christ," came the quiet voice of an American as the wheeled cannon came churning across the field. And for a long moment, those two words seemed to adequately sum up the feelings of all the folks in Ruddle's Fort. Then people up and down the palisade began clamoring for Captain Ruddle to do something—anything. But there was little that Ruddle or anyone could do against such an unexpected increase in firepower.

Ruddle peered through a shooting loop at the gaping bore of the big gun, and as a rider carrying a flag of truce broke rank and walked his horse slowly toward the fort, Ruddle's former arrogance became a mixture of fear and anger.

He swallowed, not liking what he had to say next. "We'd best listen to their offer. We have little choice, actually."

Chard rode his horse through the gate and into the common grounds that lay in the center of the fort. From the corner of his eye he could see Americans of all ages, sizes, and descriptions leaning against the wall, standing in family groups, and marching toward him with quick, angry steps. His backbone crawled, but his face was impassive as he sat his mount and waited to be addressed by the leader of the rebel forces.

People pushed in around his horse, imprisoning the animal, staring up at Chard as if he were the devil himself, and even though he continued to keep his eyes locked straight ahead, he could feel the anger, resentment, and fear that gripped the small garrison. Ruddle pushed through the crowd and caught the reins of Chard's mount.

"Get down and say your piece, mister," he said in short, clipped words, his only outward show of nervousness. "You've got our attention."

Chard touched his cocked hat in a salute. "I prefer to remain seated, sir, if that is agreeable."

"Then tell us what your commander wants. You didn't ride in here to pass the time of day."

Chard took a deep breath and let it slide between his teeth. He had first thought it a great honor to be selected to offer the terms of capitulation, but as his gaze journeyed over the motley array of sodden men, women, and children who fortified the small station, noting that no soldiers were present, not even militia, he was ashamed of his part in the surrender. He was ashamed to know that twelve hundred fighting men, not to mention six pieces of artillery, had come over six hundred miles to attack a handful of farmers and their families. And as he straightened in the saddle and looked solemnly into Ruddle's face, he could only wonder what the Royal British Army was coming to.

"Captain Henry Bird of His Majesty's Eighth Regiment demands the surrender of this fort and all its inhabitants and worldly goods," he said with what dignity he could muster. "In return, Captain Bird guarantees safe passage for your women and children to the next closest settlement. The men will become prisoners of war, with the right to keep their weapons."

Ruddle's breath burst from his lips. "That's not an ungenerous offer, sir," he said, looking up at the young British officer in surprise. "But the decision will have to be agreed to by a majority of the folks here. If you would be kind enough to wait, we will vote on it."

Chard tilted his head in a simulated bow. "I'm at your disposal, sir. Take as long as you wish." Chard waited, his eyes taking in the perimeter of the fort, the log buildings, huts, and lean-tos, and finally the roof where Bitsy, her wet, burnished hair plastered tight against her small face, was reloading her rifle. As she reached out to run the ramrod down the barrel, her rain-drenched bodice clung tightly to her small, firm breasts, and her soaked skirts closely hugged the rounded curves of her hips. Chard sucked in his breath. Never in his twenty-four years had he seen anything or anyone half so beautiful.

But if he had expected an answering smile when Bitsy felt him staring at her and turned her sea-green eyes in his direction, he was badly mistaken. The girl frowned, then scowled, then tossed her head angrily and climbed down the makeshift ladder to join her mother in the crowd of Americans, who were arguing back and forth about whether they should capitulate.

The young ensign edged his mount closer to the throng and raised himself up in the stirrups, searching for that mass of copper-colored hair that had vanished into the crowd. He spotted her standing beside a tall woman who, it was plain even from where he sat, had once been an extraordinary beauty. And even though it was evident that the harsh frontier life had taken its toll, she was still an unusually handsome woman.

"I think we should fight until help arrives," the woman was saying. "Surely someone will come to assist us if we hold out for a while longer."

"They'll blow this fort down around our ears, Mrs. Patterson," Ruddle disagreed, amid nods from many of the Kentuckians.

"Maybe so," she argued, "but at least we'll have a chance. If we surrender, we've no chance at all."

"Ma'am," interjected Chard. "'Tis not my intention to dispute your word, but there are over twelve hundred men out there." He threw his hand toward the gate. "We have six cannon trained on this fort. Ma'am, you don't have a prayer in heaven of defending this place."

"You keep your arrogant British mouth shut," exploded Bitsy, eyeing the ensign hatefully, "or so help me God, I'll forget that you're an emissary under a flag of truce and shoot you out of the saddle myself."

She raised the long rifle and took aim at the horseman.

Chard's breath caught. Never had a woman talked to him so humiliatingly. It rankled his pride that a mere Kentucky frontier girl was not only unimpressed with his grand appearance but actually hostile toward him personally—to the point of shooting him. Although Chard fully expected to feel the ball smash into his body, he neither flinched nor cringed as he looked into Bitsy's angry face.

A hush fell over the crowd, and for a long instant every eye in the fort was glued to the irate young woman.

"Bitsy," said Susan, laying a restraining hand on the rifle, "you've shot at enough soldiers this day."

"But I only hit one, Mama," complained the girl bitterly. Then, with a cry of frustration, Bitsy dropped the butt of the rifle into the mud and turned her back on the white-faced young man whose heart was trying without success to return to its normal rhythm after having been stopped for what seemed to him an eternity.

"Sir," said Ruddle, resuming his position of authority, "tell your commander that we agree to his terms. Tell him to present himself in one hour. We will have the necessary papers ready for his signature."

The ensign bowed stiffly from the waist. Then, his back ramrod straight, he carefully trotted his horse through the gate.

Captain Henry Bird, Major James Southhampton, and Ensign Richard Morgan Southhampton dismounted before the nearly three hundred subdued people of Ruddle's Fort. No swords were presented; no drums rolled; no salutes were fired. No soldiers stood at attention to honor the quiet mass of frightened frontier folk who were trying valiantly to retain a portion of their dignity while fearing what fate held in store for them. For, as the terms for surrender had stipulated, their weapons had been neatly stacked in a blockhouse. They were nervously aware that they were at the mercy of the British and; God forbid, a horde of heavily armed savage Indians.

Chard glanced uneasily over the crowd; nowhere did he see Bitsy or her mother. He wasn't sure why he was trying to locate them, only that he felt an overwhelming need to be near them while the surrender and evacuation took place.

He glanced around the fort, more uncomfortable by the minute. Something was terribly wrong. It was the same feeling that had nagged him ever since he had witnessed the look of conspiracy that had passed between his father and the Girty brothers at Detroit. That, and the undeniable fact that the Indians had broken their word to Captain Bird; instead of waiting in the forest, as he had commanded, they were advancing stealthily toward the gate, a gate he suspected had been ordered, by none other than his own father, to be thrown wide open.

Almost in panic, Chard again scanned the crowd. As he did, the small hairs on the back of his neck rose up in alarm. Hideous screams and war cries had broken the stillness, shrieks and screeches unlike any human sound he had ever heard.

Spinning toward the gate, he saw hundreds of naked red men funneling through the small opening, pushing and shoving one another in an effort to be the first to reach the Americans. Chard flung himself from the saddle and lunged into the crowd of terrified Kentuckians. "Run!" he screamed into their stunned faces. But to his horror, they stood rooted to the muddy ground as if they had grown there. "Get inside," he pleaded. "Hide until we can get control of these savages. Hurry!"

But even as he begged the people of Ruddle's Fort to heed his warning, hordes of naked savages, screaming with blood lust, were falling upon the first Americans they encountered, sinking their tomahawks deep into their skulls, hacking and slashing with razor-edged butcher knives, at point-blank range discharging Brown Bess muskets into live, quivering flesh. Yet, even then the Americans refused to flee, standing like statues, waiting to be hacked down by the bloody hatchets of the red men.

The young ensign charged through the Americans like a madman, until finally, near the back edge of the stunned crowd, he spied Susan and Bitsy huddled in a close embrace.

Pushing, punching, and elbowing, Chard beat his way toward the two women, who, like the other Kentuckians, stood waiting mutely for the inevitable outcome. When Chard finally reached Bitsy and Susan, the cries and screams and piercing war whoops of the savages had grown to such a crescendo that they drowned out all other sound. "Get inside the nearest cabin!" he shouted.

Neither moved. They, like the others, were in a state of shock that paralyzed them mentally and physically. And on top of all that, Susan seemed to have lost her mind. She was slowly caressing a small locket that dangled from her neck.

"Damn it," Chard grated, catching Bitsy around her waist, while his other arm encircled Susan in a similar fashion, "I said, get inside!"

He dragged the unresisting women to a cabin and flung them through the door. "Fort up," he ordered, "and don't open the door for anything or anybody." He turned and raced again into the mass of Americans, who were at last showing signs of life as they tried valiantly to defend themselves barehanded against the cleaving hatchets and slicing blades of the savages.

When he finally worked his way to the front of the crowd where the worst of the carnage was taking place, it took every ounce of self-discipline to keep from going to his knees and retching up what little food he had eaten that morning. He saw a baby torn from its mother's arms and tossed into a fire, and when the fear-crazed woman tried to pull the infant from the flames, a Shawnee rushed up and tomahawked her between the eyes.

Everywhere Chard looked, other atrocities were taking place. He tried to cover his ears to block out the sound of hatchets splitting skullbone, the sucking noise of a ten-inch blade being withdrawn from live flesh, the tearing swish of hair being ripped from a human skull; but even though his ears were muffled, his eyes could still see Indians shaking fresh scalps to rid them of excess blood, the tortured victims writhing amid screams of agony, and in many cases actually watching their hair being tied nonchalantly to an Indian's belt. He could see that and the hundreds of other humiliations and hurts that accompanied such butchery.

Stumbling past defenseless men, women, and children who were doing their best to keep from being decapitated by the blood-crazed savages, the ensign caught Captain Bird by his tunic lapels and snatched him to within inches of his angry face. "Stop this carnage, Bird," he shouted. "What kind of an inhumane wretch are you?"

Captain Bird stared incredulously at the young officer.

"What in God's name can I do?" he cried, flinging out his hand in a forlorn gesture. "These savages have gone completely mad. There's nothing anybody can do to stop them."

"We can get in there," Chard pointed toward the struggling mob, "and try to reason with the chiefs. Damn it, man, if we don't do something in a hurry, there won't be a live American in this fort!"

"Father!" he shouted to Major Southhampton, who was standing as far under a blockhouse overhang as the log wall permitted. "Father, we need you to help us stop this slaughter. Summon all the regulars and get them in here quick."

Staring fearfully at the crazed Indians, Southhampton plastered himself more rigidly against the barrier. "I'll not do it, Chard. We cannot risk our lives among those bloodthirsty demons. They might mistake us for Americans."

The young man gazed contemptuously at his sire, ashamed that Southhampton was his kin—and his superior.

"Little likelihood of that," Chard said turning again to the slaughter. "These Americans have courage."

With Captain Bird and what few red-coated soldiers he could gather following reluctantly in his wake, Chard raced into the carnage.

An Indian who had seen Susan and Bitsy slam and bar the cabin door rushed madly around the three exposed sides of the building in search of an opening. Finding none, he dropped to his belly and crawled under the puncheon floor.

Inside the cabin, a hatchet blade slipped between two planks and pried up a pegged corner. "Bitsy," whispered Susan, "fetch me that pot of lead off the fire."

Bitsy sprinted to the hearth, and with a small iron hook lifted a brass kettle off the swing crane. Susan wrapped pieces of heavy cloth around her hands, took the container, and moved quietly to the small crack the Indian had opened. Without a word, she tilted the pot and watched a wide stream of molten metal disappear into the opening beneath the floor.

A hideous bellow followed; the lead had caught the Indian full in his upturned face as he lay on his back and worked at the overhead planking, searing the skin off his skull and burning his eyes out of their sockets. The Indian's inhuman screams as he crawled blindly from beneath the building very probably did more to stop the bloody massacre of Ruddle's Fort than all the pleading and cajoling the king's men could have accomplished in a lifetime.

The savages released their victims and dashed to the man who was stumbling toward them, his hands groping out before him. They stared in awed silence at the bloody silver-gray metal mask that had once been the man's face.

79

It was the dead silence that drew Southhampton from his lair.

He crept from beneath the overhang and made his way toward the far end of the fort where the soldiers and British officers had congregated. He carefully avoided viewing or touching the mutilated bodies of the dead or, for that matter, those who clung to life by a thread, quivering in the mud as if attempting to hollow out their own final resting place. Just as steadfastly, he refused to gaze into the accusing eyes of those who had survived and who seemed to mock his pretense of leadership and see him for the wretched creature he actually was. He was glad the survivors were being ushered quickly out of the fort under the questionable protection of a body of British Regulars and Canadian Rangers, for he wanted them well out of his sight.

His confidence blossomed once he joined the protection of the British officers milling before the cabin where the Indian had been scalded. Without hesitation he assumed command and marched to the cabin, rapping heavily on the door with the hilt of his sword. "Unbolt this door this instant," he commanded too loudly. "If you should be so foolish as to refuse, I'll have the place burned down around your ears."

In two strides Chard was at his father's side.

"Let them be. We've enough captives to worry about now, sir; two more will be nothing but a larger burden to hamper our movements."

"Damn you!" exploded Southhampton. "Since when does an ensign give a major orders? Get your arse in hand, or I'll have you court-martialed."

Chard stared hard at his father, then drew himself to attention. The major was right. He had overstepped his authority in behalf of two American women. "I beg your pardon, sir."

Turning to the cabin, Southhampton bellowed that those inside had thirty seconds in which to surrender before he ordered the place burned to the ground. He waited impatiently for several seconds. When the door failed to open, he commenced to count out loud.

"Do you think we should give ourselves up, Mama?" whispered Bitsy as Southhampton reached twenty-five.

Susan flashed her daughter a nervous grin. "I think we should stay right where we are."

"But, Mama, he'll burn us up in here."

Susan laughed shakily. "It's been raining for weeks, darling. These logs are drenched; they won't burn, at least not from the outside."

Bitsy's worried expression vanished, and a smile lighted her face, but then it, too, faded as they heard Southhampton make good his threat.

"I hope you're right, Mama," she murmured, as the unmistakable sound of wood being stacked against the outside walls filtered through the chinking.

Stepping away from the door, Southhampton pointed at a bonfire that had been lighted by Indians who were ransacking the cabins and burning everything they didn't need or couldn't carry. "Move that fire over here," he commanded.

In minutes, Susan and Bitsy could hear the crackling of flames as furniture and household goods that had been lovingly and painstakingly hauled hundreds of miles were carelessly broken up and thrown into the fire that licked at the cabin wall. But the sodden logs did nothing more than hiss, sizzle, and smolder.

Southhampton's face grew livid when it became obvious that his efforts were wasted.

Chard approached his father cautiously: "I ask permission to speak, sir."

Southhampton eyed the young man with distaste. "I'm sure you have nothing to say that I would be the least bit interested in, boy."

"Let me talk to them," implored the young man, ignoring the insult. "I think I can get them to come out peaceably. At least let me try, Father."

Southhampton cocked his head to one side with a bored expression. "I don't give a damn whether they come out peacefully or not."

Captain Bird cleared his throat. He resented the major's interference in his command and had been searching for the opportunity to resume leadership. "Go ahead and try to get them out of there, Ensign," he said, jutting out his chin.

"Thank you, sir." Chard purposely avoided meeting his father's angry glare as he stepped around him and walked quickly to the cabin entrance.

"Ladies," he called, knocking gently on the heavy boards, "I implore you to unbar this door and give yourselves up."

" 'Tis that young officer who put us in here and told us not to open the door for anyone," said Bitsy, flushing with anger.

The girl strode to the door and pressed her cheek against the panel.

In shocked silence Susan listened as her daughter, whom she had never heard utter an obscene word in her entire life, calmly and without hesitation told the young ensign exactly where he could place his entreaties for surrender. "You are wasting your lying breath if you think you can wheedle us out of here," she continued, her normally soft voice growing loud with anger. "As far as we are concerned, you have the blood of all those folks on your head. You, sir, are a murderer."

The young man hung his head, not in shame, but in exasperation. He could hardly blame the girl for her bitterness, could even sympathize with her to a degree, for he felt much the same way. Yet, when he had implored the Americans to surrender, he had sincerely believed that he was doing the right thing for the people in Ruddle's Fort.

"Ma'am," he said, "I'm truly sorry for what has happened here. I am as upset by it as you are. You must believe that."

"Go to hell, where you belong," returned Bitsy acidly.

"That's enough," roared Southhampton, eyeing Bird as if to say, I told you so. "You've had your chance, boy, which I knew was a waste. Now stand aside. We'll break down the door."

Four soldiers carrying a large post moved to a position directly before the building and prepared their battering ram for assault.

"Please come out of there," pleaded Chard one last time.

Upon hearing Southhampton's command, Bitsy pushed herself from the door and retreated hastily to

Susan's side. Both women stared anxiously at the heavily barred entrance. They knew it could not stand the prolonged thrusts of a battering ram, but it was their only defense, and they were determined to hold out until they drew their last breath.

Chard stepped aside and turned his back on the four men who rushed against the door with such impact that the small building shook. The seasoned oak cracked and splintered, but to the amazement of all present, the door held.

Again they thrust the ram against the panels, and again the door held.

"Get more men on that ram," shouted Southhampton. "I want those women out of there this instant."

Two Indians added their weight to the heavy log; it was more than the door could stand.

Susan and Bitsy watched in undisguised fear as the crossbar bowed from the impact, then snapped like a gunshot, and their only hope of evading capture disintegrated into a crashing pile of splintered wood that would have been useful only as kindling.

The two Indians rushed into the cabin and seized Bitsy and Susan by the hair of their heads. Amid screams and kicks, the savages dragged the struggling women out into the common, where they unceremoniously threw them to the ground and fell on them with raised hatchets.

Before the deadly blows could fall, however, Southhampton raised a frenzied cry that halted the red men in their tracks.

"They are my prisoners," he screamed. "And if they are harmed, I'll see to it that you are hanged!"

Although the Indians understood little English, they did see the major's outrage. Releasing the women, they sprang to their feet and stared stone-faced at Southhampton.

The major strode haughtily to where the women lay.

"Well, well." He smiled as he squatted beside them. "I almost didn't recognize you, Susan. But you can be grateful that I did—you owe me your life."

Susan pushed herself to her elbows and gazed up at the British major. He looked vaguely familiar, but she could not remember having met him before.

He grinned sardonically, his eyes roving over her and

then Bitsy. "You also owe me the life of the lass, whoever she might be."

Susan's breath caught. "Lieutenant Southhampton?"

"Not lieutenant," corrected Southhampton with a sneer. "I'm a major now. I haven't been a lieutenant for twenty-five years."

Southhampton's eyes traveled again to Bitsy who had pushed herself to a sitting position. "And who might you be, lovely lass?" he inquired, his eyes roving boldly over her young body.

Bitsy tossed her head contemptuously. "I am Bitsy Patterson, and you can rest assured that neither my mother nor I owe you anything."

Southhampton laughed. "You'd be dead now, you little vixen, if it hadn't been for me. Yes, you owe me—and I will collect, I assure you."

"Hush, Bitsy," warned Susan, drawing herself erect and lending a helping hand to her daughter. "The less we say, the better off we'll be."

"Do you know him, Mama?"

"Yes," answered Susan, "I know him."

Southhampton was pleased with himself. Things were working out splendidly. If he couldn't wreak vengeance on Morgan Patterson, he could do the next best thing: he could make the man's family suffer in his stead. And suffer they would. He'd see to it personally.

CHAPTER
· 6 ·

"I'LL NOT LEND our cannon in the capitulation of Martin's Station," Bird said adamantly to the nearly nine hundred silent Indians standing before him, "unless you give your word of honor that there will be no repetition of the atrocities I have witnessed this day."

He waited as Simon Girty translated.

"Furthermore," he continued, "you must agree that any and all prisoners taken at Martin's Station will belong to His Majesty, George the Third, and will be marched to Fort Detroit."

Bird would have demanded that the prisoners from Ruddle's be included in the transaction, but he was afraid the Indians would staunchly refuse to give up what they already possessed. And he was quite correct, for the savages undeniably believed they had a rightful claim to every man, woman, and child captured that day. After much mumbling and shuffling of feet, the Indians, like children deprived of a toy, reluctantly agreed. They were well aware that without the cannon they would stand little chance of taking Martin's Station without losing Indian lives—and that was not part of the game.

As it turned out, at ten o'clock on the morning of the twenty-eighth of June, 1780, after Bird cunningly dispatched a small delegation of Ruddle survivors to warn the folk at Martin's what might be expected should they show resistance, Martin's Station surrendered without firing a shot.

Discontented with having given their word not to take scalps, the Indians fell upon the settlers' cattle, sheep, goats, and hogs, killing every last one of the dumb beasts. Captain Bird was furious. Nearly four hundred and seventy prisoners, counting those from Ruddle's, and not one ounce of meat with which to feed either them or his army. To make matters worse, word had it that Clark and a thousand Kentuckians were descending on Bird in rapid order.

The prisoners were quickly weighed down with what household plunder they could carry and driven like cattle into the forest. As the British and Indians fled before Clark's mythical army, the Kentuckians were caught up and hurried along in a hard scramble with little military deportment. In a letter dated July 1, 1780, Captain Bird reported to Major Arent S. DePeyster, commander of Fort Detroit: "I marched the poor women and children twenty miles in one day over very high mountains, frightening them with frequent alarms to push them forward."

The "frequent alarms" were Southhampton's brainchild: so afraid was he that Clark's forces would catch him in the wilderness that he constantly harassed the Americans with threats of "turning the bloodthirsty savages loose to kill you all." And when the strenuous pace became too much for the very young, the old, and the sickly, Southhampton made good his threat and calmly turned his back while an Indian hatchet or scalping knife did its gruesome work.

As the long line of Kentuckians trudged single file through the wilderness, the damp earth quickly became an ankle-deep bog that sucked at their feet and clung to their clothing with such weight that the women could hardly drag their long skirts behind them, making each step they took an exertion of effort that left them spent and panting for breath. And the men fared little better, for the chore of carrying the heavy plunder had fallen for the most part on their weary shoulders.

The British showed no mercy. They whipped the Americans on at every opportunity, paying not the least attention to those who could go no farther and sprawled face down in the mud. And, because of Southhampton's intimidation, the Kentuckians fortunate enough to still be on their feet stepped over those who had collapsed without giving them so much as an encouraging word or even glancing in their direction.

In the rear of the cavalcade, Chard was overseeing the tedious task of moving the wheeled cannon over the rough terrain. As the big gun lumbered sluggishly up the muddy trail, he became increasingly alarmed by the growing number of bodies that littered the makeshift road. Finally he could stand it no longer and ordered a sergeant to move the cannon to the head of the line. Chard spurred his horse up the mountainside in search of Bitsy and Susan. He told himself he was seeking the answer to a question that had lain in the back of his mind since they had been captured, an answer that could very well be the key to his mother's mysterious past. But as he walked his horse slowly along the line of Americans, he admitted that his quest was also personal. He desperately needed to assure himself that they were still alive.

Near the front of the column, he located his quarry. Touching his hat to Susan and nodding curtly at Bitsy to hide his elation, he inquired politely about their well-being.

"You can look around you and see for yourself that we are being driven like animals," cried Bitsy, indicating her fellow Kentuckians with a sweep of her hand, "and we don't need any mealymouthed British fop reminding us of it."

Chard blushed mightily. Ignoring the irate girl, he leaned from the saddle and placed a restraining hand on Susan's shoulder.

"Mrs. Patterson? Was it my imagination, or did you actually say that you knew my father?"

"Your father?" Susan raised her face to Chard. "Is James Southhampton your father?"

The young man nodded. "Yes, ma'am, he is, and I've a few questions to ask, if you will permit?"

Bitsy sprang to her mother's side and knocked Chard's hand aside.

"I might have guessed you were begat by the likes of Southhampton. You're both just alike. Murderers, both of you. You British must be so proud of yourselves! All those poor women and children . . ."

Chard looked shamefacedly at the girl. "Miss Bitsy," he said softly, "I hate this as much as you—"

"Get away from those two prisoners," commanded Southhampton, swinging his horse alongside Chard.

"They're not to speak to anyone—and most certainly not you." Southhampton eyed the young officer with such malice that Susan wondered at the relationship between father and son.

Without a word Chard turned his horse off the path and trotted into the forest. He rode a few feet into the brush, then dismounted. Exhaling his pent-up breath, he lowered himself heavily to an ancient log and cupped his chin in his hands. Vacantly he swung his eyes to the prisoners. A woman stumbled past carrying a large black iron kettle atop her head. Blood streamed down her cheeks where the heavy metal had cut into her scalp. A man, bent from the weight of a massive wooden trunk lashed to his back, shuffled awkwardly through the mud. Chard shrank from the scene, thinking that it must surely have been much the same when the Romans forced Jesus to carry his burden to Calvary. Another poor wretch moved by, holding the skin of his forehead out of his eyes. Chard gaped at the naked skullbone that was visible where the man had been scalped. These are people, a voice wailed in his brain. They are human beings. God, what have we done?

He sprang to his feet and vaulted into the saddle. Had he not absolutely refused to abandon his mother in her time of need, he most certainly would have ridden into the wilderness and not looked back. As it was, he rode to the long line of heavily burdened Americans and, dismounting, insisted that an aged white-haired woman, who appeared to have gone her last step, ride while he "stretched his legs."

So, intermittently throughout the day, oblivious to the questioning stares of his fellow officers, especially his father, the young ensign would walk while one or two captives rode. The Kentuckians considered him a godsend, even if they did detest everything he stood for.

They camped wet and hungry that night. There were no rations for the captives save a cup of moldy flour for the men and half a cup for the women and children. The prisoners huddled like whipped dogs on the muddy ground and licked at the musty food until every tiny particle had been devoured. The children cried for more. Finally, with stomachs still aching from want of nourishment and muscles so sore they could hardly stretch their bodies length-wise, they closed their eyes and tried to sleep . . . some for the last time in their lives.

Southhampton sat before his large, cheerful campfire and stared into the flames. He had paid George Girty in gold to go out and bring him meat. Girty hadn't returned. Southhampton kicked at the flames with the toe of his polished boot and cursed Girty for a lazy, no-account savage who allowed an officer of the Royal Army to go hungry.

"Major," said George Girty, stepping into the firelight with a deer hanging limply over his shoulder, "be careful how you talk about me. I don't like being cussed."

"It's about time you returned," said Southhampton crossly, "I'm starved to death."

"You ain't half as hungry as them poor bastards back there." Girty indicated the captives with a thrust of his chin as he dropped the carcass to the ground.

"And I'll tell you somethin' else, Major," he went on coldly. "These damned savages that you feel so superior to wouldn't eat high on the hog while their captives starved. They would share and share alike, even if it weren't more'n one bite each."

"You're being paid well to hunt game for me, Girty," reminded Southhampton. "And if you wish to continue to take my money, then do so with your mouth shut. I will not tolerate such insolence, sir. Furthermore, these Americans are not my problem. If they starve, it's on Bird's shoulders, not mine. Now get busy and skin that animal. I can't hold out much longer; I'm famished."

Girty expertly skinned and quartered the deer, then, without a word stalked off into the night.

Southhampton cut himself a large slab of venison and set it to roasting over the fire. He ignored the stares of the hungry captives camped not a stone's throw away, and refused to consider the thought of sharing his food with them, knowing all the while that he couldn't possibly eat even a fraction of the deer meat before it spoiled.

Southhampton smiled to himself: hungry people would do almost anything for food. With that thought in mind, he walked arrogantly to the captives' compound and sought out Susan.

"No, thank you, Major," sighed Susan with disgust. "I'm not at all hungry, for either food . . . or conversation. But there are folks here who are starving, especially the children. . . ."

Southhampton turned and strode angrily toward his campfire.

Bitsy rubbed the gooseflesh that had risen on her arms. "There is something evil about that man, Mama. He reminds me of a snake, the way he looks at you."

He's worse than you know, thought Susan. But all she said was "Don't worry about him, darling; he's no real threat to us." Somehow the words rang false, and she wondered if Bitsy had caught the doubt in her voice. She hoped not.

Before daylight, the captives were again struggling through the wilderness. They silently threaded their way through the damp undergrowth, their clothes sopping wet from the morning dew. And each time they began to dry out, they would find themselves drenched anew from crossing the muddy waters of Gray's Run, then Mill Creek, then Raven Creek.

Captain Bird and his officers hurried them on, relentlessly determined to reach the forks of the Licking River before dark. Bird reasoned that at the forks they could load the prisoners into the waiting boats and quickly descend the main branch of the Licking to the Ohio. Once they put the banks of the Ohio behind them, pursuit would be impossible.

Southhampton, his crimson uniform brilliant in the early morning light, sat his horse where the trail topped a steep ridge, watching patiently as Susan and Bitsy struggled to cross a jagged outcrop of rock. He was pleased that Susan was showing signs of exhaustion from the long climb. Perhaps four nights without food or shelter, along with the hardships of the trail, had opened her eyes to the realities of captive life. Aye, he thought, studying her closely, she just might be hungry and weary enough to listen more sociably to his offer of hot food—and a cot to rest on. With that possibility bolstering his confidence, he ordered Susan aside, commanding Bitsy, who had stopped with her mother, to get back into the line and move on.

Reluctantly, the girl rejoined the column, to be caught up and shoved along by the slow-moving force of hundreds of human beings whose one purpose in life was simply to place one tired foot in front of the other. Ignoring the hardship she placed on her fellow prisoners each time she brought the long line to a halt, Bitsy would stop and peer frantically over her shoulder, hoping to catch a glimpse of her mother. Finally, an Indian rushed up and cuffed her a vicious blow to the head. With hand signals, he informed her that she had better not look back again—and Bitsy didn't.

Southhampton led Susan to a secluded spot well hidden from the main trail.

"I wanted to talk to you alone," he said, dismounting.

"Obviously," she returned, unimpressed.

Southhampton studied her profile as she gazed wistfully across the rugged hills they had crossed, barriers between her and the freedom she had enjoyed just a few days before. He was struck by her beauty, her pride, her dignity. Yet he knew those very qualities that spoke of class and breeding were her greatest foe, for they presented a challenge that Southhampton couldn't resist. "I have plenty of food. I would share it with you, if you but say the word."

Susan shot him a cold glare. "Major Southhampton," she said, "I'd starve to death before I would share anything with you."

Southhampton grinned. "You haven't changed a bit in the last twenty-five years, have you?" Susan didn't answer. "You were a proud bitch, even then," he went on. "But it will be different this time."

"No, Major," she sighed. "You are wrong. It will be exactly like the first time. I won't sleep with you, no matter what you offer me."

"Ah, but you will," he returned easily. "You'll crawl on your belly and beg for it, and Morgan Patterson won't be here to interfere."

Susan's smile was a mixture of amusement and fear. "You didn't learn a thing the last time you were here, did

91

you? My husband will follow us into the pit of hell if that's what it takes to find me. And when he does, Major, and I assure you he will, I wouldn't want to be in your shiny new boots."

Southhampton grinned with assurance. "By the time he finds you, Susan, you'll have been serviced so many times, he'll think he's married to the whore of creation."

With that, he swung into the saddle and spurred his horse directly at Susan so that she was forced to throw herself aside to keep from being trampled.

Chard reined his prancing mount alongside Bitsy as she stepped tiredly in the footprints of the hundreds of prisoners strung out before her.

"You doing all right?" he asked, slowing his horse to match her pace.

"Leave me alone," returned the girl wearily.

"Where's your mother?" He gazed up and down the line of captives with a questioning frown.

"You know very well where she is," accused Bitsy, raising her skirt and stepping over a small tree that had fallen across the trail. "And if your father harms one hair of her head, so help me——"

"My father? What are you talking about?"

Bitsy looked at him hard. "Your father took my mother out of line this morning. I haven't seen her since." Then her chin quivered, and she knuckled her eyes as tears streamed down her dirty cheeks. "He'd better not hurt her," she finished with a slow shake of her head.

But Chard wasn't listening. He had wheeled his horse and was galloping wildly down the line, the iron-shod hooves throwing clods of mud on the startled Americans.

He found Susan near the rear of the cavalcade. An infant, obviously belonging to the deathly pale young woman who walked behind her, rode lightly on the gentle curve of Susan's hip. "I always wanted a little boy," Susan crooned, smiling into the baby's small face. "I wanted one just like you."

"Ma'am," said Chard. "Are you . . . Did my father . . . Ma'am, has anything happened? Are you hurt?"

Susan pushed past the ensign without even glancing at him.

"Ma'am," he said again, dismounting beside her. "Your daughter is worried about you."

"Tell her I'm fine."

After several moments of awkward silence, the young man said, "If you'll permit me, Mrs. Patterson, I'd like to escort you back to her. She won't believe me if I tell her you're fine. She will have to see for herself." When Susan didn't reply, he said softly, indicating the long line of prisoners, "I'm truly sorry all this happened."

Something in his voice made Susan tilt her head up and assess the young officer closely. He was sincere. He actually regretted what had happened. The thought shocked Susan. Then, in spite of all the misery, she felt a tingle of warmth steal through her. Perhaps Southhampton's son was cut from a finer bolt than his father.

The young mother had overheard the exchange. "Don't be foolish, Mrs. Patterson," she said, taking the child from Susan. "Get back to your daughter while you have the chance."

"Are you sure you have the strength to carry him?" inquired Susan with a frown. "You are awfully frail."

"I'll be fine, ma'am. Me and my husband, Walter, want to thank you kindly for givin' me the chance to catch my breath. You probably saved my life, and my baby's, too. Now go on back to Bitsy before the ensign changes his mind."

Susan timidly offered Chard her hand. With seemingly little effort, he lifted her to the saddle. "Awfully nice thing you did back there," he said, as they trotted toward the head of the line.

Susan shrugged. "Kentuckians take care of their own," she said simply. It was a statement that would eventually prove heartbreakingly false for her and Bitsy. Then she asked the question that had nagged at her since she learned Southhampton had returned to America.

"Sir," she said, tightening her arms around Chard's waist for support, "is your mother well?"

Even through the heavy fabric of his tunic, Susan could feel his muscles tense. In the instant before he answered,

93

she knew a moment of fear mixed with sadness, for she was sure that Judith was dead.

So it came as both a relief and a shock when he told her abruptly that Judith was alive and well, and then staunchly refused to elaborate on the subject.

Bitsy's face was a delight to behold when the young ensign reined in and Susan swung lightly to the ground. The girl ran to her mother and caught her hand.

Chard whipped off his cocked hat and bowed from the saddle. "Your mama, my lady, and she is safe and sound."

Bitsy ignored him, entering immediately into an animated conversation with Susan.

The young man exhaled a despondent sigh and trotted his horse toward the head of the line where the wheeled cannon was being manhandled over a two-foot stone ledge. All four of the heavy draft horses and the entire gun crew grunted in a sweat bath of strained muscles and nerves as they concentrated their overtaxed energy into one final effort to raise the gun the two feet necessary to get it over the rocks to the level ground beyond.

Chard dropped from his saddle and lent his broad shoulder to the massive wheel, a task most British officers would have considered beneath their dignity even if their refusal to help meant abandoning the armament. The red-faced soldiers, after the initial shock of seeing their superior straining alongside them, made an even greater effort, and the big gun creaked, groaned, and rolled slowly over the stone, settling with a shudder on the flat surface above. The men cheered as the young officer drew his muddy tunic sleeve across his sweat-stained brow and grinned at them.

Susan and Bitsy, who, along with the rest of the captives, had not been allowed to slacken their pace, reached the crest of the bluff just as the cannon stabilized itself on the level hilltop. "I wish that cannon had broken loose and run off the mountainside," said Bitsy. "And I wish it had run over that fancy ensign and mashed the poop out of him."

"He is rather pretty," agreed Susan, watching the gun

crew gather around Chard and clap him on the back as though he were a hero.

"Aye," admitted Bitsy, "but he is well aware of it . . . spoiled to be sure."

"Oh, I don't know about that," chided Susan. "He seems very nice."

Bitsy was aghast. "How can you say that, Mama? He is the reason we are here; he is responsible for so many of our friends being dead."

"Don't hold him personally responsible, Bitsy," returned Susan thoughtfully, her attention drawn to Southhampton who had pranced his horse to a stop and now sat stiff-backed in the saddle, eyeing his son with contempt. "He may be the only reason any of us are still alive."

Bitsy would have argued the point had not Southhampton's voice rung out loud and clear.

"Damned fine display for an officer of His Majesty's Royal forces. You make a mockery of your commission, Ensign."

Chard's proud smile vanished, and his shoulders slumped. "I apologize, sir, but the men needed help."

"We've over four hundred slaves at our disposal, Ensign. If help is needed, let them do it."

"Yes, sir," said the young man, striding to his horse and remounting.

He longed to remind his father that the Kentuckians were prisoners of war, not slaves. But his common sense told him that such an outburst would only worsen the situation.

Southhampton frowned angrily at his son's receding back as Chard rode away. The ease with which Chard had accepted his chastisement left the major with the disturbing feeling that his words had been too soft, and he deeply regretted not having given the boy a genuine tongue-lashing just to impress the troops. After all, discipline, especially among the officers, was a must if an army was to survive. He raked his spurs viciously down his horse's flank and raced toward the head of the column where Captain Bird waited.

"Major," said Bird, when Southhampton drew his lathered horse to a halt, "take some men on ahead and build a bridge where the south branch of the Licking makes its sweeping bend. If we wait much longer, the bloody river will be too wide to cross."

"I've just the man for that detail, Captain," said Southhampton smiling. "He enjoys physical labor. I'll see that he is accommodated."

"I don't care how you do it, Major. Just have that bridge built by the time our supplies and ordnance get there."

"It will be ready, sir," promised Southhampton.

Under his father's overbearing supervision, Chard and fifty hand-picked captives felled two giant trees across the south fork of the Licking River.

Using poles for leverage, they worked the timbers an inch at a time until the huge logs were spaced the approximate width of the wheeled cannon. That done, they went to work with axes and hatchets and started laying smaller logs crossways on the two large timbers.

Weary of overseeing the efforts of the workmen, especially those of his son, who had cast aside his tunic and actually seemed to be enjoying the strenuous exercise, Southhampton rode to the top of a rise and gazed anxiously up the river in search of the column that should have been in view half an hour before. Had he but listened, he would have heard the unmistakable sound of an army on the march. But to his discredit, only after he had spied the long line of British, Indians, and captives who, from such a distance, resembled a string of ants more than humans, did he hear the pounding of hundreds of feet, the rattle of equipment and weapons, the clanking of chains and harness, and the rumbling of heavy wheels as fifteen hundred people, animals, and ordnance snaked slowly up the long valley. Southhampton touched his heels to his horse and rode to meet them.

He cantered up to Bird and inclined his head in a bow. "The bridge will be ready when you get there, Captain."

"Excellent," returned Bird, smiling. "With luck, we should make the forks of the Licking before dark."

A flurry of excitement from the rear of the file caught the two officers' attention.

"What in hell's name is going on back there?" said Bird, standing in the stirrups and scanning the long train of prisoners.

"I'll ride back and find out, sir," offered Southhampton. It would be a good excuse to locate Susan and continue the conversation that had been less than satisfactory that morning.

But when he walked his horse down the line, he was met by a half-dozen Indians who pushed and prodded two out-of-breath and thoroughly terrified women before them. Forcing the women to their knees almost beneath the hooves of the major's skittish mount, the Indians began a harangue that Southhampton neither understood nor cared to understand. As far as he was concerned, the Indians could do with the captives whatever they wished so long as he was not involved.

"They say they caught these two ladies trying to escape," said George Girty, dropping the butt of his long-rifle to the ground and resting his forearm casually across the muzzle. Southhampton eyed the man with distaste. He was well aware that Girty had been deliberately avoiding him since the incident with the deer.

"They are from Martin's Station," continued Girty, "so they're the army's responsibility, Major."

Southhampton silently cursed the women for not being prisoners from Ruddle's Fort. Had they been, the Indians, who claimed all the captives from that station with the exception of Susan and Bitsy, would have merely killed them and been done with it. Then, to make matters worse, Southhampton was forced to watch with mounting resentment as Susan and Bitsy marched past without even glancing in his direction. Southhampton's face turned thunderous, and he did what came naturally to one of his caliber: he vented his anger on the two unfortunates who, by an act of God and a pack of swift-footed Indians, found themselves at his mercy.

"Get on your feet," he commanded, eyeing the pair hatefully.

"Thank the Lord," sobbed one of the women, rising and kissing Southhampton's boot, refusing to let go. "I was sure the Indians were going to torture and kill us. Thank you, Major, oh, thank you, sir, for sparing our lives."

97

Southhampton removed his boot from the stirrup and kicked the woman away. "Gunner!" He bellowed to a sergeant who was helping to maneuver the armament around a decayed log that blocked the trail. "Chain these sluts to the spokes of the cannon wheels. If they've enough energy to run off into the wilderness, they've enough energy to help push that gun carriage."

He watched with satisfaction and a deaf ear as the pleading, sobbing women were shackled, one on either side of the cannon, to the heavy spokes of the carriage wheels. And he was even more pleased with his decision when the horses pulling the gun leaned into their harnesses and the cannon lurched into motion. The women were thrown heavily to the ground, and as the wheels slowly turned, the chains dragged them to their knees, to their feet, and again to their knees. The women had to constantly bend, kneel, and straighten with each revolution of the wheel.

"You are despicable, Southhampton," spat Susan, from down the line. "There is not one ounce of kindness in you."

"I thought I was rather ingenious," he said in return. " 'Tis certain they won't feel like trying to escape again."

Then he laughed uproariously as he walked his horse alongside her. "Actually, madam, you could obtain their release quite easily . . ."

"The answer is no, Major."

"Then they can rot on those wheels for all I care," he said, spurring his horse away.

Susan turned her head and walked on, refusing to glance at the two women. In truth, she felt guilty, and somewhat responsible for their suffering, but sorry as she was, she would not under any circumstances prostitute herself to Southhampton. She would die first.

It took well over an hour for the caravan to reach the new bridge that Chard and the fifty Americans had built. And it was a worn-out, weary procession that trod cautiously across the uneven logs.

As Susan and Bitsy approached, they eyed the makeshift bridge with concern. "It doesn't look any too safe to me, Ensign," said Susan to Chard, who was standing proudly beside his hastily built span.

"It'll hold just fine, ma'am, long as you walk careful. 'Tis hard to build a sturdy bridge without nails."

He smiled and offered his arm as Bitsy stepped onto the structure. "May I escort you across, Miss Bitsy?"

"If you so much as touch me, I'll slap you silly," returned the girl, flushing with embarrassment.

"My cheeks are already stinging." Catching her elbow, he guided her across the walkway.

And, to Bitsy's surprise, she found herself not at all inclined to slap his face. In truth, she rather enjoyed his attention.

Over half of the captives were on the far side of the stream when the wheeled cannon reached the crossing. The teamsters prodded the lead team of horses onto the bridge, but the hollow sound of their hooves when they struck the logs and the rushing waters beneath threw the animals into such a frenzy of plunging and bucking that the soldiers were obliged to quickly back the horses onto solid ground before the terrified animals could harm themselves or the precious cannon.

"Blindfold those horses and get that damned cannon over here immediately," bellowed Southhampton from the far shore. "The captain wants to make the forks of the Licking before dark."

Chard, who had just handed Bitsy down from the bridge, drew himself to attention. "Sir," he said, addressing his father, "I request permission to free the two women who are chained to the wheels. The gun would be easier to manage, sir, without being encumbered by their presence."

"If they get in the way, run over them," answered Southhampton sourly.

The young ensign grimaced, then turned on his heel and trotted back the way he had come.

The teamsters had managed to wrap the heads of the frightened horses with linsey-woolsey strips cut from the dresses of the two captives, but even blindfolded the animals shivered with fear as the men whipped and prodded them onto the log framework.

And it seemed to Chard, who walked backwards just ahead of the procession, and called out warnings if the teams veered right or left, that it would have been much easier, and without a doubt less dangerous, simply to have unhooked the horses and rolled the gun across by hand. But orders were orders, and he had already disobeyed far too many. He was well aware that his present duty, that of laboring with the prisoners, was a direct result of his abuse of his commission. To him, however, it was worth it. But he had no intention of pushing himself into a corner; he could help his mother, himself, and the captives only if he was free from constant observation and attention. So he promised himself that he would follow orders no matter what.

As it turned out, it was a promise made to be broken.

Halfway across the bridge one of the lead horses lost his blindfold. The terrified animal reared and fell backwards in a tangle of broken harness and kicking hooves. The off horse and the wheelers went berserk in a world that was pitch black and completely alien to them; they, too, reared and plunged, and lashed out with steel-rimmed hooves at anything or anyone who happened to brush against them.

The gun crew sprinted for their lives as the screaming fifteen-hundred-pound horses bucked, lunged, and thrashed with such force that both wheels of the twenty-five hundred pound cannon were in the air at once. The women chained to the spokes were jerked about like rag dolls, and when the cannon crashed back onto the bridge, they were snapped about and smashed to the rough logs like sacks of flour.

Then, as if in slow motion, amid the sound of popping and cracking logs, the great gun rose up on one wheel and almost lazily toppled into the fast-moving current, taking horses, women, and a large portion of the bridge with it. For a brief second, the hundreds of people who witnessed the incident were speechless. Then a great wail arose from the family and friends of the two women who had vanished in the turmoil of screaming horses, breaking timbers, churning wheels, and rushing waters.

And in the midst of it all was Chard, who had snatched up an ax and made a long, running dive into the water almost before the women had disappeared. He fought his way to the bottom of the muddy stream and for a terrified moment became entangled in the melee of thrashing horses that were attempting to break free from the awful thing that was dragging them to their death. Yet, even as the young man frantically kicked himself free of the tangled animals, he could feel their actions become slow and labored as their great lungs burst from suffocation.

Chard's chest was a burning pain as he pushed himself deeper into the black depths of the Licking. By willpower alone he worked his way over the double trees and trace chains until he could grip the wheel of the huge gun that lay on its side, half buried in the muddy river bottom.

With pain popping behind his eyelids and his chest threatening to explode, he groped his way around the wheel until his hand touched the clammy flesh of one of the women. Quickly, he drew himself along her body until he located the fetter. But try as he might, in his fast-weakening condition, he could not cleave the lock. Again and again he fought the pressure of the strong current as he smashed the ax against the heavy steel. And finally, as unconsciousness slowly overcame him, he thought of his father, who had the only key.

Chard fought his way up from a black hole filled with slime and mud. He could hear voices, but he could neither see nor move.

"He's coming around," said a feminine voice.

"I tell you, he's dead," came Southhampton's unmistakable nasal whine.

"See," said the woman triumphantly. "His eyelids fluttered."

The young officer slowly opened his eyes. The world appeared to glow red, and only the very center of his vision seemed to be in focus. But try as he might, he still could not make out the faces that peered down at him. He attempted to shake his head, to tell them that he was indeed alive, but that required too much effort.

"Easy now," said the woman. "You'll be fine in a few minutes. Just give yourself time."

"Get up, boy," commanded Southhampton. "If you're awake enough to open your eyes, you're awake enough to stand like a man."

"Leave him be," snapped the woman. "He's not even

101

fully conscious yet." And Chard knew it was Susan, for no other person would have dared to speak to his father in such a manner. His lips formed a soft smile as the darkness again engulfed him.

He awoke the second time to the jostling of a litter that two prisoners had fashioned from a blanket and a pair of staves. Before the startled stretcher-bearers knew what was happening, Chard had flung his legs over the side and was attempting to stand.

"Easy, sir," said one of the men, dropping his stave and adding his support to the teetering ensign.

"I'm all right," rasped the young man. But a moment later, he found himself obliged to lean heavily on the man's shoulder. "Knees are a bit weak, that's all."

"You've been to hell and thumbed your nose at ol' Lucifer his self. You've a right to be a mite spent."

"Well, I am that." Chard smiled, trying his best to stand alone.

"So you're on your feet, are you?" called Susan from down the line of shuffling prisoners.

Chard waited for Susan to approach. And even though his legs were wobbly as a newborn kitten's, when she drew abreast he stepped up beside her.

"'Twas a heroic thing you tried to do, diving into the river for those women," said Susan.

Chard dropped his head. "Didn't do much good, did it?"

"Still and all," said Susan, "you did your best, and those of us who knew those poor women thank you." She smiled then. "You've gained the respect of a lot of good people, Ensign, if that means anything to you."

Chard nodded his appreciation for her kind words. But his eyes had moved to Bitsy, who was wrapped in a blanket, her hair hanging in copper strands about her face. "You probably think I did it to try and cut the horses free, don't you?" he asked the girl.

"You need to thank her," said Susan, laying her hand on Chard's arm. "She's the one who dove into the river and pulled you out."

"She saved my life?" Chard was amazed. "The women I know can't even swim. 'Tis not ladylike."

Bitsy's eyes grew round with disbelief. "Not ladylike!"

102

she cried. "Why, you pompous . . . I wish now I had let you drown."

"Oh, you do not," scoffed Susan. "Why, you were just this minute saying—"

"Mama!" cried the girl, aghast. "If you say one word, I swear by all that's holy, I'll never confide in you again."

"What was it you said about me?" asked Chard with obvious pleasure.

Bitsy shot him a bitter grimace. "I said that the offspring of swine are nothing but little pigs."

Chard's smile vanished. But before he could retort, his father appeared leading Chard's horse. "Mount up, Ensign," he commanded, flinging the reins at his son. "You've lain abed long enough."

Without a word, Chard swung into the saddle and spurred his horse away.

"Mama, don't ever embarrass me like that again," said Bitsy, watching Chard ride stiff-backed up the line. "I can't believe you did that to me."

Susan laughed lightly and laid her arm around her daughter's shoulder. "Well, you did save his life, didn't you?"

"I would have done the same thing for a puppy. And in truth, I would probably have done it quicker."

"And I suppose you would have hovered over a puppy like a concerned mother until we got it breathing again?" said Susan, tightening her embrace and smiling proudly at Bitsy. "And you did say, just before the ensign awakened, that his diving into the river was the most heroic thing you had seen anyone do in a long while. Well, darling," she concluded, "what you did was just as grand, and you should be as proud of yourself as I am of you."

Bitsy blushed, not used to being complimented. "He had it all wrong," she said with a laugh. "I was the one trying to save the horses."

CHAPTER
· 7 ·

IT WAS WELL after dark by the time the cavalcade marched wearily into the camp at the forks of the Licking River.

Chard went directly to Judith's tent.

She answered his questions. Yes, considering her status, she had been treated kindly by the guard. No, she was not hungry. Then, with her heart hammering in her chest, she asked about the invasion of the Kentucky settlements.

She listened with rapt attention while her son related the criminal offenses of the British and their Indian allies. Not wanting Judith to know of Southhampton's cowardice at the fort or his cruel treatment of the prisoners, Chard related the highlights of the siege without mentioning the names of those involved.

"Those poor people," sighed Judith. "What will become of them? Will they ever see home or family again?"

Chard shook his head sadly. "Not for a long time, Mother, maybe never. Those from Ruddle's Station, who are captives of the Indians, are the ones to be pitied. When we reach the Ohio, the tribes will take them across the river and scatter to every Indian village for five hundred miles around. The captives will probably never be heard from again."

"What about the ones from Martin's Fort?"

"They're to be taken to Detroit, Montreal, and Mackinac."

"Some of those places are fourteen hundred miles away," cried Judith. "They will never find their way back to Kentucky."

"Ma'am," said the young ensign, "when England wins this war, there may not be a Kentucky to go back to."

Judith dropped her face into her hands. "I don't understand any of this, Chard. Why is it so important for Britain to waste her time and money on an out-of-the-way place like Kentucky? We need to center our energy in the East, where the major conflict is."

Chard patted his mother's shoulder affectionately. "I haven't got the answer, Mother. I don't understand it either, except that it appears that the Crown has every intention of preventing westward growth of the American colonies."

"But why should the Crown mind? What harm is there in people building a better life for themselves?"

"It's a matter of people finding themselves in a position to be self-reliant, ma'am. And that's where the problem begins . . . with the determination to persevere. The frontier folk are no longer tied to England's apron strings, and England can't tolerate such an outward show of independence, because it is a prelude to complete freedom."

"Freedom! Lord God, I am sick of the word," cried Judith. "Don't these fool Americans realize that once you acquire anything, even if it's naught but a lowly cow, you are no longer free? You are obligated to that animal."

"It's not our worry, Mother," he said gently. "We've got more important things to consider just now. Your future, for instance."

"Is your father still determined to whip me in public?"

"Aye," said Chard, "he won't be satisfied until he makes a big show of chastising you, the worst of which will be the humiliation and embarrassment that you will be forced to suffer. Father will probably cut a green willow switch and go through the motions, as most husbands do. No, I'm not concerned about the whipping; it's the trial once we reach Detroit that has me worried."

Judith smiled sadly to herself. Chard was so naive: James Southhampton would not be satisfied with merely embarrassing her publicly. No, he would have something special in mind for his wife, something far more terrible than Chard supposed. She shuddered, but she was determined not to worry her son with her fears. "We'll cross that bridge when we come to it," she said, laying her head on Chard's shoulder. "Don't worry about me, love, the Bible says that everything happens for the best, and we've got to believe that. It's about all the encouragement we've got right now . . . but 'tis enough."

Chard took Judith's hand and kissed it. "Mother," came his soft words, "if God would be so kind as to grant me just one of your fine traits, I'd pray that it would be your unflinching bravery."

But after he was gone, after the sound of his footsteps had been drowned out by the chirping of the crickets and the croak of tree frogs and the thousands of other friendly night sounds, Judith's brave resolve crumbled. Great silent tears rolled down her cheeks to hover momentarily at the dimpled corners of a pair of lips that were created to kiss and caress, not to tremble in loneliness and fear. For indeed, that was exactly how she felt, alone in a foreign land and terrified of what tomorrow would bring.

July 1, 1780 broke bright and clear, a welcomed change after all the dreary days of rain and overcast skies. After a breakfast of more stale flour, the captives were ushered to the cleared space where the officers' tents were pitched. Captain Bird stepped out of his marquee, and a hush fell over the prisoners. To their surprise, Bird informed them that they would bivouac for a day while the gear, supplies, and ordnance were loaded into the boats.

Susan felt like cheering, so exhausted was she from the grueling overland march. But, like those around her, she remained silent for fear that it was but another ruse to further destroy their strength of mind, which had already been drawn to the breaking point.

Captain Bird was going on: "We have, this morning, a task to perform." He scowled, not liking what he was about to say, but at a loss as to how it could possibly be circumvented. He was well aware that a man's honor must not be compromised, no matter the costs. "You will witness the public whipping of a traitor to the Crown. Precisely at ten o'clock, you will present yourselves at this spot."

"Which one of us do they intend to flog?" whispered Bitsy to Susan. "We are all traitors to the Crown."

Susan frowned. "It must be someone special. They wouldn't waste their time whipping one of us; they would just kill us and be done with it."

At ten o'clock, the prisoners were again assembled at the clearing. They waited anxiously for the traitor to appear. Speculation had flapped like the wings of a bird about who the poor devil might be.

But no one was prepared for the beautiful British lady who stepped elegantly from her tent and, looking every bit the aristocrat, walked haughtily between an escort of red-coated regulars to a post that had been set in the clearing.

"Are they going to whip that lovely lady?" said Bitsy, shielding her eyes from the glare of the sun in order to see better the woman standing proudly at the post. "Surely not?" the girl continued. "She doesn't look like a traitor to me."

Susan's hand fluttered to her breast in an attempt to calm her palpitating heart. She had recognized Judith immediately, and she did not know which was greater: the shock of seeing Judith again, or the fact that a soldier was tying her hands in front of her and passing the rope through a ring in the post above her head. Susan watched in dismay as the man drew the rope tight and tied it, forcing Judith to rise to her tiptoes in an effort to spare herself the torture of dangling.

Bitsy was aghast. "Must they pull her arms so high? Why, she can hardly touch her feet to the ground."

Susan, however, wasn't listening. Her mind had raced back twenty-five years, to an eighteen-year-old girl with golden hair, an English girl of noble birth who openly professed an enduring hatred for America and the people who inhabited it. And for the life of her, Susan could not imagine that girl, even years later, having changed so drastically as to be publicly flogged as a traitor to the Crown. The very thought was incredible.

Southhampton advanced to stand behind his wife. He deliberately ripped open her fine gown from the nape of her neck to her hips, exposing a soft, feminine back that had been drawn so tight by the overhead rope that every muscle, rib, and bone in Judith's upper body stood out in vivid relief. Not satisfied, Southhampton spun her around and ripped her bodice until it hung in shreds about her narrow waist.

From where she stood, Susan could see the startled shame suffuse across Judith's face as the unexpected disrobing left her exposed to hundreds of probing male eyes. But degrading as that was, Susan knew that it amounted to nothing compared to Judith's humiliation at the speculation, comparison, and—yes, even pity—in the eyes of the gawking women. Susan turned her face away. She remembered vividly that Judith was a very modest person. And that she was especially sensitive about her underdeveloped, immature-looking breasts.

Southhampton clapped his hands theatrically, drawing Susan's attention again to the scene. A nearby soldier marched to the major and presented him with a leather case. Southhampton made a great show of slowly opening the container and withdrawing an ugly, short whip, a length of rawhide with nine individual lead-tipped lashes.

"A cat-o'-nine-tails," cried Susan, voicing the surprise of nearly everyone present, including the British and Canadians, who were aghast that Southhampton would actually consider flogging his wife with such a deadly device. "He will strip the flesh from Judith's back and leave her scarred for life," Susan whispered unbelievingly.

Bitsy studied her mother with surprise.

"Do you know her, Mama? Who is she?"

"She's Southhampton's wife," said Susan, not taking her eyes off Judith.

"His wife? She's the mother of the young man I saved?"

Susan nodded.

Bitsy's mouth drew down in disappointment as she thought about the handsome young ensign. "If I had known that he would be coward enough to stand by and let his father whip the flesh off his mother and not do a thing to stop it, I would have let him drown." She was almost in tears.

"He's not here," defended Susan. "Captain Bird sent him and several soldiers out late last night to scout the back trail in case General Clark is in pursuit. I now wonder if perhaps it wasn't Southhampton's way of getting rid of the

108

boy while he does this awful thing to Judith. Somehow I doubt that Chard would stand for such cruelty."

Bitsy exhaled. Her mother's words comforted her, and she felt better believing, as Susan did, that Chard would not approve of what was happening. And she was grateful that he would not be there to witness his mother's suffering—or, even more horrible, her possible death.

"I'm glad he isn't here, Mama," said the girl softly.

Susan glanced at her daughter. But before she could probe into the depths of Bitsy's feelings, Southhampton drew the cat over his head, and she, along with the rest of the crowd, watched in stony silence as the nine lead-tipped lashes whistled through the air.

That same morning Morgan Patterson and his exhausted companions trotted short-breathed through the gate of Clark's Fort at the falls of the Ohio.

The four woodsmen couldn't believe their eyes; the place was all but deserted. Only a handful of men were present to cheer when they made their grand entrance, and Clark was in the embarrassing position of the returned hero without the well-deserved and rightly expected welcoming.

"Where in hell are all the men?" boomed Clark when he kicked open the door to the commander's office and stood with hands on hips as if daring the man not to answer.

"General!" cried the captain, springing to his feet with a wide grin. "It's good to see you, sir."

"Never mind that," snapped Clark. "Where are the troops that should be up in arms and rarin' to go?"

"They're all over to Harrodsburg, General," answered the man lamely. "They's some big land deal goin' on over there, and that's where all the men is, 'cept for the few old-timers that served with you in 'seventy-eight. They're the only ones that waited, sir."

"Goddamn!" shouted Clark. "Has this country gone crazy? Land! We've got the best land in the world here in Kentucky. But it ought to be—it's been fertilized with American blood for years. And it will be again if Bird and his Indians aren't stopped."

"They ain't been no word about Bird, sir," came the captain's quick reply. "Nobody's seen or heard a thing about no Britishers being in the country. And they damn sure ain't come down the Ohio. We been watchin' the river night and day."

"Well, we can be glad of that," said Clark, dropping onto a bench with an exhausted sigh. "Now fill me in on this land scheme that's going on over at Harrod's."

The four frontiersmen listened silently as the captain explained that the government land office had set up headquarters at Harrodsburg. Nearly every able-bodied man in the country was there trying to get a deed to something or other—it didn't make much difference what, so long as it was land.

"I can't believe it," sighed Clark, when the captain had finished. "Bird's somewhere within a hundred miles of Kentucky, if he isn't here already, and those goddamn fools are dickering over land."

He shook his head, dead-tired. "Well, boys," he said to Patterson and the others, who silently awaited his orders. "There's not a hell of a lot we can do about it this day. Let's get some rest. We'll leave for Harrodsburg at first light."

Patterson eyed the general with a steady gaze. "With your permission, George, I'd like to push on to Ruddle's today. Susan and Bitsy are there."

Clark shook his head. "I'm going to need you tomorrow, Morgan. There's no telling what I'll find at Harrod's. Damn it, man," he said, fighting his inclination to let his friend go, "I hate like hell to refuse anything you ask, you know that. But I'm of a feeling I'm going to need every friend I've got tomorrow." He smiled sympathetically and laid a hard, callused hand on Patterson's shoulder. "I swear by all that's holy that you can leave for Ruddle's as soon as we clear up this mess about the land office. Is that fair enough?"

Patterson dropped his eyes to hide his disappointment. "That's fair enough, General."

Judith rose to the tips of her toes as the nine lashes wrapped themselves around the sensitive skin of her bare back and then whipped across her rib cage to bury their lead tips in

110

the even more delicate flesh of her exposed breasts. Her entire body writhed and convulsed as the searing pain tore through her, burning every muscle and nerve fiber in its path.

She had expected pain, but she was unprepared for the excruciating agony that seemed to attack her body from all sides, a suffering so intense that she involuntarily opened her mouth to scream. At the last moment, however, that abundance of courage and pride that was the very essence of her being snapped her teeth together with such force that they nearly severed her lower lip.

Southhampton smiled with satisfaction.

Moving to Judith's side, he leaned close. "Just think, my dear," he whispered into her ear, "only nine more to go . . . and I promise you, you *will* scream before I'm through."

Judith slowly swung her dangling body toward Southhampton, and to the astonishment of those who watched, spat a mouthful of blood and saliva into his unsuspecting face.

Susan almost wept with pride at the spectacle, for what the others had just witnessed with awe was the Judith whom Susan remembered from so long ago: the proudest and most arrogant woman she had ever encountered. And Susan recalled something else, something she had said to Judith so long ago: "If I could be like anybody I wished, I would choose you."

Susan's heart went out to the beautiful woman who hung suspended by her wrists. Softly, Susan's lips formed the words: "And I would still choose to be just like you, Judith."

Southhampton removed a lace kerchief from the cuff of his tunic and delicately dabbed at his face. "You common slut," he said softly, his eyes round with shock. "I'll have every inch of hide off your back for that." Then, in afterthought, he added, "And your breasts, too."

"What breasts?" slurred Judith, grimacing with pain as she dropped her eyes to the small, bloody mounds. "I never had any to begin with. You've told me so a thousand times."

If Judith thought the first lashing was unbearable, the second and third were even more terrible. And in spite of her vow not to allow Southhampton the pleasure of hearing her scream, she heard, as if from far off, agonizing shrieks. It dawned on her that the inhuman sounds were coming from her own lips, but at that point she no longer cared.

By the fifth fall of the whip, Judith's torture was over. She hung from the end of the rope like a pendant, her limp body revolving slowly in the morning sun.

"She's dead," whispered Bitsy, breaking into tears. "He whipped her to death, Mama. How could he do that?"

Bitsy wasn't the only person who asked that question. Such a clamor arose from the captives and soldiers that it appeared only the Indians were enjoying the spectacle. Captain Bird rushed to Southhampton and caught the man's arm as he raised the cat-o'-nine-tails for the sixth time.

"Good God, Major," he cried, "is it your intention to kill her? She's had more than enough, sir."

"'Tis my prerogative, Captain," reminded Southhampton. "As her husband, I have the right. This is no military matter, or have you forgotten, sir?"

Bird released Southhampton's arm and stepped back. "Proceed, Major. But let me remind you of one thing." He gazed steadily at Southhampton. "If Lady Southhampton dies, I'll hang you for murder. No man has the right to kill his wife, sir." With that, the captain strode angrily to his tent and, kicking the flaps away, disappeared inside.

Southhampton's face was ash gray as he studied Judith's unconscious form. He was afraid that he had pushed his luck too far. Exhaustion from wielding the whip sent large drops of perspiration trickling down his face onto his immaculate ruffled shirt front, but it was fear that caused the sweat to seep through the fabric at his armpits and soil the crimson tunic that he wore with such arrogant pride.

"Cut her down," he commanded, refusing to meet the eyes of the soldier who had tied Judith to the post. Without a word, the private marched past Southhampton and slashed the ropes that bound Judith's wrists.

Southhampton turned to the hushed crowd. "I hereby proclaim my marriage to Judith Cornwallace annulled. I publicly divorce myself from this woman, who, by her acts of treason, has disgraced not only myself, but the Almighty Lord God, King George the Third, and every loyal Englishman who ever drew breath. I separate myself from her, and from this day forward will refuse to acknowledge her existence."

Without glancing at Judith, he handed the whip to a guard and marched toward his tent.

While all eyes were on the woman who lay in a crumpled heap where she had fallen, Susan slipped quietly to Captain Bird's tent.

"Sir," she whispered through the canvas door, "may I have a word with you?"

"Come in, come in," came the officer's reply.

"Captain," said Susan as she faced Bird who was sitting at his field desk with quill and ink, "I would like permission to attend Mrs. Southhampton."

Bird eyed Susan without interest. "Your request is unwarranted, ma'am. We have a surgeon who will minister to the lady's needs."

"I know you do, sir," argued Susan, "but with all he has to do just to keep the troops fit and ready, I'm sure you would rather have him free."

"A point well taken," said the officer with a thoughtful frown. "Aye, a point well taken."

Late that evening, Susan and Bitsy moved their blankets to the supply tent that served as Judith's cell and hospital room.

Susan was stricken with pity at the welts, abrasions, and torn flesh on Judith's upper body. Silently, she thanked the Lord that the mauled woman had not regained consciousness.

She and Bitsy worked with deft fingers, gently applying an ointment obtained from the surgeon on the lacerated mess that had once been a graceful body.

"She will be scarred terribly," whispered Bitsy, as she gently rubbed the salve into the open wounds. "She will never wear an off-the-shoulder ball gown again. 'Tis a shame."

"Ladies our age don't wear such alluring dresses, darling," said Susan, thinking how much Bitsy had matured in the past few days. The girl had never even seen an off-the-shoulder gown; she had only heard about them from

113

the newcomers to Kentucky who brought news of the latest European fashions.

"Such things are for young ladies," Susan finished lamely, suddenly unhappy that Bitsy probably would never have the opportunity to wear such finery. Bitsy had grown to young womanhood in the harsh, unpretentious simplicity of the frontier wilderness, never having known the gay and carefree life that existed for those with wealth and position; neither of which meant a great deal when one survived on the fringes of civilization.

Judith cried out as Susan carefully rolled her onto her side in order to evaluate the extent of damage her chest had suffered.

"Merciful God in heaven," breathed Bitsy, as she gaped at the open slashes that crisscrossed Judith's breasts. Involuntarily, the girl's hands flew to her own bosom, and she felt sympathetic pain for the unconscious woman.

"I hurt for her, Mama," she whispered, pulling her shoulders forward and clutching her breasts tightly. "I actually ache all over."

"We both do, darling," said Susan with a shudder. "There's not a woman on earth who could look at such as that and not feel awful."

"Mama," said Bitsy hesitantly, "I don't think I would ever have the nerve to do what she did."

Susan glanced at her daughter and frowned. "What are you talking about?"

"She spit in her husband's face, knowing when she did it that she would only infuriate him all the more."

Susan didn't answer, for in all honesty, she doubted that she would have had such courage either, especially knowing that it would only worsen her punishment.

Then she smiled as she gazed tenderly, proudly at the unconscious woman. "But I love you for doing it, Judith," she said softly. "It was the grandest thing I ever saw."

She and Bitsy smoothed the salve over Judith's wounds, then sat back and observed their work. The cuts and abrasions had stopped bleeding, but it was too soon to tell what real harm Judith had sustained.

"'Tis about the best we can do tonight," sighed Susan, wiping her greasy hands on her skirt. "If she isn't better by morning, we'll call in the surgeon."

"All he'll do is bleed her," complained Bitsy, following her mother's example with her hands. "And I don't believe she can stand to lose much more blood."

Bitsy gingerly fingered a lock of hair that had fallen across Judith's forehead. "Mama, were you with her when she got this scar on her face?"

Susan glanced at the thin silver line that crossed Judith's brow. "Yes," she admitted with a sigh, "I was there."

"Has . . . has she known a lot of suffering, Mama?"

Susan took Bitsy's hand and held it tight. "Yes, darling, I'm afraid she has. We were captured by the French and Indians. Judith, Ivy, her handmaiden, your papa, and I were herded together with several other English people and taken to the Indian village, Chillicothe. One of the captive women was pregnant. Judith, Ivy, and I delivered her child. The woman knew she was dying, so she gave the baby to Judith, who promised to love and cherish it as her own. But . . . it didn't work that way." Susan looked long into her daughter's eyes. "Are you sure you want to hear this, Bitsy? It is not a pretty story."

Bitsy nodded her head. "Go on, Mama. I want to know what happened."

Susan took a deep breath. "Judith thought she was barren, so I suppose that was why she became almost fanatically attached to the child. The trouble was, not one of the captive women was fresh. There was nothing to feed the baby." Susan dropped her eyes, remembering that horrible day so long ago. "An Indian killed the child to stop it from crying. The murder of the baby broke Judith's mind."

"She . . . went insane?" inquired Bitsy aghast, drawing away from Judith.

"Not insane, exactly. She wasn't a raving lunatic . . . Anyway," said Susan, wishing she had not begun the story, "the Indian who killed the baby hit Judith in the face with his hatchet."

"My Lord!" whispered Bitsy in awe as she studied the unconscious woman. Then her young face hardened. "If seeing someone die drove her crazy, Mama, then the frontier is no place for her."

"That baby was not just someone, Bitsy. In Judith's

mind it was as much her child as Chard is," defended Susan.

Bitsy looked long at Judith. "Do you think if something happened to Chard, she would go—"

"I have no idea," interrupted Susan, wishing the girl would hush. Bitsy clearly did not understand or believe that a mother could be so wrapped up in a child or that the death of that child could drive her to madness. But Susan understood. Aye, she said to herself as she gazed at her daughter, if something happened to you, Bitsy, I would . . . She shuddered uncontrollably and turned her face away, unable to finish the thought.

An hour after full dark, Chard and his troops marched tiredly into camp. Every soldier and Indian on the premises ran to meet the small band, eager to hear whether Clark and his army were within striking distance.

Taking advantage of the confusion, John Hinkson, a captive from Ruddle's Station, bolted into the night and flung himself into the tall ferns beside a fallen log. He lay there with his eyes closed so the Indians who were passing within a rifle's length wouldn't see the reflection of the moon in his pupils. Hinkson was lucky that night, for the Indians quickly gave up the search in order to get back to camp and hear what news the soldiers brought.

Immediately after reporting to Captain Bird that he had seen nothing to indicate the army was in danger of being attacked, Chard made a mad dash for Judith's tent. He felt his way through the darkness to her pallet and knelt by her side. "Mother?" he inquired softly.

"She can't hear you," came a tired voice from the darkness.

"Who's there?" demanded the startled ensign.

"It's Susan Patterson and her daughter, Bitsy."

After a long pause, Chard murmured that he would get a light.

"No!" cried Bitsy anxiously. "Please . . . wait until morning to see your mama. She's resting now."

"What my daughter is trying to say," said Susan, "is that your mother was whipped today."

116

"Aye," returned the young man, wondering why they seemed so excited about a switching, "my father whipped her."

"You knew he intended to whip her?" came Bitsy's incredulous voice.

"Of course," answered Chard calmly. "'Tis a husband's right to publicly whip his wife if she deserves it."

"Get out of here," cried the girl. "Get out of here before I forget I am a lady and— Go on, get out!"

The young man sprang to his feet and backed to the tent flaps. "What in bloody hell is wrong with you?" he inquired harshly as he stepped out of the tent. "Are you daft?"

"Get out," repeated the girl with even more venom. "You don't deserve to be this lady's son!"

After he was gone, Bitsy slumped to her pallet and drew her knees up under her chin. "Mama," she said into the darkness, "why does he upset me so?"

"I've wondered about that myself," came Susan's reply. "Would you like to talk about it?"

"There's nothing to talk about. He reminds me of someone, but for the life of me, I don't know who."

The girl sighed and stretched out on the makeshift bed.

"I feel drawn to him, yet I despise him. It just doesn't make any sense."

"Well, he is handsome," said Susan. "He looks just like his mother, except for his eyes. They have the look of the hawk."

"It's not his looks, Mama," said the girl slowly. "It's his actions, his way of moving . . . Oh, it's not important." She rolled onto her side and dismissed the thought.

Suddenly the tent flaps flew open and Chard stood there with a lighted lamp. Bitsy and her mother shielded their eyes from the blinding glow.

"Damn it," Chard barked, "why didn't you tell me that my father used a cat-o'-nine-tails?"

"We thought you knew," came Susan's uncertain reply. "You said you knew he intended to whip her."

"With a switch! I thought he was going to use a willow branch."

"Well, he didn't," said Bitsy dryly.

Chard stalked to Judith's pallet and knelt by his mother's side. Susan and Bitsy watched with mingled anger and compassion as the young ensign moved the light across Judith's body.

For several minutes he stayed like that, poised on one knee, neither moving nor speaking and, in truth, hardly breathing.

Bitsy and Susan had to listen closely when he did speak, for the words were barely audible. "If he weren't my father, I'd kill him where he stands." Then Chard was up and stumbling blindly through the flaps.

"He didn't shed a tear," said Bitsy angrily. "'Tis his mother lying there near death, and his eyes didn't even water."

Susan took her daughter's hand. "Mayhap he is like your papa, and does all his crying on the inside."

"He's not at all like Papa," cried the girl, angered by Susan's comparison. "And he never will be. Papa is a man!"

At daylight, the camp was alive with activity. Prisoners were loaded into birch canoes, pirogues, and dugouts. Supply boats were quickly checked and rechecked. Indians herded horses down the Licking toward the Ohio some fifty miles away. And soldiers were already making last-minute preparations for shoving off.

Judith, along with Susan and Bitsy, had been placed in a thirty-foot bark canoe so that she might lie as comfortably as possible. Susan suspected that Chard had somehow managed that godsend, probably by purchasing the canoe outright from an Indian. Bending over the sick woman, Susan raised a corner of the dressing she had applied the night before. She frowned at the exposed wound. If even one of those deep slashes became infected, Judith was as good as dead.

"How is she?" asked Bitsy, from her position near the bow of the canoe.

"Not good," came Susan's worried reply. "The cuts are

puffed and red. I wish she would regain consciousness. I think that would help."

But as the flotilla progressed down the main branch of the Licking toward the Ohio, Judith's condition worsened, and by noon she was delirious. Both Susan and Bitsy had their hands full just to keep the thrashing woman from upsetting the canoe.

CHAPTER

· 8 ·

FOUR ANGRY WOODSMEN thundered their mounts through the wide open gates of Harrodsburg. The sight that awaited them did nothing to improve their mood. Hundreds of men of all descriptions milled about or stood in line before the cabin that had been designated as a land office. Very few men were under arms, and nowhere was there a guard on the palisades.

Before the lathered horses could slide to a standstill, the four officers were off and bounding toward the over-crowded cabin.

"God damn it, Harrod," raged Clark, elbowing men aside to burst through the cabin door. "What in Christ's name have you allowed to happen here?"

James Harrod took a deep breath and crossed the room to the waiting general. "Nothing I could do about it, George," he said apologetically. "Damned people are from the government—got letters of authority."

"I'm the government here," boomed Clark, turning beet red. "And I'm closing this land office, as of now."

The government land agent, who sat behind a large, crudely constructed desk, raised his head from the title he was signing and gave Clark a hard look. "You've no authority to close this office," he said crisply. "I suggest that you retract that statement, sir, or I'll have you in irons."

Clark's mouth fell open, and for a heartbeat he could do nothing but gape at the man. Morgan Patterson leaned lightly against the door and smiled sadly at the agent. The fireworks were about to begin. Clark's hand flashed out and wound itself in the commissioner's waistcoat. In the next instant, the man was over the desk and peering into Clark's cold eyes, so close that the lashes almost touched.

"You baldheaded son of a bitch," crooned Clark. "I've a damned good mind to twist your little head off and use it for a game of kick."

Before the man could swallow the lump that suddenly rose in his throat, Clark spun him around and planted his foot at the man's backside with such force that the commissioner hurtled past Patterson into the crowd that had gathered just outside the door.

As Clark brushed past Patterson in the commissioner's wake, he said, "If I wasn't so goddamn mad, Morgan, I'd probably enjoy this."

Patterson gave Clark a boyish grin. "A game of kick? I'm disappointed in you, George. Lacrosse would be more like it."

"I'm not a goddamn savage, Morgan," boomed the general as he went out the door.

"Now, you listen to me!" Clark roared at the assembled crowd. "As of this instant, you are all duly appointed privates in the Virginia Militia." He flung his hand out to stop the rumble of disapproval that was rising from the audience. "I won't listen to that horseshit, not one goddamn minute of it. Furthermore, I'm sending Major Harlan and Captain Consola with a company of men to Crab Orchard with instructions to shoot any son of a bitch who tries to leave the country."

Clark smiled acidly and examined each face. "You're stuck here, men, like it or not, and get this straight. You'll fight for this land that you thought was going to come so easy . . . or we'll bury you here. Whichever way you want it, you'll get what's comin' to you."

Patterson pushed himself erect and moved to Clark's side. Looking at the surly men, he wondered whether Clark had bitten off more than he could chew. These were a different breed from the men who had gone with the general to the Illinois country in 1778.

Patterson frowned, his attention drawn to the main gate, where a lone woodsman had staggered to the upright and was leaning heavily against the post as if he had gone his last step. That indeed was close to the truth, for John Hinkson had come seventy miles in a day and a half.

121

Nudging the general with his elbow, Patterson nodded toward the gate. "Looks like Hinkson," said Clark, following Patterson's gaze. "Some of you men help that fellow up here."

In a matter of seconds the men had half carried and half dragged Hinkson to where Clark and Patterson stood.

"What's happened, John?" said Clark, as the men eased the worn-out woodsman to a sitting position.

Several shuddering breaths and half a dozen false starts later, Hinkson gasped out the sordid story of the capture of Ruddle's and Martin's Forts. "I escaped and made it back to Ruddle's," rasped the man between breaths. "I found a horse the Indians had overlooked and rode into the Kentucky River. Overheated—killed him deader than a doornail—shoulda known better . . . I run the last ten miles without a breather."

"Well, you heard the man," said Clark to the surrounding throng of white-faced newcomers. "Do you still think Kentucky soil comes free?"

"I'm not joinin' no bloody militia to go traipsin' off after no thousand Indians," offered a surly young man standing near the front of the crowd. "Those chaps who got captured can rot in hell before I go after them."

Clark moved fast, but Patterson was quicker. His right fist smashed into the man's mouth, whipping his head back with such force that had he not been built like a bull, his neck would have snapped. In the blink of an eye, Patterson's left fist caught the point of the man's upturned chin and dropped him flat on his back in the ankle-deep mud.

Clark seized Patterson in a bone-crushing bear hug and spun him away from the prostrate form. "Don't kill him, Morgan," he barked, holding tightly to the angry woodsman. The fallen man shook his head several times to clear his sight, then pushed himself to his elbows. Hatred marred his face as he slipped his hunting knife from its sheath. "I'll kill that old son of a bitch," he mumbled through his split lips.

A moccasined foot reinforced by two hundred pounds of muscle and bone came down on the man's knife wrist, forcing it into the mud. Simon Kenton grinned down at him and wagged his head from side to side. "That old son of a bitch," he said easily, "will skin and quarter you before

122

you even get a chance to draw blood. Don't you know that's Morgan Patterson?"

Kenton grinned even wider. "He didn't live to be an old son of a bitch by being stupid like you." With that, Kenton removed his foot and ambled off good-naturedly. If the man wanted to die, that was his business; Kenton had warned him. The drama, however, wasn't quite finished. Patterson flung Clark from him and eyed the general through slitted lids. "Don't ever lay hold of me again, George."

Clark's face turned livid. He was well aware that Patterson was not making an idle threat—yet, as the commanding officer in Kentucky, he could not afford to have his authority or respect jeopardized, not even by a friend.

"Then don't ever put me in a position to have to lay hold of you, Morgan," he said with unaccustomed softness. "I'd hate to have to kill the best man I ever met."

Patterson looked hard into Clark's eyes. Then he smiled crookedly. "Reckon Kentucky could survive with the both of us dead?"

Clark's booming laughter drowned out the relieved cheers of the old-timers who knew both men and never doubted for a moment that should they tangle they would both wind up dead—for that was the kind of men Patterson and Clark were.

"Who was that big-mouth bastard that Patterson hit?" said Clark, turning to the crowd and finding the man gone.

One of the old campaigners showed a toothless grin. "Said his name was Clarke, General. He grabbed hisself a horse and lit out like he had a fire in his arse."

"Well, the son of a bitch ain't no kin of mine," roared the commander as he winked at Patterson, "and I say, good riddance."

Those were words that many Kentuckians would live to regret.

Clark was coldly serious that evening as he watched Morgan Patterson prepare for an extended journey.

"I wish you would wait and come with the army, Morgan," he said as Patterson crammed small bags of

123

provisions into his haversack. "Those men out there are rarin' to go, now that the threat is real. I wish you'd reconsider."

"George," said Patterson, slinging the haversack over his shoulder, "you won't have these men in the woods before the last of July." He held Clark's eyes. "I hope to have my wife and daughter back by then."

"Well," said the general, "they're probably beyond the Ohio by now. 'Tis no easy task you've set for yourself, my friend."

Then, in the manner of one who knows he is fighting a losing battle, he added angrily, "At least take Simon Kenton and some of the old hands with you."

"I can travel faster alone, George," returned the woodsman, stepping through the door to the horse that stood tethered just outside.

"Morgan," said Clark, following Patterson out, "with this war, a nation is being born. And, as with any birthin', blood, pain, and suffering are inevitable."

"Say what you mean, George. Quit pussyfootin' around."

Clark gripped Patterson's shoulder hard. "This infant United States ain't comin' easy, but whatever the price of labor, we've got to pay it, Morgan. It's worth it. No matter what you find out there, remember, it's worth it."

Susan stood on the Kentucky shore of the Ohio River and gazed at the uncharted wilderness beyond the distant bank. Very soon, the captives from Ruddle's Station would be crossing that river. And, likely as not, many would remain there forever.

If there was one thing that she could thank Southhampton for, Susan decided, it was that she and Bitsy were not captives of the Indians. She shuddered as she thought about the cruelty the people from Ruddle's would endure while living with the savages. They would be slaves in the truest sense of the word, unless by some trick of fate they happened to be adopted into the tribe. But that was highly unlikely except for the very young male children.

Susan stretched her cramped muscles. The fleet of canoes, pirogues, and dugouts had come fifty long miles that day, making a total of ninety miles in four days, counting the day they laid over at the forks of the Licking, the day Judith was whipped. She thought of Judith then, of the cuts and abrasions that were becoming even more inflamed by the hour. That and Judith's persistent unconsciousness were driving Susan frantic with worry. Even the surgeon had shaken his head and said there was nothing he could do.

Susan took a deep breath and let it out slowly. She wished Morgan would come and take her and Bitsy away before something even more terrible occurred. She had thought that Judith's presence, even unconscious and near death, would dampen Southhampton's advances toward her. But he acted as though Judith did not exist.

He made a point, it seemed, of treating Susan as if she were his personal property to order about as he pleased. Indeed, he had grown especially malevolent since Chard had returned and assured him that the army was well beyond the reach of danger or pursuit. And upon reaching the Ohio some two hours ago, he had become even more difficult, a man overly confident of his position, a man who acted as though he, personally, controlled not only her immediate future but her life as well. And she was truthful enough with herself to admit that his domineering, proprietary attitude had cast fear and doubt into her soul.

He had commanded her to meet him at sundown on the riverbank—and she was there. That was proof in itself of his newly acquired power to intimidate. He had used as his weapon the one thing in her life that influenced her every thought and action—her daughter, Bitsy. So she awaited the major with a sickening sense of dread.

Susan heard his footsteps, but she remained where she was, gazing across the river. She feared having to face Southhampton, for she was sure he had devised some scheme that would put her or Bitsy, or perhaps both of them, at his mercy.

"'Tis good that you came, my dear," he said, striding to her side and slipping his arm across her shoulder.

Susan shrugged from his embrace and faced him.

"Say what you came to say, Major. Your wife needs my attention."

125

"I have no wife," he returned easily. "She forfeited that sacred and honorable title when she turned traitor, madam."

"I have no idea what you are talking about," said Susan, eyeing him indifferently.

"'Tis of little consequence. Actually I came here to bargain with you."

"You have nothing I want, sir," said Susan.

"Ah, but I have. Your daughter's honor is in the palm of my hand."

"Then you have nothing," repeated Susan. "Captain Bird has assured all the women that no harm will come to us. You haven't the nerve to chance a taste of what you gave your own wife."

Southhampton's face clouded. He caught Susan's wrist and snatched her to him. "I don't give a damn about Bird's orders, nor do half the men who serve under him." He pushed his face close to hers. "Men, I might add, who have been in this damned wilderness for weeks without the taste of feminine flesh. I'm sure that you, as a protective mother, have been well aware of the hungry looks your blossoming young flower is receiving."

Susan remained quiet, but Southhampton's words had struck home. She had seen the burning lust in the eyes of the soldiers, looks that had devoured Bitsy's body as though it were a feast fit for a king. Susan's stomach tightened as an even greater fear of Southhampton filled her. "What is it that you offer, sir?"

"Your daughter can keep her precious virginity, or I can give it to the troops. The decision is entirely yours, my dear. All you have to do to secure her safety is—"

"Come to your tent," finished Susan in a dead voice.

"There is a trifle more to it than that," he said, studying her face thoughtfully, gauging the depth of her submission.

"How much more, Major? Exactly what do you expect from me?"

"James. Call me James. After all, we are going to be very close . . . friends."

Susan felt her stomach convulse. "We will never be friends," she snapped. And then added, "James."

Southhampton raised his hand to Susan's cheek and

caressed it with his fingertips, letting them travel across her lips.

"Don't be so pious, Susan. After all, you and I are two of a kind, my dear. Birds of a feather." When she didn't respond, he continued. "You accuse me of being a murderer for not attempting to save those folks at Ruddle's Station. If I am guilty, then you, madam, are equally as guilty. You allowed two women to drown, rather than compromise your . . . virtue."

Southhampton's words were like a sledgehammer blow to Susan's temples. Almost as though he were reading her mind, he could see he had indeed struck a sensitive nerve that had been paining Susan's conscience since the two women's deaths. Southhampton parted Susan's lips and flicked his fingernail across her teeth. "You will be my woman," he decreed. "You will come to my tent at midnight tonight of your own free will, and you will tell no one—absolutely no one—of our arrangement. Is that understood?"

Susan nodded, not trusting her voice.

"As far as Captain Bird or anyone else is concerned, 'tis your decision to be my mistress in my wife's stead."

Again Susan nodded, her gaze steady as Southhampton looked deep into her large black eyes. "And if you are thinking of killing me," he warned, "you can forget it. I have left orders in the right places that should any harm befall me, any harm at all, your daughter is to become the common property of the Eighth Regiment. And I can assure you, madam, when they are finished with her, she will be less than human."

And when you are through with me, wondered Susan, what will I be?

"What is wrong, Mama?" demanded Bitsy as she and Susan finished removing the soiled dressings from Judith's wounds. "You haven't said three words since you got back from the river."

Susan didn't answer. Her mind was numb and confused, and she had no idea what she could tell her daughter. She knew better than to tell the girl the truth. If she did that, Southhampton would be denied the pleasure of delivering Bitsy into the eternal fires of the hell that he called the Eighth Regiment, for the girl would perform that honor herself. She would walk into their camp and sacrifice her virtue without blinking an eye if she thought it would protect her mother's dignity and self-respect.

Thankfully, she was saved from having to answer Bitsy's question by Simon Girty, who stepped into the tent without knocking. In wide-eyed alarm, Susan and Bitsy watched him advance.

"Ladies?" he said, inclining his head in an attempt at formality.

"Aye?" said Susan, catching Bitsy's hand and drawing the girl nervously to the back of the tent. "What is it you want?"

After a moment of silence, Girty produced a small crock and quietly offered it to the women.

"'Tis salve for the woman who was whipped. 'Tis Indian medicine; it will help heal her wounds. That stuff the surgeon gave you is naught but a balm that the army uses on the horses."

"Why do you care?" whispered Susan. "'Twas you who caused her capture in the first place." But all she got in return was silence.

With a slight nod, Girty backed quietly out of the tent and walked away.

"Well, what do you make of that?" breathed Bitsy, staring after Girty.

Susan studied the crock with a critical eye and tentatively sniffed at its contents. Wrinkling her nose, she quickly turned her face away. "I have no idea why he did it," she informed her wide-eyed daughter, "but anything that smells as awful as this has to be good." And without further ado, she and Bitsy dipped their fingers into the stinking mess and, being as gentle as possible, smoothed the balm over Judith's chest and back and even managed to work a portion into the inside of her lip where she had bitten through the flesh.

"Why do you suppose he did that?" said Bitsy wonderingly as she set the crock aside.

"I haven't the faintest notion," murmured her mother. "Let's just pray his remedy works. Judith is looking worse every minute."

"Well," smiled Bitsy, "at least you are talking again. You had me worried, Mama."

"I've a lot on my mind, sweetheart. If I seem distant, don't fret about me; I'll be fine." But Susan knew that wasn't true—she would never be fine again . . . not after midnight, not after Southhampton . . .

"Is my mother any better?" Chard anxiously thrust aside the tent flap and stepped quickly to Judith's pallet.

Bitsy gazed at the young man in the flickering light of the candle lantern. His alarm appeared sincere.

"We've some new ointment," she said, handing Chard the crock. "'Tis Indian medicine, but my papa says Indian cures really work."

"Damnation!" The ensign turned his face aside. "Where'd you get that stuff?"

When Bitsy told him, Chard agreed that he couldn't imagine Simon Girty being so humane—but if the ointment eased Judith's suffering, he was beholden to the man.

Bitsy smiled into his eyes as she took the crock from him. "Maybe we'll see a difference in a day or two. Till then all we can do is pray for her."

Chard's chiseled face softened. "I don't know how to thank you . . . you and your mother."

"Just get out of here and leave us alone," snapped Susan. "I don't want you near my daughter, do you hear?"

Baffled and embarrassed, Chard eyed Susan warily. Even Bitsy's face flamed bright in the feeble light of the candle lantern. "Mama, what has come over you?" whispered the girl. "You haven't been yourself all evening."

"I don't want him ever to speak to you again," shouted Susan, pointing her finger at Chard, who was staring open-mouthed as if he, too, could not believe what he was hearing. Susan's candid honesty, sincerity, and kindness had drawn him to her. But the woman he had grown to admire in the past few days was certainly not the same person facing him at that instant, not she, with her cold, hating eyes, she who seemed on the brink of lunacy.

Chard bowed curtly to Susan and Bitsy. Without a word, he spun on his heel and stalked into the night.

"Why did you do that?" stormed Bitsy. "He has made no advance toward me. In fact, he is the only soldier with

129

this army who has not given me that dirty look that leaves me feeling cheap and unclean."

Susan turned her back on her daughter and took a deep, racking breath; her daughter's words beat at her temples like a deafening drumroll. In her mind she could see Southhampton's sardonic grin and hear his words: "When they are finished with her, she will be less than human."

"I'm leaving you tonight," Susan said harshly.

Bitsy's eyes widened until they nearly consumed her small oval face. Her mother's quavering voice continued: "In the future, I do not want you to come near me or acknowledge that I am your mother . . . I never want to speak to you again. Do you understand?"

"Mama," whispered the girl with such desolation that Susan very nearly broke her pledge to keep Southhampton's agreement secret. She wanted desperately to take her daughter into her arms and tell her the whole sordid truth behind her decision to join Southhampton. But fear for Bitsy sealed Susan's lips as surely as if she had been dead.

"What have I done?" came the girl's anguished voice, her eyes swimming with tears. "Please tell me . . . I'll do anything to make it right. Please, Mama, what have I done?"

"'Tis a decision of my own making," said Susan stonily. "Now, say no more about it."

The girl was crying openly, slowly shaking her head from side to side as if the negative movement might in some way influence her mother's monstrous decision. "But, Mama, Papa will come and take us home . . . He always comes, Mama."

Susan shrugged as if the statement were pointless, but she yearned for Morgan Patterson to arrive out of nowhere, as he had done so many times in the past, and save her from the disgrace that Southhampton planned for her. But she knew that it was only wishful thinking; Patterson would not magically appear and whisk her into the safety of his strong arms. This time there was no way out except to go forward, and when she made that final step to Southhampton's tent, even that avenue would close behind her. She shook her head. She almost wished that Morgan would not attempt to rescue her, for she was sure she would never be able to look

130

into his eyes without feeling guilty, debased and totally unworthy of such a fine man; and she would rather never see him again than be despised by the only man she had ever loved, would ever love. Taking a deep breath, Susan moved toward the tent flaps.

"I won't let you go," cried Bitsy, flinging herself to her knees and locking her arms around Susan's waist. "Please, Mama," she whispered, looking up into her mother's face. "Please don't leave me."

Susan pushed Bitsy roughly away, throwing her off balance to fall heavily to her side. Bitsy curled her body into a tight ball and cried the heartbroken tears of a child who is lost, alone, terrified, and confused.

Perhaps Judith's subconscious had heard the heart-wrenching exchange between Bitsy and Susan, or maybe it was nothing more than one of those rare moments between fever and delirium, but whatever triggered it, Judith awakened with a clear head. Her eyes traveled from Bitsy's pathetic form to Susan, and for an eternity the two women searched each other's faces. Judith fought hard to speak, but her lips were so inflamed and swollen that her broken whisper was incoherent.

Susan, however, had no trouble reading the imploring look in her long-ago acquaintance's eyes, an expression of concern that begged Susan to reconsider and stay with her daughter.

Susan wanted to scream at Judith that she had no choice at all. But instead, she raced blindly into the night, unable to endure one more second of Judith's compassionate stare. And as she stumbled through the darkness, she wondered what those eyes would hold if they knew that before the night was over, James Southhampton would be lying bathed in sweat between Susan's thighs.

Judith stared at the flickering patterns that the candle lantern cast on the tent wall. She wondered if she was still dreaming, or if the conversation had actually taken place. Even more incredible, the woman she had beheld when she regained her senses was none other than Susan Spencer —no, she corrected herself, she would be Susan Patterson now. Judith turned her gaze to the girl who lay on the floor, knees drawn up to her chin in the fetal position.

The sound of the girl's sobs pierced the very depths of

Judith's maternal instincts and, fighting against the overwhelming pain that lanced through her body each time she moved, she dragged herself to Bitsy and gathered her into her arms.

And sixteen-year-old Bitsy responded by throwing her arms tightly around Judith and pressing her wet face against the woman's raw and inflamed breast. Judith ignored the agonizing pain of the girl's embrace and forced her trembling hand to tenderly caress Bitsy's long copper hair—right up to the moment her fever-ridden body could stand no more and she slumped, unconscious, to the floor.

When Susan left the tent, she ran toward the river. Soldiers, lying leisurely around their campfires, whistled and called as she passed, but she didn't hear them.

Her mind was blank, her eyes unseeing; she could not have uttered an intelligent word had she tried. Instinct pointed her toward the Ohio, instinct and something else, something she refused to acknowledge, for never would she have openly considered taking her own life. It was as though her feet acted independently of her body as they raced in an unwavering line straight to the bluffs above the deadly, fast-flowing water.

She stood on the plateau and stared into the swirling current. It seemed to draw her toward it, calling her name, inviting her to join its cold depths as it flowed away from Kentucky and the pain and torture of the Indians, away from the disgrace and degradation of Southhampton, the guilt of knowing she had cost two innocent women their lives; away from the shame that would fill the eyes of her daughter, her countrymen, and eventually her husband if she went to Southhampton; and, most important, away from the person Susan Patterson would become.

Taking a deep breath, Susan flung herself into the emptiness above the rushing river.

A group of French-Canadian Rangers who had been visiting a Shawnee village across the Ohio stayed their paddles and let their bark canoe drift with the current. They were captivated by the sight unfolding on the moonlit bluff. They knew, even before she jumped, that the woman intended to take her life. And when she did jump, they dug their paddles deep, pointing the bow of their vessel toward the waters beneath the promontory.

They were there almost before she splashed into the icy current. And when she bobbed up, their strong hands dragged her into the boat. She coughed and spit and tried to catch her breath, and when she realized that she had blundered in her attempt to fulfill her destiny, she fought with the frenzied strength of one determined to finish what she had started. But the Canadians wrestled her to the bottom of the craft and held her still.

"Madame," commanded one ranger as he cupped Susan's head between his callused hands and peered into her wild eyes. "Madame, listen to me."

"Let me go," she cried, fighting even harder. "You have no right to interfere."

"Ah, but there you are mistaken, madame. If we permit you to take your life, my companions and I will burn in hell alongside you."

"You and your companions will burn in hell regardless," grated Susan through her teeth. "Now let me up."

"I cannot do that," shouted the Frenchman with equal venom. "Our religion does not permit suicide. If we condone such an act, we will be as guilty as you."

"Then drown with me, damn you," said Susan. She threw her weight against the side of the craft with such force that the canoe nearly capsized.

"Please, madame," begged the man, fighting to hold the canoe steady, "would you destroy our chance for the hereafter? Would you drag us to the bottom of the river with you?"

"I want to die," whispered Susan.

"We cannot permit that. One does not have the right to take one's own life. God forbids it."

"God?" she said incredulously. "There is no God."

The Canadian stared wide-eyed at Susan, then slowly crossed himself. "Madame, do not say such a thing."

"Do you think God would allow all this suffering and killing?" cried Susan. "Do you?"

The man gazed hard into her eyes. *"Oui,* madame, it is

His way. We have no right to question the ways of the Creator."

Susan slumped against the ribs of the canoe. "I'm sorry," she murmured. She closed her eyes and sighed deeply. "You can release me, sir. I will be all right now."

And, in fact, she was all right. For in that brief interval after the Frenchman had spoken, Susan had thought about Judith's beating. And the reflection left her ashamed and despising herself for what she had attempted to do. Judith had taken her punishment without so much as a whimper, until it became unbearable, while Susan had not the courage to face hers.

"Please," she implored, "you can let me up. I will give you no further problems."

The Canadian breathed a sigh of relief. He glanced at his companions; they nodded their assent. Watching her carefully, he eased his bulk from Susan's trembling body.

When it became apparent that the woman had no intention of pursuing her self-destructive course, the men again dipped their paddles deep, and the canoe shot toward the Kentucky shore.

When Susan approached Southhampton's dimly lighted tent and slipped between the door flaps, the scene she beheld made her gasp in astonishment. Southhampton and a young woman lay writhing on his cot, their sweat-soaked bodies locked in a most recreational and amorous display.

The woman peered with large, panic-stricken eyes over the glistening shoulder of her lover. At the sight of Susan, she recoiled with such startled dismay that she all but jumped from beneath Southhampton's naked form.

"Mrs. Patterson!" she wailed, shamed and startled by the discovery.

The girl sprang from the cot and with trembling hands pulled her worn shift over her head. She ran to Susan, dropped to one knee and looked imploringly into her face. "Mrs. Patterson," she whimpered in quick, nervous explanation, "Major Southhampton promised me that if I would come to him, he would see to it that me and Walter and the baby would not have to cross the river with the Indians tomorrow." The girl's eyes were wide pools of self-

134

abasement, begging Susan to understand. "Walter and the baby is all I got in this world, ma'am. I'll do anything to keep from being separated from them."

Yes, thought Susan, gently drawing the terrified young woman to her feet, I know the feeling well. We women have no shame when it comes to protecting a loved one.

"Go back to your husband," she instructed, gently directing the girl toward the exit. "Say nothing to Walter about what happened here tonight." She looked knowingly at the girl. "Forget this ever happened."

The young woman nodded gratefully and sprang through the flaps. The sound of her bare feet smacking the earth could be heard plainly as she raced toward the captives' quarters.

"Do you intend to keep your promise about their not having to cross the Ohio? Or need I ask?" said Susan, fixing Southhampton with a cold stare.

Southhampton sat up and smiled patronizingly. He let his eyes rove over Susan's sopping dress and tangled hair.

Then, pursing his thin lips, he said, "I had to pay a damned Huron Indian five shillings just to get him to let her come here tonight. I couldn't care less what happens to her tomorrow." His smile became sardonic. "You spoiled a pretty tableau by coming early. The sweet little honey was very eager to please me."

"The sweet little honey," said Susan, "was prostituting herself for her husband's sake. She gave herself to you so that her family would not be separated tomorrow. You are without a doubt the vilest piece of offal that ever drew breath."

"Now, now, my dear," said Southhampton blandly, "life is what you take from it, nothing more, nothing less. Furthermore, it might interest you to know that half the officers in Bird's command have made similar promises. Aye," he continued with amusement, "many a husband will wonder where his wife disappeared to this evening."

"I don't believe you," breathed Susan numbly.

"Then you are not only stupid but foolish as well." Southhampton swung his feet to the floor and pushed himself erect.

Susan's eyes fell to his naked body, which gleamed stark white in the candlelight, and in spite of herself, she compared the flaccid muscles and paunchy belly of the pompous officer to Morgan Patterson's lean, muscular torso and flat, hard stomach. She wondered, too, if she would actually be able to submit to his, or anyone's, physical intercourse, for she was, in every sense of the word, Morgan Patterson's mate.

"Come here," he commanded, eyeing her intently. She crossed the room and stood facing him with wide, steady eyes. If he expected her to cry or plead, he would be sadly disappointed. She had no intention of cowering before him.

"The years have been kind to you, Susan," he said, stroking her wet hair. "You wear neither powder nor rouge, yet your color is high. I always did think it a cowardly shame to allow such beauty to go to waste in a raw and unsophisticated place like America. With your looks, you would have been treated like a queen in Europe."

"Was your wife treated like a queen in Europe?" Susan asked coldly. "She is more beautiful than I could ever hope to be."

Southhampton scowled and tightened his fingers in her thick tresses. "Judith is lovely, I'll grant you that, but not as perfect as you. Her face is scarred."

"It does not impair her beauty," said Susan dryly.

"I can't stand blemishes," he said, shrugging nonchalantly. "Her face revolts me, but yours I find ... bewitching." He pressed his naked body against her, his hands moving up to capture her face and draw it toward him. "But 'tis your lips that I find most alluring," he murmured, kissing her lightly, "lips that were made to drive a man mad."

His eyes were live embers, as though a fire burned deep in his brain, the hot glow searching for an outlet through his pale irises.

Susan shuddered under their scorching scrutiny; at that moment she was seeing Southhampton in the same light as that in which Judith beheld him, as a brutal, egotistical man, completely devoid of compassion or consideration.

Southhampton wound his hand tightly in Susan's hair and slowly forced her to her knees. His voice thickened as he told her in vivid detail what she was expected to perform. Her eyes grew big, and she struggled wildly to gain her feet, but he pushed her down with such fury that she cried out in pain.

"Do it," he ordered, drawing her face against his groin. "Do it, or your daughter will do it for a hundred men."

She shut her eyes, but the image of Bitsy performing fellatio on scores of soldiers hovered beneath her eyelids. Shaking uncontrollably, she parted her lips to do as Southhampton bade, but the musky odor of the young woman he had just seduced lingered on his body, and she knew she was going to be violently sick.

Southhampton used Susan brutally all through the night. Each time he awakened, he would begin anew, inventing positions and intimacies that Susan had never even dreamed of in her wildest nightmares. It was as if he were driving himself, forcing his powers to higher peaks and longer plateaus, and he kept insisting throughout the frenzied ordeals that Susan tell him how wonderful it felt, how much a man he was. "Better than Morgan Patterson?" he would demand. "Aye," she would whisper, not trusting her voice, "you're the best I'll ever have from this day forward," and he would plunge and squirm and drive even harder for completion, until finally he closed his eyes and released the deep sigh of the exhausted.

He smiled, pleased with himself. He had wreaked a small portion of his long-awaited vengeance on Morgan Patterson.

As the eastern horizon shone with the first streaks of crimson, Morgan Patterson stood by his horse, just ninety miles from where Susan lay in wide-eyed sleepless desolation next to the snoring form of James Southhampton. The Kentuckian angrily surveyed the smoldering remains of Ruddle's Fort at the precise instant when nearly three hundred terrified Americans from that fort were being ferried across the wide Ohio River by their Indian captors.

In one canoe a young woman wept hysterically and called her husband's name. A Shawnee squatting directly behind her grunted with displeasure and, without batting an eye, snapped her head back and drew the razor-sharp edge of his scalping knife hard across her throat. Without ceremony, he cut away her long brown hair and dumped her lifeless body into the swift Ohio current. His eyes traveled to the four-month-old boy child who lay in the bottom of the canoe watching his every move. For an instant he considered throwing the baby overboard also, but the boldness of the child appealed to the savage. Reaching down, he gently covered the boy with a captured blanket.

"Wal-ter," he grunted to the Indian in front of him, as he resumed paddling. "What is a Wal-ter?"

The lead Indian shrugged and dipped his paddle deep. "It is what white people call the river and the rain."

The second Indian looked hard at the fast-flowing river and scowled. He had killed a perfectly good slave just because she wanted to drink from the river. His mouth drew down at the corners as he realized how stupid he had been. Then, as he bent again to dip his paddle into that very same water, the small leather pouch that hung suspended by a thong around his neck clinked and jingled, reminding him of Southhampton's five shillings. His painted face broke into a wide grin. The woman had not been a total loss after all.

Not an hour later, Captain Henry Bird was roused from his cot by a sleepy-eyed sentry who informed him that a man from Harrodsburg had just arrived and demanded an audience with the commander.

"Show him in," cried Bird, drawing on his breeches. "I've been expecting him for a week."

"Well, Lieutenant Clarke?" said Bird, extending his hand warmly as Clarke entered his marquee. "What did you find out at Harrodsburg?"

Clarke took a seat and commenced his report. It was a slow and cumbersome process because of his puffed and swollen lips and aching jaws. "And when I attempted to discourage the men at Harrod's from retaliating, a woodsman named Morgan Patterson caught me unawares." He pointed to his mangled mouth. "I would have killed the bloody bastard, but several of his friends jumped me—"

"What's this about Morgan Patterson?" inquired

Southhampton, entering the commander's tent unan-
nounced.

"This is Lieutenant Samuel Clarke, one of our best
intelligence officers," said Bird to Southhampton. "He
reports that General Clark is at Harrodsburg raising an
army. Damn it, Southhampton, Clark never was at the falls;
we could have taken Kentucky with ease."

"That's water over the dam, Captain," said Southhampton, with a wave of dismissal. "Once we reach Detroit, however," he said, addressing Clark, "we will have the
pleasure of hanging the party who started that rumor and
cost us our campaign. . . . Now, sir, tell me everything you
know about Morgan Patterson."

"Well, Major," said the man, rubbing his jaw, "I know
for a fact that he's a mean son of a bitch." Having said that,
he made a complete report on the happenings at Harrodsburg before and after Clark's arrival.

Morgan Patterson tied his skittish horse securely to a tree
and walked with heavy steps to the bloated bodies of the
victims of Ruddle's massacre. Try as he might, he could
recognize very few of the people. The buzzards, wolves,
and other scavengers had already done their grisly work.
What little they had left was hardly enough for identifica-
tion.

With a heavy heart, he retraced his steps and mounted
his horse. Clark and his soldiers had a terrible job ahead of
them; it would be no easy task to bury such a mangled mess
of human flesh and bones. But that was Clark's worry.
Patterson headed his horse north by west and heeled the
animal into a fast trot. It was a simple matter to follow the
trail Bird's army had taken. All he had to do was glance at
the sky and ride toward the next closest swarm of spiraling
vultures.

He wished he could cut across country and intercept
Bird at the Ohio, but that was out of the question. Hinkson
had been unable to shed any light on Susan and Bitsy's
whereabouts; indeed, the man had no notion whether they
were still alive, so Patterson was forced to follow the army's
trail and check every body he encountered along the way. It
was a time-consuming and agonizing job. When a female

victim was the same stature and build as his wife or daughter, his heart stood still while he forced himself to make certain that it was neither Bitsy nor Susan.

Although Judith's eyes were red-rimmed and bloodshot when she awoke that morning, her forehead was cool under Bitsy's palm. The cuts and lacerations that covered her upper body were definitely less angry and swollen, but it was still too soon to rejoice. She even managed a feeble smile for Chard when he came to inform the guard that as soon as the women were ready to travel, the soldiers could strike the tent and prepare to move out.

Chard avoided glancing in Bitsy's direction. Instead he walked straight to Judith's pallet and took his mother's hand. Bitsy busied herself with preparations for the journey.

"You look better, Mother," Chard said, kneeling beside Judith. "Do you feel up to the long day we have ahead of us?"

Judith clasped her son's hand and squeezed it affectionately. Chard was shocked by the weakness of her grip, and he was again reminded that, indeed, his mother was fortunate to be alive. At that moment, a deep, festering hatred for James Southhampton, one that had lain dormant for years, rose like bile to fill Chard's entire being with its burning, acid taste.

Judith read her son's face easily, and she did not like what she saw. "Promise me," she said weakly, her eyes probing deep into his, "that you will do nothing to avenge my whipping. Promise me."

Chard's mouth tightened into a thin line. For a long moment Judith was afraid he would not answer.

"I will do nothing at this time, Mother," he said finally. "But if he ever so much as lays a finger on you again, I will kill him."

Judith lay back and closed her eyes. She would see to it that Southhampton never came near her again, for her son's sake . . . and for her own. She knew she was not strong enough to shoulder the heavy burden of guilt she would carry should her son kill his father; she would not be able to live with herself knowing that such a stigma would taint

140

Chard the rest of his life, no matter how valid the reason. At that moment, Judith Ann Cornwallace Southhampton pledged in her heart that she would murder her husband in cold blood before she would let him destroy her son.

"Ensign?" said Bitsy as Chard turned to leave. "Have you seen my mama?"

"No, Miss Bitsy," he said. "I don't know where Mrs. Patterson is."

He was ashamed to look into her anxious face, ashamed that he had been forced to lie to her. Stepping through the tent flaps, Chard walked quickly toward the river, wishing with every step that the whispered rumors about Susan and his father were not true. But he knew better.

Bitsy's shoulders slumped. She was at a loss to know what to do. She wanted to search out her mother, at least find out where she was and be sure she was safe. But Susan had forbidden even that small consolation.

With a deep sigh the girl turned to Judith and began replacing the soiled bandages with clean strips of linen. Bitsy's deft fingers fairly flew over Judith's body as she hurried her ministrations, for she could hear the soldiers hammering hard at the tie-pins to loosen them so the tent could be struck and packed for travel. She intended to have the invalid presentable when the soldiers ordered their evacuation. But she had barely replaced Judith's bandages before the two guards drew back the flaps and informed her that it was time to go.

"One moment more," said Bitsy, quickly covering Judith's nudity with a light blanket.

"I'm sorry, miss," said one of the guards. "We've orders to take you to the boats now."

"She's not decent!" cried the girl.

The soldier grinned at Bitsy and entered the tent. "It makes little difference to the army whether a spy is decent or not." He brushed Bitsy aside and secured a handhold on Judith's pallet. The second guard did the same, and together they lifted the makeshift litter and carried the injured woman through the flaps.

"Be easy with her," pleaded Bitsy, as she trotted along behind the men.

"Look, girl," said the guard over his shoulder, "this

woman is a traitor. She will probably be hanged when we get to Detroit." He scowled at Bitsy. "Anyway, we're being as easy as we can."

Had Bitsy not been so wrapped up in her concern for Judith, she would have seen Susan dart quickly into Southhampton's tent and peer cautiously through the narrow opening between the flaps as the group passed. Susan's heart went out to her daughter, who trailed behind the guards, begging them to be gentle with Judith. She watched until Bitsy disappeared from view before stepping again into the sunlight.

Southhampton, approaching in the company of a young officer whose lips were swollen to twice their normal size, stopped in his tracks and gave a long low whistle of appreciation. "Clothes do make the woman," he breathed as he took a turn around Susan, admiring her from all angles as though he, personally, had created her. At his insistence, she had donned one of Judith's finest gowns and had piled her hair on top of her head so that the curve of her slender neck was set off elegantly. She was stunning.

Southhampton's lips pursed and his eyes twinkled as he surveyed her. "Lieutenant Clarke," he said to the gawking man beside him, "may I have the honor of presenting Mrs. Morgan Patterson."

The man's puffed lips fell open as he stared in disbelief at Susan.

"Aye," said Southhampton with amusement, "this is the woman I was telling you about, the wife of the man who mashed your mouth . . . the mother, I might add, of a very beautiful daughter."

Turning to Susan, he said, "Tell Lieutenant Clarke, who has just arrived from Harrodsburg, what your status is, my dear."

Susan bowed her head and studied her dress, her fingers nervously working the fabric into tight folds.

"Tell him," demanded Southhampton.

"I'm your whore," whispered the shamefaced woman, repeating the words Southhampton had forced her to say a hundred times during his sexual torments the night before.

Southhampton leaned close. "I can't hear you, my dear. Speak up."

Susan closed her eyes and took a deep breath. "I'm

Major Southhampton's personal whore, sir," she said, not looking at either of the men.

Southhampton laughed and draped his arm across Susan's shoulders. "Clarke," he said, eyeing Susan contemptuously, "have you ever had a woman who's been shot through the tittie? No? Well, even though it's a terrible blemish, it does not lessen her other charms, I can assure you."

Susan's face blanched stark white, and her hands flew to the collar of her dress, drawing the garment tight against her throat. Her eyes were terrified spheres of liquid obsidian as the two men backed her slowly through the flaps of Southhampton's tent.

CHAPTER
· 9 ·

CHARD STOOD KNEE DEEP in the swift current of the Ohio and steadied the canoe while the guards placed Judith in the bottom of the craft.

Bitsy, on the riverbank, idly stripped the leaves from a low branch of the young willow that grew at the water's edge. When Chard ordered her aboard, she snagged her foot in the sapling and fell heavily. Instantly she was up, apologizing profusely for her clumsiness as she sprang lithely into the boat to kneel beside the sick woman.

She glanced up and down the Ohio River. Something was wrong. The morning was too peaceful, too serene. Then it dawned on her: the Indians were gone, and the people from Ruddle's Fort with them. Over a thousand savages and their captives had vanished as if they had never existed.

The girl's face grew sad. She gazed at the distant wilderness across the wide expanse of water that separated Kentucky from the even more deadly Ohio country where white men, unless they were captives, had seldom trod —and lived to tell about it. Her mother and father had been there. She knew that from bits and pieces of idle conversation picked up over the years. They had lived at Chillicothe, the large Shawnee town on the banks of the Little Miami River. As for details, she knew little, because that long-ago portion of her parents' lives was a book they rarely opened.

Bitsy turned her attention to the woman lying beside her. She studied Judith's flushed face, noticing again the thin silver scar that stood in vivid contrast against her heated brow, and she wondered if Judith remembered her trip beyond the Ohio.

Bird was enraged when he learned that the Indians had abandoned the expedition, stealing off during false dawn with their prisoners, plunder, and horses.

"Not one stayed behind to do our hunting?" he demanded, eyeing Simon Girty incredulously. "You mean that every one of our bloody savages has run out on us?"

Girty nodded. "They figured their job was done."

"Jesus Christ, Girty," cried Bird. "Lorimer's Store must be nearly two hundred miles from here, and there's no guarantee that he will have provisions for us when we get there."

Girty eyed the captain with distaste. "Why don't you dine with Major Southhampton and his new lady friend? Southhampton sees to it that he eats high on the hog, and Mrs. Patterson obviously likes the idea, too."

Bird studied the man closely. "What are you talking about, Girty?"

The renegade smirked and spit a stream of tobacco juice through the captain's tent flaps. "The major has been paying my brother, George, to hunt game for him."

Bird nodded, acknowledging that he was aware Southhampton had been dining well. "Go on," he said impatiently. "What's this about Mrs. Patterson?"

"She moved in with the major last night. I passed his tent about midnight, and they was having a high time of it."

Bird shook his head and frowned. "She didn't strike me as that kind of lady."

"That's the real kick in the arse about the whole thing," agreed Girty. "She's Morgan Patterson's wife, and she ain't that kind of woman."

Bird's eyebrows drew together in thought. "The major knows my rules." He looked at Girty. "Is she there of her own free will?"

Girty shrugged noncommittally. "Captain," he said, changing the subject, "do you know Morgan Patterson?"

"I never heard of the man until we reached Kentucky. Why?"

Girty eyed the captain hard. "I've known him fo years, even hunted with him a time or two before the rebellion. He'll come after his wife, Captain, and he'll kill anything or anybody that gets in his way. And this Eighth Regiment you're so proud of won't never even lay eyes on him, much less see him over a gun barrel." Girty smiled wickedly. "Captain," he said, "Southhampton is a walking dead man and he don't even know it."

Bird shuddered under Simon Girty's intense stare, and at that moment he was glad that he was not James Southhampton.

When Captain Bird stormed into Southhampton's tent, he was shocked and embarrassed by what he saw. Southhampton and Clarke were donning their uniforms, and Susan lay on the major's cot staring with wide unblinking eyes at the ceiling. Slowly, as if it didn't matter, she drew a soiled sheet across her midsection. The effort was wasted; it did little to hide her nudity.

"Really, Captain," said Southhampton, breaking the silence. "You could have the decency to knock before entering."

"What's this woman doing here?" demanded Bird without preamble.

Southhampton tucked his shirttail into his breeches. "She's here of her own volition, Captain. 'Tis no concern of yours."

Bird addressed Susan: "Is that true, Mrs. Patterson?"

"I bloody well resent your doubting my word, Captain," said Southhampton, moving to Susan's side and eyeing Bird hotly. "'Twas her choice to come here, wasn't it, my dear?"

Susan turned her face to the wall and closed her eyes. She was tired, so very, very tired. She wished the three of them would leave. She wished the world would move on without her, that she could lie there and never move again, for that was what she wanted, just to lie there and die.

"Wasn't it, darling?" said Southhampton, digging his fingers cruelly into the soft flesh of her shoulder.

Susan turned her face to Bird. The captain frowned at

146

the bruises and cuts that showed plainly across her cheeks and lips; it was obvious that the woman had been brutally beaten.

"I want to be here," came her slurred voice.

Bird dropped his head and sighed. He knew she was lying, but he was powerless to intervene so long as she took responsibility for her actions.

"Major Southhampton," he said at last, "it has come to my attention that this woman's husband will come for her."

"We are depending on it, sir," agreed Southhampton. "Lieutenant Clarke and I have personal reasons to look forward to greeting Morgan Patterson—and when we do, it is our intention to kill the bastard."

Susan pushed herself slowly to one elbow and laughed mockingly into Southhampton's face. "You will never kill Morgan Patterson. Not you, or a hundred like you."

Bird eyed Southhampton's flaming face, and he, too, smiled, for he had a nagging suspicion that Patterson's wife knew exactly what she was talking about.

Bird cleared his throat. "The rest of the flotilla is already under way, Major. Be prepared to abandon this camp within the hour." With that, he spun on his heel and stalked out of Southhampton's tent.

Chard sat in the bow of the war canoe and watched the countryside slide past. With luck, they would make the thirty miles to the mouth of the Great Miami River long before dark. He relaxed. Were hunger not taking its toll, the trip down the Ohio would seem more like an outing than a military foray.

The weather was clear and warm, and even the insects seemed lazy and good-tempered for a change. Or perhaps it was Chard's attitude that made the difference. He felt stimulated as he surveyed the wilderness on either side of the river. It seemed to beckon to him, to draw at him like a magnet. Yes, he decided, the wilderness was in his blood.

He frowned then, wondering how it had gotten there. His father hated America, and his mother was a gentle-woman of English birth. Yet Chard felt that somewhere in his veins ran the blood of a hunter, an explorer. He sighed, puzzled by the contrariness of the world. His thoughts drifted then.

Even more puzzling and disjointed was the behavior of Susan Patterson. He wondered what had prompted her to throw her life away, especially since Morgan Patterson, aside from being a rebel and therefore an enemy, was reputed to be quite a fine man. Had not the American captives used his name along with Daniel Boone's when they spoke of frontier legends and heroes? So why in God's name would Susan cast such a man aside and replace him with someone like James Southhampton?

Chard bit his lip and grimaced. I should be ashamed, he thought, admiring and respecting a turncoat, a man I've never even seen, more than I do my own sire. I am indeed an unworthy son.

Yet the mystery of why a woman like Susan Patterson would turn to Southhampton for companionship continued to offend the ensign's natural instinct for honor and fair play. He shook his head. He would never understand the intricate workings of a woman's mind. Then, glancing at Bitsy, he thought, Nor for that matter, a girl's either. He smiled, his face turning young and boyish. Perhaps females were born with involved and complex inner selves, while males just naturally blundered through life wondering what in hell was going on.

His smile faded as he watched Bitsy fuss over and comfort his stricken mother, partly to relieve her own distress, he suspected. Although Bitsy had not again pressured him for information about Susan, he knew that the uncertainty was making her frantic. He had seen and could sympathize with the devotion and love between the mother and daughter, for it was much the same emotion he felt for his mother. And indeed, Susan's strange actions were no less perplexing and uncharacteristic than Judith's.

I wish I could confide in Bitsy, he thought wistfully; perhaps together we could sort out the mystery of our strange and unconventional parents. But that was out of the question, for he had no intention of telling the girl that her mother was living with his father. He shrank from the thought of what her actions and feelings toward him would be when she eventually did find out.

148

"Damn," he mused, under his breath. "She is the most beautiful and compelling girl I've ever met. Yet she hates everything that I am, everything that my father and I stand for."

"What's that, sir?" queried the private directly behind the ensign.

"Nothing," answered Chard. "I was just thinking out loud, soldier."

"Yes, sir," agreed the man, dipping his paddle in unison with the three other oarsmen. "This silent, godforsaken frontier has that bloody effect on a man. I'm wishing we were back at Detroit, sir."

We'll be there soon enough, thought Chard, feeling again the uncomfortable burning sensation in his stomach that seemed more frequent with each mile that brought them closer to their destination.

He wondered about his mother's trial. Would she defend herself? Did she even have a defense? *Why, Mother?* he cried silently. *Why did you do it?* He had worn himself out searching for reasons meaningful enough to cause a highborn lady of quality to willingly and knowingly betray her home, family, and country in exchange for . . . what? He had come up empty-handed time and time again. He discarded the possibility that her sole reason was to save the Kentucky settlements; that certainly had some bearing on her decision, but the principal cause lay much deeper, buried, he was afraid, beneath a sequence of events that had taken place before he was born.

I may never know the truth, he said to himself. I'm not even sure I have the right to know. It was her decision . . . hers alone.

Judith slept the day away. The gentle rocking of the canoe and tranquil serenity of the wilderness had a calming effect that worked like medicine on the injured woman.

Late that afternoon the fleet turned out of the main channel of the river and glided silently toward the half-mile-wide valley that broke the wall of an otherwise solid line of impenetrable green foliage that bordered the Ohio's north shore. They had reached the mouth of the Great Miami.

"Lady Southhampton appears to be much better," commented Bitsy to Chard as they followed the litter-carrying soldiers up the slight incline that was the bank of the Great Miami. "I think her fever has broken for good."

The girl touched the ensign's sleeve. "She needs food, Chard," she went on, using his given name for the first time, "something that will give her strength. She's so weak that it frightens me."

The young man frowned, studying the cane thickets that lined both sides of the Miami for a quarter of a mile in all directions. "I'll borrow a musket and see if I can bag a nice fat stag." He glanced at the sun. "There are still a few hours of daylight left; I should have no trouble finding one before dark."

The girl nodded, wondering why he did not just slip into the woods and kill a deer. Why, her father would have considered it an insult to his manhood had he allowed his women to go to sleep with rumbling bellies. She frowned then, wondering what a stag was, and if they were good to eat. And she wondered why, if these stags could be caught in bags, Chard had not provided them with food days ago. She eyed the young man with disgust; the English were a conceited, arrogant, selfish people, with never a thought for anyone but themselves.

Bitsy stepped up her pace. She would rather walk beside Judith's litter.

Chard pushed through the cane toward the forest beyond. He was excited, for never in his life had he been permitted to hunt alone. In England, someone else had always been present—a caretaker, an overseer, someone to help or advise. But it was different in America: all one had to do to be alone was to step off the trail. And he had done that, rushing pell-mell into the dense thickets and honeysuckle, paying no heed to the direction he was traveling, for actually, it didn't really matter so long as he was moving, free to hunt wherever he pleased. He was unaware that the woodland he was marching into with such grand and glorious disregard was larger than England and France put together, with Spain thrown in for good measure.

He stalked on, taking long strides in his hard-soled English riding boots, snapping twigs and branches, pushing aside overhanging limbs and letting them whip back into place, reveling in the confusion and unnecessary noise he was creating. As the afternoon wore on, he wondered at the scarcity of game. He had yet to see a living creature. He eased his tired frame down on a log and peered between tree trunks that were ten and twelve feet in diameter, sentinels that stood at rigid attention as far as he could see.

It dawned on him how insignificant and unimportant man actually was in the scheme of nature and wilderness, a wilderness that cared not whether man lived or died, for nature was supreme. It would feed man or feed upon him; the choice was his.

That thought sent a thrill of fear through Chard like a splash of ice water. He realized that he was out of his element—venturing into a new world that drew him to it as though he were supposed to be there, knowing well that he was not prepared for its dangers.

The wilderness is like a spiderweb, he thought, glancing cautiously about him. It appears so peaceful and inviting, yet once you venture into its depths, it closes in around you and strangles the very life from your body. And that was exactly how he felt as he looked in all directions, wondering what he should do next. He decided to backtrack, but when he stood up, he could not remember which way he had come—and the longer he studied the thick, forbidding forest, the more confused he became. Every tree looked the same.

He didn't panic, as many novice hunters or would-be woodsmen might have upon finding themselves lost and alone hundreds of miles from civilization—not immediately, anyway. He chose a likely-looking direction and struck out in a fast walk. Hunting game was forgotten; returning to the campsite was the uppermost thought in his anxious mind.

He peered at the overhead foliage in an attempt to gauge the position of the sun, but the thick canopy of leaves and branches concealed the sky as if it didn't exist. And to make matters worse, daylight was fading almost before his eyes. He studied the forest floor for shadows that would indicate the east side of a tree—there were none. The entire woods was one huge shaded arbor.

It was then, when he realized that night was fast approaching, that he began to lose control. His keen mind began to twist and tighten, coherent thoughts grew fleeting, and rationality became impossible; panic embraced him with its long, constricting tentacles and drew him into a world bereft of reason. His eyes were wild, his lungs panting as he peered at the strange and frightening forest around him. Then his self-control snapped, and he began running, heedless of obstacles that scratched, cut, or beat at him in his mad, mindless dash through the gathering twilight.

Bitsy stood at the tent flaps and listened to the night sounds of that same forest, but she didn't hear them. And, although her eyes stared at the campfires along the banks of the Great Miami, she didn't see them either. She was blind and deaf to everything except the conversation that she had heard earlier between the two guards posted outside the tent. Their words had not been pretty. Nor was the picture they painted something the young girl should ever have had to envision, for her mother had been the main topic. The guards had said with vulgar clarity that if they possessed certain feminine attributes, they, too, would be dining as well as Susan Patterson that evening. Bitsy had covered her ears to block out their suggestive laughter, but it had done no good. She had gotten angry then and told the soldiers they were lying. But when she had gone for water at sundown, she had seen Susan at Southhampton's fire. Her mother was dressed in one of Judith's gowns and looked, from where Bitsy stood, like a finely attired queen who was well satisfied with her surroundings. The girl had bitten her lip to keep from calling out to her mother and had hurried away before she did something foolish, like cry.

She had run back to Judith's tent, laid her head against the rough canvas, and gazed sightlessly at the river. How she wished she were in her father's snug log home on the Licking River in Kentucky. Lord, how she wished her father hadn't insisted that she and her mama abandon the cabin for the safety of Ruddle's Fort. How she hated

Colonel John Bowman who, in the spring of 1779, flouting better judgment, had led a large expedition of Kentuckians against the Shawnees at Chillicothe. Bowman's raid had netted two dead Indians—Chief Red Pole and the beloved principal chief, Black Fish, thus ending the protection Susan and Bitsy had enjoyed while the Indian lived. Bitsy sighed and her large green eyes misted. "Papa," she whispered, "please come and take Mama and me home. . . . *Please.*"

"Bitsy?" said Judith from her pallet.

"Yes, ma'am?" answered the girl without turning.

"Has Chard returned?"

"No, ma'am, I haven't seen him."

Judith was silent for such a long time that Bitsy thought she had gone to sleep.

"I'm worried about him," sighed Judith moments later. "He has never been alone in a forest before."

"Never? He has never hunted before?" Bitsy turned her incredulous face to Judith and studied the woman wonderingly.

Judith shook her head. "Never alone." She seemed almost ashamed as she continued: "Gentlemen in England never hunt alone. 'Tis beneath their dignity."

"Humph," snorted the girl. "We are eating this moldy old flour because none of these stupid Englishmen know how to hunt. We starve, because it is beneath their dignity."

"Well, at least Chard is out there trying," defended Judith.

Judith was sadly mistaken. Chard had ceased trying hours before when fear had stripped him of his usual common sense and judgment, stampeding him through the pitch-black woods as if there would be no tomorrow. In his panic, he had decided that, come morning, when he didn't show up at the camp, the army would move on without him, and he would surely die alone and forgotten in that godforsaken wilderness.

He blundered through the forest with no notion of direction, time, or terrain. He almost knocked himself unconscious when he ran head-on into the trunk of a shagbark hickory tree, but even then, he did not slow his pace or stop to consider his position. All he could think of was dying alone, dying before his time, dying, dying, dying. . . .

The word beat at his temples like a bass drum, drowning out all rational thoughts.

Not once did he glance at the sky to see if he could locate the North Star; nor did he stop and listen for sounds of camp life or look for fires. He ran aimlessly through the darkness, bumping into trees, falling over logs and roots, scratching and cutting himself on briars and vines.

He cursed violently when he fell headlong over a rotten stump and drove his front teeth through the tip of his tongue. That was when he lost the British-issued Brown Bess musket he had borrowed. He was up in an instant, oblivious to the searing pain in his mouth, and again running full speed into the night, forgetting completely the gun he had dropped when he fell.

Sweat burned his eyes and dripped off his chin; his cocked hat was gone, and his clothes were almost in shreds when he unexpectedly burst from the forest and fell head over heels down the muddy bank of the Ohio, tumbling heavily into its cold depths. He splashed to the surface, spitting and sputtering; the shock of the icy water had snapped him back to reality.

He stood in the waist-deep current and gazed around him, wondering how he had come to be in the river. Slowly, as if it had been a dream, he reviewed the events up to the moment he realized he was lost. Beyond that, he remembered nothing. He waded sluggishly to the bank and crawled up the incline. He was exhausted and scared, but he was thinking again, contemplating his position and the possibility of locating the encampment. He studied the broad expanse of the Ohio. The army was camped at the mouth of the Great Miami on the eastern shore. All he had to do was follow the Ohio to the Great Miami. He wondered why he had not thought of that before.

Chard worked off his boots and poured the water out of them. He slipped his tunic off and wrung it out, then did the same with his shirt and breeches. As the warm night air dried his body, he laughed aloud at how stupid he had been. Now that he was thinking straight, his headlong flight through the dark forest seemed silly and childish. He couldn't imagine having done such a thing.

He donned his damp clothing and struck off in a fast walk toward the mouth of the Miami. Thirty minutes later he stalked into camp, provoked with himself and, in truth, feeling more than a bit foolish. He had nearly beaten himself to death in the tall timber when, in fact, he had never been more than a quarter of a mile from camp the whole time.

"What happened to you?" came Bitsy's astonished voice as she gaped at the disheveled young man striding past Judith's tent.

Chard ignored her, stepping up his pace to put distance between them before she could continue her questions. He was in no mood for her sharp tongue and jeering eyes.

"Did you bring us a stag?" she called after him, leaning far out into the night and staring hard at his wet, ragged appearance. She saw his shoulders slump, but he neither slowed his pace nor acknowledged her inquiry. "I guess he didn't," she said, turning to Judith.

"What's wrong with him? I heard your questions—is he hurt?"

"He didn't seem to be hurt, but he looked as if he had been dragged through a gristmill and then dumped into the pond."

"I can't imagine him passing by without stopping," said Judith, puzzled. "'Tis not like Chard to ignore us."

Bitsy glanced at Judith. She started to remind the woman that Chard was Southhampton's son, but she could not find it in herself to be that insensitive, for it was plain that Judith adored Chard with a love that was without compromise.

"Well," said Judith with a sigh, "he will explain in his own good time."

"I'm sure he will," answered Bitsy dryly.

Chard stripped off his wet clothes and flung them into a corner of his wedge tent. He slumped to his cot and stretched out with his hands locked behind his head.

He had made a real mess of his first hunting attempt.

Not only had he not found game, he had destroyed a uniform, lost a Brown Bess musket—a borrowed government-issued gun that the owner would have to account for—and had gone berserk on becoming lost. It had been a less than productive day. He smiled then at the absurdity of his understatement, and wondered what had possessed him to believe he was cut out for a life in the wilderness.

He swung his legs off the cot and flipped back the lid of his war chest. In five minutes, he was fully dressed in his spare uniform. Stepping outside, he drew himself to his full height. He detested the thought of having to face Bitsy, but there was no way it could be avoided. Taking a deep breath, he squared his shoulders and marched to Judith's tent.

"No," he said thrusting aside the flaps, "I did not find any animals."

Bitsy put her hands on her hips and smirked. "Not even one little stag?"

"No, not even a glimpse of one. I don't believe there is any game in these woods."

Bitsy eyed him wonderingly. How could anyone, let alone a grown man, venture into a wilderness that abounded with game of all sorts, and not see a living creature? It was incredible.

"Don't look at me that way," cried Chard angrily. "Your name should be Bitchy, not Bitsy."

Bitsy's face clouded. "You've no right to talk to me like that."

"Stop it," commanded Judith. "You sound like a spoiled brother and sister." Judith's face drained of color, and her eyes grew large in her thin face. Her words hung like echoes in the small tent.

"Now look what you've done," said Bitsy, giving Chard an accusing glare as she knelt beside Judith. "You've upset your mama."

Chard shook his head in outrage, but he clamped his teeth shut and stalked to Judith's side, dropping down beside Bitsy who was delicately blotting Judith's brow with the hem of her dress.

Judith's eyes traveled from one to the other as the two young people knelt side by side. She kept her thoughts to herself, but her eyes were speculative and frightened.

"I apologize, Mother." Chard took Judith's hand. "I will try to do better in the future." He glanced sideways at Bitsy. "In finding game and otherwise."

Bitsy neither apologized nor commented, so Chard went on: "I lost my way in the forest. In fact, I even lost my gun."

Bitsy was shocked. "You lost your musket? How can anyone lose his musket? 'Tis impossible!"

"It's not impossible," said Chard patiently. "I dropped it in the dark and could not find it again. Actually, it was very simple."

Bitsy shook her head and absently rubbed her temples. Never in her sixteen years on the frontier had she heard of anyone losing his gun while hunting. She could not imagine such a thing. Then she burst out laughing. Chard was, without a doubt, one of the most blockheaded people she had ever encountered.

Before daylight the next morning, Bitsy was up and dressed. She asked the guards' permission to enter the woods, assuring him she was not attempting an escape, but was merely in need of an hour or so of privacy. The guard nodded with understanding and watched the girl walk into the dark cane patch.

Bitsy moved silently around the perimeter of the camp until, in the first rays of a sun hardly risen, she located the trail Chard had made the evening before. She shook her head; the heels of Chard's riding boots had dug into the earth with such force that a child could have tracked him through the half-lighted woods.

When she found the spot where Chard had panicked, her brows came together in wonder. Never had she seen such sign. Limbs were broken, vines were snapped or hanging free, bits of cloth were fluttering in the early morning breeze, and the trail itself was irregular and sporadic.

Bitsy squatted and studied the ground for spoor of whatever it was that had terrorized the young man. Her frown deepened; nothing animal or human had followed in his erratic path.

The girl's eyes slowly scanned the quiet forest. The first rays of the sun were slanting through the foliage, giving the woods an enchanted splendor that was peaceful and inviting. A squirrel chattered overhead, and another leaped from limb to limb, rustling the leaves in a nearby tree. Birds chirped and sang. An owl made its last mournful hoot, advising the world that it was sorry to see night fade. Nature was in order.

Bitsy was more puzzled than ever. She could not imagine what had hounded Chard into dashing madly through such dangerous obstacles; it must have been something truly awful, perhaps some kind of night demon, or will-o'-the-wisp. Smirking at the thought of Chard being frightened of the dark, she struck off in a fast walk down the lane Chard had opened in the forest.

She found the musket beside a rotten stump. The barrel had been driven into the soft loam. Other than needing a good cleaning, the weapon appeared to be undamaged. Bitsy shouldered the gun and continued in Chard's wake. She studied the riverbank carefully. It was easy to see where Chard had climbed out of the water, for there were slippery tracks up the bank. But, try as she might, she could not find where he had entered.

Then it dawned on her that he had accidentally fallen into the river. Leaning heavily on the musket, she burst into a ripple of girlish laughter so pure and clear that it sounded like music as it trilled across the fast-moving current of the wide Ohio.

Chard was astounded when he tossed back his tent flaps and found the Brown Bess musket stuck barrel-first in the earth not three feet in front of him. He glanced quickly about, but nothing was amiss. The soldiers were going about their morning chores, preparing to break camp, and the captives from Martin's Station were doing the same.

He quickly retrieved the weapon and ducked back into his tent. His eyes narrowed. Only two people besides himself knew that he had lost the gun; and one of those was bedridden.

"Damn her," he muttered below his breath, shamed that Bitsy was woodsman enough to venture into the forest before full light and find the virtual needle-in-a-haystack, a feat he was incapable of performing any time of the day.

"Damn her to hell," he said again, hating the thought of facing her when they broke camp. He slumped heavily on his cot and began the tedious task of cleaning the clogged gun barrel.

CHAPTER
· *10* ·

MORGAN PATTERSON STUDIED the remains of the log bridge that spanned the Licking River. He idly wondered what had caused the collapse of the structure, but he didn't dwell on it; he did not intend to use the bridge anyway. No self-respecting horseman would try to force his animal across such a makeshift piece of handiwork, even had it been in first-class shape.

Holding to the stirrup leathers, Patterson swam his horse across the stream without incident.

On the far side he spent considerable time examining the bodies of more Kentuckians who had been unable to continue the grueling trek and had been slain where they lay. A searing hatred welled up in him. The needless butchery, obviously condoned and perhaps even encouraged by the British, left him shaking with wrath.

For the tenth time since daylight, he thumbed open the frizzen of his rifle lock and checked the priming powder in the flash pan. If he was fortunate enough to catch a British or Indian straggler, he wanted no misfires. Touching his heels to the horse's flank, he resumed his slow and tortuous trek toward the Ohio.

He had traveled several miles before he realized that the wheeled cannon was missing. He studied the trail closely as he rode, but nowhere did he see a sign of the cannon's passing.

Then he smiled and straightened in the saddle: the gun must be at the bottom of the Licking River; it had collapsed the makeshift bridge. Patterson felt better knowing that

Kentucky had deprived the British of one of their most indispensable possessions. Then he sobered. The trade had not been worth it.

At noon, he ate as he rode, munching parched corn and jerked venison and washing it down with water from his canteen. He stopped only when he approached a murdered Kentuckian, and then just long enough to look at the body. If the corpse was that of a man, he rode on. But that was infrequent, for it appeared that the men were holding up better than the women and children.

Again Patterson cursed the British for being inhuman wretches. Not once did he lay the blame on the Indians, for they were not at fault; theirs was a life of survival of the fittest. So, weeding out the old, the sick, and the weak was justified to their way of thinking. No, he placed the entire blame on the "civilized" British for the wanton death and destruction of the Kentuckians, for they knew it was wrong in the eyes of God—and that was where the difference lay.

He reined his horse to a standstill and stared long and hard at the body of a woman lying beside a towering oak not thirty yards distant. His skin crawled, and his breathing became a shallow whisper as he slowly stepped down and leaned heavily against the saddle. It took his every ounce of self-control to walk to the body and turn it over so he could see her face.

He almost retched. The woman's skin had been eaten away by maggots. Only bits and pieces were left. Her black hair was matted with dried blood where the Indians had cut the top of it away. He studied the corpse for a long time, a thousand years it seemed, before he could summon the courage to look one last place.

He had to force his shaking hand to rip away the bodice of her dress. His pent-up breath rushed between his clenched teeth in a long sigh of relief as he gently draped the cloth back over the naked, unscarred breast.

He walked unsteadily to his horse and pressed his forehead against its mane. "I'm not sure I could have stood it had she been Susan," he murmured to the animal. Shaking his head wearily, he climbed into the saddle. There was another body just ahead.

Chard ignored Bitsy's jeering eyes as their canoe moved sluggishly up the Great Miami. His embarrassment had lessened as the day wore on, until finally he had convinced himself that she had very probably stumbled upon the gun by accident. He found it inconceivable that a mere snip of a girl—even Morgan Patterson's daughter—would have the skill to track him through the dark uncharted forest until she located the lost weapon . . . inconceivable indeed.

Deep down inside, however, Chard's basic honesty forced him to consider, reluctantly, the superiority of Bitsy's woodsmanship. But his pride fought with his integrity. He was simply unwilling to acknowledge the girl's skill. For if he admitted, even to himself, that she had indeed tracked his path to the lost weapon, he would be forced to face the truth that he had neither the experience nor the expertise to go alone into the wilderness. So he told himself again that her finding the gun had been nothing more than a freak accident.

Bitsy, kneeling beside Judith, raised her eyes at frequent intervals to study the young man sitting in the prow of the canoe.

At first she had been amused by his headlong race through the forest and subsequently into the river. But that sensation had quickly given way to contempt, which in time turned to curiosity.

She did not understand Chard. In fact, she was not sure she even wished to waste time trying. Still, he was a puzzle. She had witnessed acts of heroism by him, as when he had leaped into the river in an attempt to rescue the two captive women, and before that, when he carried her and Susan to the cabin before attempting to halt the massacre at Ruddle's Station. And he has a kindness about him that is most considerate, she mused, remembering his insistence that the elderly and weary ride his horse while he walked.

Bitsy frowned, her eyes flicking toward him again. But when it comes to acting in his own best interests, he is a coward. Had he not cowered before his father like a whipped dog when Southhampton reprimanded him for helping to move the cannon? Had he not stood idly by and done nothing after finding that his father had flogged his

162

mother to within an inch of her life? Had he not panicked, dropped his weapon, and run in fear when he became lost in the forest? Bitsy eyed Chard with disappointment. No woman would ever feel safe with him as her sole means of protection, she told herself, for he is unpredictable . . . and even worse, he is undependable.

The girl turned her melancholy face to Judith.

"I'd give a gold sovereign to know what was going through your pretty head a moment ago," Judith said.

Bitsy's cheeks dimpled as she smiled wistfully. "It was of no importance, ma'am."

"Somehow," said the blonde woman, "I have the feeling that for one so young, very few of your thoughts are 'of no importance.'"

Bitsy blushed and changed the subject. "Your wounds are healing nicely. You should be up and about in a day or two."

Judith smiled at the girl's obvious tact. "I intend to try to stand on my own when we camp for the evening. I've lain on my sides so long I doubt if I've any curve left in my hips."

"Don't be too anxious to get back on your feet, ma'am," cautioned Bitsy. "We wouldn't want to take the chance of breaking open those cuts."

"I'll be fine," assured Judith, delighted by Bitsy's concern. It was refreshing to find such thoughtfulness in one so young. Aye, thought Judith, Americans are an entirely different breed of people than the arrogant, self-centered English aristocracy.

She prayed that Chard would recognize and respect the unselfish willingness of Americans to be concerned for others, that give-and-share trait that abounded in the frontier folk, and that he not look upon it as a detestable weakness as Southhampton was so quick to proclaim.

Judith took Bitsy's hand. "Thank you, Bitsy."

"For what?"

"For being you, for being what you are . . . and for being who you are."

Bitsy shook her lovely head and frowned at Judith. "I'd give a gold sovereign to know what you meant by that."

Judith laughed. "It was of no importance," she said mockingly.

Both women erupted into a gale of feminine laughter that made every boat crew within hearing smile in appreciation. Even Chard turned and grinned at the women, for it had been a long time since he had heard such welcome music. Not since leaving England had he heard his mother laugh with such abandon, and he loved it.

Bitsy approached Chard cautiously. He was personally overseeing the erection of Judith's tent. She waited patiently as he gave orders that the shelter be raised on a small knoll well away from the river.

"Perhaps the insects won't be so bothersome up there," he said to Bitsy when he found her standing behind him.

"It will be a help," admitted the girl.

The two stood in awkward silence as the soldiers, grumbling and complaining, did as they were ordered.

"Chard," blurted Bitsy, her eyes averted, "would you allow me to take the musket into the woods this evening? I might find something to shoot . . . a squirrel or a rabbit or something."

Chard's face drained, then flushed a bright crimson. "Damn you, Bitsy, do you poke fun at me? I knew you would. I knew you'd not have the decency to let it pass."

"Let it pass?" Bitsy spun toward the young man and lifted her chin menacingly. "Your mother and I are starving, and all you can think about is your manly pride —which isn't manly at all." She moved a step closer. "I can hunt circles around you, blindfolded. I'll not let your mama go hungry just because you need to feed your silly pride!" She was so angry she was on the verge of tears. "Damn you," she whispered. "I'll not cry in front of you no matter how much you upset me—nor will I beg you for the right to feed myself." She turned and started toward Judith's tent.

Chard caught her before she had gone ten feet. "Wait," he said, taking her hand. "I didn't say I wouldn't let you use the gun."

"Then you will?"

"Not exactly." Then, seeing her face harden, he quickly added, "But I will allow you to accompany me when I go hunting this evening."

Bitsy scowled but refrained from speaking her mind. She longed to make it plain that he would be doing her no favors by giving her permission to follow along behind like a good and trusted dog.

"Thank you," she said finally. "'Tis very nice of you."

"I intend to enter the forest just as soon as we have mother resting comfortably." He indicated the soldiers with a tilt of his head. "They've almost finished raising her tent, so it shouldn't be long. Can you be ready that quickly?"

"I'm ready now," answered the girl, wondering what he thought she might wish to prepare. Everything she owned was on her person.

"Surely you do not intend to venture into the wilderness without boots?" he asked.

Bitsy glanced at her bare feet. "Why would I want to wear boots? Kentuckians don't wear boots when they hunt. No one even wears moccasins after the weather gets halfway warm."

"Well, regardless of what you frontier people do," returned Chard, "a British gentleman wouldn't be caught dead without his boots."

Bitsy studied the young man thoroughly. "In Kentucky, sir, those boots you're so proud of might very well be the reason a British gentleman *would* be caught dead."

"You talk in riddles, Bitsy."

"Perhaps," said the girl, refusing to argue when it was obvious it would be a waste of time.

"Anyway," he continued, "there're snakes out there, and I have no intention of being bitten."

"Snakes don't bite other snakes," Bitsy said scornfully. With that, she stalked off to help settle Judith comfortably for the night.

Bitsy followed close behind Chard as he marched brashly between the giant trees. She cringed each time he cracked a limb, stumbled over a root, or broke brush.

"Chard," she said finally, "if you would put your toe down first, then ease your heel gently to the ground, you will find that you move a lot more quietly."

Chard scowled, but he remained silent. Finally he

nodded, and put his toe to the earth, then his heel. He nodded his head at Bitsy: it did seem to work better. After that, he blundered through the woods making only half as much racket as before. They had gone a half-mile without so much as glimpsing an animal when Bitsy caught Chard's arm.

"We'll never see anything this way. We've got to be quiet; we've got to slip through the woods."

"How does one slip through dead leaves, twigs, and branches?" he asked irritably.

"Move slowly," said the girl. "Take a few steps and stop. Look way out ahead of you . . . and listen."

Chard's brow wrinkled. "What would we be listening for?"

Bitsy looked at him, dumbfounded. "Do you not know that animals and birds make a world of noise when they believe that they are alone in the woods?"

"They do not," scoffed Chard. "They're as silent as a shadow."

"Not when they feel safe," argued Bitsy.

They discussed it back and forth for several minutes. Chard finally agreed to let Bitsy take the lead some fifty yards ahead of him. She was to signal if she saw anything.

Bitsy made a wide loop toward the river. As twilight fell, she motioned for Chard to stop. Dropping to her hands and knees, she crawled to the top of a rise and then flattened out on her stomach. Slowly she wriggled to the lip of the knoll and peered intently toward the riverbank not forty yards distant. A buck and two does with fawns were feeding on the tender shoots of the young saplings that grew near the slow-moving water.

Bitsy motioned Chard forward, making hand signals that he stay low and move cautiously.

Chard dropped to a crouch and slipped as quietly as he could toward the knoll. Even then, Bitsy could hear the crunch of his boots with each step he took. She grimaced and motioned that he drop to his belly and crawl as she had done. Chard reluctantly followed her suggestion.

After what seemed to Bitsy an eternity, Chard crawled to her side and peered intently in the direction she indicated.

"What do you see?" he whispered, staring into the

deepening gloom as the fading rays of the sun threatened to plunge the forest into darkness.

"Can't you see those deer feeding by the river?" she said in a hushed voice.

"Where?" Chard squinted through a break in the trees at the span of the Great Miami.

"Right down there below those big poplars." Bitsy pointed toward two huge trees on the riverbank.

Chard studied the shadowed area carefully. Then, before the girl knew what was happening, he jumped to his feet and shouted: "'Tis a magnificent stag!" He shouldered the musket and fired into the underbrush at the river's edge.

Bitsy watched in startled dismay as the small herd of deer bounded into the forest and vanished. She flipped onto her back and flung her arm across her eyes.

Chard waved the smoke away and scrutinized the empty woods.

"I missed," he ventured lamely, dropping the butt of the gun to the ground and leaning heavily on the barrel.

"Why did you shoot at the buck when the does and fawns were closer and standing in the open?" asked Bitsy from beneath her arm.

"For the trophy, of course," said Chard as if her question was absurd.

Bitsy pushed herself upright and frowned. "What trophy?"

Chard blinked at the girl. "The keepsake, the stag's antlers. The trophy."

Bitsy's face gathered thunder. "Are you not hungry, Chard? Does your belly not ache as mine does? You can't eat deer horns! Furthermore, they are in the velvet and not even fit to make knife handles."

Chard eyed her hotly. "All right! I made a mistake and I'm sorry! And yes, I, too, am hungry. I don't like eating moldy flour any more than you do."

"Then listen to what the lass has to say," came a soft reply from the nearby brush as Simon Girty stepped through the leafy screen and dropped a young doe to the ground.

Bitsy jumped to her feet, and Chard spun toward the man, raising the musket at the same instant.

Girty pushed the gun barrel aside. "It's not loaded," he said with a smirk. Then he turned to Bitsy. "This woman knows more about the forest than most long-hunters. She can teach you much, if you let her."

"She's just a girl," argued the ensign lamely. But he considered Girty's words, for he had already realized that Bitsy had been right about where the deer would feed at dusk. Furthermore, she had been correct about watching and listening and slipping up on unsuspecting animals. He frowned, considering Bitsy in a new light. Perhaps she was also right about his manly pride. He didn't like that thought at all.

"I'm leaving you this deer," said Girty to Bitsy. "You and Mrs. Southhampton eat well tonight, lass."

Bitsy started to protest. She did not trust the Girty brothers, especially the notorious Simon. But her better judgment prevailed, and she curtly thanked the man.

He nodded, expecting nothing more from the girl, then faded back into the brush.

"That's the second time he has helped us," said Chard, gazing after Girty. "I wonder why?"

"Before the war, he and my papa were friends," admitted the girl. "The three Girty brothers have eaten at our table several times, but that was before they chose to become traitors."

"They're not traitors," said Chard angrily. "You Kentuckians are the ones who are rebelling, not us."

"Because you haven't got the nerve," returned Bitsy with equal venom. "You highbrow Britishers will never want anything more than what you have now—to be *subjects*. Aye, the king doesn't even call you people; he calls you loyal British subjects." The girl looked hard at the angry ensign. "We Americans will never be *subjects*, Chard, whether we lose this war or not."

The young man looked deep into Bitsy's fierce eyes, and he knew a moment of deep admiration for her. He had no doubt that she spoke the truth: she would never bow down to anyone.

"You had better load your gun," she said. "'Tis the first thing a hunter does after he shoots."

Chard blushed and withdrew the ramrod.

They wolfed down venison until they made themselves sick. Then they ate again, chewing slowly, savoring every bite.

Judith was able to sit upright beside the fire and feed herself, a great improvement that made Chard and Bitsy smile with satisfaction. Judith was well on the road to recovery.

"Bitsy's going to teach me to hunt American style," Chard said unexpectedly to his mother.

Judith's pale face turned ashen, her eyes jerking from Chard to Bitsy.

Bitsy blushed under Judith's disapproving gaze. She didn't understand it. She had thought Judith would be pleased.

"I forbid you to take this young woman into the woods, Chard," said Judith flatly. When Chard didn't answer, Judith pierced him with a cold glare. "You are not to be alone with her. Have I made myself plain?"

"Yes, Mother, very plain, indeed."

Does she not trust her son? wondered Bitsy. Or does she not trust me? Bitsy's face paled as a new question wormed its way into her mind. Or does she not think I am good enough for him?

The thought left Bitsy angry and resentful. Why, the very idea that she and Chard would even become friends was utterly ridiculous.

Snatching up the remainder of the venison, Bitsy marched off toward the captives' area. What meat that was left wouldn't fill their bellies, but it might give each of the one hundred thirty Kentuckians a bite—which was better than nothing.

Even though they did not hesitate to accept the food, the people of Martin's Station gave Bitsy a cold reception. Not one word was spoken to her, not even a thank-you. Bitsy wondered at their scornful stares and angry glances. Bewildered, she retraced her footsteps toward Judith's tent. She wished that she could go to her mother and just talk to her. There were so many things that needed answers. Was she wrong to give her people food? Why did they treat her with such contempt? Was she wrong to teach Chard to hunt? Were her actions brazen or cheap? Why did people dislike her so? Bitsy shook her head. She had never been looked down upon in her life, and the fact that Judith and the Kentuckians did so made her feel insecure and self-conscious. At that moment she would readily have welcomed her mother's friendship, guidance, and understanding, while a month earlier, she might have spurned it all with violent independence.

Without being aware of it, Bitsy had walked nearly to Southhampton's tent before she realized where she was. She drew up abruptly and stared at the people sitting around a large campfire blazing brightly in front of his marquee. One of them was her mother.

The loud laughter of Southhampton, three junior officers, and the spy, Clarke, who sat beside Susan, suggested that they were well into their cups. And, in fact, one of the men was making rounds, refilling each person's tankard, including Susan's.

Bitsy stood dumbstruck. She had never seen her mother touch a drop of spirits. Yet there she was, drinking rum as though it were water. The man with the bottle eyed Susan speculatively when she immediately tilted the pewter goblet to her lips and drank it dry, then, grinning drunkenly, held it out so that he could fill it again.

She's trying to kill herself, thought Bitsy, horrified at the scene. No one can drink rum that fast and live.

She would have rushed to the fire and knocked the cup from her mother's hand had not one of the officers taken the goblet from Susan's unresisting fingers and set it casually aside. Then he whispered something to Susan, swept her into his arms, and staggered drunkenly through Southhampton's tent flaps.

Bitsy stood transfixed. She had never seen or experienced a sexual act, so she could only guess at what was taking place in the confines of the small room. But naive as she was, she knew enough to be terrified by what she had just witnessed.

Crying out to her mother, she made a mad dash for Southhampton's tent.

Southhampton caught the girl as she sped past the fire. Clamping his hand over her mouth, he snatched her off her feet and dragged her, kicking and struggling, toward the forest. At the woods' edge, he flung her against a tree and pinioned her there. "What in hell do you think you are doing?" he demanded, pushing hard against her chest so the rough bark of the tree cut into her back.

Bitsy's eyes were wild. "My mama!" she cried. "I've got to help my mama!"

"Your mother is exactly where she wants to be," said Southhampton. "And the best thing you can do is mind your own business."

Bitsy shook her head. "You're lying!"

Southhampton released her and crossed his arms. "If you think I'm lying, then go down to the tent and see for yourself. Go on down there and watch what your mother is doing. Go on! You might enjoy it."

Bitsy put her hands over her ears, her face drawing into a hideous mask. The first heart-wrenching pains of humiliation welled up within her, engulfing her as surely as if it had been she who had allowed a stranger to carry her to his bed, a stranger who acted as though he had every right to believe Susan would go with him unresisting—which she had done.

Blindly, Bitsy pushed past Southhampton and stumbled into the dark forest. Slumping down among the roots of a giant oak, she cried silently, great shuddering sobs for a mother she no longer knew, and for a sixteen-year-old girl who was fast learning the meaning of the word *self-hatred*. For Bitsy believed that somehow it was she who was to blame for the contempt of her fellow prisoners, for Judith's unbridled animosity, and for the wanton, uncaring actions of a mother she adored.

It was best that Bitsy had run from the scene at Southhampton's camp. For while the girl cried herself to sleep beneath the huge tree, Southhampton's four "guests" paid their respects to the woman who lay in a state of drunken semiconsciousness on the major's cot. Having failed to drink herself into total oblivion, as she had tried so hard to do, Susan knew exactly what was happening to her. She lay there as they took their pleasure and wished that they would hurry and get their fill.

But even that small kindness was denied her, for when Southhampton finally lowered his bulk to her aching body,

171

he was so excited by the graphic comments of his fellow officers who had just finished with her that he used Susan viciously for the remainder of the night.

Throughout the ordeal, Susan's befuddled mind kept returning to something Southhampton had said days before, something she would never have believed: "We are two of a kind, my dear. Birds of a feather." And that thought followed her into the oblivion she so desperately sought, for finally, hours too late, the rum and the exhaustion closed Susan's eyes in tormented slumber.

"I tell you she's gone," said Chard, as he paced the length of Judith's tent for the hundredth time.

"She couldn't have just vanished, Chard. She's got to be around here somewhere." But even as she said it, Judith was wondering if the girl had slipped away during the night.

"Has your musket disappeared, too?" she asked.

"It's still here. And that's what's bothering me. Nothing is missing, except her."

Chard stopped pacing and faced Judith. "I'll have to report her disappearance to Captain Bird. He might send out a search party, but my guess is he'll go on without her." He smashed his fist angrily into his open palm. "Damn it all. Why didn't she stay in camp last night?" He faced Judith squarely. "I'm not leaving here without her, Mother."

"Chard." Judith rose painfully to her feet. "Perhaps it's best if you let her go."

"How can you say such a thing?" he shouted. "She's just a girl, Mother. Suppose she's lost or hurt. . . ."

"Chard," said Judith, holding his gaze steadily, "if she's gone, you can bet she's not lost or hurt. She's Morgan Patterson's daughter. She knows more about surviving in the wilderness than those Tories, Elliott and McGee. Maybe even as much as the Girty brothers."

"She's just a girl," repeated Chard.

Judith's eyes flashed. "Chard, you are fooling yourself about Bitsy, placing her in the same category as the young ladies who move in our social circles. She's not a lady,

172

Chard. She's a frontier woman who can plow the fields, chop wood, shoot a gun, and raise a cabin full of runny-nosed children, all at the same time. She's not delicate, tender, or squeamish at the sight of blood. When I was in America the first time, I watched her mother use a tomahawk to hammer that pearl-handled dagger of yours out of Morgan Patterson's leg—without batting an eye. Bitsy would do the same thing in those circumstances. No, son, if Bitsy has run away, she knows exactly what she's doing."

"She wouldn't leave her mother," argued Chard, but his words sounded hollow even to him.

"Morgan Patterson would leave her," said Judith dryly. "He would disappear into the night and stay out of sight until he found an opportunity to save her. Then he would calmly kill anyone who got in his way. And Bitsy is just like him."

Chard ran his fingers wearily through his hair. "Perhaps you are right, ma'am, but I would rest easier if I knew for sure what had become of her."

"She will be all right," Judith assured him. "Women like her can take care of themselves."

Yes, thought Judith, as she watched Chard stalk off to inform Captain Bird that Bitsy had vanished, women like Bitsy are survivors. She knew that for certain, for she had traveled hundreds of miles through the wilderness with Bitsy's mother and father. Yes, the girl would endure and be the stronger for it.

Then Judith's face hardened. "I hope, for your sake, Chard," she whispered to the empty tent, "that Bitsy never comes back. It will be far better for all concerned if you never see her again."

After Chard left Bird's marquee, Southhampton, who had been present during the report, cleared his throat and nonchalantly approached the commander.

"If I were you, Captain," he said, "I would be bloody sure that word of the girl's escape did not go beyond this tent."

Bird studied Southhampton questioningly. "What are you getting at, Major?"

173

"It would not do for the captives to get the idea that they are not being properly guarded—as they would, knowing that a girl strolled off into the night and kept right on walking."

Bird chewed his lower lip, his brows knitting together. "Perhaps you are right, but I do think Mrs. Patterson should be informed of her daughter's disappearance. She might even be able to shed more light on it. I really can't believe a sixteen-year-old girl would prefer to face the dangers of the forest, and almost certain death, rather than remain in captivity with us."

"One never knows what these stupid Americans might do," said Southhampton. "But I will see to it that Mrs. Patterson is advised of what has happened. You can leave that to me, sir."

"Very good, Major," returned Bird, glad to have that responsibility taken from his shoulders. "Inform me if she has any suggestions that might help us locate the girl."

"I'll do that, sir." Southhampton then promptly put the thought out of his mind.

So, as the army and captives struck camp and resumed their slow journey up the Great Miami River, only Chard and Judith missed the copper-haired girl who normally occupied the vacant spot in the center of the large war canoe. Chard was fuming. Southhampton had sought him out before their evacuation and ordered him in no uncertain terms to keep silent about Bitsy's disappearance.

"'Twould be a breach of security," said the major, thus reminding the ensign that an escaped prisoner was a military matter, which, in truth, was exactly the issue—to everyone except Chard.

The young ensign glanced over his shoulder and stared hard at the campsite they had just abandoned. He watched until the view was blocked by a bend in the river, but Bitsy did not appear as he prayed she would. He reluctantly turned his attention to the canoes dotting the river as far as he could see.

He wished he could speak to Susan, but his father had forbidden it with such venom that the young man wondered what he had said to bring on such a display of temper. However, Chard made up his mind that, should the occasion present itself, he would indeed question Susan, for he still did not believe that Bitsy had run off in the night . . . no matter what anybody else said.

Bitsy had awakened just before daylight. It had taken a moment to orient herself when she realized she was not in Judith's tent. Climbing to her feet and stretching her cramped muscles, she had started toward the camp on the knoll.

The hand that clamped itself firmly over her mouth stank of rancid bear grease. Bitsy froze. She neither struggled nor attempted to scream. Only her widening eyes showed any response to her capture.

For years, her father had lectured her on the ways of the red man. He had always emphasized that if she were ever seized by Indians, she should go along peaceably and do exactly as she was told. Above all, she was never to lag behind, complain, or show fear. So she stood unresisting as the Indian removed his hand and prodded her sharply with his musket barrel toward the interior of the forest. He propelled her forward with such vicious thrusts and jabs that she had to run in an effort to avoid the brutal punishment.

The Indian pushed her mercilessly through the dew-covered mayapple and knee-high ferns that covered the sloping hillsides. In minutes, Bitsy's long dress was sopping wet from her hips to her bare toes. She caught hold of the rear hem of the heavy fabric and, drawing it between her thighs, tucked it through the sash she wore at her waist.

The trailing Indian watched the girl's actions with interest. He was impressed by her stamina and presence of mind; she would make a good slave and perhaps bear many fine sons for the Wyandot tribe.

As daylight grew stronger, the Indian guided Bitsy down a long valley and into a sparse clearing where six Wyandot warriors were squatting around a small fire. Bitsy could smell roasting meat even before she saw the haunch of venison spitted on a green hickory stick just above the flames.

The Indians jumped to their feet and grinned at her captor, who strutted proudly as he prodded Bitsy toward the campfire. The men looked the girl over critically, then gestured toward the roasting meat, indicating that she eat.

Although terror drew Bitsy's stomach into tight knots, she forced herself to fall upon the venison with nearly as much enthusiasm as did the Indians. For, like them, she was unsure when she might have the opportunity to eat again.

She swallowed the seared meat without chewing, and then wiped her greasy hands on her dress tail.

The Indians grunted their approval, and her captor's chest swelled with pride.

Bitsy was glad that she hadn't taken the time to chew her food, because without a word the red men suddenly sprang to their feet and gestured for her to fall into line. They struck out in a fast trot toward the far side of the clearing—away from the river, away from pursuit.

Morgan Patterson carefully studied the abandoned campsite at the mouth of the Licking River where it entered the Ohio. He was well aware that he might just as soon clutch at the wind as try to find signs of his wife and daughter in the chaotic scramble of tracks and footprints. Yet he knew he must try. So he painstakingly covered every inch of ground for a half-mile in all directions.

He finally gave up and walked to the shore of the Ohio. His weathered face hardened as he gazed across the river to the awesome wilderness beyond. If they are over there, he said to himself, I might spend years looking and never find them.

His lips formed a determined line. He had the rest of his life, if that's how long it would take, but he *would* find them.

He turned and started up the bank. Then, stopping suddenly, he gazed hard at a broken willow branch at the water's edge. He moved carefully to the small sapling and studied it with the experienced eye of one who understood the silent language of the forest.

He squatted and studied the ground beneath the branch.

One corner of his lips twitched into a smile and his hawklike eyes softened; Bitsy had left a trail a child could have followed. She must think I'm getting old, he decided, looking at the broken branch that pointed downstream and then at the obvious marks beneath the tree where she had dragged her foot the same direction.

He shook his head and grinned, feeling years younger and alive for the first time in days.

Leaving Bird's war road and any known trails far behind, he turned his horse downstream, west, toward the mouth of the Great Miami River some thirty miles away. His eyes searched the terrain, scanning the trees, the brush, the knolls for anything unusual, anything out of the ordinary.

He did not expect an ambush, but he never took anything for granted when it involved an Indian. He felt sure that the savages had crossed the river with their hostages and had wasted no time securing themselves in some large fortified village. Still, he took no chances, his eyes moving constantly, seeking out movement or color, his ears in tune with the sounds of the forest—searching, listening.

He cursed the necessity for caution, knowing well that the British were making as much speed as possible while he was forced to creep along at a snail's pace. Yet he was too much the professional to hurry his pursuit; he was the only hope his family had of rescue.

He wove in and out among the trees, guiding his horse steadily north by west and glancing often at the river, which was never out of sight for more than ten minutes at a time. He dared not miss the break in the wilderness that would indicate the mouth of the Great Miami where it emptied into the Ohio.

"Girty?" Chard hailed him as he worked his way up the bank from the canoes they had just beached for the evening.

"Aye," said Simon Girty, slouching on his long-gun.

"Tell me the truth," Chard demanded when he was close enough to be sure he was not overheard. "What are the chances of Bitsy Patterson making it back to the Kentucky settlements alive?"

Girty studied the young man intently. Then, nodding as if he had reached a conclusion, he said, "The truth is, she

177

ain't got a chance in hell of ever layin' eyes on Kentucky again . . . 'cause she ain't headed that way."

Chard frowned. "What do you mean?"

Girty spat a stream of tobacco juice over his shoulder. "They's been six or seven Wyandots followin' us for days, hopin' to steal themselves a prisoner."

"For Christ's sake," blurted Chard, "haven't they got enough prisoners already?"

"The Wyandot wasn't invited on our foray, and they got their hackles up somethin' fierce. Anyhow, they caught Bitsy Patterson and headed off toward the north."

"Why in hell didn't you say something about it sooner? We could have gone after her."

"They'd have killed her before you soldiers could have got within ten mile of her. Anyhow, it weren't none of my concern."

"You don't really give a damn about anyone, do you, Girty?"

Girty eyed the ensign coldly. "Careful, lad," he said with slow deliberation. "I like you . . . but not much." He raised his deerskin hunting frock and turned his back to Chard. "You see these scars?"

Chard's breath caught. Girty's entire upper body was crisscrossed with hideous rigid welts.

"I offered my services to the Continentals, and this was what I got for my troubles. Because I was raised by the Delaware, the Americans called me an Indian lover, whipped me half to death. I vowed in return to kill every one of the sons of bitches I could, and I've damn near done it. Caused 'em a mite of grief, I have."

Girty's face was vicious. "I hate Americans almost as much as I hate the whip . . . most Americans, anyway."

"So that's why you took that awful-smelling salve to my mother's tent," said Chard. "Because you hate the whip."

Girty nodded. "I hate the whip more than I hate a traitor."

Girty studied Chard thoroughly. "Listen," he said in his rasping voice. "Me and George is goin' after the girl. We ain't supposed to tell anyone, but if you was to meet us in thirty minutes at that big hollow sycamore"—Girty pointed at a treetop visible above the other towering

178

branches simply because it was snow white and leafless —"we just might take you with us."

Girty turned then and worked his way into a dense thicket. He wondered what had possessed him to give a damn about the ensign. Perhaps, he decided, it was because the young officer had helped shove that cannon up the mountainside. Aye, he showed promise of growing into a real man, maybe even a frontiersman.

After Girty had disappeared, Chard realized that he had not even thanked the man for what he had done for his mother. Shaking his head, he turned and bounded down the incline to give Judith a hand out of the canoe. For even though she was moving more easily with each passing day, was even walking for short distances so long as the terrain wasn't rough, he did not want her doing any strenuous climbing without assistance.

Judith smiled at her son as he guided her slowly up the bank. "It feels good to be up and about. I do not think I could have stood that litter . . ." Her voice trailed off as she studied Chard's face. "What is it, Chard?" she asked, bothered. "I saw you talking to Simon Girty. What did he say to upset you so?"

"Bitsy was captured by Wyandot Indians."

Judith was silent for a long moment. "How does Girty know? Is he sure?"

"He knows. He even knows how many Indians there were. Says they've been following us since we entered the Miami, just waiting for a chance to steal a captive."

"Why in the world didn't Girty warn Captain Bird?"

"Because Girty is fighting a war of his own. He doesn't give a damn about the British. He uses them . . . us"—he blushed at the afterthought—"to get at the Americans. The man is full of hate and vengeance, so he did nothing when Bitsy was taken."

Chard refrained from mentioning that Girty was responsible for Judith's speedy recovery, perhaps even for saving her life. He certainly did not want his mother beholden to a white Indian, a renegade whom even the British soldiers feared and abhorred.

Yet he wondered, not for the first time, at the puzzling scheme of things: the Girtys were responsible for Judith's capture and subsequent flogging, and then they helped to

179

heal her; they were indirectly responsible for the fall of Ruddle's and Martin's Forts and the starvation of the prisoners, and then they helped to feed them. And, although Simon Girty considered Morgan Patterson a friend, he had not raised a finger to help the man's wife or daughter in their time of need.

Chard shook his head. He was getting his first real insight into the intricate—or perhaps *un*intricate—workings of the Indian mind. It suddenly dawned on him that an Indian did what he thought was right at that particular moment, regardless of past or future developments. And right then, Chard Southhampton, having been in the wilderness but a few short weeks, understood more about the eastern Indian than his father had learned in a lifetime. He felt no elation, however, for the knowledge had come too late. Bitsy was gone, probably never to be seen again, and the responsibility lay on the shoulders of every British soldier present, including himself, for none had considered it worthwhile to understand or appreciate the inner nature of their savage allies.

Chard grimaced. Bitsy had said it all when she had bitterly pointed out that Englishmen would let the whole world go to hell, so long as it didn't jeopardize their supreme self-centered "dignity." Clenching his teeth, he muttered, "One of these days our stupid British self-importance is going to cost us dearly." Then he corrected himself. It had already cost him more than he was willing to pay.

The soldiers had nearly finished erecting Judith's tent by the time she and Chard climbed the bank and walked to the spot Southhampton had ordered hacked out of the thicket that grew near the river. Judith studied the small cleared space with a skeptical eye. "I don't like this place, Chard. It's too isolated. I can't see any of the other camps."

Chard glanced at the saplings, vines, and brambles that enclosed the small tent. He didn't tell her that his father had insisted on her being segregated from the other captives, that the major had convinced Captain Bird that Judith would be less dangerous in solitary confinement.

Dangerous to whom? wondered Chard. She could hardly walk, and it still pained her to speak through lips that had not completely healed.

It never entered Chard's mind that Southhampton had insisted on removing Judith from society simply because he was afraid that Susan, who spent nearly all her spare moments secretly watching Judith's tent in the hope of seeing her daughter, would discover that Bitsy was missing. And he knew without a doubt that if she learned of Bitsy's disappearance, his hold over her was gone. Worse yet, she would go straight to Bird and tell the commander the incriminating truth.

He had nearly panicked when he realized how vulnerable his position actually was without Bitsy for security. That fearful discovery had prompted him to pay the Girtys handsomely in gold to search out the missing girl and bring her back safely. The Girtys had promised nothing—but they had taken the money.

Simon and George Girty were standing by the hollow sycamore when Chard arrived.

"What's he doin' here?" demanded George Girty.

"He's goin' with us," said Simon.

George looked hard at his brother, but something in Simon's eyes warned him to tread lightly. George grunted his displeasure but said nothing, for Simon was one of the few men on earth whom George Girty feared.

"We leave him if he can't keep up," Simon said to George, but Chard knew the man was speaking directly to him. He nodded his understanding.

Simon drew his hunting shirt over his head and handed it to Chard.

Without being told, Chard shucked off his red tunic and slipped the buckskin on.

"Can't do nothin' about them trousers," said Simon, "but them boots is stayin' here."

Chard kicked off the boots and stood awkwardly in his knee stockings. Girty withdrew a pair of moccasins from his haversack and flipped them to Chard. "We travel fast, hard, and quiet. You got any questions?" Girty said, unblinking.

Chard shook his head.

The Girtys struck off in a mile-eating woodsman's trot with Chard hot on their heels. Within a mile, Chard had already thanked his mother a hundred times for insisting that he stay in good physical condition instead of allowing himself to become lazy with overconfidence, as many young British officers often did. Yet even the strenuous exercises he had done daily, prior to coming to the colonies, had not prepared him for the superhuman endurance the frontiersmen took for granted.

Within three miles, Chard's breath was coming in great gasps. At five, he was almost staggering. At six miles, he had gone his last step. But so had the Girtys, who drew up abruptly and began preparing their night camp. Only then did Chard realize that the sun was gone and the forest almost totally dark.

In seconds Simon had a fire going, and Chard realized that George was nowhere about. In fact, he couldn't remember having seen George for the last two miles of that exhausting run.

"Where's George?" he asked, as he sank wearily to the ground.

Simon glanced up from the fire. "He cut off two, three miles back. He'll be in directly."

Chard stretched out, groaning as his body protested the grueling treatment it had just endured.

"It'll be worse tomorrow," promised Girty.

"I'm not sure I'll be able to keep up such a pace," admitted Chard honestly.

Girty's eyes leveled on the young man.

"You lag, you find your own way back to the river."

"Fair enough," said the ensign, sorry he had complained, knowing that he would run himself to death before he would ever mention such a thought again.

George Girty trotted into the light of the campfire and dropped the hindquarter of a young deer beside the flame.

"Cook that," he ordered Chard, who had moved to a large elm and lay propped against its trunk.

Simon Girty, who was also relaxing, slowly lifted his eyes to the ensign.

Chard studied the two brothers in the flickering firelight. Simon's expression was neutral, but George's was openly hostile. It was the time of reckoning.

"Go to hell," said Chard softly.

George Girty's eyes narrowed, and he stepped toward the reclining ensign.

"If you take one more step, George," came Chard's easy voice, "I'll kill you."

Girty stopped abruptly, looking at him with keen interest.

"You're bluffin'," he said.

Chard smiled crookedly, almost as though he were enjoying himself. "I've lost a good deal of sleep over my failure to shoot you the night you laid your hands on my mother. Take the final step, Girty . . . I wish you would."

George Girty laughed harshly and returned to the fire. "There lies a British arsehole what's got teeth, Simon," he said, too low for Chard to hear.

"You're gettin' so's you can't read sign, George," said Simon, "or you'd have knowed better than to brace the lad. He's got that big-bore pistol hid beside his leg. It's cocked and pointed at your big mouth."

"When I go for him again," grunted George, "I'll kill him."

"You'd better bloody well see that you do," came Simon's reply. "I like the lad and wouldn't want to have to finish what you start."

CHAPTER
· *11* ·

BITSY WAS more than intimidated; she was scared half to death by the mass of silent Indians who lined the wide path through the Wyandot village. Everywhere the girl looked, black, expressionless eyes followed her—glittering, unblinking eyes that showed neither pleasure nor bitterness, animosity nor compassion; they were the eyes of animals that had trapped their prey and were biding their time for the kill.

The girl trembled almost imperceptibly as she and her captors stopped before a half-round bark longhouse. The Indian who had captured Bitsy caught her by the hair and forced her to her knees. She bit her lip to keep from crying out when he put his foot on the back of her neck and pushed her face into the dusty street.

He called out to the multitude that had gathered, using a dialect that Bitsy had never heard before, and the crowd shouted their response in the same tongue. Again the Indian caught the girl by her hair. Drawing her upright, he flung her through the door of the longhouse.

Bitsy sprawled face down on the hard-packed earthen floor and lay there unmoving. I won't cry, she promised herself over and over—but she did, the quiet sobs of a terrified young woman who is sure that all is lost: family, friends, home, and even life itself.

After the tears had subsided, Bitsy still did not move or raise her head. She lay there listening to the sounds around her, trying to place each rustle, but all she could pinpoint was the noise that filtered through the building from the outside. She could hear people talking and laughing, could make out the sounds of wood being chopped, could distinguish children's voices as they darted past the longhouse.

Without turning her head, she opened her eyes and rolled them each direction as far as her vision would allow. There was no one else in the room. Cautiously, Bitsy climbed to her feet and moved to the bark-sided wall that faced the broad path the Indians used for a street. She pressed her eye against a crack and studied the village with care. It was an impressive sight, boasting a hundred or more wigwams. It was the largest village, white or Indian, she had ever seen in the wilderness. In fact, to the terrified girl, it looked bigger than Williamsburg, Virginia, the home of her grandparents.

As Bitsy watched the hordes of Indians who were within her field of vision, she began to tremble anew, shuddering with such violence that she was forced to clutch the wall for support. She would not live to see the sun come up tomorrow, for the Indians were cutting limbs and staves; They intended to burn her at the stake.

The activity outside the building picked up tempo as Indians gathered in the street, chanting and wailing and beating their freshly cut weapons against the ground with such unbridled passion that the sound grew to a deafening crescendo. Bitsy's lips drew tight across her teeth, and she clamped her hands over her ears in an effort to shut out the awful noise. Still it vibrated through her mind with such force that she feared for her sanity.

She ran to the farthest wall and pressed herself against the rough wooden slabs. She watched the hide-covered doorway through dilated, unblinking eyes, waiting for the skin covering to be whipped aside for the last time. Then, knowing that any chance of escape or rescue was nonexistent, she turned to the only source she felt might give her the strength to face death bravely.

Slowly she slid down the wall to a kneeling position. "Dearest God in heaven," she whispered, raising her face to the ceiling, "let me be as courageous as Mrs. Southhampton was, and . . . please, God, don't let me suffer too long."

Chard was sure that every bone in his body would snap as he rose painfully to his feet at false dawn. Electing to keep a close watch on George Girty, he had passed the night in wide-eyed wakefulness, propped against a tree with his cocked pistol in his hand.

He joined the brothers at the fire and helped himself to a slab of venison. It tasted better than it had the night before when he had been too exhausted to eat.

"How far is this town, or village, or whatever it is?" he asked Simon Girty.

"Another hard day's run," answered Girty, "but we gained a day on the Wyandots by stickin' to the river, which they was afraid to do. We won't beat 'em to the village, but we won't be far behind."

Chard flinched. A full day of what he suffered for three hours yesterday. He wasn't sure he could do it. But he knew better than to voice his doubt.

"You look a mite peaked this mornin'," sneered George Girty. "Didn't sleep much last night, did you."

Chard smiled across the flames at Girty.

"There's only one way you would know that for sure, George."

"I sleep with one eye open," bragged Girty.

"Then you only get half as much sleep as I do," came Chard's soft reply, and he returned his attention to the venison.

Simon Girty squatted beside Chard and cut a long, thin slice of meat from the hindquarter. "Don't push your luck, boy. My brother will chew you up and spit you out in little pieces."

Anger surged through the ensign like a tidal wave as Simon Girty's words struck home. The Girty brothers considered him a pompous ass who didn't have sense enough to take care of himself.

"Simon," said Chard through his teeth, "if your brother ever lays a hand on me, I'll kill him."

Simon Girty smiled and shook his head slowly as if he were confronting a child.

"Son," he said, ripping off another piece of meat, "if my brother touches you with his hand, you'll already be dead."

"I'll keep that in mind," Chard said after a long silence, aware that he had once again spoken when he should have listened.

186

George Girty kicked dirt over the fire and without so much as a glance in Chard's direction, trotted into the predawn light. They ran without a break until noon. Chard was amazed that he was able to keep up the grueling pace, but he was more than ready for a rest when the signal finally came.

They relaxed beside a spring, drinking sparingly from time to time, and eating cold venison and parched corn. Chard caught himself dozing in the midday warmth, and struggled to his feet. The Girtys jumped up, too, supposing that Chard had signaled that he was ready to resume their journey. Silently they headed north. Throughout the remainder of the afternoon they kept up that grinding trot, until finally Simon Girty called a halt.

Chard watched as the brothers drew paint and turkey-feathered headbands from their haversacks. In minutes, they had wiped away any semblance of civilization; Chard hardly recognized them as white men.

Simon Girty faced Chard squarely. "We leave you here."

Chard was taken aback. Girty had a reason for not wanting him along, but, by the same token, Chard had a reason for wanting to be there.

"I'm going with you, Girty," he said simply.

Simon Girty's expression didn't alter, but Chard sensed the man's displeasure. They stood for a long moment gauging one another.

"All right," said Girty finally, "but there's no telling what we'll find when we get down there. Whatever happens, you are to say and do nothing. Understood?"

Chard nodded.

Girty eyed Chard's appearance. "You can't go into a Wyandot village looking like you do; those trousers is a dead giveaway."

While Chard kicked off his white pants, rolled them into a ball, then concealed them at the base of a tree, Girty was mixing paint and painstakingly spreading it over the ensign's face.

"Shake out your queue and let your hair hang free," Girty instructed, when he was satisfied with the paint.

Chard did as he was told.

Girty surveyed the young man intently. "You might

187

pass, if it wasn't for your legs—they're white as snow." The man frowned. "Ain't the sun ever burned your hide?"

Chard shook his head. "Only my face and hands."

Girty exhaled in disgust. "Put a coat of mud on them legs."

Chard glanced quickly around for a stream and, seeing none, asked Girty how he was supposed to make mud from dry dirt.

"Rake back the leaves and piss on the ground," came George Girty's exasperated response.

Chard didn't hesitate. He urinated on a small cleared spot and mixed the soft loam into a thick muddy paste, which he hurriedly plastered on his legs from foot to groin.

The Girtys eyed him critically, then nodded. He looked almost right.

They had gone less than a mile when they topped a rise that overlooked a long, open plateau where hundreds of Indians were milling about, shouting and laughing, as if waiting for something or someone special.

"Looks like they're plannin' some entertainment for the evening," said George Girty to his brother.

Simon didn't take his eyes off the village. "They're goin' to run her, George. They done made up their minds."

Chard wondered what Simon meant, but he kept his mouth shut. They moved off the hill, rifles propped in the crooks of their arms, and trotted slowly down the main thoroughfare of the village. With fixed smiles, the Girtys called out jovial greetings to the Indians, ignoring the fact that the tribe had grown quiet and were watching the three interlopers suspiciously, dangerously.

"This could get real tricky," said George Girty out of the corner of his mouth to Simon.

"'Tis a bit late to worry about it now," returned Simon without expression. "I just hope to bloody hell they recognize our names."

The three stopped before a large wigwam and, in a singsong dialect, Simon Girty addressed the building. The skin flap was thrust aside and a middle-aged Indian stepped into the waning sunlight. The Girtys dropped the butts of their rifles to the ground and leaned on the barrels. Chard followed suit.

188

"How do?" said Simon in what he hoped was passable Wyandot. "I am Simon Girty. This is my brother, George, and my brother Chard."

"We know you, Simon Girty of the Seneca," said the Indian soberly. "We are honored to have you visit the Wyandot. Come into my home and be welcome."

The three men entered the longhouse and squatted beside the fire pit. An Indian woman appeared with a long-stem pipe and tamped it full of tobacco. Picking a coal from the fire with her bare fingers, she laid it in the pipe bowl. She presented the pipe to the chief, who took a deep draw before passing it to Simon Girty who, after several puffs, passed it to George and on to Chard.

The men smoked in silence, passing the pipe until the last puff was drawn.

"What is the purpose of your visit?" asked the Indian, politely getting to the point.

"Just passin' through," returned Simon easily.

The Indian's eyes twinkled. "The gods smile on you."

"Why is that?"

"We have a captive," said the Indian, watching the men intently. "And shortly she will run the gauntlet. Then, after the feast tonight, the women have demanded that she burn at the stake. I have given my permission." He studied the three white men through hooded eyes.

He's a tricky bastard, thought Simon Girty, and he knows exactly why we are here. But all Girty did was shrug eloquently. "It will be a sight to behold."

"You are welcome to join the gauntlet line," offered the Indian, not at all pleased by Girty's reaction. "You would honor the Wyandot with your presence."

Simon Girty nodded. "The honor is ours."

With Chard sitting there wondering what was being said, Girty and the Indian talked of the weather, hunting, and finally of the war between America and Britain. Not once did the Girtys show interest in the Wyandots' captive. In fact, they carefully steered the conversation down a different avenue each time the Indian approached the subject.

They knew the Wyandot chief was aware that they were part of Bird's expedition. And they knew, also, that he was no fool; he understood perfectly that they had come in search of the girl. Their caginess was meant to baffle and irritate the Indian.

"Come, join the game." The chief rose to his feet. "My people are anxious to begin."

The three white men followed the chief to a spot near the end of a long double line of excited Indians.

As Chard took his position, an Indian thrust a three-foot stick into his hand, Chard wondered about it, but neither of the Girtys seemed disposed to enlighten the young man's ignorance, forcing him to figure it out for himself. Yet, nothing his keen mind had imagined prepared Chard for the performance he was about to witness.

The Indian who had captured Bitsy ushered her roughly through the door of the longhouse and prodded her to within ten feet of the waiting men, women, and children who lined both sides of the walkway for nearly two hundred yards. Each of the participants, including the Girtys and Chard, held a switch, staff, or whip.

Without preliminaries, her captor commanded Bitsy to take off her dress. At first, she did not understand the man's instructions. She stared at his hand signals with an open, uncomprehending face. Then her face turned the sickly color of one who is about to faint. But after a moment of deep breathing, Bitsy slowly drew the garment over her head and dropped it in the dust.

Chard wanted to look away, but he couldn't. He could no more tear his eyes from Bitsy than he could stop breathing, for she was more beautiful than he had ever dreamed. Her legs were long and shapely and molded smoothly into hips that flared with such delicacy that they enhanced and emphasized her tiny waist. Her breasts were firm and upthrust and pleasing to the eye, which naturally traveled upward to her elegant neck and small proud face.

Head held nervously high, Bitsy stepped to the opening between the human chain.

The Indians eyed her covetously, anticipating the beating they would inflict on her, and raised their weapons in preparation for Bitsy's passing. Each and every one was intent on what individual punishment he or she might inflict on the young white girl.

190

In their greedy lust for blood, they were totally unprepared for what came next. Instead of waiting for the signal, Bitsy burst into action and leaped past the first few Indians before they knew what happened. She ran like a deer, and the confused savages flailed one another's bodies more often than they did the unprotected skin of the fleet young woman.

Chard forgot Bitsy's nudity as he watched her approach. And each time a switch cut into her or a stick slashed her skin, he had to grit his teeth to keep from running to meet her, to keep from shouting encouragement; to keep from screaming to the world how very grand and glorious she was for outsmarting her adversaries. But even as he watched, an old crone thrust her staff between the girl's knees, sending Bitsy sprawling headlong in the dusty lane between two lines of savages gone berserk with blood lust.

Chard was white-faced. They'll beat her to death before she can gain her feet, he cried, standing on tiptoe as the mass of Indians flocked around the fallen girl, shutting off his view.

Bitsy came to the same conclusion. So instead of trying to rise, she flung herself sideways into the shins of the Indian woman nearest her, bringing the squaw down in a cloud of dust amid the thrashing clubs and switches of her companions.

Indians farther down the line, afraid they would miss their opportunity to inflict pain on Bitsy, converged on the downed women with a vengeance, rushing pell-mell into one another and striking anyone who got in their way. In the confusion of the melee, Bitsy squirmed on her stomach through the churning, stomping feet of her tormentors. And while the crazed savages beat one another unmercifully in an attempt to get to the spot where she had fallen, Bitsy, having worked her way through the line, bounded erect and streaked behind the screaming mob.

She might have made good her escape had not an Indian farther down the line picked that particular moment to glance behind him. Seeing Bitsy, the man broke ranks and bounded toward her. Obviously, he expected her to break away from the line, for he angled outward in an attempt to head her off when she made her move. The entire line turned when they realized what was taking place, and many a shin was barked and arm flailed as they strove to bring up their clubs and resume the gauntlet.

Again Bitsy did the unexpected. She burst back through the line, not away from it, and stretched her long legs toward the end of the gauntlet. The confusion was total, with people striking at her from all sides but very few scoring a direct hit. When Bitsy sped past Chard, he was so relieved he very nearly reached out to embrace her. He watched her race past the last of the gauntlet, but instead of stopping, she increased her speed, darting between buildings until she was lost from sight.

Then, he, along with the entire population of the village, was bounding after her through the little puffs of dust her bare feet had stirred up in her headlong flight toward the security of the nearby forest. They pursued Bitsy for an incredible half-mile before an Indian club brought her down. Chard was sick with the surety that the Indians would beat Bitsy to death for attempting to escape. Raising his club above his head, he took a step toward the savages who were dragging Bitsy to her feet. But whatever Chard intended to do to protect Bitsy, it was not necessary for, to his amazement, it was a town full of happy, chattering savages who paraded the gasping young woman back the way she had come.

Simon Girty later told Chard that never had the Indians enjoyed a gauntlet more. They bragged that Bitsy's run had been more entertaining than a game of lacrosse, a deadly form of racquetball that the Indians took very seriously. Girty also told Chard that several Indians had suffered broken arms, legs, and bashed skulls, but that all in all they considered Bitsy's run well worth it.

At the time, however, Chard had no idea that Bitsy was being hailed as the heroine of the day. He was beside himself with fear for her safety, for he could see that she was cut and bleeding in a dozen places, half of her body bruised black and blue, and that she was limping badly on her right leg. So great was his compassion that when the girl drew near Chard involuntarily extended his arms toward her. But the second before he would have embraced her, Simon Girty brushed between Chard and Bitsy and, as if by accident, knocked the ensign's hands aside.

"You fool," he said under his breath, "you'll spoil everything."

Bitsy passed the disguised white men without recognizing them. Chard gazed into her despondent eyes, the eyes of one who has found herself returned to a situation without hope and is awaiting the end. Yet, hopeless as they were, Bitsy's eyes did not have the look of surrender about them, and Chard wished he could reassure her that he and the Girtys would do everything possible to secure her release. But he could only watch with an aching heart as the jubilant Indians prodded and pushed her toward the dark longhouse she had just vacated.

It had been another long, tiring day for Judith, but the canoes were finally being steered toward shore. She missed Chard, and yes, she missed Bitsy, too. Where were they? Had Chard and the Girtys even located the girl? And if they did rescue her, would Bitsy be the same young woman she had been before her capture?

Judith pitied Bitsy. She doubted very seriously that the girl would be unchanged by her ordeal with the savages; very few people came out of the forest unaltered by such an experience. Judith had undergone a complete metamorphosis, both mentally and physically, during her sojourn through the American wilderness in 1755.

Judith sighed heavily. Even a quarter of a century couldn't erase the scars of that tragedy. Her fingers absently traced the long, thin mark on her forehead, but it was the invisible scars that were most disturbing; there were weeks and weeks of her life at that time which she had absolutely no recollection of, except in recurring nightmares from which she awakened drenched in perspiration.

Judith shuddered and tried to dwell on something more pleasant, such as what had occurred the night before when the army had made camp. She smiled, thinking about it. She had been applying ointment to her rapidly healing body when the tent flap had been thrown aside and her husband and Lieutenant Clarke had marched in.

She had quickly drawn the blanket around her, but she was sure that, even in the dim light of the candle, they had seen the ugly damage caused by the cat-o'-nine-tails.

"It doesn't look as bad as I had imagined," said Southhampton.

Judith's eyes mocked him. "Disappointed?"

Southhampton's mouth drew into a thin line. "For one who is destined to be hanged, your asinine attempts at ridicule are wasted, my dear."

"I rather like them," she returned, "and if you do not, then you can kiss my—"

"Damn your foul mouth, Judith!" shouted Southhampton. "The whipping I gave you taught you naught about respect."

Judith laughed gleefully, then sobered. "To what do I owe this joyful visit, James? I'm sure you didn't come here to show pity for my delicate condition."

"As a matter of fact, I didn't. I brought Lieutenant Clarke to talk to you. He is with our intelligence department and will testify at your trial."

"How nice."

Southhampton turned to Clarke. "She's all yours, Lieutenant." With that, he marched staunchly into the night.

Clarke studied Judith for a long moment. She was not at all what Southhampton had described. The scar on her face, instead of marring her, only enhanced her beauty with a rakish, alluring air that made Clarke's pulse quicken. And that moment before she had hastily covered herself with the blanket had allowed him a brief glance at her more intimate and womanly charms.

"What is it you want to know?" asked Judith, drawing the blanket more securely about her, for his obvious interest made her skin crawl.

"Lady Southhampton," he said easily, sure that she would listen to reason and jump at the chance to improve her situation, "I must say that I am pleasantly surprised. You are not at all what I expected. You are quite beautiful, aye, quite beautiful indeed."

"Did you come here to interrogate me or seduce me, Lieutenant?"

"I came to talk to you," he said, frowning, not liking the fact that she was openly unimpressed by his flattery. "I can be of great service to you, you know."

194

"I can guess what service you have in mind, sir. The answer is no."

Clarke's frown deepened. He had not expected her to be so insolent. "I can see to it that your confinement is not at all unpleasant. Good food, new dresses, certain liberties . . . Perhaps I can even keep them from hanging you. Have you ever seen a hanging, Lady Southhampton?"

"As a matter of fact, I have, Lieutenant. I loved every minute of it."

Clarke was outraged. He could see why Southhampton abhorred her. Still, she was a challenge, and he enjoyed a clever adversary; it made the final conquest all the more meaningful. "I can see to it that you experience it again, from a firsthand point of view," he said with a pleased smile. "Will you love that, madam?"

"More than I would love rutting with you" came Judith's soft reply.

"That remains to be seen." His confidence grew in leaps and bounds. "You are nothing but a traitor and, according to your husband, a highborn whore. And whether you wish to acknowledge it or not, you, my dear, are at my disposal. You must know that I can have you whenever I choose." He laughed aloud at the skeptical expression that crossed Judith's face. He was on firm ground and he knew it. Pressing his advantage, he continued, "If you were half as intelligent as you think you are, you would cease this silly charade and lie back and enjoy yourself. After all, who are you going to run to if I take you by force? Who would care?"

Judith's face drained of color. He was perfectly correct. No one save Chard would blink an eye should Clarke—or anyone else—choose to rape her. She was a traitor to the Crown, and any hardships or unpleasantness that befell her were justified in the eyes of her countrymen.

Clarke's confident eyes held Judith's as he patiently pressed one button at a time through the eyelets of his tunic. Folding the coat neatly, he laid it at the foot of her pallet, then repeated the performance with his white ruffled shirt.

Judith interrupted him as he untied the drawstrings at the back of his drop-front breeches. "Lieutenant," she said, "if you would move a little more to your left, I would appreciate it."

"Why so?" asked Clarke, taking a sidestep as he fumbled with his pants.

"Because, when I blow your guts out through your backbone, I don't want them to splatter on the wall of my tent." She smiled prettily as Clarke looked quickly behind him. He was standing directly in front of the flaps Southhampton had failed to close. When his eyes swung again to Judith, he saw that a big-bore pistol was aimed at his naked abdomen.

"Sweet Jesus," he breathed, stumbling backwards while attempting to wiggle back into his breeches, which had fallen to his knees, "where did that come from?"

Judith steadied the gun that Chard had left with her. "Why, you gave it to me," she said, lying smoothly, "when you tried to talk me into escaping with you."

Clarke's face went rigid. "Nobody will believe that cock-and-bull story."

"Of course not," admitted Judith, "but you will have to prove it's not true, because I intend to shout it to the heavens when they hang me, and everyone knows that people don't lie with their last breath. The best thing you can do, Lieutenant Clarke, is walk out of here and forget you ever saw me, or this gun."

Her contempt made the short hairs on the back of his neck bristle, and he knew a moment of real down-to-earth fear as she cocked the heavy pistol.

"I'm leaving," he said quickly. "Just let me get my clothes . . . if I may?"

Judith nodded toward the pallet. "Get them, and get out."

As Clarke retrieved his shirt and tunic, Judith laughed joyfully. "Tell my husband, who I'm sure is anxiously awaiting the outcome of this most pleasant evening, that he is indeed correct."

"Correct, ma'am?" said the man, baffled.

"Aye." Judith smiled grimly. "Tell him that you, too, found me most unpleasant in bed."

But Clarke didn't tell Southhampton anything. When he went to the major's camp and found the man gone, he

196

sought to salve his wounded pride the only way he was capable: by abusing another member of the very sex that had damaged it. So, ironically, while Judith Southhampton lay on her pallet and laughed out loud at having shattered Clarke's fragile male ego, Susan Patterson lay on Southhampton's cot and cried silent, bitter tears while Clarke strove to rebuild it. Neither woman had the remotest idea that the comedy turned tragedy was Judith's salvation and Susan's hell.

Judith's smile at the memory of her final comment to Clarke vanished with the shuddering of the canoe as it nosed against the bank. She stepped carefully from the craft and studied the spot Southhampton had designated for her tent. Again it was well away from the main camp, almost hidden in a small clearing amid a tangle of brush and thickets.

Judith was lonely, and longed for companionship. Not the kind that Clarke had offered, just the people kind, the gratification that comes from hearing human voices, seeing people's faces, watching their movements. Isolation was by far the worst part of being an outcast. She could endure the physical self-denial, but she was not at all sure she could combat the loneliness.

For the first time since her ordeal began, Judith felt an uncharacteristic stab of self-pity. Slowly she walked to the tent the guards were raising.

Chard had understood not one word that passed between the Indians and the Girtys, and he was growing more nervous and impatient by the minute. It was obvious from their actions that the council of Wyandot chieftains sitting stone-faced around the fire pit were opposed to giving up the white girl who had so impressed them with her running of the gauntlet.

Simon Girty had said before entering the council that buying Bitsy's release was not going to be easy because of the boldness of spirit and bravery she had displayed. He said that Indians loved a courageous enemy and that the Wyandot were looking forward to burning Bitsy at the stake.

"We will have to play it slow and careful," Girty had told Chard. "No matter what is said or done, don't act overanxious, or we'll never get her back."

But as Chard watched the proceedings in the long-house that served as a council room, he was not at all encouraged by the hand signals and singsong conversation between the Indians and the renegades. To make matters worse, neither of the Girtys felt compelled to translate for him, thereby leaving the entire transaction more or less to his imagination, which was running wild.

The council broke up just after midnight, and Chard had to grit his teeth to keep from firing questions at his companions the moment they were beyond hearing of the longhouse. As the three men walked haughtily through the village to their sleeping quarters, Chard glanced at the dark, silent building where Bitsy was kept. No guard was by the door, but Chard knew the place was being watched. He didn't think it a coincidence that he and the Girtys had been quartered in a small wigwam at the edge of the woods, at the opposite end of town from the captive.

"What went on in the council?" he demanded the moment they were inside.

Simon Girty shrugged. "'Tis nip and tuck, lad. We'll know for sure after they've slept on it."

"They ain't none too keen on lettin' her go," admitted George. "I'm goin' to be some surprised if we get her out of here."

Chard was dissatisfied with the Girty brothers' laconic comments, but he was at a loss as to what he could do. Bitsy's future depended solely on the ability of the two renegades to persuade the Wyandots to trade, sell, or whatever it took to give her up.

In minutes the Girtys were asleep, but Chard lay there wide-eyed, wondering what he would do if the Indians refused their proposals. There was one thing he knew for certain: Bitsy would not burn at the stake. Yet, when he finally did drift off to sleep, he dreamed of flames leaping high around her until, burned to a crisp, she disintegrated into a pile of soft white ashes, which the Indians cast into the wind to be carried by the breeze and distributed throughout the virgin wilderness.

* * *

When Chard stepped out of the wigwam the next morning, the Girtys were already breakfasting on stewed squirrel that a Wyandot woman had brought to their camp. Helping himself to the food, Chard asked point-blank what the Girtys intended to do about Bitsy.

As usual, George had little to say, and even Simon was noncommittal.

"You can't pressure these people," Simon grunted. "They'll either barter or they won't—'tis the way they are."

Chard had the annoying impression that the Girtys weren't telling him the truth, not all of it, anyway. He would have enjoyed snatching them up and shaking them until their teeth rattled, but he knew better. If they didn't kill him outright, they most definitely would confide nothing to him thereafter, for in that respect they were true Indians: they would not be intimidated.

So he ate his stew in silence, hating everything and everybody in sight.

The councils convened before the sun was two hours high and lasted until well past noon. Chard tried unsuccessfully to read the faces of the men who sat cross-legged around the fire pit. Finally, when they all arose and with grave dignity clasped arms with Simon Girty, Chard still did not know whether the renegade had accomplished his mission. It was the most frustrating moment of his entire life.

"Damn it, Girty, what happened in there?" he demanded when they stepped outside.

"We got her" was all the man said.

The Girtys went straight to their wigwam and ducked inside, with Chard hot on their heels.

He had a thousand questions, but he was afraid to ask. He did, however, phrase the question uppermost in his mind: "When can we get her away from here?" As if in answer, the flap of the wigwam was thrown aside and Bitsy was thrust into the small enclosure. The chief followed close behind and stood with his arms folded across his chest.

While the Indian spoke rapidly to Simon Girty, Chard scrutinized the disheveled girl. Her hair was matted and dirty, as was the exposed portion of her skin. The dress was torn and shredded. Her bare feet were crusted with dirt and grime. In total contrast to her filthy appearance, however, the whites of her large eyes gleamed like the purest snow, unblemished, clean, and untainted. On closer inspection, however, Chard noticed something in their depths that he had not seen before: her eyes were filled with pain. And why not? He remembered the beating she had taken while running the gauntlet. She was probably hurting all over.

Bitsy had not looked directly at the men, as was the Indian women's custom when in the presence of males, so Chard doubted that she had recognized either him or the Girtys—especially him, with his hair hanging in tangles about his green and red painted face. He longed to catch her attention, to give her a reassuring signal that all was well, but she kept her eyes averted to a spot just in front of her bare feet.

The Indian walked to Chard and, gazing haughtily into the ensign's face, snatched Chard's pearl-handled dagger from its sheath. Chard stood unmoving, as the Girtys had instructed, but it took his entire reserve of self-control to let the heirloom go without an argument.

The Indian clasped arms with Simon Girty, then stalked from the building.

"Let's get out of here afore he changes his mind," said Simon Girty, snatching up his rifle and stepping outside. Without a word, George Girty followed.

Bitsy raised her head and glanced at Chard to see if he wanted her to fall into line behind George. Beneath its coating of grime, her face drained of color as she looked into his blue eyes. "You!" she whispered, then quickly glanced through the open doorway. "Is that the Girtys?"

Chard nodded. "We'd best be getting away from here, Bitsy. I've no idea what Simon promised these Indians to get them to release you, but the Girtys seem to be in a hurry to put distance between us and them."

With Bitsy in the lead, she and Chard fell into line behind the renegades and trotted up the path they had used when they entered the village. When they reached the tree where they had stopped the day before, Chard snatched up his breeches and continued on. He was afraid to stop even for the short space of time it would take to dress, afraid to let Bitsy out of his sight.

They traveled throughout the remainder of the day

200

without a rest. Then, just before full dark, Simon Girty picked a campsite beneath a blow-down. George Girty nodded to his brother and continued on without breaking his stride.

By the time George returned, Simon had the fire going and a good bed of white-hot coals waiting. George flung a small hen turkey to the ground and glared at Chard, but it was Bitsy he addressed: "Clean that, and cook it." His eyes held Chard's as if to dare the young man to intervene on the girl's behalf. But he was wasting his energy, for Chard, too, considered that type of chore woman's work.

The men watched idly while the girl struggled with the turkey. George Girty finally asked what was taking her so long. It was obvious that he was displeased with her slow progress.

Chard, who had been watching Bitsy's awkward movements, climbed to his feet and walked to her side. Without a word, he took the knife from her and finished skinning the turkey. After spitting it on a green stick, he laid it over the coals.

The girl watched him, wide-eyed. And when he grinned into her upturned face, he saw a tear break free and trickle down her cheek.

"What is it, Bitsy?"

She shook her head. "'Tis nothing. I am fine, just a bit slow, is all."

She started to rise, and Chard caught her hand in an attempt to assist. The girl cried out and slumped against him, weeping pathetically. Chard eased her to the ground, baffled by her reaction. He reached again for her hand, but she drew it beneath her arm and rolled onto her side.

"What's wrong with your hand, Bitsy?" asked Chard gently.

"Nothing," cried the girl, weeping louder.

"Let me see it."

"No."

"Let me see it," he demanded, catching her wrist and drawing the hand into the open, where, even in the feeble light, the swollen, grotesque fingers were clearly visible.

"Jesus Christ," he breathed.

"Please," whimpered the girl, "please don't let Simon Girty cut it off."

201

"Cut it off!" cried Chard, his skin crawling. "Nobody's going to cut your hand off."

Bitsy shook her head and cried even harder. "Everyone on the frontier knows that the Girtys save fingers, and toes and ears, and scalps. . . . Everyone knows it, especially you British bastards who pay them to do it."

Simon Girty climbed lightly to his feet. "Missy," he said in his soft rasp, "I couldn't help overhearing what you said. And while I'll admit that I've taken a scalp or two, I've got to deny that I ever took any fingers or other human parts." He laughed as he looked into the girl's woebegone face. "'Tis naught but frontier folks' way of keepin' you youngsters in line. I heard 'em say it my own self: 'If you don't straighten up and be good, Simon Girty will cut your ears off.'" He grinned at the girl. "Maybe Susan Patterson's said that a time or two to you?"

Bitsy's face flamed. Girty broke into silent laughter.

"Now," he said when his mirth had subsided, "let's see if we can do something for your hand, short of cutting it off."

It took both Chard and George to hold Bitsy down while Simon snapped the bones into place. The girl's face streamed perspiration, and her lips were bloodless as Simon pulled and pushed and finally said he'd done all he could.

He walked into the dark forest and returned minutes later with a flat piece of bark, which he laid against the girl's palm, binding it tight with strips cut from her dress. Then he went to a small spring and returned with a double handful of thick mud, which he plastered over the entire splint.

"Don't move that hand until the mud dries," he cautioned Bitsy.

She nodded her understanding, studying the man with open admiration. "I'm sorry for what I said, Mr. Girty."

Simon smiled easily. "I'm not as bad as they make me out to be, missy."

Chard saw the respect on Bitsy's face. She had never looked at him like that, and it rankled that she would show such an emotion for a renegade, even one who had helped her. Chard climbed angrily to his feet and stalked off to the tree he had chosen to sleep under.

From under her lashes, Bitsy watched Chard seat himself against the trunk. Disappointment drew the corners of her lips down. She had intended to thank him for his concern and perhaps, if he would permit, even sit next to him when they shared the turkey. But obviously he did not want her companionship. She turned to the fire and pretended to inspect the roasting meat.

As they ate, Chard questioned Simon Girty about the Wyandot.

Girty explained that of all the Ohio Indians the Wyandots were the only ones who fought like white men. "They have a completely different notion about warfare than the Huron, Ottawa, Cherokee, or Shawnee," he said. The Wyandot would employ siege warfare and then follow it through no matter how long it took. Most tribes, he said, grew bored with the endless waiting and went off in search of better sport, but the Wyandot would stay put till hell froze over.

He told Chard that he had had to walk lightly in the Wyandot village because the tribe was displeased with the British for not having invited them on the invasion of Kentucky. The Wyandot were also well aware that they had broken their treaty with the British by abducting the girl, so he had had to handle them carefully, for like white men they were dangerous and unreasonable when angered.

Chard nodded his understanding and changed the subject. "How come we're going back to the river the same way we came? Wouldn't it be shorter to cut across country and catch the army somewhere upstream when they make camp?"

"We could do that," agreed Girty, "but our plunder is still in that hollow sycamore tree." He grinned with amusement. "Me and George hid a canoe just below it, by the river."

Chard scowled. He should have known the Girtys never did anything without a reason. He shook his head. Would he never learn to keep his big mouth shut? He ate in silence after that, which was fine for all concerned, because the Girtys were natural loners and Chard had already talked more than they would have liked.

Bitsy also ate in silence. She was in deep thought about her mother and what she had witnessed at Southhampton's tent the night before she was captured. Susan Patterson didn't drink, and she most definitely was not a loose woman, yet she had appeared to be both that night. Bitsy pondered the problem, making excuses for Susan, dreaming up all manner of circumstances that would justify such behavior, but after all the whitewashing and lying to herself was over, the girl hung her head and cried silently.

Simon Girty watched the young woman out of the corners of his permanently squinted eyes. Her courage had impressed him, especially when he had worked on her broken fingers, for although she had been in excruciating pain, the only sounds that had escaped her lips had been her intake of breath and several soft whimpers each time he had snapped a bone into place. They had placed a stick in her mouth for her to bite down on. She had bitten it in half—but she had not cried. So he could not help wondering at the tears she shed. They must surely be for someone other than herself, he decided.

As Bitsy wept, anger began building in her, anger at herself, her weaknesses, her self-pity. I'm not a crybaby, she insisted silently. I've never been afraid to face my problems, so what has come over me all of a sudden? All I've done since my mother left is cry. 'Tis silly, just childishly silly.

Bitsy fought back her tears, tore another chunk of turkey from the roasted bird, and stuffed it into her mouth. She chewed absently, continuing her contemplation: I'm a grown woman now, and I've got to start acting like one. She took a deep breath and swallowed the meat, feeling better about herself than she had in days.

CHAPTER
· *12* ·

MORGAN PATTERSON CAMPED that night on the Kentucky side of the Ohio, directly across from the mouth of the Great Miami.

He had spent the last two hours of daylight searching for a canoe. He knew that the Indians frequently sank several craft in the shallow water at the river's edge so they would have boats on both sides of the river at all times. But, much to his disappointment, he had not located one. He squinted at the far bank. The Indians had taken all craft to the Ohio side, which proved beyond a doubt that they expected retaliation from the Kentuckians.

But that was General Clark's worry. Patterson's immediate problem was finding a way to cross the river. He discarded the idea of swimming his horse across. The wilderness on the other side would be swarming with savages, and the conspicuous horse would probably get him killed. He shook his head. If he intended to survive, he would have to travel light and quiet.

He lay on his back and gazed at a break in the foliage overhead. Thousands of stars sparkled in that small, dark patch of sky like tiny glowworms, and he wondered if, perhaps, they were nothing but a reflection of the Indian campfires burning beyond the Ohio.

Before those stars faded into the dawn, Patterson hid his saddle and bridle beneath a pile of brush and slipped the tether from his horse's neck. He watched the animal make its way uncertainly into the forest. Yet, even then, it hesitated, reluctant to leave its master and the security of companionship.

Finally, it tossed its head and trotted into the gathering light.

Patterson caught up his rifle and walked to the riverbank, where he squatted and studied the expanse of fast-moving water. Far out, barely larger than a speck, a movement caught his attention: a canoe making its way toward Kentucky. Gradually it took on shape and distinction until finally it came close enough for him to count the six Indians paddling in unison.

Patterson wriggled his way into a cane patch and hunkered down to wait.

The Indians beached the boat not a hundred yards from where the woodsman knelt. As quiet as snakes, they slipped from the craft and slithered into the forest. Patterson guessed that they were a scouting party in search of Clark and his army. They had not sunk their canoe, which indicated that their stay on the Kentucky side would be a short one.

Patterson intended to give the Indians enough time to get well into the forest before stealing their boat. But he knew that the best-laid plans could go awry when one depended on nature, savage Indians, and luck. About ten minutes had passed when the frontiersman heard the chilling whoops and excited cries of the Indians. He gritted his teeth. The Indians had spotted his horse.

Oblivious to the noise he was making, Patterson burst out of the cane thicket and bounded in long lopes toward the canoe. He didn't see the young Indian who had been left to guard the craft until the boy rose up out of the brush directly in his path and aimed his musket at the woodsman's chest. Patterson saw the hammer of the gun fall. And he saw the look of disbelief that filled the Indian's face when he realized the gun had misfired.

For a startled moment the Indian stood awestruck as the woodsman came toward him like a charging buffalo. Then, casting the musket aside, he drew his knife and dropped into a crouch. He had only trod the warrior's path once, and that was with Bird's army when they invaded

Kentucky. So the young man believed all white men would behave like those at Ruddle's and Martin's Forts —intimidated into immobility by war paint and flashing steel. He died with that thought on his mind, for Patterson did not hesitate as he charged into the waiting Indian. He merely pressed his gun against the boy's face and blew the back of his roached head away.

Without breaking his stride, Patterson jumped the body and bounded into the canoe, using his momentum to launch the light craft. Dropping his empty rifle into the bottom of the boat, he snatched up a paddle and sank it deep and powerfully into the swift current. The canoe shot forward with a speed that put yards of safe water between the riverbank and the woodsman. But when Patterson glanced over his shoulder to be sure he was beyond reach of the war party, he was appalled to find that they had already gathered at the water's edge and were sighting their muskets on his broad back.

A sledgehammer blow tore into his shoulder with such force that it spun him halfway around, nearly upsetting the boat. By reflex alone, he dug the paddle deep, again and again. The Indians reloaded quickly, not patching the ball or measuring the powder charge, but by the time they had finished, Patterson was almost a quarter of the way across the wide river, well out of musket range.

He stayed his paddle, letting the canoe drift with the current while he eased his hunting frock off his shoulder. The ball had passed through the trapezius muscle just above his collarbone. He thanked God that it had not been an inch lower. Slipping the buckskin back into place, he painfully resumed paddling toward the distant shore.

He was in midstream before he realized the canoe was taking on water. He ran his hands along the ribs below the float line and found two ragged tears in the birchbark. Only then did he realize that all the Indians had emptied their weapons at him—for he had not heard even that first gun go off. Ignoring the pain in his shoulder, he dug the paddle deep and pushed hard for the Ohio bank, still a good quarter of a mile away. But even as he stroked with all his might, he knew he would never make it.

On that same morning, a hundred miles from Patterson, Chard burned with jealousy. Simon Girty had just finished replastering Bitsy's hand. Chard told himself that he didn't mind Bitsy's easy attitude with the white Indian. He even managed to remain impassive when she smiled gratefully at Girty and thanked him for his trouble. But he could not keep himself from stalking over and reminding the white savage that if he was finished with Bitsy, the sun was up and the trail awaited.

Simon Girty's eyes turned hard as agate. He did not like being chastised, especially by a lad who didn't know which end was up about anything, much less the frontier.

George Girty had the same notion as Chard, and without realizing it, he came to the ensign's rescue. "The man's right, Simon," he said, scowling. "We've tarried here long enough."

Simon swung his eyes to his brother and, after a long interval, nodded his agreement. Without a word, he sprang to his feet and trotted toward the river. Bitsy slipped her mud cast into a sling Girty had fashioned from a strip cut from her dress and fell into line behind George.

Feeling angry at the world, Chard brought up the rear. He watched Bitsy run gracefully before him, and try as he might to push aside the mental image of how proud and beautiful she had been standing naked before the Wyandot nation his mind refused to be sidetracked. His eyes, as though drawn by a magnet, kept returning to the rhythm of her hips as she stretched out her long legs in an effort to keep stride with the Girtys. Chard began to entertain fantasies about the girl, talking to himself and even managing an occasional answer.

By the time they reached the hollow sycamore by the river, he had succeeded in convincing himself that Bitsy was but a replica of her mother. If his father could sleep with Susan Patterson, then it stood to reason that he, Chard, could sleep with her daughter. He told himself that everyone knew that mothers and daughters were one and the same for, after all, everything a girl learned was nothing but a hand-me-down from her mother. And it was obvious that Susan Patterson believed in freely sharing her favors.

With that thought burning his mind, Chard retrieved his scarlet tunic from the hollow tree and went to the river to wash the mud and paint from his face and legs. He was sick of being an Indian; he was sick of the Girtys; he was sick of Bitsy; and he was beginning to be sick of himself and the childish way they all treated him. Flinging his clothes aside, he waded knee deep into the river and, using handfuls of sand, scrubbed his skin until it shone. Then he splashed into the deeper water to rinse his body.

Realizing the need to give the men privacy while they changed into their hunters' garb, Bitsy walked to the river and gazed upstream in the direction she knew her mother and the flotilla had traveled. She heard a splash, swung her attention downstream, and beheld Chard wading toward the shore. With a startled cry, her face as crimson as a British tunic, she dashed into the security of the dark forest.

For an instant Chard stared after her. Then he, too, was running. He overtook her before she had gone a hundred yards and, slipping his arm around her waist, he snatched the kicking, struggling girl off the ground and crushed her to him.

"Spying on me, were you?" he laughed into her ear.

"I was not," she cried, fighting hard to break his grip.

He freed one hand and used it to force her face around until he could capture her lips with his. Bitsy's mouth was cold and hard and unyielding.

Angrily, he drew away. "Kiss me, damn you," he commanded, staring hard into her great green eyes. "Everyone knows that you frontier girls will tumble in a haymow with any man who asks."

Bitsy's eyes went even wider. Then she clutched him tight and kissed him full on the mouth, her lips warm, soft, inviting.

Chard's heart leaped with passion. She was everything he had expected—no, she was that and more; she was everything he had dreamed. He relaxed his hold and bent to sweep her into his arms. But Bitsy darted to the side and, spinning about, kicked him savagely in his unprotected groin. Chard doubled over and sank to his knees. Then, his face drawn and pinched from a pain far greater than anything he had ever experienced, he slowly rolled onto his side.

Bitsy danced around her would-be seducer in a state of

anger so intense that she didn't know what to do next. She kicked him again, but that wasn't enough; she searched frantically for a stone big enough to kill him, but luckily for Chard, none was handy. She looked for a tree limb to use as a cudgel, but there was none.

She stopped then, and panting as though she were out of breath, she spat: "My papa taught me that trick when I was fourteen years old, to use on people like you who think that frontier girls will jump in the haymow with any man who comes along. Let me tell you something, Mr. High-and-Mighty, you think you are God's gift to womankind, but you are wrong. We so-called frontier girls only jump in the haymow with men we have chosen." Her own words made her so furious she could hardly breathe, for she had never been in a haymow with anyone, at any time. "I wish we were in a haymow right now," she cried. "I'd set it afire and watch it burn your naked little butt to a crisp!"

She kicked him again, but much of her anger had abated. Tossing her head, she stalked off toward the dead sycamore where the Girtys awaited.

If Simon or George was aware of what had just passed, neither showed it. In fact, they appeared to be uncommonly busy with their rifles and shooting gear. After a while, Simon looked up and said: "You didn't kill him, did you?"

Bitsy broke into a gale of laughter. "Simon Girty," she said, "why don't you change sides and fight with us Americans? You're not a bad fellow."

Girty's face turned sour. "Don't you believe it, missy," he said softly. "If'n the ensign had taken you to the ground and raped you to a fare-thee-well, I would not have raised a hand to stop him. Remember that."

Bitsy's smile died on her lips. She slowly nodded her understanding. "I'll remember," she said with equal softness.

Chard moved as gingerly as an old man when he finally made his way down the incline to the waiting canoe. The others had already taken their positions in the craft and were patiently awaiting his appearance.

George Girty sniggered when the ensign was forced to

pick up one foot at a time and place it in the canoe. Then, obviously in great pain, Chard eased his body into a kneeling position in the bottom of the boat. He avoided the faces of his comrades, especially Bitsy.

Simon Girty guided the canoe into midstream and, together with George, dug his paddle into the sluggish Miami.

Chard closed his eyes and fought hard the wave of nausea that threatened to send his head over the side—an act that he would rather have died than given in to. He swallowed several times and thought about England. How he wished he had stayed there.

But Chard's concern about Bitsy's attitude was indeed wasted, for the girl refused to acknowledge his presence in any form or fashion. She spoke lightly to the Girtys, even joked with them occasionally, and once in a while was rewarded with a grunt or a smile for her efforts.

She watched the wilderness slide past and seemed to take great interest in the different types of trees that grew at the river's edge. She laughed quietly when they rounded a bend in the river and startled a black bear and her cubs who were about midstream in their effort to cross the expanse. And she complimented the Girtys on their decision to let the canoe drift until the animals climbed onto the bank, for even in the river, one swipe of a bear's paw could rip a canoe to shreds. But as the day droned on, mile upon mile, not once did she look, speak, or in any way show Chard a moment's notice.

On the other hand, when he was sure he could do so unobserved, Chard watched her every move.

He wanted to apologize for his actions, to assure her he had never behaved that way before, to tell her how proud he was that she had stood strong and unbending in her beliefs. And how foolish and ashamed he felt for assuming she was anything but what she appeared. But he said none of those things, for each time he worked up the courage, his grand British pride choked his throat until not even a whisper could slip past his lips.

They pushed hard into the night, stopping only once and then just long enough to stretch their weary limbs and eat sparingly of the turkey that was left. And as the first rays of the rising sun reflected off the river, they beached the canoe beside the flotilla and headed directly for their respected places, Chard and Bitsy to Judith's tent, the Girtys seeking out Southhampton.

"What did she cost?" were the major's first words, after he had led the Girtys well away from Susan's hearing.

The Girtys crossed their arms, their faces infuriatingly blank and unreadable. "It took all your gold, a knife, and a substitute," said Simon Girty.

Southhampton's mouth fell open. "She's not worth it," he cried. "'Twas a poor bargain."

George Girty's eyes bored into Southhampton like a lance.

"Your orders, Major, were to bring her back at all costs."

"I did not think they would value her so highly," hedged Southhampton, "My God, man, 'twas a king's ransom you paid for the sniveling brat."

Simon Girty considered telling the major that Bitsy was worth every penny he paid, but he was not one to argue, and certainly not with a fool. He spat tobacco juice next to Southhampton's highly polished boot. "We can take her back if you're not satisfied, Major."

Southhampton ignored the threat. "What do you mean, a substitute?"

Girty told Southhampton that the only way they could secure Bitsy's release was to promise the Wyandots a captive in return.

"They will be waiting for the flotilla at Standing Stone, Major," he said. "The whole tribe will be there—and they will expect a prisoner." He gazed warningly at Southhampton. "You'd best be figurin' a way to give them what they want."

With that, the Girtys stalked off toward the forest.

Southhampton watched through narrowed eyes as the brothers made their way into the timber. He was certain that they had intentionally spent all his gold, very probably keeping half for themselves. Aye, they had undoubtedly robbed him. He reminded himself that the moment he no

212

longer needed the Girtys he would see to it that they were locked away somewhere and forgotten. The thought raised a smug smile; rank did have privileges that could be useful.

Judith welcomed Chard with open arms. With Bitsy, however, she was more reserved, asking the girl how she fared and, finally, what had happened to her hand.

Chard interrupted before Bitsy could reply and told Judith the whole story of the girl's brave and quick-minded tricks when she ran the gauntlet. Judith was aghast. She had once seen a full-grown frontiersman run the gauntlet; he had not survived the ordeal.

"Chard makes you sound very heroic," said Judith crisply.

"Not really, ma'am," returned Bitsy, amazed that she was no longer in awe of Judith or, for that matter, of Chard either. "Simon Kenton, a friend of my papa's, ran the gauntlet nine times. The tricks I used were his."

Judith studied the girl thoughtfully. She has changed, Judith told herself, just as I changed, as everyone changes who gets taken by the wilderness and the savage people who live there. No, she thought, 'tis not merely the Indians and the wilderness that have altered her. 'Tis something I can't define. . . . Then Judith's face hardened: it was the way Chard looked at Bitsy and his tone when he had described her heroics . . . almost as though he adored her. Judith looked from one to the other and felt nausea rise up within her. Something had taken place while they were together, something she could only guess at.

"Bitsy," she said, giving way to her suspicions, "I would prefer for you to move back to the captives' quarters."

Bitsy was crushed, but she strove to keep it from her voice. "Ma'am," she said evenly, "I would not wish to stay here if you think I should be elsewhere."

"It would be better for all concerned," said Judith, dropping her eyes.

Bitsy stared at the woman. She did not want to leave Judith. In truth, she had looked forward to confiding in Judith the nightmarish scene she had witnessed at Southhampton's tent. She needed help from someone older and wiser than herself, someone who might explain why her world had gone crazy.

Judith raised her eyes to Chard and looked long at the young man's flushed face. Although he remained silent, it was obvious he was not at all pleased with her resolution. Oh, Chard, she wailed silently, why did you choose Bitsy? Of all the young women you could have, why her? Why? Why?

"Perhaps it would be best if you left immediately, Bitsy," she said. She turned her back to the girl, afraid Bitsy would see the anguish Judith's unjust decision had kindled in her heart.

As if in a trance, Bitsy moved to the corner of the tent and awkwardly rolled her blanket into a ball. Without a word of farewell, she walked silently through the door. Outside the tent she stopped and gazed sightlessly toward the captives' quarters. She dreaded facing the Americans, her people, for the cold reception she had received when she delivered the venison still caused an ache in her breast.

Her anxiety was not unjustified; the faces in the compound were just as she remembered—cold, hard, and unforgiving. What is wrong with you people? she thought in bewilderment. Why do you look at me as though I were trash? I'm Morgan and Susan Patterson's daughter. You all know me.

But even as she moved toward them, they turned their backs on her and busied themselves with their morning chores. Bitsy walked slowly to a spot well away from her countrymen and dropped her blanket to the ground.

She almost wished that Chard and the Girtys had not rescued her. Then she grimaced. *Chard and the Girtys.* She wondered why his name had come to her lips first. Normally, when one spoke of more than one person, the strongest or most significant person's name came first, and Chard was most definitely neither of those.

She scowled, angry with herself for even thinking of Chard when there were so many other things that needed considering—important things, like assuring her mother that she was alive and well, for Bitsy was certain that Susan would be frantic with worry. She must also try to find out why her countrymen so detested her. And she must mix more mud and replaster her hand. She decided to plaster her hand first.

Bitsy dipped her tin cup into the captives' water bucket and walked as far from the Kentuckians as the confines of the compound would allow. Scraping the leaves from under a tree, she mixed the contents of the cup with the soft loam until she had a thick, sticky paste. Doing exactly as Girty had done, she spread a fresh layer of the pungent mud over the existing cast.

It was a tedious task. And by the time she was finished, her good hand ached nearly as badly as her damaged one. Her heart almost broke when she turned from her undertaking to find the Kentuckians watching her every move —yet, not one had offered assistance. Bitsy rinsed her cup and trudged to the end of the line that was forming for the morning ration of flour.

The Ohio shore was still an eighth of a mile distant when Morgan Patterson decided to abandon ship. The canoe was two-thirds full of water and sinking fast.

Using his belt, Patterson quickly strapped his rifle to his chest. Then, careful of his wounded shoulder, he rolled the canoe over.

The Shawnees, watching from the Kentucky bank, yelled, hooted, and shook their fists in the sign of victory as the craft turned upside down and the woodsman sank beneath the swift current. They congratulated themselves on their marksmanship, for they were sure that they had killed the white man. Still, they watched the river to be sure he did not resurface. Yet, even as they strained their far-reaching eyes, they failed to detect Patterson's head when it broke water, or his arm as it slowly and painfully snaked its way across the upturned bottom of the canoe to grasp a handhold in a small cut he had punched in the craft's floor before capsizing.

He didn't attempt to guide the boat, for that would have been an obvious giveaway. Instead, he used it as a buoy, allowing it to drift of its own accord, and occasionally kicking deep under the water in an effort to guide it gradually toward the bank.

It took the better part of two hours before the canoe floated close enough to shore for Patterson to find the bottom and wade into a dense thicket of tall reeds that grew at the water's edge. He turned and peered through the tangle of stems and leaves as the craft drifted with the current. A grimace drew his lips into a thin line for he hated to lose such a fast and effective means of transportation.

Wading farther into the reeds and overhanging brush, he concealed himself and waited. When an hour had passed and no sound had broken the tranquil stillness, Patterson crawled out of the water and pushed himself up the bank and into a patch of dry, sweet-smelling sawgrass that grew in a sunny spot provided by a break in the trees.

He would have liked nothing better than to give in to the exhaustion that was threatening total collapse and bask in the warm sunlight, but he fought that urge, forcing himself instead to slip off his hunting frock and reexamine his shoulder. The torn flesh was ragged and inflamed. He scraped moss from the bark of a black oak tree and sprinkled it over the bloody gash, then turned his attention to a more pressing problem—his rifle. His wound made it almost impossible to draw the ball, clean the weapon, and reload it. The process, which should have taken twenty minutes, took nearly an hour. Even so, Patterson thanked the Lord that he had been able to accomplish the feat at all. Finally giving in to the fatigue that made his eyelids feel as though they supported a fifty-pound weight, he stretched out in the lush grass and slept the morning away.

He was up by the time the sun was directly overhead. Feeling worse than before, he fought his way through cane that grew twelve to fifteen feet tall across the floodplain at the mouth of the Great Miami. He longed for the canoe that had sunk in the Ohio, for even though he would have been forced to travel at night, he could have covered twice the distance on water that he would now have to traverse on land. It took until midafternoon to cross the natural obstacles that the half-mile of floodplain presented and arrive at the mouth of the Great Miami. Still, all in all, he was elated to be heading in the right direction again.

He had gone but a short distance upstream when he found the abandoned campsite used by the British the night Chard had gotten lost. The cold ashes and trampled weeds and bushes indicated that camp was days old—possibly even a week. Patterson's high spirits plummeted. It was heartbreaking to know that while he had been forced to travel so slowly and carefully, Bird's army was floundering along with over a hundred captives and still making two miles to Patterson's one. But for the woodsman there had been no other choice—there still wasn't.

He cradled his rifle in the crook of his fast stiffening wounded arm and continued north, following the twisting, turning Miami River Valley.

He increased his vigilance, his eyes and ears alert, for he was in an alien land. Ohio was the red man's domain, and Patterson's life was on the line with every step he took, day and night. If he was captured, he was dead. It was as simple as that.

The need for extreme caution, combined with his impatient anxiety to find Susan and Bitsy, played havoc with his nerves.

When he topped a rise, he had to force himself to stop and carefully study the terrain below until he was sure the area was uninhabited. And then, when he did decide to go forward, it was all he could do to keep from rushing pell-mell in the direction Bird had taken his family.

CHAPTER
· *13* ·

BITSY, IN A CANOE at the rear of the flotilla which was strung out for nearly half a mile on the Great Miami, turned and gazed downriver. She hadn't expected to see Judith's canoe, for she had heard her tell Chard that she had been ordered to follow behind the others at a respectable distance —which was no less than a quarter of a mile. But Bitsy was disappointed, nevertheless, for she wished she were still with the English lady instead of traveling amid a boat full of loud, foul-talking soldiers.

She trailed her fingers in the current and wondered for the hundredth time what terrible thing she might have done that had turned every living soul she met against her. Even the soldiers in the canoe treated her like a trollop; and Chard had attempted to molest her as though she were a common whore. What is wrong with me? she wondered, closing her eyes and taking a deep, shuddering breath. Do I appear cheap, or easy? Am I not a lady? She turned her face downriver again. She was not searching for Judith's canoe this time, but was looking beyond the horizon—toward Kentucky. "I need you, Papa," she whispered. "You are all I have left."

When the canoes turned toward the shore that evening, Bitsy's depression increased even more. She anticipated another miserable night of ostracism by the other Americans. She was so apprehensive that she waited until last before following the captives up the sloping bank. Even then, Bitsy blushed self-consciously, sure that each time the Americans looked over their shoulders, she was the object of their accusing glances.

Wretched and unhappy, she moved off to herself and spread her blanket, a difficult one-handed chore made worse by a throbbing pain that traveled the entire length of her injured arm. She wished she could wash away the mud cast and flex her fingers—anything to relieve the ache—but Girty had insisted that she leave it on for at least another week.

Sighing deeply, she lay back on the blanket, only to jerk herself erect moments later when an elderly woman, glancing about as though afraid of being seen, squatted nervously beside her.

"If you'd rather no one saw you with me," said Bitsy bitterly, "come back after dark."

The woman shook her head. "I come to say my piece, and I'll say it." She cleared her throat noisily, then continued, "I ain't forgettin' that you give us the only bite of meat we've had since we been took. I come to thank you for that, and no matter that your ma'am has went to the British and become a . . . fancy lady, me and my kin are beholden to you."

Bitsy stared at the woman. "That's ridiculous," she said. "My mama wouldn't betray her own people; she hasn't gone to the British."

A rage began building in the girl greater than any she had yet experienced. She bounded to her feet and marched to the center of the compound that housed the Americans. "You self-righteous bigots, listen to me!" she cried, drawing every face in the camp toward her. "You people are from Martin's Fort. You don't even know my mother or me, and yet you have condemned us without benefit of trial or hearing. Well, you're going to hear me now!" She had their attention, for they were sure she intended to make excuses for her and Susan's actions—but they were wrong.

"When Ruddle's Fort talked of surrender," she said in a loud, clear voice, "my mother begged Captain Ruddle to fight till the end. When he didn't, she and I barricaded ourselves in a cabin. The British tried to scare us out; that didn't work. The Indians tried to burn us out; that didn't work. They had to break down the door and drag us out by the hair of our heads. But we didn't surrender—we never surrendered." She eyed the assembled crowd with disgust. "But you people from Martin's, you who look down your noses at my mama and me, you cried and pleaded and gave up everything you owned . . . and you never fired a shot."

The crowd began to shift uncomfortably and find other things that attracted their attention. But Bitsy was going on: "I can't speak for my mother, for I have no idea why she is doing . . . what she is. But I do know that I will someday find out that she did it because it was the right thing to do . . . because she was protecting someone other than herself. As for my actions, I went to the British because a woman was beaten to within an inch of her life. She needed help." Bitsy's eyes were afire with loathing for the mob that surrounded her. "Do you not remember why she needed help?" When no one answered, the girl continued, "She was whipped with a cat-o'-nine-tails because she was a traitor to the Crown. A traitor! That makes her one of us." She sighed deeply and gazed at the Kentuckians. "But you don't understand that, do you? You don't understand that we are all traitors to the Crown."

Shaking her head sadly, she brushed through the crowd and started toward her blanket.

Several people broke from the mob and trailed after her. "Miss Patterson?" said one. "Wait just a minute."

Bitsy spun to face the small congregation. "Leave me alone," she said, fighting back the tears that had filled her eyes. "Just leave me alone." And at that moment, she wondered how she and Susan could ever have believed themselves fortunate not to have been taken beyond the Ohio with their friends from Ruddle's Fort.

Chard slipped silently through the forest. He was wearing a hunting frock, knee-length leggings, and moccasins. He carried a long Pennsylvania rifle that he had confiscated from Ruddle's Station, one that had belonged to Bitsy Patterson. He had taken great pains at Ruddle's Fort to keep that particular weapon from falling into the hands of the savages. He had also been careful not to let Bitsy know that he possessed the gun. He was afraid that she would misunderstand and think that he, like the other soldiers, had pillaged and plundered when the truth was that he had coveted the beautiful gun because it reminded him of its owner.

He missed Bitsy's presence on the hunt, which surprised him, and he had missed her at his mother's tent. It had made a difference just knowing that someone was with Judith—no, he decided truthfully, it was knowing that *Bitsy* was there, for the girl had been truly concerned for Judith's well-being.

Well, he told himself bitterly, if I hadn't been such a fool, she would still be there . . . and here, hunting with me. He shook his head and lovingly caressed the long-rifle that Bitsy had been carrying the first time he saw her.

"I've never met a more desirable woman," he murmured as he stroked the weapon. "I wanted her the first time I saw her." Then he blushed, remembering her words: "We frontier girls only jump in the haymow with men we have chosen." Obviously, he did not appeal to her. And, really, he could not blame her, coming at her the way he had, as though she were a barroom wench from lower London. He smiled then, knowing she had never seen a barroom, much less set foot in one, and the thought sobered him. It was suddenly clear, the thing about her that had nagged at him ever since he'd first met her. Regardless of what his mother had said about Bitsy being different from the highborn young ladies with whom he was acquainted, in her own way she was as much a lady as any. No, he corrected himself, she was more a lady, because her femininity was genuine, not the coyness that came of being born to the proper family and raised in the right social circles.

A nearby movement suddenly caught Chard's attention. He slipped behind a tree and peered cautiously around the trunk. A hundred yards away, a black bear in search of grubs was clawing at a rotten stump. Raising the rifle, Chard sighted on the beast, then squeezed the trigger. The bear spun angrily, nipping at its hindquarters as if a hornet had flown into its fur. Rearing to its hind legs, the beast raised its long snout and sniffed in all directions. Catching wind of rifle smoke or perhaps spying the man trying frantically to reload, the animal released a terrible roar and lumbered toward the startled hunter with earth-shaking strides.

Attempting to watch the bear and reload at the same time, Chard missed the muzzle of his rifle with his powder charge, pouring the granules over his shaking hand and into

221

the ferns below. When he looked up, the bear was so close he could see the pain and hatred in its piglike eyes.

Chard's first impulse was to flee the vicious teeth that were snapping together like the jaws of a steel trap. Then he thought of Bitsy's reaction when he had missed the buck that first time they had hunted together, and something hardened inside him. Something made him stand firm and gave him the strength and courage to face the furious beast.

With a speed and force that was terrifying, the bear lunged at Chard, but the ensign had anticipated its move and at the last moment darted behind the tree. The momentum of the charging animal sent it crashing past. It skidded to a halt, wheeled, and reared to its hind legs, looking down its muzzle at the man who had stepped into the open. Chard raised his dueling pistol, took careful aim, and shot the bear through the throat. With a mighty roar that shattered the forest's silence, the beast collapsed and lay still.

Chard's knees were weak and shaking. He eased down beside the black, shaggy mound of fur and took a deep, shuddering breath, the first he had taken since the ordeal began. When the enormity of what he had done hit him, Chard jumped to his feet and shouted triumphantly at the heavens. He had killed a bear! With a light heart and lighter feet, he raced toward the camp. Going directly to the captives' area, he found Bitsy easily, since she was isolated from the other Kentuckians.

"There will be food for all of us, Bitsy!" he shouted proudly as he approached.

The girl neither smiled nor spoke. Instead, she turned her back on the exhilarated young ensign and stared at the gathering darkness.

"I thought you would be happy," he said, circling around so she would be forced to look at him. "I killed a bear, all by myself."

"Congratulations," she said dryly.

"Look here, Bitsy." He caught her arm to keep her from turning aside. "I want to share the meat with you . . . and the captives. . . ."

"No, you look here," interrupted the girl as she broke from his grasp. "If you think the fact that you have food changes anything, you are mistaken. Your father tried to buy my mother with venison. . . . Now, here you are offering bear meat. Get out of my sight, Chard. . . . And stay out!"

"Very well," he said, hurt replacing his elation. "I shall honor your request. In the future, madam, I shall avoid you like the plague . . . that you are!"

As he stalked away, he told himself that her angry reaction was of no consequence, but it was a subdued, joyless young hunter who ordered several Kentuckians to bring in the meat.

Susan refilled her cup, spilling a good portion of rum on her bare thighs. She had been drinking since sundown, some four hours earlier.

She grinned drunkenly at Southhampton. "Would you like some more?" She jerked the bottle toward him, sloshing rum on his immaculate white breeches.

Southhampton jumped to his feet and brushed angrily at the stain. "You drunken bitch," he whispered. "'Tis all you ever do anymore. From morning till night, you stay befuddled . . . and naked."

Susan laughed bitterly. "You encouraged it. Thought it was amusing, remember?" She took a sip from the cup. "Your friends thought it was high fun to get me drunk."

Southhampton slapped the cup from her hand, flinging its contents against the tent flaps.

"Go to bed and sleep it off," he commanded, eyeing her with distaste.

Susan toasted Southhampton, then tipped the bottle to her lips.

"You slut," he breathed. "You common slut. Drinking straight from the bottle like a woman without any breeding or refinement. How dare you be so brazen in my presence?"

Susan almost choked on the fiery liquid as the irony of his words penetrated her rum-soaked mind. Then she burst out in the high-pitched, frenzied laughter of the intoxicated.

Disgusted, Southhampton whipped aside the tent flaps and strode into the night.

Susan turned the bottle up and drank several large swallows. Then, staring glassy-eyed at the partially closed flaps, she drew the bottle over her head and hurled it at the canvas curtains.

"Without breeding indeed!" she shouted at the empty tent. She was the best-bred whore in camp—just ask anybody, any man you wished, for she had been with them all. She swayed groggily to the rear of the tent where Southhampton kept his private stock. Selecting a full bottle, she twisted out the cork and drank deeply.

Staggering to Southhampton's field desk, she threw back the lid and withdrew Judith's silver-rimmed looking glass. Holding tight to the desk, she eased herself slowly to the cot. Then, hesitantly, almost fearfully, she studied her image in the mirror—her high-piled black hair; her sad, red-rimmed puffy eyes; her sunken cheeks; her pouting, sensual lips.

I look the part of the whore, she decided. I even feel that way inside. I've grown to accept it, even to embrace it. I *am* the best-bred whore in camp—just look at me.

She turned the small hand mirror in all directions so she could see, on each portion of her naked body, all the ugly bruises administered by her lovers, for she almost reveled in hurt and pain. It was punishment for the wanton role she had been forced to play. Then she moved the mirror slowly down her body, past her bruised and swollen nipples, past her flat stomach, until it reflected her most intimate places.

Dropping back upon the cot, she flung the mirror to the floor and laughed bitterly, the terrible sound of one who is condemned, for the mirror had confirmed her most feared suspicions: she was infected and diseased.

While they were cooking bear steaks, Judith realized Chard's pearl-handled knife was missing. When she questioned him, Chard explained that the Wyandot chief had taken it in return for Bitsy's release.

Judith was disappointed that Chard had given up the knife; it showed in her voice. "That was the knife Ivy used to stab Morgan Patterson. It nearly killed him."

"Then 'tis only fitting that it should buy his daughter's life in return," the ensign said. "I'm not sorry that it is gone, Mother. And you shouldn't be either."

Judith smiled at her son's generosity, but she could not feel guilty for wishing Chard had refused to give up the knife. It had been passed down through her family for generations, and she had taken it for granted that Chard would continue the tradition.

"Tell me how it nearly ended Patterson's life," prompted Chard as he turned the spit, sending the grease from the bear steaks sizzling into the open fire.

Judith drew her knees up under her chin and smoothed out her dress.

"At that time," she began, "the dagger belonged to my handmaiden, Ivy. She had accompanied me to the new world."

Chard nodded, watching his mother intently. He knew that Ivy was his mother's childhood companion and later her abigail. He also knew that Ivy was the daughter of the old black woman who still oversaw the management of his grandfather's house.

"Anyway," continued Judith, "Ivy and I were separated from General Braddock's army and became lost in the forest. Morgan Patterson found us and had all the best intentions of returning us to the column." Judith laughed and looked into Chard's anxious face. "Ivy thought he was an Indian, and in truth he did resemble one, with his long black hair and painted face." Judith sighed, remembering that day so long ago. "So Ivy naturally mistook him for a savage. She caught him completely off guard and drove her dagger through his thigh. He nearly died from loss of blood."

"She attacked Morgan Patterson?" Chard was in awe.

"Aye," answered Judith. "Nearly killed him, too. And while we worked to save Patterson's life, the army ran off and left us."

Chard's brows drew together. "The army left you in the wilderness . . . ?"

Judith nodded. "They did."

"Wasn't Father with the army?"

Judith glanced away, refusing to meet Chard's eyes. "He was there, Chard. He said later that he had sent Morgan Patterson to find us."

Chard blanched. "Well, after all," he replied uncertainly, "Father was an officer in His Majesty's forces. Perhaps he couldn't leave his command."

"Perhaps," said Judith. She took a deep breath and let it out slowly. "Well, 'twas a long time ago—and 'tis best forgotten."

Chard took Judith's hand. "I'm sorry to ask you to recall such painful memories, Mother. I know you hate to think of that awful time."

Judith smiled at her son. "Not all of them were bad times, Chard. But to be quite honest, most of the time it was a nightmare." Judith squeezed Chard's hand. "Ivy used that same dagger when an Indian had Patterson down and was in the process of killing him. Ivy cut the savage's head off."

"Good Lord!" said Chard. "Ivy must have been quite a woman."

"She was the best," answered Judith slowly, "right alongside Susan Spencer Patterson."

"Mrs. Patterson was there, too?"

"Aye," said Judith, with a faraway look in her eyes. "And two finer women never drew breath than Susan and Ivy."

Chard drew Judith to him and embraced her. "There's one more name you need to add to the list," he said, kissing her cheek. "You, too, are the best."

Judith stiffened at the compliment. She wondered what her son would think if he knew the truth of those days so long forgotten.

"I believe the meat is ready," she said quickly.

While Chard and Judith savored the taste of hot bear steaks, Morgan Patterson lay beneath a blow-down and dined on water-soaked jerked venison. He had spent the entire day traveling the east bank of the Miami in search of the second British campsite. Then, just before dark, he had discovered the wide trail up the far bank. Grimacing, he had studied the river, wondering how he was going to manage the crossing.

Hours later, long after the venison was gone, he was still mulling over the problem of crossing the river. Finally, his mind rebelled from sheer strain and drifted to pleasanter thoughts. He saw Susan's soft smile and warm, friendly eyes, heard her easy, laughing voice. He remembered the nights when she came to him; the special feeling he always had when they made love. It was the feeling God intended for two people who were meant for each other. And what made it so touchingly beautiful was that she was as much in love with him as he was with her.

Patterson's face became determined. God had brought him and Susan together. God had given them Bitsy. And he would be damned if he would let man destroy what God had created.

He sighed then. He was well aware that since the beginning of time man had jealously set out to destroy what the Creator had molded with such careful skill and understanding. And if the Almighty Himself was unable to curb man's wanton carnage, what made Patterson—a weak, sinful mortal—think he could succeed where the Lord had failed?

Patterson gripped his rifle savagely. There was one avenue open to him that the Creator seemed hesitant to pursue—and it was a far cry from turning the other cheek. If God, in his weakness, watched passively while the British triumphed over trusting souls like Susan and Bitsy who believed in Him, then Patterson, who in essence lived by the writings of the Old Testament, would take matters into his own hands. An "eye for an eye" would be an understatement. He would, without conscience or mercy, kill his enemies until either he or they were wiped from the face of the earth. And that was God's own truth.

When the flotilla reached Standing Stone, they found the entire Wyandot tribe waiting silently on the banks of the Miami.

Hundreds of hastily erected wigwams covered the area, and the British were hard put to find decent accommodations for their tents and gear.

Simon Girty sought out Southhampton and inquired whether the major had chosen the unfortunate American who would take Bitsy's place at the stake.

"Damn it, Girty," said Southhampton. "Go choose one of the bloody bastards yourself."

Simon Girty eyed the major with loathing. "Kill your own snakes, Southhampton. And you'd better give them somebody quick, or you'll have the whole Wyandot nation after your pretty powdered wig."

Southhampton turned toward Judith's tent. It would be so easy . . . so damned easy.

Sighing in disgust, he spun on his heel and stalked to the captives' area and hailed the first man he saw.

"You there? What's your name?"

"Ravencraft, Major," said the Kentuckian respectfully.

"I've a chore for you, my good man. Follow me, if you please."

Ravencraft fell in behind the major. He walked with his head held high, his Kentucky pride worn like a badge, straight to the Wyandot chief and the stake the Indians had set in the middle of the clearing.

Ravencraft's skin crawled and his breathing became shallow when it became apparent that he was being delivered to the savages.

"You British son of a bitch," he breathed fiercely to Southhampton. "I pray your bones will burn in hell from this day forward."

"Your bones will burn in hell before this evening is over, sir," returned Southhampton, "and all your traitorous friends can watch them."

The Indians caught the Kentuckian's wrists and wrenched them behind his back, binding them tightly with rawhide. They ripped away his clothes, then smeared a mixture of bear grease and charcoal over his face until the whites of his eyes shone like two holes in a hangman's mask. Without further ado, they dragged him to the tall, thick stake and slipped a rawhide noose around his neck, tying the loose end to the pole.

"What's going on here?" inquired Chard, who had just approached the outer circle of spectators and stood watching while Indians of all ages gathered brush and twigs, which they stacked in a large circle around the naked white man.

"They're going to burn 'em a Kentuckian tonight," said George Girty, grinning. "In place of your sweetheart."

"What do you mean, in place of Bitsy?"

"It was part of the trade," said Girty. "Your daddy agreed to trade Ravencraft for the girl. You didn't think that silly little knife of yours bought her freedom, did you? Not even you could be that stupid."

Chard didn't know he was going to hit George Girty. It was more a reflex than a planned assault. Nevertheless, the blow left the renegade lying flat on his back staring blankly at the sky-high trees overhead.

George Girty shook his head to clear his dizziness, then climbed slowly to his feet. He held a tomahawk in one hand, a skinning knife in the other.

Chard could see the intent to kill that danced in the renegade's eyes, but, strangely, it didn't bother him. He had had his fill of ridicule and snide comments from scum like George Girty. He was through with disrespect and mockery. He was a man, and he was well aware that he had been behaving like a child. But those days were over.

He smiled crookedly at Girty and took a step toward the man. Girty crouched low and made ready to cut the young officer into doll rags.

A squad of red-coated soldiers with fixed bayonets rushed to Chard's aid, surrounding the two men and advancing slowly toward the renegade. "Stand firm!" ordered Chard.

The soldiers drew to a halt, bayonets low and steady. "Shall we place this man under arrest, sir?" said the corporal of the guard.

"'Tis a personal matter, Corporal," returned Chard, holding Girty with a level gaze. "Mr. Girty is free to go."

Girty drew himself to full height and slipped his weapons through his belt. Without a word, he pushed through the ring of soldiers.

Chard followed him with his eyes, appraising Girty's heavy shoulders and narrow waist. He believed he was a match for the man physically, but he had neither the experience of hand-to-hand combat nor the inclination to kill that would be necessary if he intended to confront George Girty. He knew that he had surprised Girty when he hit him. Otherwise he would never have gotten close enough to lay a hand on the man. Chard made his mind up that if he was forced to fight Girty again, he would shoot the man dead and be through with it.

He glanced again at the ring of kindling the Indians were placing around Ravencraft. He wondered if Bitsy was aware that her fellow Kentuckian was destined to die a horrible death in her stead. No, he thought, she would never allow such a thing. He dreaded looking toward the captives' quarters, and yet he could not help himself. His gaze met Bitsy's. Along with the other Kentuckians, she had witnessed his fight with Girty. They stood for a long moment, looking deep into each other's eyes, before the girl turned and disappeared into the crowd.

Chard contemplated the look she had given him. Was it wonder or fear for his life? Probably neither, he decided. But at least it wasn't the jeering, disgusted glance she normally wore—and most important, it was not the look of one who would let an innocent man burn to death without knowing the true reason.

Sighing with relief, Chard squared his shoulders and hurried off to find Captain Bird.

Captain Bird, in deep thought, hands locked behind his back, took a turn around the interior of his marquee. "Major Southhampton assures me that if we do not give the Wyandot a prisoner, we will surely lose them as allies." He eyed Chard stonily. "We can't afford to antagonize these savages, Ensign."

The muscles in Chard's jaws were knotted cords. It was beyond his understanding how an officer of the king's army would be intimidated by a horde of bloodthirsty Indians, regardless of their professed loyalty to the British cause. The only thing that kept Chard from accusing Bird of cowardice was that the captain was ignorant of Bitsy's involvement in the arrangement. And that only strengthened Chard's belief that Bird was unfit to represent the Crown or command His Majesty's forces.

Chard's unrelenting expression made the captain blush. "'Tis not to my liking, Ensign. But we are at a disadvantage as long as we are in this damnable wilder ness. I swear to you it would be different if we were at Detroit."

Chard had to bite his tongue to keep from criticizing Bird for his inability to show responsibility and leadership.

"Captain Bird," he said, barely hiding his disgust, "have you forgotten, sir, that Ravencraft is a British prisoner of war? It is our sworn duty, sir, to protect him."

"It is my duty, Ensign, to return this command to Detroit without incident. That is my first and only consideration."

The conversation was cut short; the Indians had begun their ceremony. Drums sounded their monotonous rhythm. The eerie wailing chants of the Wyandot women joined the beat, and the shuffling of hundreds of bare feet grew to a thundering crescendo. It was as though Ravencraft had stepped into the very bowels of hell and was witnessing Satan's demonical welcome.

"I've never heard anything like that in my life," breathed Bird. He pushed aside the flaps and peered white-faced toward the Indian encampment.

Chard eyed the commander with a mixture of scorn and pity. Bird was out of his element. He should have stayed safe and sound in Detroit or, better yet, in England.

"I ask the captain's permission to be excused, sir," said Chard, nodding in a curt bow. Not waiting for dismissal, Chard rushed past the captain to intercept his father, who, with Lieutenant Clarke, was walking toward his marquee.

"Father," he called, "may I have a word with you, sir?"

"What is it?" said Southhampton irritably. "I'm rather in a hurry."

"It's about the Indian hostage, sir." Chard looked deep into his father's face, afraid he already knew the answer. "George Girty said you traded Ravencraft for Bitsy. Is that true, sir?"

Southhampton caught the ensign's arm and propelled him away from the tent.

"Damn you. I took great pains not to upset Mrs. Patterson with the fact that her daughter was missing. And now you blurt it to the whole world."

Susan, draped in a blanket, staggered through the tent

231

flaps and blinked her unfocused eyes at Chard. "Did I hear you say something about Bitsy?"

"You're drunk, my dear," came Southhampton's quick interruption. "Go back into the tent before someone sees you."

"Not until I find out what the ensign said. Is something wrong with Bitsy?"

Susan swayed toward Chard, but Clarke barred her way. "Get back inside, woman, or you will get a beating you won't forget."

Chard's brows came together in anger. He flung his father's hand aside and stepped to Clarke. "Just who in hell are you to be threatening this lady with a beating, Lieutenant?"

"I'll have you in irons for insubordination, Ensign," said Clarke. "You are interfering with an order given by a superior officer."

"Chard," cried Southhampton with bulging eyes, "you'd best remember your rank and position. Lieutenant Clarke is quite correct. You are insubordinate, and you most definitely are impeding a direct order. You have overstepped your authority, sir, yes, indeed."

"There's a hell of a lot going on here that's not military, Father," came Chard's bristling reply as he turned to Susan. "Your daughter was captured by Indians, ma'am," he said, ignoring the thunderous faces of Southhampton and Clarke, "but we got her back. She's safe with your fellow Kentuckians."

Susan lurched toward Southhampton, almost falling in the process. Righting herself, she demanded, "Why didn't you tell me that my daughter was in danger? Why didn't you tell me!"

"Get her inside," said Southhampton to Clarke. "And you, Ensign, are under arrest. You will present yourself to the sergeant of the guard immediately. Do you understand, sir?"

Chard drew himself to full height and bowed to his father. "Yes, Major, I understand perfectly."

Clarke stiff-armed Susan toward Southhampton's tent, making her stumble and fall. Catching her roughly by the arm, he snatched her to her feet and propelled her on tiptoe through the canvas flaps. He followed her inside.

As Chard moved off to report to the sergeant of the guard, a muffled scream filtered through the thin walls of his father's tent. He gritted his teeth and kept walking.

Confined to quarters, Chard stood just inside his tent and watched with frustration as the shuffling, milling Indians worked themselves into a frenzy. Even though night had fallen, the area was lighted almost as bright as day by scores of huge bonfires.

He wondered how Bird, or his father, or anyone who considered himself a Christian could simply turn his back on a fellow human being, a former Englishman, and rationalize such behavior. He shook his head. Blundering as his attempt may have been, at least he had tried to stop Ravencraft's torture. Chard felt a pang of guilt shoot through him; he had not tried hard enough.

Ravencraft, still tethered to the pole by a thong around his neck, dodged and darted as far as the leash would permit in an attempt to avoid the thrusts and jabs of the flaming pointed sticks and white-hot lance heads the Indian women and children took great pleasure in forcing just beneath the surface of his skin. They were expert at inflicting tremendous pain while not doing enough damage to kill the poor wretch, who writhed and screamed and endured, when he wished to God he would die.

The torture increased as the Indians' excitement intensified. Warriors, their muskets loaded with nothing but powder, pushed the muzzles against the Kentuckian's naked body and pulled the trigger. Ravencraft bellowed with rage and pain as the black granules of ignited powder burned deep into his flesh, making it smolder like charred cloth. Had he been able, he would have joyfully loaded the weapons with shot or ball, for he wanted his torment to end. Small children ventured close, slashed the man's skin with razor-sharp knives, and then darted safely away to hoot and jeer and dance delightedly as his blood ran in crimson rivulets down his pale flesh.

Night brought a cool, sharp breeze. And when the moon rose, it was hidden behind a mass of boiling thunderheads. Chard raised his face to the sky. Lord, he prayed, if

233

you ever intended for it to rain, you have my permission to let it do so immediately.

The Indians, too, felt the weather change. They hurriedly snatched flaming staves from the campfires and cast them into the brush that surrounded Ravencraft's pole. As the kindling caught and flamed up, the tortured Kentuckian bounded awkwardly around the stake until the tightly wound leash forced him to backtrack. Yet, no matter how fast or hard he ran, he was unable to evade the blistering heat that burned away his body hair and seared his skin like a piece of raw meat. He lurched and howled, sounding more animal than human, until the Americans, British, and Canadians watching his torment wished he would hurry and die and end his ghastly suffering.

Perhaps Chard's prayer was answered, or perhaps the Creator had had his fill of the inhuman torture, for without so much as a roll of thunder the heavens opened and pounded the Ohio country with a downpour of such ferocity that white and red men alike were forced to flee for cover. Ravencraft sagged against the sizzling pole and sobbed his thanks to God. And Chard, the only person who had not sought sanctuary, stood outside his tent and raised his drenched face to the heavens. "If this is a man," he cried, pointing at Ravencraft, "then man is a strange-looking thing, God." And indeed it was true, for Ravencraft had been burned and butchered until he no longer resembled a human being—but he was alive.

"Can't you do anything with her?" said Clarke, flinging his hand toward Susan, who lay huddled in a corner of the marquee, crying softly. "She stays so drunk most of the time she don't even know what in bloody hell goes on around her."

"'Tis depressing," admitted Southhampton with a sigh. "But we're stuck with her whether we like it or not. She knows enough to get us both flogged or maybe even hanged. Bird would jump at the chance to court-martial me. He needs a scapegoat for the mess this expedition has turned into."

Clarke nodded his agreement, then looking at Susan, he clenched his fingers into a tight fist.

Southhampton laid a restraining hand on the lieutenant's arm. "You're going to hit her too hard one of these days, my friend."

"I would be doing the world a bloody favor," said Clarke, shaking his fist at Susan. "She's nothing but a worthless slut."

Susan cringed harder against the tent wall. Her lips were puffed and bleeding, and both jaws ached with such pain that she could barely open her mouth. She could not stand another beating. She closed her eyes and listened to the rain drum harshly against the canvas. Perhaps Southhampton and Clarke would demand her services tonight. Rain did that to people. She hoped they would desire her. It was by far the lesser of the two evils, for they couldn't hurt her any more that way: she felt thoroughly debased. But the beatings, which were becoming more frequent with each passing day, were a torture she could not endure much longer. She could hardly breathe without coughing, and a lacerating pain had developed deep in her chest. The only thing that eased her suffering was to drink herself into a stupor. And that was self-defeating, for the more she drank to ease the pain, the more they beat her for being drunk.

She listened to the downpour. The rhythm of the rain soothed her, and her thoughts drifted to a day long ago, and a cabin on the Licking River in Kentucky. It had been raining then, too, raindrops tapping on a split-shingle roof. She saw Morgan Patterson sitting before the hearth with five-year-old Bitsy on his knee, and they were laughing together while Susan finished baking bread for the evening meal. Those were good days. The Indians weren't stirred up, the British were across the ocean, Kentucky was a wild, beautiful land, and she and Morgan were happily in love. They still were. Or at least she was.

Her undying devotion to Morgan Patterson was the one thing Southhampton couldn't ruin or spoil. It would endure as long as she drew breath. She wished she could tell Morgan that, could somehow let him know that she would always be his no matter who possessed her body or what Southhampton said about "birds of a feather." She cried then, for she would never be his again. Even if he found her, she could never go back to the carefree, happy days of before, because she would never be the same person she had been before coming to Southhampton. "You can't go back," she whispered aloud, "because the empty space that is created when you leave shrinks with time. And no matter how hard you work at it, you can't ever wriggle back into that space."

"What's she mumbling about?" said Clarke, cutting an angry glance at the pitiful woman huddled in the dark corner of the tent.

"Forget her," Southhampton grunted, lifting the tent flap and gazing at the violent storm. "I think her mind has gone to hell along with her body."

CHAPTER

· *14* ·

CROSSING THE TWO-HUNDRED-YARD-WIDE Miami River the next morning presented a real problem for Patterson. Because of his wound, he was unable to wade in and swim the tributary as he would normally have done. In fact, the shoulder was so stiff and sore that he couldn't even swing his hatchet to fashion a raft.

So he hunted along the banks of the stream until he located a place where limbs and driftwood had created a log jam close to the bank. The first jam was unproductive. But in the second was a log some four feet long and eighteen inches in diameter, wedged securely in the tangled branches of a sycamore whose roots had eroded and toppled the tree into the river.

Walking carefully down the trunk, which lay precariously between the bank and the stream, Patterson made his way to the tangled debris. He hung his shot pouch, powder horn, and rifle in the fork of a branch and, leaning close to the water, chopped away at the limbs and snags that held the small log in place.

It was time-consuming, dangerous work. His wounded shoulder prevented him from grasping anything to counterbalance his weight when he bent to wield the hatchet. And even with his legs braced against an upright limb, it was still hazardous to use the small ax with any authority. But with each stroke, the log came that much closer to being free.

Sweat streamed down his forehead and into his eyes. Still he chopped away, afraid to sacrifice even the small amount of time it would take to wipe his face. He was well aware that the sound of his hatchet would carry far on the open river.

When the log finally broke loose, it came free so unexpectedly that Patterson lost his balance and nearly plunged headlong into the current. Flipping his leg around the upright, he hung there, watching with dismay as the log drifted almost beyond reach. Taking a deep breath, he leaned far out and made a desperate thrust with his hatchet. The blade struck the edge of the wood and bit deep. Patterson's knuckles stood out like knobs, and he gritted his teeth to keep from moaning, for the effort required to drive the blade into the moving target had ripped open his partially knitted shoulder wound.

Moving carefully, he inched into the water. Then, dragging the log after him, he side-stroked the few feet it took to put him in shallow water. He hurriedly retrieved his shooting gear and strapped the cargo to the log with his belt. Then, driving his hatchet into the log beside the shot pouch, he wedged his rifle tightly between the two and pushed the make-shift float into the current.

By the time he reached the distant bank, it was all he could do to haul himself out of the water and pull the log after him. But he knew that no matter how tired he might be, he must push on; the British would not be resting, not for one minute. He retrieved his rifle and crawled on his hands and knees up the steep incline, dragging his plunder behind him. After a long interval, ages it seemed, he finally found the strength to push himself erect.

Keeping abreast of the river, Patterson worked his way north in search of the next British campsite—which he prayed would be on his side of the river.

The bivouac areas were no trouble to locate. Even though they were only used one night and part of a day, he could smell them a mile away. A camp with over three hundred people and no latrines would always be easy to find. He reached the abandoned site as the sun was fading. After studying it thoroughly and finding nothing he could definitely attribute to either Susan or Bitsy, he pushed deeper into the woods to search out a shelter for the night.

Turning in all directions, Patterson sniffed the air like a wolf. He could smell the change in the breeze that spoke of

238

rain even though the skies showed no sign. With that in mind, he searched for another blow-down like the one he had slept under the night before. But short of traveling a half-mile or more across the floodplain to the hills that flanked the valley, he could find nothing suitable. So, as darkness fell, he crawled beneath the thick, matted foliage of a fir tree whose interlaced branches almost swept the ground, and stretched out on the soft needles. He tried to go immediately to sleep, for he was sure it would be a short rest.

He was right.

It was the very same downpour that had saved Ravencraft's life. With galelike force, it whipped the fir tree first this way then that, forcing Patterson to fuse himself closely against the trunk in an attempt to stay dry. But the violence of the late spring storm was such that the thick overhead branches quickly became saturated with water. Drips appeared, soon turning into full-fledged streams that seemed bent on searching out and falling directly on Patterson. And even though he kept the lock of his rifle wedged tightly between his thighs, with the tail of the hunting frock wrapped around the lock in an effort to keep the flash pan dry, he was unsure if the gun would weather the storm in firing condition.

He lay there, wet and miserable, and hoped that Susan and Bitsy had been given shelter; surely the British would see to it that the captives were as comfortable as possible.

While Patterson huddled under the sodden fir tree and waited for daylight, a Wyandot hunter who had lost the woodsman's trail at the mouth of the Miami the day before was making his way through the rain-lashed forest toward the British camp at Standing Stone, forty miles away. The Indian ran through the downpour in high spirits, for he felt sure the man he had been following would prove to be easy prey for a war party who knew the country as the Wyandot did.

It would be no trouble to search him out and take his scalp.

* * *
239

Patterson was dead wrong in his assumption that the captives had been given shelter.

Neither Bitsy nor any of the Kentuckians had slept a wink that night. Those lucky enough to possess blankets had crouched like animals beneath them, their lips turning blue, their bodies shivering under the sopping cover as the cold rain lashed the countryside. Out of pure misery, Bitsy finally climbed to her feet and walked the perimeter of the compound in an effort to preserve what little body heat she still retained. She drew up short when she noticed movement in the Indian sector. It took her a moment to realize they were breaking camp. It was eerie the way they ghosted about, striking shelters and preparing for the trail without a sound, not even a whimper from a child.

She wondered if Ravencraft was still alive. She doubted it.

A party of warriors broke from the main group and trotted toward the river, their silhouettes flickering like will-o'-the-wisps through the predawn darkness. A hunting party, she assumed. Without a murmur, the tribe filtered past the sleeping British tents and vanished into the misty wilderness. Bitsy breathed a sigh of relief. Indians unnerved her with their animallike ways and snakelike movements.

Putting them from her mind, she continued her pacing, her water-soaked blanket heavy about her shoulders, her teeth chattering uncontrollably.

As full dawn fought its way through the dripping haze, the world began to come alive. Soldiers stumbled from their tents, stretching and cursing and tending to their morning duties. They were dumbfounded to find the Indians gone, especially since no one had heard even the softest whisper when they took Ravencraft and slipped away.

"The Wyandot considered it a bad omen, that rain," said Simon Girty to his brother as he studied the empty area where the camp had been.

"This whole venture is a bad omen, Simon," returned George. "Maybe we should slip away ourselves."

"Can't do that, George. Bird has ordered me to cut

240

across country and see to it that Lorimer is prepared to feed the army when it gets to his store." Simon grinned widely. "You ain't gone soft, have you, George? That young pup didn't slap you down and skeer you into leavin', did he?"

George's face clouded. "Knocked the shit outa me. I ain't forgettin' it, Simon. I'll kill him for that."

"Maybe," agreed Simon.

George studied his brother's profile. "You're the one who's gone soft, Simon. You've taken a likin' to that boy. I ain't never seen you do that before."

"He's got the makin's."

"He's too old to train right, Simon. Anyway, he's too highbrow. It would be a waste of time."

"Killed that bear, didn't he?"

George snorted and looked hard at his brother. "Any fool worth his salt would've knowed better than to take a hundred-yard shot with an untried rifle gun. It was pure ole luck that he hit that bear at all, much less killed it."

Simon raised his eyebrows. "He dropped that bear with a hand pistol at five yards, George. That took guts."

George Girty scowled with surprise. He had not heard that part of the story. It was something to consider.

"Ain't but five men I know who's got that kind of nerve," continued Simon. "Boone, Patterson, Kenton, and you and me." He glanced at his brother. "On second thought, ain't but four men, George. . . . I would have run."

George laughed gruffly. "That jest leaves three, then. A hand pistol, you say?"

Simon nodded. "Blowed its head off."

George pursed his thin lips. "Makes no never mind, Simon. He'll never live long enough to make a woodsman, 'cause if'n I meet him in the timber, he ain't comin' out."

"'Tis none of my affair," said Simon without interest. Then, rising to his feet, he caught up his rifle and stepped lightly down the trail the Indians had taken. He didn't like conversation, not even with his brother.

He frowned, thinking about George's accusation that he was getting soft. Perhaps George was right. Both Chard and Bitsy had impressed him with their young and vigorous headlong dash after life and everything it offered. They might even find whatever it is they're lookin' for, he decided. That thought prompted another. He was thirty-nine years old and had never married. He was past his prime and had not sired a legitimate offspring.

His mind sprang to Catharine Malott, a white captive with the Delaware tribe in upper Ohio. She was a comely woman, aye, comely indeed. Almost as pretty as Susan Patterson. His frown deepened. Perhaps Catharine's beauty would be a drawback? It seemed that handsome women had trouble being faithful to their husbands. Still, he needed a wife, and he was sure the Delaware would trade Catharine to him.

"Girty?" shouted a private, running down the path from the campsite. "Captain Bird wants to see you, sir. He sent me to catch you before you left for Lorimer's."

Girty leaned on his long-gun and waited for the soldier to catch up. "You go back and tell the captain that I've already gone. Tell him you looked high and low and couldn't find me."

"I can't do that, sir. He said for me to bring you back, said it was important."

Girty scowled at the private, who stepped backward quickly.

"I'm just following orders, Mr. Girty."

Girty sighed. He did not want to answer any foolish inquiries about why the Wyandot had left or what would be the fate of the army if the Indians blamed the British for the rain that had saved Ravencraft's life, or the hundreds of other asinine questions that he knew the captain would ask, but he saw no way to escape. Disgustedly, he shouldered his rifle and marched back the way he had come.

"I'm goin' to be travelin' fast and hard, Captain," argued Girty, suppressing a growing anger. "And if Lorimer ain't got enough provisions for the army and these prisoners of yours—which he ain't—then I'm going to be huntin' game even faster and harder. I don't need no tenderfoot ensign taggin' along for me to have to look after, sir."

"I appreciate your predicament, Girty. But I must consider the morale of the troops, and the good of this expedition. Ensign Southhampton's arrest was the worst thing Major Southhampton could have ordered, what with everyone already upset by the burning of that prisoner, what's his name." Girty didn't answer, so Bird continued, "I want the ensign away from here. Give the major time to cool down. So I am asking you to take Chard with you to Lorimer's. I would consider it a favor."

"I ain't no nursemaid, Captain," said Girty, turning to leave. "I want you to remember that. I'll take the ensign with me, but he's on his own."

"Very good," returned Bird, pleased with the bargain. He wished he could dispose of all his problems so easily. "Tell the sergeant of the guard that I've ordered the ensign paroled to your custody. Good luck on your hunt, Girty."

Girty spit tobacco juice out of the side of his mouth and eyed Bird with distaste. The man was disgusting, not fit to lead men. Nor were his junior officers any better, for they only increased the confusion and discontent, especially Major Southhampton, who seemed bent on destroying everything he touched, his family included.

Of all the officers in His Majesty's army, decided Girty, Fort Detroit had drawn the dregs. The whole lot of them were pompous, overconfident fools—and the ones who weren't fools were arrested for insubordination or some other equally silly reason, because only a fool would follow a fool and keep his mouth shut.

Bitsy watched as Chard and Simon Girty trotted toward the forest. She thought that Chard glanced in her direction just before passing from sight, but in the dim light she wasn't sure. It bothered her, his going off with Girty, for although she had to admit a grudging respect for the renegade, she knew he was dangerous and untrustworthy.

Shrugging, she told herself Chard was a grown man and could look out for himself. But she didn't really believe it. 'Tis his business, she told herself again. If he wants to go traipsing off through the wilds with people like Simon Girty, why should I get upset about it?

But she was upset. She liked Chard, in spite of what she had said the day he killed the bear. She would never forgive him for his disgraceful conduct or for the pain he had caused by thinking her easy prey, but she still liked him. The conflict tore at her young heart like the talons of an eagle, leaving it ripped and bleeding and open to the world. The worst part was that she had no idea how to stop liking him.

"Time to move out!" The command rang loud and clear in the heavy morning air that was already turning sticky and hot, promising a steaming, sultry day.

Bitsy and the other wretched Kentuckians made a slow exodus toward the waiting flotilla, their steps labored, not only because of the long, oppressing night, but because of the horrible event they had witnessed the evening before. It had brought into vivid relief the very real dangers that attended their captivity. They had mistakenly allowed themselves to breathe a bit easier after the tribes had abandoned the army at the Ohio, but the burning of Ravencraft had made it glaringly clear how vulnerable they actually were. The incident had left them scared, depressed, and desolate.

When they reached the river, Bitsy stood on tiptoe and gazed beyond the crowd of shuffling Americans, but she was unable to locate her mother in the large group of British personnel who were already paddling into midstream. Nor was she able to see Judith, who would be the last to leave, as usual. She shook her head as she looked at the canoes, dugouts, and bateaux. Only a few short weeks ago, all those people, the Americans and the British, had been moving forward at a normal pace, if not happy, at least satisfied with their progress. Now everything was confused and complicated.

She wondered who was to blame for it all. Try as she might, she could not pin the responsibility on one individual but finally decided that everyone was to blame: England, for its unjust tyranny; America, for its grand desire to be free; the people of both countries, for their selfishness and jealousy.

Bitsy massaged her temples, then laughed bitterly as she thought back to a few short weeks ago, when her greatest vexation was the belief that Susan was being unreasonably strict. A person surely has life too easy when all she can find to be displeased with is the people who love her most, the girl thought guiltily.

Bitsy longed to take her mother into her arms and tell her what a silly, self-centered daughter she had been. She vowed to herself that if, the opportunity ever presented itself, she would make it up to Susan—even if it took the rest of her life. Bitsy smiled suddenly. Her promise gave her something to look forward to. She gazed up the Miami with renewed interest, glorying in the chirping of the birds, the croak of the bullfrogs, the buzzing of the insects that, because of the recent storm, were almost insufferable in the early morning heat. Little did she realize as she basked in the pleasure of her noble, self-sacrificing resolve that it was nothing but a young girl's fancy; for she and Susan would never be that close and uncomplicated again. Life would not permit it.

CHAPTER
· 15 ·

ALTHOUGH ANOTHER DAY and night had passed since the storm, Patterson's damp buckskins still chafed the skin where they had rubbed it raw when sopping wet. He hated wet leather. There was nothing comfortable about it, for unlike wool, which kept its shape and even retained a certain amount of warmth when soaked, buckskin stretched and sagged and held the cold until it dried out—which seemed to take forever. Yet it was that very nuisance and discomfort that kept him from running headlong into an ambush.

He had squatted beside a fallen chestnut log and was basking in the drying rays of the early morning sun when the Wyandot appeared. They were moving slowly, heads down, searching for sign. He froze as the Indians fanned out and hid themselves in places where one would swear men could not hide, becoming an integral part of their surroundings.

Patterson dropped to his stomach and pushed himself as far under the log as possible. He knew very well the Indians were hunting him.

The Wyandot chief surveyed the quiet forest through slitted eyes. He had seen no sign of the white man's passing, so he felt sure he was still somewhere close ahead. The feeling left him tingling with anticipation and with a confidence that made him abnormally careless. Signaling for his companions to remain where they were, the chief sprang from his hiding place and sprinted ahead, checking the ground as he ran. He knew the man was near; he could smell him.

Smiling wolfishly with satisfaction, the Indian dropped to his belly and squirmed like a serpent through the ferns, bloodroot, and mayapple toward a clump of honeysuckle that had wound itself around a huge lightning-struck chestnut log a hundred yards away. When he reached the fallen tree, he lay there listening carefully to the sounds of the woodland: the breeze in the trees, the humming and droning of insects, the chirping of birds. Everything seemed in order except the wind; it had shifted, carrying with it the smell of the white man, that slight advantage that often meant the difference between life and death.

Cautiously he inched his roached head around the end of the log. The sickening sound of metal striking flesh and bone blended into the other forest noises. A hatchet blade had caught the Indian squarely between the eyes, driving deep into his skull. The red man recoiled with such force that his backward lunge snatched the tomahawk handle from Patterson's grip.

Lying flat on his back, the Wyandot grasped the hatchet with both hands and began working the blade out of his forehead. Blood fountained out as the metal slipped free, covering the painted face and chest with a bright crimson that sparkled in the early morning light like a brilliant ruby. Pushing himself to his elbows and wiping at the flow of blood with a twitching hand, the Indian stared expressionlessly at Patterson, who was staring in return, incredulity etched across his rugged features.

The Indian tried to speak, but words would not come. He groped at his waistband and withdrew a small, pearl-handled dagger, which he pointed menacingly at the woodsman. But even as he attempted to drag himself toward Patterson, his eyes glazed over and his head fell sideways into the thick tangle of honeysuckle.

Patterson exhaled through his teeth. He had never encountered such a strong-willed human being. And as the Indian's body jerked and quivered and finally stiffened in one mighty shudder of death, Patterson truly regretted having been forced to kill such a fine specimen of a human being. Patterson slithered around the log and crawled to the

247

Indian's side. He retrieved his hatchet, then gathered the Wyandot's musket and powder horn.

Light glinting on steel drew his eyes to the knife still gripped tightly in the Indian's hand. Patterson studied the blade; it looked familiar. He pried the Indian's fingers apart and held the small dagger aloft, turning it over and over in the filtering rays of the sun.

Recognition and wonder flooded through him; the knife had long ago belonged to Judith Cornwallace's servant girl, Ivy. What was a Wyandot Indian doing with it in a wilderness thousands of miles from England? It was a small world, indeed.

Thrusting the knife into his belt, he caught up his rifle and the Indian musket, crawled to a slight rise, and scanned the forest. After several minutes of intense scrutiny that reaped him nothing, he settled among the ferns and waited.

The morning droned on, slow, sultry, and nerve-racking. Flies buzzed around his head, and gnats and mosquitoes raised welts on his face and hands, but still he waited. Near noon, one of the Indians slipped from cover and sprinted to a companion hidden beneath a blow-down. They talked for several seconds. Then both men moved cautiously toward Patterson, obviously following the trail of the chief.

Patterson's heart surged. It was exactly the move he had hoped they would make. Sighting down his rifle barrel, he touched the trigger and watched the lead Indian flip backwards as if he had been kicked in the chest by a draft horse. Before the smoke had cleared, Patterson had the chief's musket in action. The second Indian, believing that the woodsman had but one gun, let out a bloodcurdling scream that immediately silenced the wilderness sounds, and rushed headlong toward the ball of smoke that hung heavy above the gentle incline. Patterson shouldered the musket, biting his bottom lip to reduce the excitement that urged him to shoot the man immediately, instead of letting him get close enough for a sure hit.

The other three Indians had broken cover also, and, screaming like fiends, they too bounded toward the hill at full speed. Patterson let his breath slide between his teeth as he touched the trigger. The musket erupted, sending out an even greater cloud of smoke than the rifle. The woodsman quickly rolled to one side and peered beneath the blue-white haze to see if his shot had been true.

Patterson was elated. The Indian was spinning sideways, only to career into the trunk of a slender oak, which propelled him into the air like a springboard. He hit the ground as limp as a rag doll and lay still. Patterson swung his attention to the remaining Indians, but the unexpected second shot had sent the red men scurrying for cover.

Drawing his rifle across his chest, Patterson poured a charge of powder down the barrel. Then, without patching, he rammed the ball to the breech. Even more quickly, he ripped the stopper from his priming horn and dashed a small portion of the fine granules into the flash pan. He breathed more easily knowing his gun was charged and primed. Taking his time, he reloaded the Indian's musket.

He scanned the forest, searching for movement, for noise, for color, but try as he might, he could not locate even one of his red assailants, and he cursed himself for his bad luck. If the Indians had been Shawnee or Delaware or Seneca, or almost any tribe except Wyandot, they would have fled when the first two Indians went down. But not the Wyandot. They would lie in wait until their adversary made a mistake. Then they would kill him.

What they failed to consider, however, was that their quarry was as good an Indian as they. And if anyone made a mistake, it might very well be the Wyandot, as two of them had just demonstrated.

The stalemate lasted for over two hours. It was finally shattered by groans from the second Indian Patterson had shot. The musket ball had taken the man high in the chest, missing his lungs and heart. The Indian, just barely conscious, thrashed heavily in the leaves beneath the tree, the sounds clearly audible in the stone-dead stillness.

Patterson considered shooting the Indian again to put him out of his misery, but an idea flashed through his mind, and he quickly decided that it was worth trying, for as it was, neither he nor the Indians were going anywhere fast.

"Wyandot brothers," he called in Shawnee. "While we lie here and wait for someone to show himself, one of your brethren bleeds his life away under yon oak tree." Patterson paused and watched the forest through squinted eyes. Nothing moved.

"I am searching for my family," he continued, "and have nothing against the Wyandot. You can collect your wounded friend and leave here, or you can die with him. I have spoken."

If the Wyandot understood the Shawnee dialect, Patterson felt that he might stand a chance of persuading them to take the wounded warrior and withdraw. He waited. After a long interval, the three Indians began a harangue among themselves that the woodsman was unable to follow. He doubled his vigilance.

"Brother," came the reply in Shawnee. "We have decided to accept your generous offer. We were not aware that we hunted a Shawnee. We are sorry we interrupted you in your search for your family."

Patterson breathed deeply, but he did not relax. For, although the Wyandot were known for their honesty, they were still Indians, and as such, they were unpredictable, especially since he had already killed two of their tribesmen and wounded another.

"Wyandot," called Patterson. "Too much blood has fed the roots of the ferns. Come and get your friend. My gun will stay silent."

Two Indians broke cover and darted to the wounded warrior. Catching him by his wrists, they hastily dragged him farther into the forest.

The third man stepped haughtily from behind a tall elm and stood facing Patterson. "Brother," he said, "we go now, but we will return to bury our dead."

"I will not be here," answered Patterson.

The Indian nodded. "You had best run far, for in my grief I may forget that we have pledged our word of honor."

Patterson sighed, knowing that the man was telling him it wasn't over, that he would be on Patterson's trail the moment the burial was finished. Patterson took a fine bead as the Indian turned to follow his comrades and shot the man through the back of the head.

In the distance, he saw the two remaining Indians drop their wounded comrade and run wildly through the forest until they were lost from sight. But he knew they would be back; and they would not rest until he or they were dead.

Patterson hid the Wyandot's musket and powder horn in a hollow tree. He would have preferred to keep the musket, but his wounded shoulder was too weak to support the weight of two guns.

He drove himself to his limit to put distance between him and the two remaining warriors. He had no doubt that they would be on his trail like mastiffs, to avenge the men he had killed, especially the last one, whom they assumed he had slain for no reason after giving his word that he would allow them to leave in peace. Although he didn't expect the Indians to show up for another day or two, he knew the savage mind too well to take that assumption for granted. So he watched his back trail constantly.

He didn't bother to cover his tracks, because the Indians knew where he was headed. The best he could hope for was that they would be so angry that both would come after him rather than one breaking away to go for reinforcements. If that happened, Patterson was a dead man.

The situation angered him; he had no quarrel with the Wyandot. In fact, the entire episode had been a waste of time he could not afford to lose. It seemed that the Lord was taking great pleasure in putting obstacles in his path.

Patterson was not a God-fearing man. He did believe in the Bible, and he believed in Christ, but he feared neither. He believed that he had as much right to question the Lord's ways as the Almighty did his.

As he trotted, he raised his eyes to a speck of sky that peeped through the treetops. "I once asked you, Lord," he shouted silently, "if You had turned your back on us Americans. Well, I'm asking again. Have You turned your face away from Kentucky as You did the Virginia Militia when Braddock was defeated? Have You forsaken my wife and daughter like You did those poor devils during the French and Indian War? If not, then leave me alone to seek them without all these interruptions."

He felt better after that, and with a satisfied grunt, he dropped his head and stepped up his pace.

Patterson was jerked awake the next morning by the warble of a tom turkey.

His first thought was how good a slab of meat would taste. His second thought was that it was too late in the summer for a turkey to gobble. Normally the birds did that only during mating season in the early spring.

Patterson scowled, distressed that the Indians had found him so quickly. He surmised that they had left their dead where they lay and had taken directly to his trail. If so, they wanted him powerfully badly. He cocked his head and listened again for the call.

When it came, it was from his left. Patterson smiled. His luck was holding; both Indians had followed him. That suited him fine. Still, he wished he could just slip into the wilderness, cover his tracks, and try to elude them. But, persistent as they were, that was out of the question; the two Wyandot would hound him to death. No, he told himself, he had no choice except to finish it once and for all, for there would be no rest for either him or the Indians until it was over.

He flipped the frizzen of his flintlock open, blew the powder from the flash pan, and carefully reprimed the rifle.

He moved like a shadow, the hunted becoming the hunter, his squinted eyes darting ahead and to all sides, missing nothing. He plastered himself against the trunk of a huge elm and listened intently. Not a sound. He cast a slow glance in all directions. Nothing moved. His skin crawled; he knew the Indians were near.

Inching into a crouch, he leaned around the tree trunk and viewed the woods directly ahead of him.

Bark exploded next to his head, filling his face and eyes with bits of flying debris, and somewhere through the blinding pain he heard the unmistakable roar of a musket. Patterson fought frantically to clear his sight, for even louder than the echo of the blast was the sound of breaking brush as the Indian raced toward him.

Tears streaming down his cheeks and his eyelids fluttering like a butterfly, the woodsman raised his gun and pointed the barrel toward the sound. Through a watery haze he could see the silhouette of something moving toward him. He fired. Before the smoke had cleared, Patterson was running as if Satan himself were after him. He knew he had missed the Indian, and he knew the man would waste no time hunting him down now that his rifle was empty.

Patterson, however, had not survived all those years in

the wilderness without picking up a point or two that very few hunters acquired. He, Boone, and Simon Kenton had painstakingly learned the art of loading while on the run. And he put that knowledge to good use. He poured a charge of powder into the palm of his hand, but still nearly blind, he stumbled over a fallen log and lost the powder when he used the hand to break his fall.

He was up and running immediately. Even though he couldn't see his pursuer, he knew the Indian was closing the distance between them in startlingly swift strides. He almost panicked as he poured another charge into his palm and clamped it over the rifle's muzzle. He popped a bullet into his mouth and worked it around until it was saliva-covered. Then he spit the ball down the barrel. Still running hard, he slammed the butt of the rifle against the ground, seating the charge against the breech.

The Indian was so close that Patterson could hear the man's breath whistling through his teeth, could smell the rancid bear grease, could feel the man's hatred. He spun on his heel and dropped to one knee. Sure that Patterson's gun was not loaded, the Indian screamed triumphantly and, raising his tomahawk for the kill, rushed straight toward the woodsman's leveled rifle.

Patterson blinked rapidly as he sighted down the barrel. He was staking his life on the chance that his rifle would fire unprimed. It would be a delayed ignition, but he had done it several times in the past and it had worked.

The Indian was fifteen yards away when the woodsman squeezed the trigger. The hammer dropped, and as the flint raked down the steel frizzen, a minute shower of sparks danced and rolled in the empty flash pan, but the gun remained silent. The woodsman clenched his teeth and steadied himself, raising the gun barrel a hairsbreadth as the Indian's silhouette loomed larger and larger in his sights.

It was the hardest thing he had ever done, holding that gun steady as the red man covered yard after yard, for Patterson's every instinct screamed for him to throw the rifle aside and flee for his life.

When the weapon erupted, it was as though the Indian had run into an invisible wall. The ball took the man in the chest, flipping his feet so high that the back of his head was

253

the first thing that hit the ground. His body followed, crumpling to the earth like a sack of flour. Patterson reached out cautiously with his gun barrel and nudged the man's lifeless body.

"Too close," he breathed raggedly, trying to stop the shaking of his hands. "Too damned close."

He reloaded quickly, measuring the charge, patching the ball, priming the flash pan. Yet all the while, he was scanning the forest for the remaining Indian. It bothered him that in the space of two days he had killed nearly as many Indians as he had in his entire life, but nevertheless, he wished that the last Wyandot was dead.

He did not like killing human beings, red or white. But the choice was not his, so he gritted his teeth and crawled through the forest. He was as quiet as any Indian, and much more deadly, for Patterson had the best of two worlds tucked neatly inside his being. Having been raised through adolescence by Black Fish, the Shawnee chieftain, he knew and understood the red men's cunning, bravery, and patience; and having spent his adult life with the English, he possessed their skill, understanding, and prudence.

Patterson knew the Indian was wondering if his tribesman had been the one who had died. He also knew that the enemy was as nervous as he, probably even more so, because Indians enjoyed fighting when the advantage, either in numbers or in surprise, was on their side. This man had neither. Patterson guessed that the Indian, too, wished he could back out of the fight, but his Wyandot pride would not permit him to quit until it was finished. It was a shame.

Although Patterson's eyes still stung, his vision was clearing rapidly. What bothered him most was the need to blink more often than usual, for in the wilderness the bat of an eye could be detected quite easily, almost like a flashing lantern. Patterson knew that it was often the small blunders that proved fatal.

He darted from tree to tree, flattening himself against their trunks to make as small a target as possible. Only his narrowed eyes moved as he probed the landscape for sign of his enemy, letting his gaze rove slowly from shadow to shadow, trunk to trunk, bush to bush. He did it with infinite care, taking in every detail of his surroundings.

It was just such waiting that was the undoing of most

white men: not knowing what might happen next, jumping at each small sound, allowing the mind to run wild with anxiety until finally, a man grew so nervous and distraught that he would force something to happen. And that was the mistake that nine times out of ten cost him his life.

Under normal circumstances, Patterson had the patience of a cat lying beside a mouse hole, watching his prey for hours, waiting for the right moment to strike. But this was different. He had to act immediately, for every minute he lost meant that Bird was taking his wife and daughter farther and farther into enemy territory.

A flicker of movement caught Patterson's attention. Not moving his head, the woodsman let his eyes slowly swivel to the spot. The Indian's head rose above a cluster of ferns as he surveyed the forest. The man stayed like that for several minutes, watching, listening, looking. Every muscle in Patterson's body screamed for release from the strain of remaining absolutely frozen, but he knew full well that if he so much as crooked his little finger the Indian would be gone.

When the Indian dropped his head to gather himself before standing erect, Patterson slowly lifted his gun and thumbed back the hammer. But even that slight movement was enough. The Indian sprang sideways, flinging himself toward the protection of a huge hemlock.

Patterson's rifle barrel followed the man's quick actions, bellowing its defiance, shaking the quiet forest with its thundering denial of his intended escape. The ball took the Indian in the hip, shattering his pelvic bone with such impact that it sent him tumbling sideways, end over end. The Wyandot lost his grip on his musket, and it spun to one side and disappeared beneath the thick carpet of mayapple and fern.

Patterson quickly reloaded and trained his gun on the spot where he had seen the Indian go down. He watched for several minutes, but nothing moved. Hesitantly, his eyes riveted to that spot, his gun at the ready, Patterson stepped into the open.

He knew the Indian was wounded, but he had no idea whether the man was down for good or was merely baiting him into making the wrong move. With the short hairs standing rigid on his neck, he advanced slowly toward the place where the Indian had disappeared. The woodsman studied the blood-splattered leaves. Even the greenest hunter could have told from the quantity of thick red drops and bone fragments that the man was hard hit. Patterson breathed more easily.

Yet even then he did not relax. A wounded savage was just as dangerous as any other injured wild beast. Patterson stalked even more cautiously when he found the spot where, after having been knocked sideways, the Indian had quickly crawled away, leaving large puddles of blood plainly visible beneath the ferns where he had dragged his useless legs.

Patterson took slow steps as he followed the path, his eyes probing every inch of the wilderness that stretched out before him. No human could go far, shot up as badly as the Wyandot, and in that respect, Patterson was correct. He came upon the man less than a hundred yards farther on, and he was forced to admire the Indian's cunning. Like many wounded animals, the savage had burrowed beneath the vines and leaves in an attempt to hide himself. And had the woodsman not been wise to such tricks, he might have walked over the man without seeing him.

Knowing that he had been detected, the Indian erupted out of his cover like a snarling animal, dragging himself forward on his elbows, lashing out at the woodsman with his scalping knife. Patterson felt both sadness and admiration for the man's bravery in the face of sure death.

Clinching his teeth with self-loathing, Patterson raised his rifle and shot the man between the eyes.

CHAPTER
· *16* ·

CHARD AND SIMON GIRTY worked their way across the flat woodlands toward Lorimer's Store.

As they traveled, Chard paid close attention to Girty's every move, his every gesture, and tried hard to imitate the frontiersman's ways.

Approving of the young man's interest, Girty took the time to explain and demonstrate those portions of woodsman's lore he felt the newcomer could grasp and retain. He showed Chard how to move quietly through the brush, how to stand for long periods of time and still be at ease, how to stalk game, how to track and read sign, and many more small points that kept a man alive in the out-of-doors. And much to Girty's surprise, Chard learned quickly and easily; he was a natural woodsman who lacked only instruction.

The white Indian demonstrated how to quick-load and fire Bitsy's Pennsylvania gun, commenting that it was probably one of the finest rifles in Ohio. Chard was pleased by the praise and strove hard to prove worthy of such a fine weapon. As a result, he took pains not to miss when he sighted on bird or animal.

Another thing Girty noticed was that the more Chard learned the quieter he became, and when he did ask a question, it had a significant point.

Girty explained that when they got to Lorimer's they would pick up a pack horse or two and go after big game: elk, bear, moose, and deer. Enough meat to feed the army and their captives all the way to Detroit.

The mention of Detroit brought Chard abruptly to reality.

His mother's impending trial was the one dark spot or his horizon. No, he told himself, that wasn't true. His involvement with Bitsy had also clouded his skies. But that was minor when compared to the very real prospect that Judith might face a dishonorable death at the hands of the military. With each mile the army traveled, that possibility was coming closer to being a reality. He knew that if his father's rank and influence carried enough weight, Judith would be hanged. With a sigh, Chard pushed those thoughts to the back of his mind. At present, the wilderness demanded his undivided attention—if he wanted to learn to stay alive in a land that seemed to thrive on death.

The churning sensation in Chard's stomach, which had subsided briefly during the excitement of Bitsy's capture and rescue, returned in full measure, bringing to life his nearly constant companion and tormentor, nausea.

But he dared not let that emotion surface, for throughout his days and nights with Girty, he had never been sure of how the man felt or what he thought, unless Girty offered such information freely. So Chard, swallowing his bile to keep his sickness a secret, worked hard to emulate Girty's privacy and aloofness. And strange as it was, the young man enjoyed the responsibility of keeping his own counsel and depending on his own initiative, stamina, and perseverance. It was a new way of life for him, and he cherished it with the passion of one who has discovered the meaning of freedom and is terrified that it may be only an illusion.

Chard and Girty reached Lorimer's on the sixth day after leaving the camp on the Miami River. Chard was amazed by the size of the place. He had expected a one-room log cabin, but saw instead an assortment of buildings, large and small. The main structure, a store, was at least forty feet long with a twenty-foot wing off the back. To the side was a small cabin that served as temporary quarters for travelers, and beyond that stood a corncrib and blacksmith shop. To the right, in a clearing that flanked the Pickawillany Creek, was one of the ever-present Indian villages that seemed to spring up when a trading post was founded.

Chard was all eyes as he followed Girty across Lorimer's stump-dotted field to the store. He was even more dumbstruck when they entered. The interior was a confusion of merchandise: blankets, traps, guns, flints, powder, shot, tobacco, cooking utensils, knives, horns, shot pouches, saws, hatchets, axes, bolts of cloth, and, of course, the inevitable mind-fogging American drink called Monongahela whiskey.

Even the trader was an imposing sight. He was at least six feet tall, weighing two hundred pounds or more. But what caught Chard's attention was the coal-black braided queue that fell to the man's waist, that and the fact that Peter Lorimer was not English at all. His swarthy skin and dark eyes leaned more toward French Canadian, more Indian than white.

Girty, with Chard at his side, walked to the far end of the rough-hewn counter where Lorimer was dickering with an Indian over the price of a pile of furs. Acting uninterested in the pelts, Lorimer hailed Girty in a gruff voice and strode arrogantly toward him and Chard.

The Indian gathered his catch into a bundle and stalked from the building.

"Lost you a customer, Lorimer," said Girty, looking after the Indian.

"He'll be back, M'sieur Girty. There's no place else for him to trade, unless he takes the furs to Detroit—and Detroit is a far piece away, no?"

"Give me a taste of Monongahela," said Girty, changing the subject. "And one for my friend." He indicated Chard with a nod of his head.

Lorimer poured two goblets of whiskey and pushed them across the planks.

Girty drank deeply, but Chard, who had never tasted corn whiskey, took a small sip and let it run slowly down his throat. The fiery liquid burned a trail all the way to his stomach.

He set the cup on the counter and moved off to investigate the trade goods that were displayed over every square inch of available space.

"Are you not intending to drink the whiskey, m'sieur?" called Lorimer, staring sullenly at Chard.

"I don't like the taste of it, sir," returned Chard easily

"Not man enough to drink it, eh?" challenged Lorimer.

"I suppose not," said Chard. "But I would give half my life for a cup of East India tea, Mr. Lorimer."

"Tea? We have no tea, m'sieur," scoffed Lorimer, turning an angry shade of red. "Do you think you are in Boston or New York or Philadelphia, m'sieur?"

Chard smiled at the Frenchman. "I've nothing against your Monongahela, sir. It's just that I've not had a good cup of tea in weeks."

Lorimer leaned across the counter and scowled at the young man.

"M'sieur, I would not like to think that you are too good to drink my whiskey."

Girty sipped at his drink, his small black eyes traveling from one man to the other. Lorimer was known to be a rough-and-tumble fighter who was mean when aroused, and Girty doubted that Chard had ever engaged in that type of combat. The truth was, very few British gentlemen had ever seen a frontier fight, much less allowed themselves to become involved in one.

"Sir," said Chard, walking to the door, "if I have offended you, I apologize. But corn liquor does not set well with me. I will be more than glad to pay for it, however."

The Canadian snatched up the goblet and poured the contents back into the barrel, then slammed the empty vessel down on the counter. He had not vented his spleen on anyone in weeks, and he was well overdue. The pretentious, handsome young man with his quiet, mannerly attitude had triggered the violent streak that lay just beneath Lorimer's swarthy surface.

Sensing the unreasonable animosity that was building in the storekeeper, Chard decided to avoid a confrontation that to him seemed utterly ridiculous and without purpose. He turned his back on Lorimer and stepped through the door to the hard-packed dirt of the common grounds that stretched to the wood line some one hundred yards away.

Lorimer burst from the building and lunged headlong into the unsuspecting ensign. They went down in a cloud of

260

dust, the impact forcing the breath from Chard's chest with such violence that he felt as if his lungs had collapsed. The only thing Chard could concentrate on was getting oxygen into his system, and Lorimer, taking advantage of his opponent's plight, pounded the young man mercilessly. His powerful knuckles opened a deep gash on Chard's cheek, and another blow split his lips, knocking him half-unconscious. The ensign was whipped before he knew what was happening. He had no chance to retaliate or defend himself, so quick and ruthless were Lorimer's attack and execution.

Lorimer sprang lightly to his feet and stood glaring at Chard. "Too good for Pierre Lorimer, eh?" he said in French. Turning disgustedly, he stalked into the store, beckoning to the Indian with whom he had been trading.

Girty stood beside the doorway sipping his whiskey, and then he, too, turned and followed Lorimer inside.

The Indians who had gathered to watch the fight filtered soundlessly back to whatever they were doing, indifferent to the whole affair. No one offered Chard a helping hand as he tried unsuccessfully to get to his feet. He made it to his hands and knees, his head hanging, blood dripping into the dust, but he could not stop the world from spinning. For a full five minutes he held that position before trying to stand erect.

The earth spun sickeningly, and Chard braced his legs wide to keep from falling. He drew the back of his hand across his mouth and wiped it on his hunting frock, leaving a bloody streak on the fawn-colored leather. He shook his head, blinked, and breathed deeply several times. He squinted toward the store as if trying to figure out what had taken place. Then, as his memory returned and the episode became clear in his befuddled mind, an overwhelming anger raged through him.

He took a few tentative steps to be sure his legs worked properly, then resolutely stalked to the chopping block and snatched a broadax out of the wood. He pounded the butt of the handle against the block until the ax head came free. Then, hefting the hickory handle several times to test its weight, he walked into the storeroom.

261

Girty was sipping his whiskey at the far end of the counter. The Indian was standing by the door with his arms crossed. Lorimer was bent over the furs, sorting them out to be graded.

Girty's eyes narrowed when Chard entered the room, and he slowly lowered the goblet. The Indian, however, merely stepped aside to be sure he was out of the line of fire, and waited.

Arrogant and self-important man that he was, Lorimer did not even look up to see who had entered. So when Chard reared back and brought the ax handle down on Lorimer's bent head, driving the man's face into the peltry, Lorimer never knew what hit him. Dragging the furs with him, the storekeeper melted down the counter and sprawled on the earthen floor.

Without changing expressions, the Indian gathered his furs, nodded at Chard, and walked through the door.

Girty set his goblet on the counter and glanced at Lorimer's prostrate body. Then, without a word, he retrieved his goblet, walked to the whiskey barrel, and drew himself a full draft.

Chard flipped the ax handle through the door and, catching up a mug, dipped himself a cup of the strong drink.

He took several deep swallows, and then, cutting a length of cloth from a bolt behind the counter, he soaked it in the mug and dabbed at the cuts and scrapes on his battered face. That done, he leaned over the counter and poured the remainder on the deep gash in the top of Lorimer's head.

"Let the son of a bitch die," said Girty, walking toward the door. "He would have let you."

"And so would you," said Chard, pushing himself away from the counter and following the renegade outside. "Why did he attack me, Girty? He doesn't even know me."

"The way you speak," said Girty. "You sound like a British dandy, and Lorimer ain't got no use for weaklin's."

"I'm no weakling, Girty."

"He didn't know that. He's been around Indians all his life. He's a hard man, a resentful man, and when you refused whiskey and asked for tea, he took an instant dislike to you, had to try you out." Girty stared hard at Chard. "Indians will do the same thing. They ain't got nothin' but contempt for a man that ain't meaner than they are. You'd best remember that. Furthermore, you knew Lorimer was spoilin' for a fight, yet you turned your back on him. 'Tis a wonder he didn't beat you to death."

Chard blushed. Girty was right. Gentlemanly ways would get a man killed on the frontier. His attempt to avoid trouble had given Lorimer the impression he was a coward. Chard would not forget that.

Girty caught up four horses from Lorimer's holding pens, and in twenty minutes he and Chard were lost in the wilderness surrounding the outpost.

They traveled north by west over flat, monotonous terrain that seemed to stretch to the ends of the earth. But the easy traveling was a novelty that Chard welcomed. They shot a young doe at sundown and butchered out the sirloin strips, leaving the remainder of the carcass to the wolves and other wilderness predators.

They picketed the horses, then spread their gear close to the animals, for even though the local Indians were friendly, four horses would be hard to pass up should a hunting party happen upon them. They built a fire and roasted the meat, and ate in the silence of two men who had their own thoughts to pursue. Then they rolled in their blankets and were immediately asleep.

As daylight approached, they left the horses hoppled in a small field where they could forage without the need to travel far, and made their way on foot through the forest to a large body of water that Girty said the Indians called Grand Lake. They approached the lake with care, well aware that the game they stalked would be nervous as the brightening of dawn shattered their concealing cloak of safety and left them vulnerable to daylight predators.

Girty and Chard belly-crawled to a small rise overlooking the silver-black water that was just beginning to show ripples of rose-gold from the lightening of the sky in the east. As the glow increased and the shadows took on definite shape, Chard could make out several large animals standing quietly at the water's edge, their dripping muzzles creating small rippling circles in the lake's surface.

263

"Elk," whispered Girty out of the corner of his mouth. "Seven, maybe eight of them." Chard nodded his understanding.

"I'll take that big 'un that's standin' off to himself over by that pine tree." Girty used his rifle barrel as a pointer.

Chard's eyes followed to a lone pine tree twenty yards beyond the small herd. A huge animal stood beneath its branches, its nose raised so that the back of its head appeared to be resting on its neck.

Before Chard had a chance to react or pick an animal for himself, Girty's gun bellowed. The bull elk dropped to its front knees, then slowly flopped onto its side. The remainder of the herd began to mill nervously, not sure what had taken place.

Chard picked a large cow elk and sighted down his barrel. His rifle roared. The cow staggered, then raced into the forest, following the headlong flight of the remaining herd. Chard cursed under his breath. Girty's shot had been a clean kill, while Chard's had missed its mark. The wounded animal would require tracking, which could be an all-day job—if they were lucky enough to get the beast at all. The two men trotted to the carcass of the bull. Girty laid his rifle aside and drew his skinning knife.

"Hadn't we best be tracking the one I shot before it gets away?" said Chard.

"If'n it's hit hard, we'll find it. If'n it ain't, we won't."

Girty slipped his knife beneath the skin and split the belly of the elk from its crotch to its rib cage. In short order, he had the animal field-dressed. Then, after wiping his hands and forearms with dead leaves, he gathered up the liver and walked to the lake.

Chard had observed Girty's every move as the man cleaned the animal. And he watched with equal interest as the hunter washed the raw liver and cut it into thick slices. Handing one to the ensign, Girty stuffed a slice into his own mouth and chewed vigorously.

Chard followed suit, surprised that the dripping red mess stayed down when he swallowed. But it did, and he found himself asking for more. The meat had a bitter taste that was different, but not at all displeasing to the hungry young man.

Girty slipped the remainder of the liver into his

hunting pouch and returned to the elk, where he propped open the chest cavity of the animal with a two-foot-long staff. He explained to Chard that the meat needed to air-cure as quickly as possible, but that the flies would probably blow it regardless of what they did.

When he had finished, Girty trotted to the edge of the forest where the wounded cow had disappeared. He squatted and ran his hand through the fallen leaves. Chard knelt beside him and studied the sticky blood that Girty rubbed between his fingertips.

"See how bright red and frothy this is," said the hunter, offering his fingers for Chard's inspection. "You shot her through the lungs."

Before Chard could ask the inevitable question, Girty went on, "If the blood had been blue-red, it would mean you hit an artery or vein or such."

"What're the chances of getting her, lung-shot as she is?"

"We'll take it slow. We'll get her."

They tracked the blood sign for three miles before they came upon the dead elk. She was lying in a small creek where she had obviously lain down to try to stop the bleeding. Chard was elated. He hated the thought of losing a wounded animal, for he detested suffering. Nor did he approve of waste. So even though his face was as unreadable as Girty's, he felt jubilant that they had tracked the elk to completion.

Chard leaned his rifle against a tree and stepped into the ankle-deep water where the elk lay. With Girty's help, he dragged the carcass to the bank and began field-dressing the animal, taking pains to do exactly as Girty had done.

Girty hunkered down and watched Chard work. Occasionally he would offer a word of advice, but for the most part he did nothing but observe.

"Right good job, son," he said when Chard finished.

"Could have been better," grunted the young ensign, pleased by the compliment but bound not to show it.

Girty climbed to his feet and stretched. "I'm goin' for the horses. You keep an eye on the meat."

Chard nodded.

Girty eyed the young man intently, but all he said was

"Take care of your hair." Then he was gone, trotting silently back the way they had come.

Glancing at the sun, which was only three hours high, Chard, as Girty had done earlier, slipped the heart and liver into his haversack, then decided to scout the area.

The terrain was flat woodlands that frequently opened onto small plains. It was some of the most fertile land Chard had ever seen. He wondered how the British Crown intended to keep people from moving into such a productive region once England won the war. And how would the British ministry handle the Indian problem that would arise, especially since the Ohio tribes were allies to the king? He doubted that would carry much weight should the Crown decide to open the country to settlement. Treaties with the Indians had never been honored in the past, and Chard did not believe the British code of justice had changed one whit.

He crept quietly through the shaded woods that skirted an open, grassy meadow, and surprised himself by slipping up on and shooting a big buck deer feeding on tender shoots growing in the edge of the natural field.

After dressing it out, he followed Girty's example by propping the chest cavity open with a stick, pleased at how easily the skills had come to him.

He smiled to himself. Everything considered, it had been a good hunt. Bitsy would be proud of him. He scowled, wondering why she had sprung into his thoughts —and worse, why he cared what her feelings were one way or the other. He shook his head, irritated with himself, because there was no denying that, before Bitsy, he had never longed to impress any woman, at least not the way he did the Kentucky girl. But try as he might, all he had accomplished thus far was to provoke her scorn and anger; every move he made was wrong.

If he could become a good hunter and woodsman, he reasoned, perhaps she would see that he wasn't entirely the self-centered weakling she believed him to be. That thought perked him up so much that he fairly flew through the woods toward the cache of elk meat where he was to rendezvous with Girty.

A more experienced woodsman would never have let exhilaration override caution, but Chard, in spite of his recent accomplishments, was still, for all practical purposes, a tenderfoot. Instead of approaching the elk with care, he trotted straight in as though he were on a hunting reserve in some British hamlet.

If he had been paying attention, he would have noticed the stillness, the absence of normal forest sounds, the fact that not a cricket chirped or a bird sang. But Chard noticed none of those things. He propped his gun against a tree and squatted beside the elk carcass. Flies were swarming over the raw meat, and Chard waved them away. They immediately settled at new locations, and he was forced to wave them away again. He decided to cut a bough from a fir tree to use as a fan. When he turned, his mouth dropped open. Not ten feet away, stood a dozen warriors, their roached heads and heavily greased bodies mirroring in the morning sunlight.

They all held muskets pointed at Chard's chest. He glanced at the tree where he had leaned his rifle. The gun was gone. He cursed himself for a fool; Girty had cautioned him always to keep his rifle within reach.

Chard crossed his arms as he had seen Girty do, and waited.

The Indians moved quickly to him and snatched his arms behind his back, drawing his elbows close and lashing them with rawhide. They rummaged through his haversack, scattering the contents on the ground.

Chard considered telling them he was a British officer, but he doubted that they would be impressed. He had heard too many stories of how British soldiers were killed for the price their scalps would bring in Detroit and how the army never seemed able to find an Indian who knew anything about the murders. Indeed, all the red men would ever say on the subject was that the scalpings were done by another tribe and that they knew nothing about it. And the army had no choice but to accept the savages' word and pay for the hair of their countrymen.

Chard wondered if it was to be his fate simply to disappear into the wilderness. He gritted his teeth as he realized that in all likelihood one day soon his hair would lie on DePeyster's desk in Detroit.

He thought of his mother and what the outcome of her trial would be if he wasn't there to see that she got a fair hearing. Then in spite of himself, his mind slipped to Bitsy. What would happen to her when the prisoners reached Detroit? Would she be imprisoned there or at Montreal or one of the other British outposts in the northwest area? Or would she be taken into someone's home as a servant? Or, heaven forbid, would she be bound out to a tavern keeper for illicit purposes? That last reflection left Chard's mouth dry, for even though he had been as guilty as any man when it came to satisfying his lust with barmaids or house servants, never taking into consideration the desires of the girl involved, he was outraged at the thought of Bitsy being forced to participate in the very same acts that he had practiced with such callousness.

"I am a British officer," he blurted out in desperation. "I am under the command of Captain Henry Bird of the Eighth Regiment. Do you speak English?"

Ignoring his outburst, the Indians dragged Chard to the elk. They quickly hacked off a hindquarter, and lashed it tightly to his shoulders, allowing the weight of the meat to rest heavily on his elbows. The young man's knees almost buckled under the enormous load.

They turned due north and struck off in a fast walk. In less than a mile, Chard's arms and shoulders ached with a pain that drew his lips into a grimace.

He remembered the Kentuckians, weighted down with plunder from Ruddle's and Martin's, and the miles upon miles they had staggered through the wilderness under their heavy burdens. He wondered how they had done it. Then he sighed and gritted his teeth, remembering that the bodies of those who had not been able to carry their loads lay scattered from the Licking River all the way to the Ohio. And there was no telling how many more had died in the wilderness beyond the river. Chard was determined to survive. Leaning forward to shift the load higher on his neck and shoulders, he quickened his step, which brought a grunt of approval from his captors.

Fortunately for Chard, the Indians were a hunting party whose main camp was only five miles away. So, just past noon, Chard found himself amid a throng of temporary lean-tos and shelters where a half-dozen women and children awaited their men's return.

The women were elated to see Chard stumbling into camp, bent at the waist under the weight of the meat, and they made clicking sounds with their tongues as though they were calling a dog. Chard wondered at the contempt in the eyes of the female savages, until one walked boldly to him, ran her hands inside his breeches, and grasped his penis and testicles. His face flushed with angry embarrassment, for it was plain that the woman was investigating his body to be sure he was a man. He remembered then that Girty had told him it was beneath the red man's dignity to carry such a burden. That was for women, or horses.

One of his captors stepped forward and slashed the rawhide thongs, and the meat dropped to the ground with a resounding thud. Chard stepped aside and drew himself to full height, fighting hard not to show the pain that shot through his body when he straightened his spine. His arms had nearly lost their feeling from being tied so tightly, and when the Indians cut the lash that bound his elbows Chard sucked in his breath to keep from crying out as the blood began circulating through his hands and fingers.

As he massaged his arms and elbows, he surveyed the camp. Racks of drying meat stood in the sun, curing as though in a slow-burning oven. The women were fleshing out hides and slicing the carcasses of two deer into thin strips for jerky.

One of the men poked the ensign in the ribs with his gun barrel and motioned for him to pick up the hindquarter and carry it to the women. Chard shook his head and scowled at the man. He flung out his hand, pointing to the women, and then crossed his arms and stared at the forest. The Indians glanced at one another, not knowing what to do. They understood Chard's sign and grudgingly admired his stand, for they, too, would have refused to carry such a load when women were present.

The women jumped to their feet and barraged the warriors with such shouting and finger-pointing that Chard was sure they would irritate the men into forcing him to carry the meat or killing him if he again refused. But the Indians turned their backs on the women and, pushing Chard before them, moved to the shade of a giant elm and relaxed into a squatting position.

They talked softly among themselves, indicating Chard with occasional nods of their heads. He guessed they were discussing his future—or his lack of one. Obviously they had never encountered a white captive who refused to do as he was told, and it upset their expectations. And, like many who depend on fear and intimidation to cow their adversaries, they were bewildered by Chard's behavior.

He could tell by their gestures that some were for killing him outright, while others shook their heads and spoke in their singsong voices, evidently talking against it. Chard felt his stomach rise up in his throat as he waited to see which faction won out.

An Indian jumped to his feet and shook his tomahawk in the ensign's face, but to Chard's relief, he slipped the weapon through his waistband and resumed his seat. Although fear still gripped at his insides, his mind wandered again to Bitsy. Had she felt the same nerve-racking terror when captured by the Wyandots? Surely she had. Yet she had never let it show. She had faced the Indians and the gauntlet with her head held high, her eyes level, unwavering.

Chard felt pride well up within him. He had not truly appreciated the girl's courage until that very moment. And he realized that had he not been captured he might never have understood just how brave she was. He wished he could tell her of the admiration and respect he felt for her, and he deeply regretted that he would not have the chance to do so. With a sinking heart, Chard realized his appreciation of Bitsy had come too late. The Indians were taking him to their village to run the gauntlet or to burn at the stake, or whatever else their fiendish minds could conjure up, and it was almost certain that he would never see the girl again.

The Indians rose as one and, pushing Chard before them, trotted down a well-worn path. As he ran, all Chard could think about was the unjust trick that fate had played on him. Then suddenly he knew he was experiencing exactly what Bitsy, Susan, and the other Kentuckians were enduring at the hands of the British and their Indian allies. He laughed, a loathing, self-accusing sound. Perhaps it was not an unjust trick after all.

270

They trotted without a break for the remainder of the day and far into the night before finally reaching a small clearing that was, judging by the numerous fire pits, a much used layover point. After a supper of hastily cooked venison, the Indians lay down with their feet to the fire and went immediately to sleep.

Chard, who had been tethered to a tree, watched for an opportunity to escape, but none presented itself. One or two of the Indians always seemed to be jumping up to replenish the fire. Finally, Chard fell asleep from sheer exhaustion.

They were up and running before dawn. Near noon, they reached the St. Mary's River and followed it due north. Two hours later, they reached a vast meadow with an Indian village visible on the far side.

One of Chard's captors gave a hideous yell that was a mixture of turkey gobble and wildcat's screech: it was the Indians' way of warning a camp or village that a prisoner was approaching. The camp sprang to life. Guns were fired, shouts and yells echoed up and down the river, and a gauntlet was hastily formed.

With his heart hammering wildly, as if trying to pound its way out of his chest, Chard faced a much shorter version of the same narrow human-lined avenue that Bitsy had confronted. The anxious faces of his antagonists blurred as nervous perspiration dripped into his eyes, and he wished they would free his hands so he could wipe it away.

The ground vibrated with a resonant tattoo as the savages began pounding the earth with their staves, signaling that they were ready. It was what Chard had been waiting for. He remembered Bitsy's tricks when she had sped down that line, and he silently thanked her, for he intended to use the same tactics. Before the waiting Indians could raise their weapons and settle themselves, the young man burst into action. He was a third of the way down the gauntlet before a club so much as touched him.

When an Indian finally did lay a hickory staff alongside of Chard's head, the ensign spun away from the jarring impact and, dropping his shoulders, plowed heavily into a warrior on one side of the line. Then without a moment's hesitation he darted forward and threw his weight into

271

another Indian on the opposite side, knocking both men into their companions.

Chard felt satisfaction wash over him as pandemonium erupted.

He dashed on, watching his assailants closely for an opportunity to butt, kick, or slam into them, knowing that each time he did the unexpected, he created more havoc, which increased his chances for survival. He was well aware that the Indians were screaming for his blood, for he could see their mouths moving rapidly, but all he heard was the constant roaring of his heart that left him deaf to all other sounds.

Blows assailed him from all sides, but such was his fear and anxiety that he felt no pain—that would come later when his adrenaline ebbed. He flung himself toward the end of the line, his breath rasping through his teeth, his muscles trembling from raw abuse.

An Indian ran toward him, flourishing a heavy war club. When the man raised the deadly cudgel above his head, Chard kicked him viciously in the groin. The Indian went down as though he had been poleaxed. Chard silently thanked Bitsy for that trick, too.

But the delay, however short, was disastrous. Clubs rained down on him from all sides, hammering him into the earth like a tent peg being driven into hard, unyielding soil.

He regained consciousness to the sensation of water splashing in his face. When he opened his eyes, he saw that it was not water at all, but a young Indian boy standing over him with widespread legs, urinating. The tribe shouted encouragement to the youngster, cheering him on when he began to trickle, applauding him when he stepped aside to make room for yet another lad who sprang to take his place. Chard had never been so humiliated; it superseded the pain in his limbs, the dizziness in his head, the fear in his heart. And as the youth fumbled beneath his breechclout, Chard pushed himself to his elbow and threw his strength into a backhand blow that sent the boy sprawling into the laughing, hooting congregation that ringed the white man.

An immediate hush fell over the crowd. Chard lay there looking into a hundred expressionless faces more menacing than before. Then the Indians converged on him, dragging him to his feet and propelling him to a nearby tree, where they tied him securely.

The young man's heart almost stopped as they blackened his face and stacked brush in a circle around him, leaving a three-foot open space between him and the eventual fire. He would cook slowly as Ravencraft had done, until, like that poor wretch, he would be more vegetable than human. But unluckily for Chard, rain would not extinguish the flames that would torture his body. Chard leaned into his bonds and worked at the rawhide. He remembered the way Ravencraft had screamed and writhed and begged for someone to kill him, and the memory drove Chard berserk. "You bloody heathen bastards!" he cried. "Cut me loose and let me fight like a man! I demand the right to die in battle as a soldier should!"

But they, not understanding English, thought he was pleading for his life, and they despised him for it.

A stately old man, the gray hair of his roach standing tall, came forward and studied Chard for a long while. He spoke to the men who had captured the ensign, making motions with his hands and counting on his fingers. They crossed their arms and stared into space. The old Indian hastened off and returned shortly with an armload of deerskins.

Chard counted as the ancient warrior laid out ten buckskins.

The Indians shook their heads and encouraged the women and children to pile more brush around the ensign. The old man added five more skins to the pile.

The warriors hesitated, then shook their heads again.

The elderly warrior walked to a tree where the guns were stacked and caught up Chard's rifle. He returned to the waiting men and counted out three more skins. A third time the Indians shook their heads. The old man shrugged and, laying the rifle aside, gathered up the skins and turned to leave. One of Chard's captors stalked forward and laid a restraining hand on the old man's arm. For a brief moment the captors held a muffled conference. The way their roached heads bobbed and swayed with the rhythm of their movements as they argued the old man's offer back and forth reminded Chard of a flock of wild turkeys. Finally, they turned to the warrior and held up two fingers.

For a moment Chard was sure the Indian was going to back out of the transaction, and he cursed himself for entertaining the luxury of hope when there was none. After a long moment, however, the old man threw the skins to the ground and stomped off, leaving Chard to wonder what was taking place. In a few minutes he was back, and muttering to himself, he dropped two additional pelts on the pile.

Scowling darkly, the old warrior hacked away the bonds that secured Chard to the tree, then slipped a rawhide noose over the ensign's head. The rough texture of the uncured leather cut into Chard's neck like wire, but the old man paid it no mind. Tying the end of the six-foot thong to his wrist, he struck off in a fast trot that left Chard hobbling along behind like a semiinvalid.

The Indian led Chard to a lean-to at the edge of the river and motioned for him to sit. Chard slumped to the ground and rubbed his aching arms and legs. He hadn't realized that he had taken such a beating until his fingers explored his bruised and battered muscles.

Chard asked if the man understood English. The Indian shook his head. You are a liar, thought Chard, but he had enough presence of mind not to voice his opinion.

They sat like that, staring at each other, for over an hour. Then, just as Chard decided to venture another question, the old man jumped to his feet, gathered up Chard's rifle and shot pouch, and, yanking at Chard's thong, struck off in the woodsman's trot down a narrow game trail.

At dusk, the Indian slowed his pace, and after several minutes of watching and listening, he abandoned the trail and struck out through the woods. With Chard following, he crept silently to the edge of an open meadow and squatted in the cover of a bramble thicket. Laying Chard's rifle aside, he slipped his hickory bow off his shoulder and selected an arrow from the quiver that hung at his side. He nocked the shaft and waited.

Chard's eyes traveled toward the gun. He felt sure he could snatch it up before the Indian could stop him. And he felt equally sure the old man expected him to make such a move. Chard's eyes narrowed in speculation. He wished he
274

understood the red man as Simon Girty did; maybe then he would know what to do.

Deciding to go for the gun, he lunged toward the rifle, fingers groping frantically in the leaves for the stock. Just as his hand tightened around the smooth wood, the Indian snatched the noose with such force that Chard felt the thong bite deep into his throat, cutting off his breath and driving a white-hot bolt of lightning through his brain. Chard was terrified that the old man intended to strangle him to death or, worse yet, continue to draw the noose gradually tighter until it severed his head.

Chard thrashed and flopped, his fingers tearing at the noose.

The Indian laughed and allowed the line to slacken. Chard frantically worked his fingers under the rawhide. Spots swam before his eyes, and there was a great roaring in his ears, but he was breathing again. He slumped into the foliage, gasping and heaving and cursing himself for being an idiot.

The old man reached out with his bow and popped Chard hard on the top of the head. When Chard looked into the man's wrinkled face, the old Indian wagged his head from side to side as if disappointed that Chard had tried such a foolish stunt. Still coughing, his lips white and pinched, Chard pushed himself to a sitting position and massaged his throat, feeling the bloody gash that would scar him for the rest of his life, a reminder that he was a captive of a savage people who did not know the meaning of mercy.

Savage people? Mercy? Silently, Chard mocked his own simplicity. Were his own people, the British, any less savage? He was sure the Kentuckians, especially the two women who had drowned, would argue that point. There was actually no meaning to the word "civilized," for no matter a man's race, creed, or color, all of them were savages at heart. The only difference was that some were forced by written laws to hide their fiendish nature for fear of their own lives.

His mind leaped to the jail in Detroit, and he conjured up a picture of his mother, shackled and chained while patiently awaiting her trial. He almost wept just thinking about it. After the searing pain of his own rawhide bond, he could not stand the thought of his beloved mother undergoing such mental and physical torture. At that precise moment, Chard Southhampton's blind faith in humanity came to an abrupt end, but he didn't understand the significance of the sadness and bitterness that consumed him. Nor would he have believed it possible that the events of the past few weeks, especially the past few days, would alter ideas and loyalties instilled in him in childhood. But the Indian, who had been observing Chard closely, saw and understood the hard, brittle light that came into the young man's eyes. And he grunted his satisfaction, for he had no time for childishness in full-grown adults. His lips compressed into the slightest of smiles, and he was pleased that he had traded for the white boy who had just become a man.

The Indian settled on his haunches and pulled his gaze to the knee-high grassy plain that stretched out before him. The stems of the wild oats and wheat rippled in the evening breeze like a deep green sea, with an occasional whitecap appearing when the wind bent the dark tips and revealed the lighter undersides of the leaves. It was as if swell after swell rolled headlong into one another as invisible gusts darted across the open meadow.

Then, ever so slowly, the Indian drew the bowstring taut, the fletchings of the arrow resting against the side of his hooked nose. Chard heard the hum of the release, but his eyes were unable to follow the flight of the shaft as it sped toward its unseen mark. The old man gave several quick jerks on Chard's leash, then bounded into the field. Chard flung himself after the man, doing his best to keep slack in the line.

After crossing more than thirty yards of field, Chard was amazed to find that the arrow had taken a groundhog through the head. He felt like a fool. For while he had been straining his eyes for deer or elk, and in truth wondering if the old man had lost his eyesight—and his mind—the Indian had been closely watching the rodent as it periodically raised its head above the grass to scan the field for predators. It was during one of those brief moments that the savage had loosed his arrow.

The red man removed the shaft, checked the flint head to be sure it was tight, then slipped it back into the quiver. Chard had wondered why the Indian did not use the rifle, but after such a display with the bow and arrow, it was easy to see that the primitive weapon was more than adequate.

The young ensign shook his head. What a blessing it was that the white man possessed such superior firepower; for if the British had not possessed the advantage of long-range armament, they would have stood no chance at all against the red man's cunning, strength, and mastery of such ancient weapons.

He was still considering that thought when the Indian handed him flint and steel and, without glancing again at Chard, began skinning the animal.

Chard lay back and watched the flickering light of the campfire play in and out of the pitch-black overhead foliage. He wondered about Girty. Why had he not come to his rescue?

With a hard yank on the thong, the Indian jerked Chard from his speculations, making motions for the young man to go to sleep.

Chard rolled onto his side and closed his eyes. Almost immediately, it seemed, he was awakened by another tug on the leash. It surprised him that daylight had already broken; he didn't remember having fallen asleep.

CHAPTER

· 17 ·

CHARD WAS DUMBSTRUCK when the Indian led him into the clearing behind Lorimer's Store. He had lost his sense of direction days before and had no idea they were anywhere near the establishment.

He quickly scanned the area; Bird and his officers had raised their tents and marquees in the shade of a great elm on the far side of the common grounds well away from the orderly rows of wedge tents that housed the troops. Indian huts and skin shelters were pitched close together near the edge of the forest, many more than Chard remembered when he and Girty had been there, so he assumed that word of the army's arrival had spread quickly, drawing savages from afar. The captives were housed in a cramped compound behind the trading post, between the forest and the necessary building. Then his eyes narrowed. By the numerous fires and the aroma of roasting meat, Chard surmised that Girty had made it back with the elk. Resentment surged through him; he had longed so very much to feed the captives with his own kill.

His face flamed with embarrassment when the entire group of Kentuckians left their fires and stood in silent wonder as the Indian led him past. But as bad as that was, his shame multiplied tenfold when Bitsy pushed her way to the front ranks and stood gawking at him as though he were a freak on display in London's Piccadilly Circus. Chard came to an abrupt halt: he would be damned if he would be a spectacle for Bitsy's entertainment.

The old Indian snatched viciously on the leash, causing

the rawhide to bite painfully into Chard's already lacerated flesh. Ignoring the noose, Chard forced his head around and looked again at the girl, seeing the flash of her white teeth in the sunlight. And in that split second, the respect, tenderness, and understanding that he had felt toward Bitsy since having experienced many of the same hardships that she encountered rose like bile in his throat, nearly choking him.

His eyes flashed her a look akin to hatred, daring her to jeer, or smirk, or make sport of him. With a silent oath, he turned his face away and followed the Indian to the back door of Lorimer's Store.

Bitsy, however, was neither jeering nor smirking. She was shocked by the parade. Her mouth had dropped open in surprise to see an officer of the king's Royal Army being treated like an Indian captive, and her lips had drawn across her teeth in a painful grimace when she realized that Chard was being trotted through camp tethered like a cur dog.

Under normal circumstances she very probably would have reacted with contempt, for she had no love of the British and would gladly have endorsed any torment that befell the soldiers who had brought death and destruction to her country and the people she loved. But the sight of Chard's humiliation struck a nerve deep within her soul. She felt a sympathy and compassion for him that surpassed any emotion she had ever felt for a man.

She cursed herself for having run to the front of the crowd to stare as he passed—it had been childishly stupid. Bitsy wished she could rip the thong from his neck, wipe the traces of black grease from his face, and tell him that she did not take pleasure in his ridicule, that, in truth, it only reinforced her belief that he was different from the other officers she had encountered. Indeed, he was the only person among the British who had shown any consideration for the captives, and she longed to return his kindness. But, being a captive herself, she was forced to stand idly by, unable to venture one step from the area assigned to the Kentuckians, and watch the hatred in his eyes build to a loathing so great that she wished she had not been present to witness his return.

279

The Indian tied the thong to the door of Lorimer's Store, then inspected the bindings that secured Chard's wrists.

Striding haughtily into the building, the old man moved to the end of the counter and crossed his arms. Whiskey fumes and the stench of unwashed bodies almost choked him. His nostrils flared in protest. He did not like being imprisoned inside four walls with a bunch of stinking soldiers. He caught Lorimer's eye and flicked his head toward the rear of the store.

Lorimer waved him away and continued pouring whiskey into the cups of the eager soldiers. He did not intend to miss a shilling's profit on the whim of an ancient Indian. The old man waited patiently for several minutes. Then, careful to avoid touching any of the white men, he leaned across the counter and spoke rapidly to Lorimer.

Throwing his hands into the air in a manner of agitated resignation, the storekeeper drove the bung into the whiskey barrel and followed the Indian toward the door. "Hold your tongues," Lorimer snapped, as the soldiers set up a clamor of protest. "I'll be but one moment, and I'd best not find that bung tampered with when I return, eh?" He shouldered his way through the soldiers and followed the Indian outside to where Chard stood. "What have we here?" he cried, a wide grin flashing across his swarthy face.

Chard smiled back, taking a measure of satisfaction in the sight of the dirty bandage Lorimer wore around his head.

The Indian spoke rapidly, pointing at the ensign periodically, and Lorimer answered in the same language.

"He wants me to buy you, m'sieur," chuckled Lorimer to Chard. "I believe I'll do just that. I could use the free labor, and five pounds is not a bad price. I'll have that much out of your hide in a month's time, eh?"

The storekeeper's face turned ugly. "I still owe you, m'sieur, for damn near breaking my brains out." He fingered the dirty bandage. "I will take great pleasure in repaying the debt."

Chard grinned crookedly. "Better make him throw in my rifle, Lorimer. I might not be worth five pounds."

The storekeeper removed his wallet and counted out the money. "That's why I said you was free labor, m'sieur. The rifle gun, she is worth much more than five pounds."

Chard cast a level gaze at the Indian when Lorimer passed him the money. "Mister," he said to the red man, "if you understand any English at all, take your money and get the bloody hell away from this place."

The Indian's flintlike eyes held Chard's for a long moment.

Lorimer cleared his throat. "Pay no attention to him," he told the Indian. "Come in and have some Monongahela. Come, my friend, see the new shipment of pretties that will strike your fancy. I've got beads, and bracelets . . ."

The Indian swung his eyes toward the forest and trotted toward where he was looking.

"M'sieur," said Lorimer, waving his heavy fist in Chard's face, "I believe I will beat hell out of you here and now."

Chard raised himself to his full height. "Lorimer, I am placing you under arrest for knowingly and willfully purchasing the king's property for the purposes of gainful profit."

Lorimer laughed loudly, clutching the rifle possessively to his chest. "M'sieur, you have been in the woodlands too long. This is a Pennsylvania rifle gun. It has never been the property of the British Army."

"I'm not speaking of the gun," said Chard dryly. "I'm talking about the fact that you have purchased an officer of His Majesty's Royal Army." Chard hesitated as the storekeeper's face turned stormy. "I believe, sir, the punishment for such a crime is hanging by the neck until dead."

"I do not believe you! You are no officer, you are nothing but a popinjay that M'sieur Girty picked up at Detroit."

Chard's eyes narrowed to mere slits. "Cut these bonds, Lorimer." Something in the young man's voice left the storekeeper uncertain and nervous.

Moving to the door, he summoned the soldiers. "Do you know this man?" he demanded when they emerged.

The men stared hard at Chard, seeing the thong that had slashed his neck, the bruises that were visible from his running of the gauntlet, his bleeding wrists where the rawhide had been drawn too tight.

"'Tis Ensign Southhampton," they said angrily to Lorimer, who, seeing the danger of his predicament, hastily cut away the rawhide thongs that bound Chard's neck and hands.

"Drinks are on the house, m'sieur," he said apologetically, forcing a broad smile at the young officer who but a split second before had been his property.

Chard eyed the man coldly. Then, snatching his rifle from the storekeeper, he turned on his heel and strode off in search of Girty.

"What about my five pounds?" called Lorimer angrily.

"See Captain Bird," said Chard over his shoulder. "Perhaps he will reimburse you."

He knew Lorimer would not go to Bird, and he hoped the Indian was long gone, for nothing would infuriate the storekeeper more than losing his precious money.

Chard found Girty at Lorimer's barn. If the man was surprised to see him, his face didn't show it.

"You knew the Indians had taken me," accused Chard without prelude. "Why in hell didn't you come after me?"

Girty eyed Chard with indifference. "Way I saw it," he said, shrugging, "it was one man's problems against the plight of many. If I had come after you, the meat would have spoiled. You wasn't worth it."

Anger made Chard clench his teeth so tightly that the muscles in his jaws stood out like knots. He realized the man's words contained a measure of truth, for feeding the starving soldiers and captives had been the direct object of his and Girty's mission. But still he resented Girty's assumption that his life was not worth letting the people go hungry for a few days more, especially since they had survived for weeks on little more than half a cup of flour per day.

"Don't ever put a price on my life again, Girty," he said levelly. "You may find that you can't afford me. . . . That's not a threat, Simon, it's a fact."

Girty shrugged and walked toward Lorimer's Store.

Chard struck off in a fast stride toward Judith's tent.

Judith had not seen, spoken with, touched, or been touched by a single human being since Chard had been gone, and the solitary confinement that Southhampton had forced on her was taking its toll. She looked absolutely haggard.

She threw her arms around her son and clung tightly to him as if she were terrified to let go. Finally, she laid her cheek against his unshaven jaw and cried and talked, and cried again.

She told him that the flotilla had reached Lorimer's that morning, having pushed hard up Pickawillany Creek without a break, except to sleep at night. Everyone, including Bird and his staff, was nearly dead from exhaustion and malnutrition.

"Thank God," she said, "that Girty was waiting with two elk butchered and ready. He saved our lives, for we were just about starved to death."

Judith looked deep into Chard's eyes, and he saw a glimmer of panic in hers. "When you didn't come to me immediately, as you always do," she said, stroking his cheek, "I was frantic with worry. If anything should happen to you, Chard, I would welcome the hangman's rope."

"Hush," he said gently, deciding to keep his capture by the Indians to himself. "Nothing is going to happen to me."

He held her at arm's length, studying her gaunt and sunken face. "Did they bring you a portion of the elk?"

"Not yet," she murmured. She had seen the pain in his eyes when he gazed at her, and it had hurt her far more deeply than the humiliation of having to beg for food and water.

Chard's face turned murderous. Easing Judith aside, he charged through the tent flaps and flung himself on the startled soldier who stood guard.

"Have you eaten?" he demanded, twisting his fist in the man's tunic and snatching him close.

"Aye, sir, I've et twice today, sir."

"Then why in hell hasn't the prisoner been fed?"

"Major Southhampton said to feed the other prisoners

283

first, sir. Our orders are not to speak to Mrs. Southhampton, nor to pass her any information. Major Southhampton insists that she is to be treated as a spy, sir. She's not to receive any special treatment because of her former social position."

Chard glared at the soldier. He did not have the rank or position to countermand the major's orders. And he knew it would be a waste of time arguing with his father in Judith's behalf. But he would be damned if he would stand idly by and watch his mother starve. "The other prisoners were fed hours ago," he said, facing the soldier squarely so that the man was forced to look into his eyes. "Get Lady Southhampton some food, and do it now."

"Aye, sir."

Chard watched the man race toward the compound, but it brought little consolation. He clenched his fists so tightly that his fingernails cut into his palms. He hated the feeling of inadequacy forced upon him by his military rank and position; his hands were tied as surely as though the army had bound them in chains.

For the first time since becoming a professional soldier, Chard considered resigning his commission—throwing his career to the winds, and freeing himself of the millstone that had hung around his neck since his mother's arrest. He was sick of being part of a group that brought death, destruction, and enslavement to hundreds of innocent people who had done nothing to jeopardize the British Crown. In fact, the whole invasion of Kentucky stank of wasted time and manpower as well as political incompetence. A real war was raging in the East, a war with meaning and substance, a war in which a soldier could fight for his country against a trained army on a field of battle and be proud to wear the colors of the Royal Army. But Chard felt none of that. He was ashamed of the part that the Eighth Regiment had played in the war thus far; ashamed of his role as an officer and leader in such a farce.

Judith hated to see the meal come to an end. She had savored not only the elk steaks but also the closeness and conversation. She was as starved for companionship as for food. So it was with a sinking heart that she embraced Chard and watched him walk away.

She stood in the doorway of her tent and waved until he was out of sight, then raised her eyes longingly to the rooftops of Lorimer's buildings, which rose above the shrubs and bushes surrounding her enclosure. It seemed brutally cold-blooded that she should be stuck off by herself, especially since they had reached the outskirts of civilization. Bird and her husband knew there was no way for her to escape, so the policy of keeping her confined to a solitary existence was not only unnecessary but malicious and cruel as well.

It would have seemed like a holiday to Judith if she could have ventured to the store and gazed at the trade goods, especially the bolts of cloth that Lorimer kept for barter with the Indians.

She glanced at her filthy dress, the same one she had worn when she was whipped. She seethed as she thought about the trunkful of beautiful clothes that Southhampton refused to allow her access to—clothes that he insisted were his property to do with as he pleased.

Judith fingered the ragged fabric of her skirt, her face drawing into a thoughtful frown. Perhaps she had been a bit too hasty when she refused Lieutenant Clarke's proposition? She wasn't a virgin, so what difference did it make if she gave him what he wanted in return for what she so desperately needed? It would almost be worth it just to be allowed to bathe. No! she decided vehemently. As dirty and grimy as she was, she was still cleaner than she would be if she prostituted herself for a hot bath and a new dress.

She stepped inside her tent and sank wearily to the blanket that served as a pallet. "I must be going mad," she murmured aloud. "For years I've been forced to sleep with a man I detest." She tilted her face toward the ceiling of her tent and raised her voice. "I swear to you, Lord, that I would rather die the filthy prisoner that I am than submit to that hell on earth again. No matter what happens to me." Her voice dropped to a whisper, "I'll not abase myself by sleeping with a man I do not love. I'll not!"

She laughed bitterly then, as it dawned on her that very

likely she wouldn't live long enough for it to make any difference whom she slept with.

The guard stuck his head through the flaps of Judith's tent and stared questioningly at her. "I thought you had a visitor, ma'am. I heard talking and laughter."

"I was talking to someone you don't know, soldier," she replied softly.

The man glanced uneasily around the tent. "Orders are that you are not to have company, ma'am."

"He's been here all the time," returned Judith, her eyes brimming with tears. "I just never spoke to Him before."

The soldier frowned and glanced again at the vacant interior. "Lady," he said, backing hastily through the flaps, "you've gone bloody crazy."

Judith heard him move to the second guard and speak in hushed tones. She smiled sadly to herself. Let them think what they would, she wasn't at all sure they were wrong.

Upon reaching Lorimer's, Major Southhampton, as the only officer with a female companion, requisitioned and received permission to bunk in the storekeeper's spare cabin. He wasted no time moving Susan and their belongings into the one-room log building.

Southhampton paced the floor in short, clipped strides.

"You should feel flattered, my dear," he said, scowling at Susan. "Mr. Lorimer has offered to host a party tonight, and you will be the only white woman present. And I think a *champêtre,* as he calls it, celebrating the fact that we are once again in British territory and out of General Clark's reach, is a splendid idea."

"James," returned Susan, weary of the argument that had been raging for nearly an hour, "I am exhausted. You go to Mr. Lorimer's party. I am sure no one will miss one white woman when there will be so many dark-skinned beauties present who will be more than willing to please. I am tired, James. All I want to do this night is rest."

Southhampton eyed the drawn face of his mistress. She had aged ten years since coming to his tent.

The deeply etched crow's-feet seemed even more pronounced because of the dark circles under her eyes. Her full lips were pinched at the corners, and they, too, were crosshatched with lines.

Southhampton was impatient with her seemingly endless fatigue. And her slight, hacking cough was becoming a nuisance, especially at night when he so desperately needed his sleep. His scowl darkened as his eyes moved down Susan's body. She had lost such a startling amount of weight that Judith's dresses no longer hung well on her thin frame; in fact, her body was so changed that he no longer found it appealing. He sighed in disgust. The truth was, he was tired of her. He had used her so many times in every way imaginable that he no longer desired her physically. Even her spirit was broken; she had become too submissive, too uncaring. There was no challenge to her, no fight left in her. Aye, she was a monstrous bore.

He wished he could send her back to the captives' quarters and bring her daughter to his tent in her stead, but that was out of the question. For if she were free to tell Bird the truth, which he was sure she would do, his career would be ruined. Furthermore, he would lose the opportunity to do what he most desired on the face of this earth: witness the death and destruction of Morgan Patterson.

"You will go to Lorimer's party," he instructed coldly, "and, tired or not, you will serve as bar wench for the evening." He smiled arrogantly, and slapped her thin buttocks. "You should have no trouble acting the part. 'Twas your occupation when I first met you."

Pleased by her flush of embarrassment, he laughed and patted her cheek with mock affection. "You amaze me, my dear. I did not think there was another blush in you."

"I was an indentured servant when you met me," she said bitterly, hating him for baiting her this way. "I worked at an inn in Williamsburg. I was not a bar wench or a trollop or a loose woman. I resent your insinuation that I was a whore."

Southhampton smiled sarcastically, his hand dipping beneath the neckline of her bodice to the soft mound below. "Whatever you were, my dear, has little to do with what you are now . . . and you know as well as I that you have become a whore. Surely you can't deny that."

"No, James," she returned, catching his wrist in a futile attempt to draw his hand from her bodice. "I am not a whore . . . I am a prostitute. There is a difference, you know."

Southhampton started to speak, but Susan ignored his intended interruption. "I sold myself to you for my daughter's sake. I've lain with nearly every officer on the expedition because you gave me to them . . . but I didn't come free, as they suppose. My price was high, James . . . very high." She laughed mockingly. "But I am worth it, my dear, for you have made a professional of me. I know every filthy way there is to please a man, thanks to you."

"Have you been charging for your services?" He gripped her breast savagely, his fingernails slicing into the tender flesh.

Susan's knees went weak from pain. "Not in coin, James," she managed through a low moan. "In truth, I have received no profit at all."

"I'm in no mood for games, damn you," he said, releasing her. "What have you charged my fellow officers to sleep with you? Whatever it is, I want my share."

Susan longed to laugh in his face. Every time Southhampton had forced her to submit to his sadistic desires and whims, she had prayed that he would get his "share." She had even enticed him to the cot on several occasions and tried hard to see to it that he benefited from her prostitution. But to her dismay, he thus far appeared to be immune to what she had to offer.

She thought how ironic it was that he had forced a social disease on her, and she could not repay the compliment. And her chances were fast growing slim, for with each passing day, he was becoming more distant toward her, making fewer and fewer personal demands on her body, preferring instead to take his pleasure by watching other men vent their lust between her thighs.

A wave of nausea churned in her stomach as her mind filled with images of what she could expect should Southhampton demand that she join the Indian women in pleasuring the men who attended the party. She ran to her trunk and rummaged through its contents until she located a decanter of rum. Her hand shook as she hastily uncorked the bottle and stared into its fiery contents. Drunkenness was her only asylum. Tipping the bottle to her lips, she drank deeply, again and again.

Bitsy bent over her small fire and awkwardly turned the slab of elk meat. The flame sizzled and sputtered as grease dripped into the hot embers. Even though she no longer had to pack her broken hand in mud, it was still all but useless. She absently tried to flex the thin, twisted fingers, but the pain was so acute that she ceased the endeavor.

"Does the hand bother you, my dear?"

Bitsy looked up, startled by the unexpected intrusion. Southhampton was striding arrogantly toward her.

She immediately busied herself with the food. In the past few days, she had noticed the major eyeing her on several occasions, and it chilled her to the bone.

"I asked you a question."

Bitsy turned the meat again, her eyes downcast. "You can see that I have little use of it, sir."

"That hand should have been splinted properly by the regiment physician."

"'Tis a bit late for that, Major," murmured the girl.

"Let me see it. Perhaps something can yet be done to improve it."

Southhampton caught Bitsy's elbow and drew her upright.

"'Tis a shame," he said, taking her injured hand and stroking it softly. "A girl as lovely as you should not go through life disfigured."

"I'll manage, thank you," said Bitsy, wishing he would leave. The way his eyes roved over her was unsettling. It was a dirty look that left her nervous and shaken. Unruffled by Bitsy's brisk refusal, Southhampton openly caressed her maimed fingers, then drew them to his lips and kissed them.

Bitsy recoiled and tried to break free, but the major gripped the broken hand tightly, putting undue pressure on the newly knitted fractures.

"Please, Major," whispered the girl, her eyes big with pain. "You are hurting me, sir."

"I wouldn't hurt a pretty little thing like you," he said,

releasing her. "No, indeed, I wouldn't think of hurting you. . . . Why that would be a sacrilege. You were born for pleasure, my dear, strictly for pleasure."

Bitsy cupped her aching hand to her breast in alarm. She understood the underlying threat beneath Southhampton's softspoken words, and it turned her knees to water. She had never been afraid of a man in her life, but she was terrified of the major.

"How is my mother?" she asked, desperately choosing a parental figure for protection, as most children will do.

Southhampton frowned. The mention of Susan had neatly blocked his advance. And for a split second his face was ugly and repulsive, but he hurriedly disguised the expression with a smile that extended only to his lips. "She is quite happy, my dear, quite happy indeed."

Bitsy's heart broke. A more experienced woman would have known instantly that he was lying. But Bitsy had yet to gain that particular wisdom which is acquired through close acquaintance with devious people of the opposite sex.

Bitsy sighed deeply, wondering how her mother could have changed so drastically in such a short while. Indeed, Susan had certainly seemed happy the night Bitsy had watched the man carry her to Southhampton's marquee.

"Perhaps sometime in the near future, I could arrange for you to see Susan," suggested Southhampton.

Bitsy shook her head. "No, thank you, Major. I want no favors. Not from you, not from anyone."

She could have added that of all the British officers present he was the last one from whom she would accept a favor, but she let it pass, for in truth, she felt sick and wished he would simply go away.

"You are a foolish young woman, Bitsy," he said irritably. "I've come to offer you friendship."

Bitsy bent again to the cooking meat, ending the conversation. She glanced out of the corner of her eye as Southhampton stalked away. She knew exactly what he had come to offer.

Chard had not been invited to Lorimer's party. But as the noise and merrymaking grew louder and louder, curiosity nagged at him until he couldn't resist the temptation to see what all the revelry was about.

He shucked off his buckskins and cold-shaved his bristling jawline. Slipping into his red tunic and carrying his tricorne under his arm, he walked to Lorimer's Store and leaned against the jamb of the open door.

Red- and green-coated officers were clustered in small groups, singing boisterous songs and toasting their Indian women with goblets of Monongahela. The Tories, McGee and Elliott, stood off by themselves and drank quietly as if they were ill at ease. The Girtys were absent, and Chard guessed they had not been invited.

Lorimer was dipping drinks as fast as Susan could carry them to the impatient celebrants. Everyone, including the Indian women, seemed bent on getting drunk as quickly as possible. Chard saw his father in deep conversation with Captain Bird, and he had to smile. The captain looked bored, as though he wished he were elsewhere.

Susan flitted across the floor to where Chard stood. "Hello, soldier," she slurred, her breath reeking so strongly of whiskey that the young ensign was forced to turn his head. As recognition penetrated her dull mind, Susan took a step backward, her bleary eyes trying hard to focus, her flushed face draining to a pasty gray.

"I did not think you would come to such a place as this," she said almost soberly. "I thought that somehow you were different." She dropped her gaze and stared at the floor. "I had hoped that you were different," she finished, her voice small.

Chard studied her for a long moment. "What are you talking about, Mrs. Patterson?"

Susan raised her eyes, and Chard saw the shame in their depths. "What kind of party is this, Mrs. Patterson?" he inquired.

"Well, Chard," interrupted Southhampton before Susan could reply, "you and Susan seem to have a great deal to say to each other."

The ensign cleared his throat. "Mrs. Patterson was merely offering me a cup of whiskey."

"Really? I thought perhaps she was trying to entice you to the stockroom, to offer you a taste of her . . . wine."

Chard's face flamed, and he glanced apologetically at Susan. "No, sir," he said in a cool voice that belied his embarrassment. "In fact, sir, I have no idea of what you are talking about, nor do I wish to know."

"Well, well," laughed Southhampton, "we have a true gentleman among us."

"Leave him alone, James," pleaded Susan. "He's a decent young man, the only one I've met lately."

"Obviously," said the major with a mock smile, "he has been too busy running through the woods to know what has been going on."

Susan eyed Southhampton coldly. "I'm sure you are just dying to enlighten him, but I shall do it for you." She turned to Chard and smiled acidly, but before she could speak, Chard spun on his heel and walked into the night.

He was shocked by what he had witnessed, and it had nothing to do with the fact that Susan was drunk, for he, like every other soldier under Bird's command, was well aware of her fondness for liquor. No, it was more than that. Something was physically wrong with her; any fool with half an eye could see that. She was a mere shadow of the beautiful woman she had been, and without a doubt, she should be under the doctor's care. He changed course and strode quickly to the surgeon's tent.

"Has Mrs. Patterson been to see you?" he demanded, bursting through the flaps.

The surgeon looked up from the report he was writing, the candlelight casting small flashing prisms off his square wire-rimmed spectacles. "You know I don't treat captives," he barked, obviously displeased at having been interrupted. "And I damn sure won't tend that slut."

"Why the bloody hell not?" asked Chard angrily. "The woman's sick, she needs attention."

The doctor laid his quill aside and frowned. "Half the officers in this company have come down with the clap. They all claim it come from her—which is a damned lie. They caught it from them female savages and gave it to her. But they're blaming her anyway, which, I might point out, they couldn't do if they hadn't lain with her. And now you're here. . . . Have you got it too?"

"Doctor," said Chard softly, taking a long step into the tent, "if you say one more word concerning Mrs. Patterson's virtue, I'll forget that you are my superior and knock your teeth down your throat."

"Now, see here," cried the man, jumping to his feet so hastily that he overturned the inkwell and knocked his papers to the floor. "I'll have none of that talk. Whether you wish to acknowledge it or not, sir, the woman is a whore, and you had best accept the fact."

The doctor's face softened, and he laid his hand gently on Chard's arm. "Hell, Ensign, I admire your chivalry, but you need to grow up a bit and face the facts. Mrs. Patterson has bedded nearly every officer in Bird's command, from the youngest to the oldest. She has diseased several who are married, men who haven't been with an Indian woman. I apologize for implying that you, too, might have bedded her, but it was the first thought that entered my mind when you asked about her."

Chard's shoulders slumped. He felt foolish for his outburst, but he was even more embarrassed by the cause of Susan's poor health. He had intended to demand that the surgeon examine her, but he could forget that; no army doctor would waste a minute of his time on a civilian woman with a social disease, even if she infected the whole command. He would treat the men, but not the women.

"Forget about her, son," said the doctor. "She's not worthy of your concern. Obviously, she's doing what comes naturally to her."

"I suppose you're right. . . . It's just that when I first met her, she didn't seem like that kind of woman."

"Lots of people have a base streak in them that they keep well hidden until time or circumstance allows it to surface. Mayhap that is Mrs. Patterson's case." The doctor raised his eyebrows and stared wisely at Chard. "After all, she is away from her husband and probably will be for the rest of her life. People do strange things when they find themselves free of commitment, especially those who fear that their youth and beauty are waning."

"She didn't strike me as a vain woman, doctor. In fact, she appeared completely devoted to her daughter and her husband."

"Well, as I said"—the doctor turned and began gathering his scattered papers—"you never know about people."

293

Chard left the tent and headed for Lorimer's Store. He couldn't believe he had been so wrong about Susan.

He entered the establishment and glanced quickly around the interior. Susan was not in sight. Nor were his father, Lorimer, or Captain Bird.

"Where's Mrs. Patterson?" he asked a group of howling officers who were all trying at once to disrobe a giggling young Indian girl who had fallen drunkenly to the floor.

"In the storeroom," said one of the men, obviously displeased at having been interrupted, "probably giving a dose—"

Chard stiff-armed the man aside and walked to the closed door. He didn't knock, but flung the door open and angrily surveyed the room.

Southhampton, Bird, Clarke, and Lorimer were sitting at a small table, their heads bent in deep conversation. Susan stood huddled in a corner, her face as white as death.

"What in hell do you mean by bursting in on a private meeting, Chard?" demanded Southhampton, rising slowly off his stool and facing his son. "Have you taken leave of what little sense you have?"

"M'sieur," said Lorimer to Southhampton, "you flatter the man. He has no goddamn sense at all."

"If you please, Mr. Lorimer," interjected Bird, "you are speaking of an officer of His Majesty's Royal Army, sir. And I'll have no disrespect from a civilian."

Lorimer dropped heavily onto his stool, his face flushed with embarrassment.

"What do you want, Ensign?" The captain turned to Chard.

Chard stalked to the table and leaned on his knuckles. "With all due respect, Captain Bird, I request permission to inquire into the nature of this business meeting, especially if it has anything to do with Mrs. Patterson."

"Mrs. Patterson is none of your business, Ensign," cried Southhampton, "and I am damned tired of your interference!"

"Captain Bird," said Chard, holding his commanding officer in an iron gaze, "my honor and integrity as a British officer and a gentleman are held above reproach, as are yours, sir. And when either of those traits is being compromised, I believe I have the right to interfere as I see fit."

Bird eyed the young man with interest. "What does Mrs. Patterson have to do with your honor and integrity, sir?"

Chard's eyes flashed as he leaned farther across the table and spoke directly into the captain's face. "You, sir," he said deliberately, "sent me into Ruddle's Fort under a flag of truce. I carried your articles of surrender to the Americans and read them aloud in your behalf." Chard's gaze turned hard and demanding, giving Bird a moment of awkward embarrassment. "Acting in good faith, sir, I personally promised Susan Patterson and her daughter safe passage to the next settlement, as you stated in your terms of surrender.

"I am honor bound," he continued flatly, "to protect these prisoners to the best of my ability until they are safely delivered to Detroit . . . as is every officer on this expedition, including yourself, sir."

Bird leaned back and observed Chard thoughtfully. "You've made a point, Ensign. But my first consideration is to my command." Bird made a tent with his fingers and pursed his lips. "Mrs. Patterson has become quite a liability to this expedition, and although I am most sympathetic toward the undesirable position Major Southhampton and I have placed you in, the health and well-being of the officers and enlisted men of the Eighth Regiment come before all else."

Southhampton smiled arrogantly as Bird looked up through his brows at Chard and continued, "Normally, a commander would flog a woman with Mrs. Patterson's morals and abandon her without food or water. But I am too compassionate and reasonable to do that, and so I have decided to consider Major Southhampton's proposal that the army sell Mrs. Patterson to Mr. Lorimer."

"Sell her to Lorimer!" cried Chard, turning to the storekeeper in surprise. "The army doesn't have the right to sell people. Even if it did, what in bloody hell does Lorimer want with her? 'Tis obvious she would be of no use as a slave; she hasn't the strength to last a week in the fields."

Lorimer leaned back on the stool and laughed loudly. "I have no intention of putting her to hard labor, m'sieur. To the contrary, she will pursue the trade which she plies so well. The only difference will be the clientele."

295

"What in hell does that mean?" asked Chard angrily.

"Men are men, m'sieur," shrugged Lorimer. "Red or white, after they have a cup or two of Monongahela, they will trade everything they own for a piece of her pale-skinned arse."

Not waiting for more, Chard flung himself across the table and smashed his fist into the storekeeper's mouth, overturning the Frenchman's chair so that, amid a flurry of flailing fists and elbows, both men fell heavily against Southhampton. White-faced and panting, the major kicked the struggling men from him and quickly ran to the door, screaming for help as he went.

Even though Chard had the element of surprise in his favor and an abounding desire to beat Lorimer to a pulp, in hand-to-hand combat he was no match for a man who had spent his entire life on the frontier. So, try as he might, when the men burst into the room, Chard was already taking a terrible beating.

The soldiers dragged Lorimer to the far side of the room and slammed him against the wall, instructing him to stay there. Chard was not quite so easy to handle. Although Lorimer had pounded him nearly senseless, he plunged and thrashed and kicked in a frenzied attempt to renew the fight. But the soldiers pinioned his arms behind him and manhandled him through the door that separated the two rooms.

"Calm down, for Christ's sake," said one of the officers who were struggling to hold Chard steady while another forced a shot of whiskey down his throat. "Your arse is in enough trouble. Captain Bird is furious. Now drink this Monongahela and quit fighting us; we're only trying to help you."

Chard flinched as the raw alcohol scorched his lace-rated mouth and burned its way toward his stomach. He pushed the drink aside and gazed angrily at the storeroom. He didn't give a damn if Bird was furious. In fact, he didn't care if the whole army was furious. What was taking place behind that door was wrong—morally, spiritually, and militarily wrong, and he had it in mind to go back in there and finish what he had started.

At that moment, however, Susan emerged with South-hampton yanking her roughly by the arm. The major looked threateningly at Chard. Then, pushing Susan before him with short, stiff jabs, he propelled her across the floor and into the night. The sight of Susan, downcast and unresisting, brought Chard to his senses, his anger abating as quickly as it had arisen. She was certainly not the brave lady who had staunchly refused to accept surrender at Ruddle's Fort; nor was she the strong-willed woman who had marched across the mountains, steadfastly encouraging her countrymen not to lose heart; nor was she the same softspoken woman who had insisted on carrying the children of those who had gone their last step when she was, in truth, in worse physical condition than they.

Chard shook his head in bewilderment. Something had changed Susan into a mockery of what she had been, and Chard was beginning to suspect that there was a lot more involved than the simple vanity and inborn baseness the doctor had mentioned. No, James Southhampton knew the answer, but Chard was sure he would never reveal the truth, for somehow, some way, he was directly involved with the change in her behavior. But try as he might, Chard could not figure how his father could have gained such a stranglehold on a person of Susan's character. It was a mystery indeed, but he intended to get to the bottom of it.

Chard found Bitsy asleep in her blankets. In the moonlight, with her thick copper hair billowing in disarray around her small face, she appeared angelic, childlike. He knelt, almost hating to wake her, but his urgent desire to get to the heart of Susan's dilemma was uppermost in his mind, and he gently shook her shoulder.

Bitsy awoke instantly, peering into his face in wide-eyed alarm. He admired her for not crying out or making any unnecessary noise, for he had it in mind to slip her away so they could talk privately. Chard put his finger to his lips and, walking quietly toward the woods, beckoned for her to follow.

Bitsy sat up and stared at him. She had no intention of following him anywhere. Chard retraced his steps and put his lips close to her ear. "I've got to talk to you. Please come."

The seriousness in his voice disturbed her, but his plea

297

for her to accompany him left her tingling with curiosity. Still, she was reluctant, remembering his hate-filled eyes when the Indian led him past the prisoners' compound.

"What do you want?" she asked hesitantly.

"I want to talk to you, damnit. It's important."

Bitsy drew herself erect, clutching the blanket tightly about her shoulders. He had changed since she had last seen him; he was a stranger who frightened and intimidated her, and she was not at all sure that she wished to be alone with him in the dark forest. But she did not resist when Chard caught her by the elbow and guided her silently away from the sleeping compound.

Chard had already bribed the guard, who smiled knowingly as the two approached and continued to walk his beat as if he had seen nothing. Bitsy bristled. She resented the guard's unspoken implication, for even in the darkness she had seen his conspiring grin—the look normally reserved for one who is helping young lovers to find time alone—and she wondered what Chard had told the man. But then Chard's hand was at the small of her back, forcefully guiding her toward the silent forest. She found herself both apprehensive and excited by his assertive behavior.

Yet, as Chard drew her farther and farther into the timber, suspicion overrode curiosity, and Bitsy drew to an abrupt halt. "We've gone far enough, Chard." She glanced over her shoulder and gauged the distance to the camp should she be forced to scream for help.

"Listen, Bitsy," said Chard peevishly, "I don't like this any more than you do, so you can get the chip off your shoulder. I'm sick of your jeers and taunts. And don't flatter yourself; you've nothing I want except information."

Although the girl's expression remained unchanged, she knew a moment of galling embarrassment. Then his final word penetrated her humiliation. Drawing herself indignantly to her full height, she eyed him hatefully. "I have no information that would do you any good, and I resent your assumption that I would betray my countrymen."

Chard stepped close and peered angrily into her face. "I wish to hell that, just once, you would get off your goddamn high horse and listen to what someone has to say.

I wouldn't ask or expect you to betray your countrymen. Damn it, Bitsy, that's not why I asked you out here."

Again Bitsy had the feeling that she was facing a stranger, and she was not at all sure that she enjoyed the sensation.

"I asked you out here to discuss your mother."

Bitsy stared at him for a long incredulous moment. Then she wheeled and raced toward the darkened compound. Chard caught her in three strides, slipping his arm around her waist and pinning her against him.

Bitsy struggled with a fury born of outrage, but Chard's strong arms were like bands of steel as they closed more tightly around her, drawing her securely into his embrace.

"There's been some talk about your mother," he said into her ear as she thrashed and kicked and wished that she were facing him so she could again use the trick her father had taught her. But held as she was, and entangled in the blanket she carried, she found herself completely at his mercy, and hated it—and him.

"My father has a saying about gossip," she hissed, still struggling to break free. "He says that words are like feathers flung into the wind. They travel far, and no matter how hard you try, they are almost impossible to gather up again. So take your gossip, Chard, and carry it straight to hell."

Chard spun Bitsy around and shook her savagely. "Listen to me, damn you. I'm not interested in gossip any more than you are. I'm concerned for your mother!"

"Why?" she cried. "My mother is sleeping with your father! Is that what you wanted to hear?"

Chard could feel the girl's shoulders shake, and although he did not hear a sound, he knew she was crying.

"No," he said softly, releasing his grip and drawing her tenderly to him. "What I want to know is *why* she is sleeping with him."

Bitsy found herself comforted by the gentle strength of his embrace. She felt secure and protected for the first time in weeks; it was as though someone had lifted a heavy burden from her shoulders, and without thinking, she laid her cheek against Chard's chest and clung tightly to him.

"I've lain awake every night since she went to him and asked myself that same question," she admitted with a sob.

Chard sensed her need for reassurance, understanding, and compassion; the simple, uncomplicated desire to be held. Her unspoken yet clear acknowledgment of dependence humbled him, making him even more aware of the responsibility her fledgling trust placed on him. He tightened his arms about her and laid his lips against her rumpled hair. Lord, how he wished he could protect her from the hurt and disgrace of her mother's sordid behavior.

"I'm sorry," said Bitsy, turning reluctantly from his embrace and walking a few feet away. "I guess I'm not as strong as I thought I was."

"'Tis not weakness that causes one to seek strength in the arms of another," Chard said softly. "'Tis courage. It takes a brave person to admit that she is not the most powerful human in the world. I admire you for it, Bitsy."

Bitsy wished that she could be honest enough with Chard to tell him how truly tired she sometimes was of putting on a courageous face. But she was afraid he would think her a whiner, so she said nothing. And Chard, being equally as hesitant to reveal his true self, longed to take her in his arms again and tell her how very brave she actually was. But he resisted that simple impulse for fear that his intentions might be misunderstood and spoil the closeness of the moment. So he, too, said nothing.

Bitsy spread her blanket on the ground and sat down wearily, her chin resting on bent knees. Chard dropped down beside her and gazed at her profile in the dim light of the crescent moon.

She's so damn beautiful, he thought, and she doesn't even know it.

"Chard," she said, not looking at him, "I . . . Is it true . . . about my mama?"

The young ensign's mouth went dry. He wanted to tell her what he had seen and heard in Lorimer's Store, but he couldn't bring himself to hurt her.

"Bitsy," he said, touching her cheek and gently turning her face toward him, "I didn't ask you out here to repeat malicious tattle—and that's all it would be. Lord knows, there's been enough of that already. I was hoping you might know the reason she sacrificed her honor and virtue to assume the role of harlot?"

He immediately regretted his choice of words. For

300

even in the darkness, he could see the hurt in Bitsy's face as she dropped her eyes and studied the hem of her dress, her fingers nervously working the fabric.

"I won't sit here and act as though I don't know what you are talking about," she said, avoiding his eyes. "But I have no idea why she is . . . doing what she is. I do know this for certain, Chard: she loves my papa. And neither you nor your father nor anyone else will ever convince me differently."

"I feel the same way as you," he said earnestly. "I don't believe for a minute that she went to my father willingly." He frowned into the darkness. "Something happened to change her, and I was hoping you and I might figure out what it is."

"Why are you so interested? After all, we are nothing but captives, people without names or faces or lives of our own."

"Don't be bitter," he said gently. "I know you have a right to be, but let's just talk as friends should talk. Perhaps together we can shed some light on this puzzle."

"We're not friends, Chard," she returned, studying his face soberly. "We are enemies, drawn together in a war that has no meaning . . . to us Kentuckians anyway."

"We're not enemies tonight," he said seriously. "Tonight there's just you and me."

"I won't discuss my mother with you, Chard," she said flatly.

Chard exhaled through his teeth. She was right. Susan Patterson was none of his business any more than Judith's treasonous actions were Bitsy's. And he was forced to admit that he would not tolerate an outsider probing into his mother's private life.

"Please accept my apology, Bitsy. I had no right to presume."

"You don't have to apologize, Chard. You are too much a gentleman to intentionally insult or hurt anyone. . . . Well, almost too much a gentleman," she said, remembering the day he tried to seduce her. She smiled then, her eyes roaming over his battered face. "Although, from the looks of you, George Girty must have retaliated for your knocking him down the other day."

Her grin was contagious. And in spite of the ache that

spread through him because her assumption was so far from the pathetic truth, he could not help laughing with her. They sat there, two young people talking in the night, sharing thoughts and dreams—and nightmares. They talked of their homes and their childhood. Bitsy told him of her birth and her first recollections of Kentucky, so different, so beautiful compared to the Kentucky Chard had seen. Chard found Bitsy's description of frontier life astounding and exciting. And Bitsy listened with equal fascination while he painted her a picture of England and his boyhood days.

They talked of hunting and eventually of Indians, and Chard told her of his running of the gauntlet and the tricks he had used—*her* tricks—and they laughed as they remembered the confusion and exasperated rage of the Indians when they had flailed one another with their staves. Bitsy self-consciously touched Chard's neck where the lash had cut into his throat, her gnarled fingers gently caressing the tender flesh. "We will both carry scars of the gauntlet for the rest of our lives," she said with a sigh.

"Aye," he returned, gently taking her twisted fingers in his strong hands. "But we survived . . . and I have you to thank for that."

Bitsy blushed under the compliment, and they sat like that for a long time, saying nothing, not needing to. Chard covertly studied her profile, admiring her high forehead, her small, straight nose, her full, sensuous lips that turned up at the corners in a shy smile. He longed to take her in his arms and kiss her, to experience the sweet softness of her mouth, the same yielding, searching warmth of the kiss she had returned the moment before she had kicked him. Remembering that last part, he grimaced and allowed the desire to pass, not because he was frightened that she would hurt him but because he was afraid he might offend her.

They were amazed when they finally looked around and found that dawn was breaking.

Chard helped Bitsy to her feet. "I've enjoyed this evening," he said honestly. "Will you meet me again tonight? I want to see you, Bitsy."

Bitsy shook her head. "No, Chard. No matter how beautiful this night has been, it has to stop here."

She eyed him levelly. "You are British and I am American."

"I know." He smiled. "I am the enemy."

Bitsy dropped her gaze. "'Tis not funny, Chard. You are the son of a man I loathe, and of a woman who detests the ground I walk on. No, Chard, there's no use in our seeing each other again. Half your family doesn't approve of me, and I despise the other half."

Bitsy's heart skipped a beat as Chard's lips thinned into a determined line. She stared hopefully into his eyes, praying that he had found the confidence to stand on his own two feet, to be his own man. And at that crucial moment, if Chard had only hinted that regardless of what she or anyone else had to say about it, he intended to see her again, Bitsy very likely would have thrown herself into his arms and given him the kiss he so desperately desired; for even though she was young and inexperienced, she saw in him the making of a good and decent man.

"Perhaps you are right," he said, shattering her hopes. "I owe my parents the courtesy of being a dutiful son."

Chard read the disappointment in her face, and he knew that once again he had somehow failed her.

"I suppose you do," she said, turning away.

He caught her arm and drew her to him. "Damn it, Bitsy, why does every pleasant moment we share always end on a sour note?"

Bitsy raised her head and studied his face searchingly. "You've changed a great deal in the past few weeks, Chard . . . but you haven't changed enough."

Before he could question her further, she slipped from his embrace and fled headlong down the path toward the prisoners' compound.

The same guard who had helped the two young people slip away the night before blocked her approach as she attempted to sneak into the camp. He smiled brazenly, eyeing the blanket she carried. "The bloody officers have all the fun," he said, his eyes sliding along her body.

Bitsy's shoulders slumped. She had hoped to steal back into the camp unobserved, but the soldier had spoiled any
303

chance of that. Refusing to add dignity to his statement by commenting one way or the other, she stepped off the path and started around him.

The guard caught her arm and snatched her roughly against his body. "I know what you did last night," he said, his face close to hers, "so don't play the grand lady with me. You American sluts are all alike: you turn your noses up at us that don't have rank or title, and turn your arses up for those that does."

Bitsy felt a volcanic rage well up within her. Shaking with fury, she transferred the blanket to her broken hand and balled her small uninjured fist into a tight knot. Before she could vent her wrath, however, Captain Bird intervened and saved the unsuspecting private a clout to the head that very likely would have left its mark on his unsuspecting mouth for a long while.

Bird, who was accompanying a group of officers to Lorimer's Store, broke away and hurried toward the struggling couple. "What the bloody hell is going on here?" he demanded angrily. "Unhand that woman, Private. You know my orders concerning the female captives."

"Aye, sir!" The private released Bitsy so quickly that she lost her balance and sprawled heavily in the grass. She was up immediately, glaring angrily at the soldier.

"Again I say, what is the meaning of this?" Bird looked from Bitsy to the guard. "Speak up, Private."

The man took a deep breath. He was well aware that the captain had issued an order prohibiting the soldiers from fraternizing with the prisoners. The punishment was the same terrible penalty that Mrs. Southhampton had undergone, except that Bird's orders were fifty lashes with the cat-o'-nine-tails instead of ten.

Sweat popped out on his face. "This woman approached me with a proposition, sir. She even brung her blanket." He grabbed a corner of the cover and shook it for emphasis. "I told her to return to the compound, sir, but she got mean about it. 'Tis not the first time she has tried it, sir."

Bitsy was speechless. She could only stare at Captain Bird in open-mouthed shock as he gazed furiously into her face. "You are Mrs. Patterson's daughter, are you not?"

"I am, sir." Bitsy was astonished that Bird would believe such an obvious, bare-faced lie.

"I might have known," he said, disgusted. Then his face hardened, and Bitsy was sure he intended to strike her. Instead, he pointed toward the campground. "Take your blanket and get back where you belong, and don't solicit my men again. One American whore in camp is quite enough."

With that, he turned on his heel and stalked off to the waiting officers.

Bitsy knew the captain was speaking of her mother, and her lips trembled with outrage, not for herself but for Susan, who could not come to her own defense. She quickly glanced toward the captive area to see if Bird's statement had reached the ears of the prisoners. It had. The Kentuckians were staring hard at her with the same righteous look they had given her when she moved from Judith's tent to the prisoners' compound.

It would have been a difficult task for a person twice Bitsy's age to hold her head up in front of the silent, accusing people who waited for her when she faced the camp, but, blessed with a young, courageous heart, she tried. With a vow not to crumple in the face of their malice, she drew herself to her full height and walked with unwavering dignity toward the hard-eyed congregation who stood in self-appointed judgment of her and Susan. She probably would have succeeded in her attempt had not one of the women pointed an accusing finger at her and cried, "Morgan Patterson will rue the day he ever called you daughter!"

Bitsy felt the tears coming. She took her lower lip between her teeth and bit hard, determined not to cry. But the physical pain was an insufficient distraction from the total devastation of mind and heart caused by the cruel words. Bitsy's tears triggered an avalanche of suppressed emotions that had long since passed the point of healthy restraint, and her proud carriage slumped as though the lightweight blanket had suddenly become too heavy a burden for her to support. She turned her face away from the woman who had spoken and, with a questioning frown, as though it required all her concentration just to put one foot before the other, she passed slowly through her countrymen.

CHAPTER
· 18 ·

SUSAN AWOKE ALONE, her head splitting. She had drunk so much the night before that she had passed out on the floor of the cabin, and Southhampton had left her where she lay. Slowly, her befuddled mind recalled the conversation in Lorimer's storeroom. She shook her head and massaged her throbbing temples; surely she had been dreaming. But deep down inside, she knew that it was no dream; Southhampton had insisted that Captain Bird sell her to Lorimer, and Bird was seriously considering the proposal.

Susan crawled to the bed and, after several unsuccessful attempts, finally managed to pull herself atop the straw-filled mattress. Burying her face in the bedcovers, she cried softly. Susan knew she had made a grave error; she should have gone to Captain Bird weeks ago when Southhampton first approached her. But the major had so thoroughly terrified and demoralized her with his threats against Bitsy and successfully filled her with guilt for the two women who drowned that she had panicked and made a momentous mistake. Now it was too late.

She picked up Judith's hand mirror and studied the woman who stared back at her. She was a stranger. Her eyes were puffed and bloodshot, underlined by dark circles. Her cheeks were sunken, yet at the same time bloated from excess alcohol.

"I don't know you anymore," she whispered to the haggard woman in the glass.

No one does, returned the image in the mirror. I don't even know myself.

With a sigh, Susan laid the mirror aside.

She had reached a decision: if Captain Bird sold her to Lorimer, she would wait until the army and captives evacuated for Detroit. Then she would see to it that the storekeeper lost his opportunity to profit from her body —and this time, she would not allow anyone to interfere.

Grimacing from the pounding in her temples, she rose unsteadily and walked to the cabin door. The sun was already high, and its glaring light pierced her head like a thousand tiny spears. She squinted, trying to filter the blinding rays through her eyelashes, but the effort was wasted. She retreated into the shaded interior until her eyes became better adjusted to the light, then again stepped to the door. Captain Bird, angry and determined-looking, was marching purposefully toward the trading post.

Susan straightened her rumpled dress and, patting her disheveled hair into a semblance of order, stepped out of the cabin and walked uncertainly toward the building into which Bird had disappeared. Off-duty soldiers lounging in the shade near the store held their cups high and toasted her as the officers' whore, and some, bolder, asked her to slip into the woods with them. Susan hastened her pace, praying that they would let her pass without incident.

A sergeant shoved himself away from the wall where he had been leaning and fixed Susan with a hard glare. "Don't look so fearful, missy," he said drunkenly. "The whole camp knows you got the French pox. Ain't a man here would give a shilling to raise your dress."

Susan rushed through the open door of Lorimer's Store and sagged heavily against the inside facing, her heart pounding wildly. Taking a deep breath, she pushed herself erect, walked unsteadily to Bird, and asked to speak to him in private. A look of annoyance crossed his face, but he followed her to a secluded corner.

"Have you made your mind up, sir, concerning Major Southhampton's proposal?" she asked pointedly.

Bird scowled at her and turned his head. Her stale breath was nauseating.

"Madam, I am still giving the matter serious consideration. If you have called me aside to plead your case, you are wasting your time and mine. When I reach a decision, you will be advised."

307

"That's very kind of you, Captain," she said, "but I did not come to plead; I came to bargain."

"Madam . . ." said Bird, shaking his head.

"Hear me out, Captain. 'Tis the least you can do."

Bird nodded for her to continue.

"I will stay here at Lorimer's willingly if you will promise me one small favor."

"Mrs. Patterson," said Bird wearily, "you are in no position to ask for favors or to bargain in any fashion. However, what is the favor you ask?"

"Only that you, personally, keep a close eye on my daughter."

Bird's face turned livid. "Your daughter!"

"Yes, sir." Susan frowned at the man, perplexed by his open hostility. "I only ask that you see to it that no harm befalls her."

"Madam, you insult my intelligence. I spoke with your daughter not an hour ago, and I'm of a mind to sell the both of you to Lorimer."

Susan's face turned gray. "Surely you wouldn't do that, Captain. She's a good and decent child."

Bird's mouth twisted skeptically. "She follows in her mother's footsteps, and you damn well know it. Why, just this morning she was trying to entice one of the privates—"

"Liar!" cried Susan, striking Bird openhandedly across the face. "You British are nothing but liars!"

"Very well, Mrs. Patterson," he said slowly, touching the imprint her fingers had left on his cheek, "that settles it. Both of you shall become the property of Mr. Lorimer."

Susan's knees turned to water and she groped at Bird's shoulder for support. She had unwittingly condemned her daughter to the very existence that she had sacrificed everything to protect her from.

Bird shoved Susan roughly aside and walked to the counter where Lorimer, who had witnessed the confrontation, lounged insolently. Bird spoke briefly to the storekeeper, then without glancing at Susan strode angrily through the door.

Susan ran to the entrance and clung to the doorframe. She wanted to scream at Bird, to let him know what a wretched beast he was, an inhuman, senseless creature who had no right to dictate her daughter's future. She wanted to tell him that neither he nor any other human being could assume the privilege of playing God when an innocent girl's life was at stake. Susan's trembling fingers dug into the door facing with such force that her fingernails were ripped from their quicks and large drops of blood stained the rough-hewn wooden frame. She didn't feel a thing.

Chard stood at attention inside Captain Bird's marquee. "You sent for me, sir?"

Bird looked up from his notes and studied the young officer intently. "Stand at ease, Ensign."

Chard eased his rigid stance, but he didn't relax. He guessed that the senior officer intended to reprimand him for his outlandish conduct at Lorimer's the previous night —and in that respect he was quite correct.

"You have pushed me past the limit of my patience, Ensign," said Bird flatly. "Your outburst against Lorimer was conduct unbecoming an officer of His Majesty's Royal Army, sir. Such a display of physical violence certainly does not befit a British gentleman."

When Chard remained silent, the captain continued, "You have been a troublemaker throughout this entire campaign, sir, and frankly, I am disappointed. The army is no place for idealism or unconformity."

"Idealism! Unconformity!" shouted Chard. "This whole bloody farce that you refer to as a campaign has been nothing but unconformity. We haven't been an army since we left Detroit, and you damn well know it. Hell, everyone knows it, including the Indians. If we had been an army, the Indians would never have demanded—and gotten—the captives from Ruddle's Fort. And since when does the British Army take people who have honorably surrendered and sell them into prostitution? Answer me that, Captain!"

Bird's face mottled with outrage. "Hold your tongue, Ensign, or I'll have you in irons. I, sir, am in no way obligated to answer to you, or anyone else on this expedition."

"Then I pray that God may have mercy on your soul, Captain Bird, because you will sure as hell have to answer to Him."

Bird rose slowly from his field desk, his anger so

intense that his hands were shaking. "Not one more god-damn word, Ensign. Not one more word!"

Chard drew himself to rigid attention and stared unblinkingly into Bird's face. "I purchased my commission in the Eighth Regiment believing that I could serve the king and Britain in honorable service, sir. But I find that an impossibility, for a man cannot conduct himself honorably when he is constantly thwarted by the debasing and self-serving behavior of his superior officers. I am ashamed to be attached to your command, Captain Bird."

Bird was speechless. His mouth gaped, and his face paled with total incredulity. "You conceited bastard," he breathed. "You dare point your finger at me? You, who have done nothing but disrupt this venture from the beginning with your sniveling concern for the enemy? You, sir, are a disgrace to the Eighth Regiment. You have no right to wear the uniform of a soldier."

"I proudly wore the principles of a man before I became a soldier, sir," said Chard. "And if the British tunic is too small to cover that cloak, then I'll not be bound by its cloth, Captain."

"Indeed you shan't!" cried Bird. "You are relieved of your commission until such time as a court-martial can convene in Detroit. You can rest assured, sir, that I will personally see to it that you never wear the British colors again."

"Am I under arrest, Captain Bird?" Chard asked bitterly.

Bird crossed his arms and studied Chard arrogantly. "Major Southhampton insists that you are dangerous and should be put under guard. I disagree. I will not confine you to quarters if you give me your word of honor as a gentleman that you will cause no further disruptive actions while on this excursion. Do I have your word, sir?"

Chard took a deep breath. "Aye, Captain Bird, you have my word."

Chard stepped out of Bird's marquee and ran his fingers through his hair. He was angry and dazed. He had expected a reprimand, but somehow the interchange had gotten completely out of hand.

Bitsy's words echoed in his ear: "You've changed a

great deal in the past few weeks, Chard, but you haven't changed enough."

Well, she was right, he had changed just enough to throw his career, his future, and very probably his birthright to the four winds.

As though in a trance, he walked through the campgrounds, not seeing the tents of the soldiers, the stacked arms, the company standards hanging limp in the still air; not hearing the voices of the enlisted men as they paid him their respect when he passed; not seeing the regret on their faces. For as it always does in the service, the news had already spread that Chard had been relieved of his rank, and the men were sorry, for he was the only officer they respected for the man that he was instead of for the commission his family had bought. But Chard knew none of that, and if he had known, it would not have changed the great sense of failure he harbored or the peculiar notion that somehow his whole world had crashed down and buried him beneath its rubble.

He passed the captives' area without glancing in its direction. So he did not notice Bitsy standing alone, as dejected and miserable as he.

She waved, but he passed without responding. She dropped her hand self-consciously, thinking he had purposely ignored her. Her shoulders sagged, and she withdrew into herself, more lost and alone than before. She had considered Chard a friend—perhaps her only friend—and it hurt to be shunned by the one person in whom she had dared to believe. She stood there, her face expressionless, her eyes bleak, and watched Chard until he was out of sight.

The smile that lit up Judith's face when Chard entered her tent died instantly.

Chard looked at her as though he were seeing her for the very first time in his life. His penetrating gaze left Judith shaken; he seemed to see into the darkest corners of her soul, searching for the hidden meaning of her existence.

"What is it, Chard?" she asked, her hand moving to her throat apprehensively. She knew a moment of cold fear as she awaited his answer, for she was sure that Southhampton had finally broken his pledge and told Chard the truth.

311

"The captain just relieved me of my commission."

"Why?" she breathed, praying that he could not hear the relief in her voice.

"For conduct unbecoming an officer and a gentleman. He said I was not fit to be a soldier."

"That's ridiculous. What possible reason could he have to make such a decision?"

Chard told her everything that had taken place in Bird's tent. "I am sorry if I have disappointed you, Mother. It certainly was not my intention."

Judith took her son in her arms and put her cheek against his. "I could never be disappointed in you, Chard, no matter what happens."

Chard pushed her to arm's length. "You knew this would happen. You tried to tell me so on board the ship the day you presented me with the pistols. You told me then that this trip would not be what I expected. You said I would see and hear things that would go against all I believed in."

"I didn't know for sure, Chard, I only guessed—"

"I won't accept that, Mother. You knew very well that I would not be able to tolerate the tortures and cruelties that this so-called army has inflicted on the people of Kentucky." He eyed her hard. "I want the truth, Mother. I think I am entitled to know what all this mystery is about."

Judith evaded her son's eyes. "I knew you were not the kind of man who could stand idly by and watch people be mistreated. I knew that you would loathe such injustice and that it would only be a matter of time before your honor forced you to do what you considered right. You are not like most Englishmen, Chard. I've known that ever since you were a child. You are not cold and harsh, nor do you have the ability to turn your back on suffering, no matter the circumstances."

"I do not want to be different from my countrymen," cried Chard. "Even my own father despises me. What is wrong with me, Mother?"

"There is nothing wrong with you, Chard. Your father fears your strength of character. He sees in you qualities that he doesn't possess—chivalry, kindness, compassion."

"Those are weaknesses, Mother!" said Chard, his voice rising in anger. He stopped short and blushed. "I'm sorry,

312

ma'am. I did not mean to shout at you. But all my life I have lived with the knowledge that I am an embarrassment to my father. I used to worry about it. I worked hard to be just like him, but I could not, and so I finally accepted the fact that I am weak and unmanly."

"Chard," said Judith, smiling sadly at her son, "caring about people is not weak or unmanly. In truth, the mark of a coward is the *fear* of acknowledging those feelings." She sighed wearily and touched Chard's cheek. "But most Englishmen, including your father, would argue that point, I'm afraid."

"Am I not English? You keep speaking as though I were a foreigner."

"You are English," assured Judith. She turned her head, afraid that Chard might read her face. But you are not British, she thought, and that is where the trouble lies. She had seen the difference when he was a child. Even then he'd had a deeply ingrained sense of right and wrong, and that trait, that inclination to be fair to other children, often ended in ridicule and abuse. When he got older, however, even though they considered his attitude soft and feminine, they knew better than to try and bully him, because he had a side to him that was quietly dangerous. It thrilled Judith, for she was sure that particular trait was indeed inherited from his father.

"Mother," said Chard sternly, "you have evaded explanations and changed the subject and turned your back on me ever since we left Detroit. You even fear—or hate —Bitsy, who is nothing but a snip of a girl who would harm no one. What in hell is happening?"

"I'm not afraid of Bitsy, nor do I hate her. She is a fine person . . . I just don't want you to get involved with her."

"Why not? She's the first girl I've ever met who has any substance to her. She's a real person, Mother, not some simpering pretty face who can do nothing but bat her eyelashes and coo the right words . . . whether they're right or not."

Judith took Chard's hand and laughed shakily. "You are infatuated with her, Chard. She is the first girl you've met who hasn't flung herself at your feet."

"I will admit that she is most definitely a challenge. But that has nothing to do with the issue. You've never

313

concerned yourself with my conquests in the past. Ye
suddenly you are overly protective . . . no, not overly pro
tective, overly demanding that I stay away from Bitsy."

"There are very good reasons why I must insist tha
you not see her, Chard."

"Well, what are they? Or is this some more of you
mystery of twenty-five years ago?"

"Don't raise your voice to me," snapped Judith. "But
yes, it does have to do with when I was in America the firs
time." Judith squeezed her son's hand. "Trust me, Chard
Is that asking too much?"

Chard looked squarely into her eyes. "Yes, Mother, i
is."

Judith's heart stopped. Chard had never refused her
requests or questioned her judgment. For him to do so now
scared her almost senseless. A voice inside her screamed for
her to tell him the truth, to get it out in the open, to break
the stranglehold that Southhampton had used to squeeze
the life out of her for so long.

"Chard," she said, "I . . . I can't tell you why I must
insist that you stay away from Bitsy, but I can tell you this:
should you and she become romantically involved, you
would end up hating me. More important, you would
despise yourself as well. Please, son, don't . . ."

"Then answer my questions."

Judith turned her back on him and walked to the door
of her tent. She paused at the flap and, after a long silence,
whispered, "I can't do that, Chard."

Chard stared at her. He had come to her hoping that
she would shed a ray of light on the confusing puzzle that
was playing havoc with his life. She had the missing pieces,
and he felt sure that his questions, like fingers groping in the
dark, had touched them, only to have her move them
farther out of his reach.

"I don't understand you, Mother," he said, pushing
past her and walking quickly away.

Southhampton also stepped into the hot sunlight. But
unlike Chard, he wasn't confused or disappointed; he was
mad clear through.

Bird had just told him of his decision to sell both Susan

and Bitsy to Lorimer. The mere thought of Bitsy belonging to Lorimer left Southhampton white around the mouth and trembling with jealousy. But even more bitter was the realization that with both Susan and Bitsy at the trading post, all his well laid plans to entice Patterson to follow the army were wasted. His dreams of bringing the high-and-mighty woodsman to his knees had been cast to the winds by a stupid commander who refused to listen to reason.

Southhampton's boot heels shook the hard-packed earth as he stomped to the cabin he and Susan shared. Susan was sitting on the bed with her head in her hands. She looked up quickly as Southhampton entered.

"Did he change his mind? Will he let Bitsy travel with the army?"

Southhampton scowled at her and poured himself a cup of rum. "She stays with Lorimer," he said, taking a deep swallow.

"You promised me that you would see to it that Bird changed his mind. You promised!"

"Shut your bloody mouth. I did the best I could. Bird has a feather up his arse. All of a sudden he has decided to take command of this mess he calls a military expedition. He even went so far as to insinuate that he has allowed me—me! who was honored for valor in battle during the French and Indian War—to cloud his better judgment. 'Tis unbelievable to think that he could find fault with my military expertise. . . . It wouldn't surprise me if Commandant DePeyster breaks the stupid sonofabitch's commission when we get to Detroit. Bird has made a farce of this whole venture from the start."

Susan looked at Southhampton with scorn and pity. He was one of those people who were capable of casting all blame for failure, shortcomings, and guilt upon those around him. Yet Susan was amazed by the ease with which he shrugged off the responsibility for all the chaos of the Kentucky venture. And she was sure he would do everything in his power to make Captain Bird appear incompetent should DePeyster hold a hearing questioning Bird's command.

"Bird's asinine determination to sell Bitsy to Lorimer," he continued, "has spoiled all my plans."

Susan's eyes narrowed angrily as it became clear why

Southhampton was so concerned about Bird's decision to leave Bitsy behind. "If you are still foolishly considering killing my husband, then you can thank Captain Bird for saving your cowardly hide, James."

Southhampton sneered at Susan's choice of words.

"A coward, my dear, is one who has lost control of his courage. I cannot be considered in that category, for I know exactly what I am doing."

"You are sick, James. Your mind is so twisted, you have no notion of reality."

Southhampton's face mottled with rage. "You filthy pig," he rasped, flinging the contents of his cup into her face. "How dare you—you, a common slut with the pox running out of you like slime off a snail's belly—have the nerve to accuse me of being sick?"

Susan blinked slowly as the burning alcohol streamed down her face and dripped onto the front of her elegant dress.

"I have venereal disease, James, but unlike the mental derangement that plagues you, my problem will eventually kill me, while you, my dear, will live on and on until they finally lock you away. . . ."

Southhampton hit her so hard that she did not remember falling from the bed. But a moment later she found herself being dragged from the floor and flung unceremoniously against the wall. The impact snapped the gold chain of her locket and sent it sailing into a dark corner. But Susan didn't notice, for a white-hot pain seared her chest, a pain so intense that it blotted all thought from her mind— except for the prayer to God to please let her die.

Southhampton watched her slide to the floor, gasping for breath. Her lips were drawn tightly across her clenched teeth in a grimace of agony so acute that her eyelids fluttered spasmodically as she tried desperately to pass out. But she couldn't do even that.

Southhampton flexed his aching fist, scowling at his bloody knuckles where her teeth had raked his skin when her head had snapped back. Then he beamed, smiling broadly as he studied the bleeding flesh, excited by the sensation of power, superiority, and manliness that the broken skin represented. He was lord and master over the weak, sniveling woman who lay huddled at his feet.

He put the toe of his boot under her chin and raised her face so that she was forced to look into his eyes.

"I will kill Morgan Patterson, my dear," he promised, "but it will be a long and lingering death instead of a quick and easy one. Aye"—he laughed, digging his boot into her throat—"before I'm through, he will suffer a fate that for an 'honorable' man like him will be far more cruel than a bullet. He will look forward to death the way a starving man does a morsel of food."

Southhampton laughed, then turned and marched through the door.

Susan shuddered as he swaggered away, and even the deep burning pain in her chest didn't diminish the fear his words had caused. She was afraid of Southhampton when he set his mind to scheming and planning. For she knew he would stop at nothing, no matter how many lives were ruined, to achieve his goal. It bothered her that she did not know who or what he intended to use to hurt her husband. It was certainly not her, for he would have said so. No, his plans involved someone other than herself—who would have a direct bearing on Morgan's life.

Bitsy immediately crossed her mind. But try as she might, she could not see how Southhampton could possibly use her to destroy Patterson. Bitsy would be staying behind when the army evacuated Lorimer's.

Susan racked her aching brain for the answer but was finally forced to give up. The fire in her chest was making it difficult to breathe, much less attempt an intelligent thought.

She dragged herself to the bed and strained hard to pull herself onto the mattress. But the effort demanded more strength than she could summon, and she let her head sink to the floor, too weak and faint to try again. She coughed, and her body arched and twisted with convulsions. Blood formed at the corners of her pale lips, intermingling with the scarlet smear where Southhampton had struck her. She coughed again, and more blood welled up, almost choking her. Susan's lips curved wistfully. Southhampton has finally done it, she mused, he damaged me internally when he flung me against the wall. But in that respect, Susan was only half right; Southhampton and Clarke had accomplished that feat weeks earlier, the first time they had beaten her nearly into unconsciousness before she finally submitted and serviced them both. Hurling her against the log wall had merely compounded the condition, freeing the bullet that she carried above her left breast to complete its journey toward her heart.

Susan pillowed her head in the crook of her arm and closed her eyes. She needed rest, an eternity of rest.

Southhampton ventured to the outskirts of the captives' area and observed the Kentucky women. Most of them stood in line, waiting to receive their daily rations so they could begin the evening meal for the American men who had been put to work carrying stones for the foundation of a gristmill Lorimer intended to build. But he wasn't interested in the plight of the Kentucky men and women. He was studying Bitsy, wondering if she knew of Bird's decision to leave her at Lorimer's. He hoped she did not, for such knowledge could very well hamper his plans.

After observing her a moment longer, Southhampton turned on his heel and stalked off in search of Lieutenant Clarke. He found the officer in Lorimer's, sipping whiskey and conversing with several young Indian women. Southhampton poured himself a noggin and joined the crowd.

"The army is pulling out tomorrow, Major," cried Clarke, pleased that they would soon be out of the wilderness.

"So I've been informed," returned Southhampton. "I personally think we should extend our stay until we've provisions enough to carry us to Detroit."

"The Girtys have been bringing in game aplenty. We've got full bellies, and I'm restless to be going. I've a wife at Detroit."

Southhampton nodded his understanding, but at that instant there were other matters that required their immediate attention, matters much more important than Clarke's wife. Motioning for the lieutenant to follow, Southhampton strode purposefully to the storage room.

Morgan Patterson was in a quandary. He had reached the mouth of Pickawillany Creek where it emptied into the big Miami. Both streams were navigable, so Bird could have taken either branch to Detroit. Patterson gazed smaller stream. It was several miles longer than the Miami, up the but a trader named Lorimer had a store near its headwaters. And food and supplies, plus a few days of rest, might appeal to Bird after his long and difficult flight.

"No," decided Patterson, contemplating Bird's strategy. "The captain has pushed all out to put distance between his army and Kentucky, and if he hasn't changed his tactics, he will press on for Detroit, taking the shortest route possible." Using that reasoning, Patterson began searching for a way to cross the Pickawillany and continue his trek up the main branch of the Miami.

He searched the bank for hidden canoes but found none. He considered swimming the stream, then discarded the thought; his shoulder was by no means strong enough to stand the strain. Patterson leaned on his rifle and stared at the water. He cursed his injured shoulder, he cursed the river, and he cursed himself for being helpless.

A hawk soared silently across the river and lit in the lofty branches of a dead tree. Patterson would have given ten years of his life to have been able to do that. Shaking his head in frustration, he considered his alternatives. He could try floating across on his back, kicking his feet for momentum; or he could search for a free log and use it as a float. Or he could go upstream until the river became shallow enough to wade. He decided to combine the last two choices: he would travel upstream in search of a log or a ford, whichever came first.

Patterson begrudged every step he took as he turned northwest and followed the stream toward Lorimer's. The detour would cost him precious time and no telling how many extra miles. And for what? To cross a creek only fifty yards wide! Patterson's thoughts anxiously turned to his family.

He wished he knew how they were faring or, for that matter, whether they were even alive. He doubted that the British had bent over backwards to see to it that their prisoners had even the barest necessities for survival—it was not the king's way.

Still, knowing Susan and Bitsy as he did, he felt that if any of the Americans lived to tell the story of Bird's invasion, the two of them would stand up to be counted; they were not newcomers to the tricks of surviving in hostile surroundings.

Pride surged through him as he remembered his wife and daughter the last time he had seen them: standing tall and smiling bravely, they had waved him off to join Colonel Clark at Corn Island just above the falls of the Ohio. He sighed. That had been over two long years ago. And he knew a moment of shame. It had taken a catastrophe to make him realize how very much he loved and missed them. And, guilt-stricken, he vowed to spend the rest of his life making things right between them, paying more attention to their wants and needs, listening to their ideas and desires. Aye, he would be a better husband and father if the good Lord could see fit to deliver them to him unharmed. Patterson's face softened, and he reconsidered his prayer: "I'll take them any way you give them to me, Lord. Just let them be alive."

Patterson trotted steadily on, watching the river for a shoal, drift, or any other means of reaching the far side. But the river was uncooperative, and its sluggish current seemed to mock Patterson's anxiety with its persistent inaccessibility.

And, although the woodsman had been contrite only moments before, bitter anger surged through him, and he cast aside his humble petition to the Lord. "God damn you!" he cried. "You let Jesus Christ walk on the water. And you parted the Red Sea for Moses, yet you won't even send me a log to cross a stinking little river. Damn it, Lord, help me!"

Angrily Patterson pushed on, watching the river through the eyes of one who expected a godsend. But as night approached, it was evident that there would be no miracles that day.

Chard watched his father leave the cabin and walk quickly to Lorimer's Store. He wondered what could have provoked Southhampton to move with such deliberate haste. It was unlike the major to hurry unless something or someone was threatening his very existence.

Chard waited until Southhampton had disappeared into the tavern, then he strode to Susan's cabin door and knocked gently. He prayed that she would be more open than Judith, for he had the nagging suspicion that if he didn't find the answer soon, something awful would happen, something he might be able to stop if he knew about it in time.

After several long moments, he knocked louder and called Susan's name. When she failed to respond, Chard slipped the latch and stepped into the dark interior. He halted just inside and waited for his eyes to adjust to the change in lighting. He was glad that he did. Susan lay a step away, sprawled beside the bed. Chard dropped to one knee and cradled her in the crook of his arm. Fury surged through him at the sight of her puffed, swollen lips and the thin red line of blood that trickled from her mouth and puddled on her arm.

Chard gritted his teeth. Nobody deserved the treatment Susan had endured since she had become a captive.

Gathering her in his arms, he gently laid her on the bed. He rummaged in Judith's trunk for a handkerchief, which he saturated in the water bucket before painstakingly cleansing Susan's face. That done, he wet the cloth a second time and folded it into a compress for her forehead.

Still unconscious, Susan moaned painfully, her hand creeping to the area above her left breast. Hesitantly, Chard unhooked the neck of her dress and eased the garment off her shoulders. He sucked in his breath, appalled by the angry black-and-blue flesh that met his eye.

In a panic, he quickly slipped the dress farther down until the swell of her breast was exposed. His face turned ashen at the sight of an ugly puckered scar surrounded by a blue-red bruise so inflamed that Chard was terrified it would burst if he touched it. For even he, who had no medical knowledge at all, could see that Susan Patterson was bleeding internally.

Chard lunged through the door and ran full speed to the surgeon's tent.

"Mrs. Patterson needs help immediately," he shouted as he raced through the open flaps. "Blood is welling up under her skin."

The surgeon raised his head and scowled at Chard. "I told you before, she is not my problem. Now, get out of here. I've got to finish sewing up this knife wound. Lorimer's whiskey has caused more bloody trouble than anything we encountered when we took Kentucky."

Chard eyed the man hotly. "That lady might die if she doesn't receive medical help."

"Good riddance," said the surgeon, excusing Chard. Then, amid howls of pain from his patient, he forced a long, curved needle through the man's slashed flesh.

"You bastard," whispered Chard, stepping angrily toward the doctor.

The surgeon looked up at Chard over his spectacles. "If you take one more step into this tent, I'll call the sergeant of the guard. You are already on parole, and I'd be thinking you wouldn't want more trouble."

The doctor's threat stopped Chard in his tracks. The man was quite correct; he did not need more trouble. Still, it took every ounce of self-control he could muster to keep from snatching up the surgeon and dragging him to Southhampton's cabin.

Chard exhaled through his teeth. "You're a poor excuse for a doctor and even a poorer excuse for a man."

"What the bloody hell is wrong with you, Chard? Have you gone mad? Whether I tend her or not makes no difference; she and her daughter are staying here when the army evacuates in the morning."

Chard's mouth dropped open. "What are you talking about?"

The doctor squirmed, nervous and uneasy under Chard's intimidating eyes. "Were you not aware that Captain Bird intends to leave them both here when we pull out?"

"No, I wasn't." Chard leaned heavily against the tent pole. The nausea that had plagued him since the beginning of the trip suddenly rose up in his throat and choked him, making him gag on his own bile. He forced himself to swallow the vomit rather than prove how unmanly he was by throwing up in the presence of the doctor and his

322

patient. He plunged from the tent and ran headlong into the privacy of the nearby forest, where he hung limply against a giant hickory and waited for the sickness to pass.

Too much was happening too fast; all of a sudden, life was not only chaotic but frightening as well. Lord God! he cried, wondering at Bird's decision to leave Bitsy with Lorimer. Did not the captain have sense enough to realize the terrible mistake he was making? Lorimer would ruin Bitsy. Not only would he rejoice in physical cruelty but he would laugh at the fact that she was a virgin.

Chard clutched the rough bark of the tree and moaned aloud. Never in his life had he felt so helpless. Always before when he needed assistance, he had turned to his mother. But she might as well have been thousands of miles away for all the good she could do—or would do.

Chard almost wept; he was totally isolated for the first time in his life, and he had no idea which way to turn. With the slow, shuffling steps of an old man, he trudged farther into the forest until he reached the banks of the Pick-awillany, where he sank wearily down on a large, flat rock and stared at the wilderness beyond the sluggish water.

He wished he could simply cross the creek, and disappear into the forest. It was the same feeling he had experienced a thousand years before when he had sat on a log and watched the prisoners from Ruddle's and Martin's stumble past, carrying the booty of their Indian captors on their backs. But if he threw up his hands and walked away, he would be deserting the only people in the world who meant anything to him.

Hating the responsibility that nagged at him, he dropped his head into his hands. I'm just not man enough to shoulder the burdens of Judith, Bitsy, and now Susan, he thought bitterly. Yet, as he sat there feeling sorry for himself, not once did it enter his mind to blame the women for his entanglement. Nor did it occur to him that at that moment he was a much better man than he gave himself credit for being.

Absently, he selected a small stone from the thousands that lay baking on the sun-speckled creek bank and flipped it into the stream. "That stone is just like me," he whispered, watching the pebble strike the surface. "For a split instant it comes to life with a big splash, then it is gone, to lie on the bottom of the stream and be obscured by the mud and slime of the world. But its repercussions will live on in ever-widening ripples that distort everything they touch. And those poor unfortunates in its path will be jerked, tossed, and beaten for no other reason except they had the misfortune to be in the same stream as I."

Climbing to his feet, Chard walked to the water's edge and dipped up a double handful. It felt cool and refreshing to his feverish, sweat-drenched skin . . . feverish skin . . . "Good Lord!" he cried, bounding to his feet and running up the bank toward the cabin where he had left Susan unconscious and unattended.

When he burst into the cabin, however, he was startled to find Susan on her feet. Though it was obvious that she was in terrible pain, she was packing Judith's trunk while Southhampton and Clarke looked on.

"Can't you move any faster?" demanded Southhampton. "I want you out of here immediately. Other arrangements have been made for this cabin."

"I'm going as fast as I can, James," gasped Susan, grimacing as she laid the last article in the chest. When she bent to close the heavy lid, Chard thought surely she would collapse.

He darted to her side and laid a supporting arm around her waist.

"This lady is deathly ill, Father, she should be in bed resting, not packing a trunk."

"You're just a busybody, Chard," said Southhampton. "Always sticking your nose where it don't belong. Get out of here before I box your ears."

Chard eased Susan to one side and faced his father. "What did you say, Major?"

Susan's heart skipped a beat, and her hand fluttered to her breast. But it wasn't pain that had caused the sensation —it was the look on Chard's face. For a moment, something in his flinty eyes and the set of his jaw had reminded her so much of Morgan Patterson that it was breath-taking.

"It's all right, Ensign. I've finished packing," she said quickly, hoping to ease the tension before Chard made matters worse.

Chard ignored her. "Did you say something about boxing my ears, Major?"

"Please, Chard," whispered Susan, nearly in tears. "Please . . ."

"Better listen to her, boy," said Clarke from across the room.

Susan saw the man's hand creep to the pistol that he wore in his sash. For a moment she was too stunned to move. Then, regaining her senses, she quickly stepped between Clarke and Chard, who, because he was facing Southhampton, was unaware of the danger.

"I am ready to go, James," she said to Southhampton while eyeing Clarke fearfully as he half-drew the weapon. "Please, let's leave . . . now."

Clarke silently cursed Susan through his teeth. The fool woman had deliberately placed herself in the line of fire. Angrily, he shoved the pistol back into place.

"Where are you taking her?" demanded Chard, ignorant of the deadly drama that had played itself out behind his back.

"'Tis none of your business, Chard," said Southhampton with a shrug, "but Lorimer has other plans for this cabin." He smiled delightedly as the color drained from his son's face, pleased that Chard understood who would occupy the premises, and why. "Lorimer is looking forward to breaking her in," he continued, twisting the verbal knife that he had driven into Chard's guts. "Or so he thinks."

"What, exactly, does that mean?" demanded Chard in a whisper.

"Nothing," returned Southhampton, glancing conspiratorially at Clarke. "Not a damned thing."

Turning abruptly, he caught Susan by the arm and propelled her toward the door. "But since you insist upon interfering, Chard, make yourself useful and escort Mrs. Patterson to Lorimer's Store."

Chard studied his father for a long moment, wondering if he had actually understood what his father had insinuated. Surely not. He looked at Susan, but her face was so pinched with pain, he doubted that she had heard the exchange. Aye, he was mistaken—he must be. Admonishing himself for jumping to conclusions, he bent to lift Susan's trunk.

325

"Not so fast, old chap," said Clarke, striding to the camelback and leaning heavily on it, a possessive gesture that dared Chard to interfere. "The trunk stays here. Lorimer intends to dress his prize in silks and satins. She'll make a fine-looking whore."

Chard raised his head slowly to stare at the man. The look in his eyes froze Clarke's smirk into a waxen effigy that would have been comical had the circumstances been less dangerous. Slowly, Clarke pushed himself off the trunk and took a long step backwards. He had the queerest sensation that he was looking into the eyes of the man who had beaten him senseless at Harrodsburg. "Damn you!" he whispered fearfully, blaming Chard for that fear, hating him for bringing it to the surface for all to see. "Don't come near me, or I'll kill you." He clawed the pistol from his sash and nervously cocked it.

Chard smiled crookedly and took a step forward.

"Stand firm, Chard!" commanded Southhampton. "That is an order."

"Go to hell," said Chard, taking another step toward Clarke.

"Please, Chard," cried Susan. "He will shoot you, coward that he is. Please, don't give him the excuse." Susan burst into a fit of strangled coughing that left her so faint she was forced to cling to the door facing in an attempt to keep from falling. The effort was wasted. Just as her knees buckled, Chard sprang to her side and gently swung her into his arms. Susan clung to him like a sick child, comforted by his strength and reassured by his tenderness. Nestling her forehead against his shoulder, she sighed serenely, for there was a vague familiarity about Chard that made her feel secure and protected. As Susan drifted into semiconsciousness, her brow puckered in bewilderment; Morgan Patterson was the only man who had ever inspired that trust.

Chard eyed his father threateningly as he carried Susan to the bed. "Mrs. Patterson is too sick to be moved, and if you, Lorimer, Bird, or anyone lays a hand on her, I will write a complete and detailed account of this entire despicable expedition. And I assure you, sir, when George the Third, our sovereign king, reads it, he will issue an immediate recall of certain high-ranking officers, who I feel sure would rather not undergo the indignity of defending their actions before the king's court in England."

Southhampton's mouth drew to a grim line. "I told Bird that he should have locked you in irons. You are nothing but a troublemaker, Chard. 'Tis all you will ever be. I wish to God you had never been born."

"You've made that plain ever since I was a child, Major," said Chard, staring solemnly at his father.

He had not expected to be hurt by anything Southhampton might have said, for he thought he had long since grown callous to his father's abuse. So it came as quite a blow to realize, after all that had happened, that he still harbored a degree of love for the man, still longed to be a son of whom Southhampton could be proud, for deep down inside, he felt that somehow he had always failed to measure up to his father's expectations.

He squared his shoulders. "I meant what I said, Major. I'll see to it that the king hears of what went on in this cabin."

Southhampton's expression grew thunderous. "Get out of here, Chard. She can stay, but you get out. Damn you, get out!"

Chard bowed stiffly to Southhampton. Then, facing Clarke, he backed through the door, for he was not at all sure the man would hesitate to shoot him in the back. When he felt the ground beneath his feet, he spun on his heel and strode quickly toward Judith's tent.

He walked with his head down, his eyes narrowed in thought. His father's evasiveness about Bitsy kept nagging at him. He tried to rationalize it, telling himself that since Susan would be spending the night in the cabin, her presence would surely spoil any plans Southhampton might have cooked up to have the girl to himself. He shook his head, telling himself that not even the major would stoop so low as to rape a sixteen-year-old girl in the presence of her mother. But he had a sickening feeling that he knew better.

"Bird is leaving Mrs. Patterson and Bitsy with Lorimer when the army pulls out tomorrow," he announced as he entered his mother's tent. "And Mrs. Patterson is so ill 'tis all she can do to get her breath."

Judith's eyes widened in alarm. "What is wrong with Susan? Is it serious? Has the surgeon examined her?"

327

"The surgeon won't see her," he said angrily. "And yes, I believe it's serious. She is bleeding inside, here." Chard pulled his shirt aside and pointed to the spot.

Judith gasped, her face paling in the dim light. "Years ago, she was shot there, Chard. We could not remove the bullet because it was too close to her heart. Susan nearly died from that wound, and the surgeon said she would have to be careful of it the rest of her life."

"You said, 'we could not remove the bullet.' Were you there when she was shot?"

"Not exactly," said Judith, her eyes taking on a far-away expression as her mind receded to a wintery day in 1755. "We were a mile from Fort Cumberland when we were surprised by Indians. Morgan Patterson shouted for Susan and me to run for our lives. We did, leaving him to face the Hurons alone. We had run but a short distance when Susan turned back. She insisted that I go on to the fort, for I was heavy with— I was not well. She went back to fight beside Morgan, to give me—to give me a chance to live."

Chard frowned at his mother, not understanding her hesitations and the nervous twisting of her fingers as she related her story.

"Susan took a ball through the chest," continued Judith. "When Morgan carried her into the fort, we all thought she was dead . . . but she wasn't. I assisted the doctor who saved her life."

Chard was astounded. He couldn't visualize his elegant mother tending a gunshot wound, and his disbelief showed on his face.

Judith smiled nervously. "Aye, son, I know 'tis hard for you to imagine me with blood on my hands, but I assure you that before the doctor and I were finished with Susan Spencer, I was covered with the stuff from head to toe."

"Why have you never talked of these things, Mother?"

Judith shook her head. "Perhaps someday we will talk of them, but right now 'tis better to leave them unsaid."

Chard eyed Judith with pity. "I guess it doesn't make any difference. There is nothing we can do for Susan, nor would Captain Bird or the major allow it, if we could.

328

That's the sad part of it all, Mother. Susan Patterson is dying, and nobody gives a damn . . . not even you."

Judith moved to her son and clutched him frantically. "That's not true, Chard! But there's nothing we can do. None of this is our fault. Try not to think about it, Chard. You cannot be held responsible for your superior officers' actions—"

"But I am responsible, Mother. I talked Ruddle into surrendering."

"You did your duty, nothing more, nothing less. The fort would have fallen regardless."

Chard exhaled through his teeth. "I wish I had never come on this expedition. I wish you and I had stayed in England where we belonged."

"Don't feel that way, Chard. No matter what happens, I know we have done the right thing. My life may end at Detroit, but if I had it to live over, I would not hesitate to make the same decision." She hugged Chard close. "I believe that what little I did to slow Bird's army saved hundreds of lives. . . . I must believe that, Chard, for if I didn't, I would not have the courage to face another day of this hell."

Chard raised his mother's hand to his lips and kissed it. "If England were fighting a nation of people with your courage and selflessness, my lady, she would have no chance at all of winning this war."

Judith gave Chard a dismal smile. "If that's true, Chard, then England is doomed. For in my heart, I am an American—and have been for nearly twenty-five years."

CHAPTER
· *19* ·

SOUTHHAMPTON WAITED FOR night to fall before approaching the prisoners' compound. He went directly to Bitsy's blanket and shook her.

"Your mother is ill," he whispered, careful not to awaken the other captives. "She is asking for you."

Bitsy jumped to her feet, alarmed by Southhampton's words.

"Come," he said, taking her hand and drawing her to him. "I'll show you the way." He smiled into the darkness as she came immediately to his side. She had reacted exactly as he knew she would. It was so easy to fool American women; their loyalty toward their kin was almost comic in its simplicity. The girl didn't falter when she reached the cabin. Calling her mother's name, she burst headlong into the room.

Southhampton stepped in behind her and quietly shut and barred the door.

Chard left Judith's tent and strode purposefully through the darkness toward the captives' area. He had an urgent desire to see Bitsy one last time before he and Judith were taken to Detroit to stand trial. He walked through the compound from one end to the other, but in the darkness it was almost impossible to tell one Kentuckian from another.

Hesitantly, a voice came out of the night. "If you are looking for the Patterson girl, you're a bit too late."

"What do you mean?" Chard peered hard, straining his eyes to see who had spoken.

"I shouldn't be saying nothin', to you, 'specially about her," came the woman's nervous voice, "but you let me ride your horse over the mountains whilst I was sick . . ."

"I remember," said Chard anxiously, wishing the woman would get to the point. "What about Bitsy? Where is she?"

"Some officer came for her, told her that her ma'am was sick."

"How long ago?" demanded Chard fiercely.

"Just a while, sir," came the woman's timid voice, "not over thirty minutes."

Chard stood stock still. He wanted to cry out to the heavens, to beg the gods to make time stand still until he could get to Southhampton's cabin, but he knew he was too late. *Too late.* The words reverberated in his mind like the booming chimes of Westminster Abbey at midnight.

And Chard was correct: it was too late. The hands of the timepiece that governed Bitsy's innocence and virtue, the same ones that had started ticking that day at Ruddle's Fort when Bitsy asked her mother to explain about sex and Susan had declined, had suddenly moved to the straight-up position—time had run out.

Susan lay huddled against the cabin wall, her eyes wide with terror.

Lieutenant Clarke was sitting beside her, one hand wound tightly in her hair, the muzzle of his pistol pushed hard against her forehead.

"Please, James," she said, attempting to pull away from the gun barrel, only to be drawn more tightly against its cold steel by Clarke.

"Please," she whispered again, her eyes beseeching Southhampton in the dim lanternlight, "don't do this awful thing. She's just a child."

Southhampton ignored Susan, moving instead to Bitsy, who stood frozen, staring wide-eyed at Clarke and the cocked pistol.

331

"If you don't do exactly as I say," Southhampton threatened in Bitsy's ear, "you will, in essence, be the murderer of your own mother. Do I make myself clear?"

He smiled as huge tears filled the girl's eyes. But it wasn't Southhampton's threat that shattered the girl, it was the sight of Susan.

"Don't believe him, Bitsy!" cried Susan. "He used that same ruse on me about the women who'd drowned."

Susan struggled violently to free herself of Clarke's grip, but the exertion brought on such an uncontrollable fit of coughing that had it not been for the lieutenant's hand woven tightly into her hair, she would have collapsed. Bitsy sprang toward her mother, but Southhampton caught her by the arm and flung her across the bed. The girl bounced off the straw-filled mattress, as lithe as a cat, and attacked the major with just as much ferocity. Snarling like an animal, she raked his face with her nails, kicked his shins, and tried her best to sink her teeth into the flesh of his forearm as he tried to ward her off.

"Shut her up, Southhampton!" cried Clarke, glancing nervously at the door. "She'll stir up the whole camp!"

Southhampton pushed the enraged girl from him, then smashed his fist into her face, sending her sprawling across the bed.

And as Bitsy lay there stunned by a blow that had nearly rendered her unconscious, Southhampton, in full view of Susan, who was paralyzed with shock, calmly ripped Bitsy's dress away. Then, without any preliminaries other than dropping his trousers, he spread her thighs and with intentional cruelty drove himself deep inside her.

The girl's young body arched and thrashed beneath him, and a long heart-wrenching scream echoed off the cabin walls. Southhampton caught her wrists and forced her arms above her head where he pinioned them to the bed. Then, with deliberate leisure, he bent his head and covered her mouth with his.

Bitsy shuddered violently, then went limp. Her scream became a muted whimper that faded into absolute silence until finally the only sound in the room was the slap of Southhampton's bare skin against Bitsy's naked thighs, and only her small hands, clenching and unclenching in slow agony, gave proof that she was still conscious.

Susan's head tilted slowly to the side so that her cheek lay softly against her shoulder, and great sympathetic tears spilled over the rims of her half-closed eyes to run silently down her face and make tiny splashes on the hard-packed earthen floor. "I tried to spare you this, my darling," she whispered as Southhampton made one final thrust then collapsed heavily over the sweat-spattered body of her daughter. "But I know now that no matter what I did, he would never have been satisfied until he destroyed every bit of goodness in you."

"Shut up," growled Clarke, pushing the pistol barrel so far into the soft skin of Susan's forehead that a drop of blood appeared from beneath the muzzle and oozed slowly to the bridge of her nose, where it separated and mingled with her tears, staining both sides of her face a dingy red.

"Kill me," Susan implored, turning her sad eyes to Clarke. "Do one decent thing in your life . . . kill me."

"Shut up," repeated Clarke, his eyes glued to the nude body of Bitsy, who lay unmoving beneath Southhampton's bulk.

"Get off her, Southhampton," he said, moving to the bedside and prodding the major's naked buttocks with the pistol barrel. "'Tis my turn to pay my respects, and I must say she looked to be a most enjoyable ride."

Southhampton rolled off Bitsy and drew himself to a sitting position. "Not this time, old chap," he said, smiling with satisfaction. "When Morgan Patterson comes for his family, I want him to know that I, James Southhampton, spoiled his precious daughter. I want the son of a bitch to feel what I felt when I found out he had seduced my wife!"

"Morgan didn't rape Judith," said Susan, without emotion. "She went to him willingly. In fact, she begged him to seduce her."

"He took Judith's virginity!" screamed Southhampton.

"And you took his daughter's," sighed Susan. "The only difference is that your wife gave hers freely. She *gave* herself to Morgan Patterson."

"You are all whores underneath that facade of decency and respectability that you wear like a cloak," shouted Southhampton angrily. "You shed it along with the rest of your attire any time the fancy strikes. Every goddamn woman who draws breath is nothing but a common whore at heart!"

He jumped from the bed and strode angrily to Susan. "Say it!" he yelled, his face inches from hers. "You've said it a hundred times since coming to me. Say it again, damn you!"

Although it took all the strength she could muster, Susan raised her head and, remembering how proud she had been of Judith the day Southhampton whipped her, she spat full into his unsuspecting face.

Southhampton sat back on his haunches. He was speechless. Hate danced in his eyes as he slowly wiped the spittle from his face. He wanted nothing more than to beat Susan to death with his bare hands, but he was afraid of what he saw in her eyes, or possibly what he didn't see, for there was no trace of fear there. And in that instant, he knew that he had lost his hold over her. The woman he faced would welcome death, even embrace it, and the cowardice that was his constant companion rose up in his throat and choked him.

He spun on his heel and stalked to the door. "Come, Clarke," he said arrogantly. "We have accomplished what we came for."

Chard pushed his way through the surly crowd of Americans who had gathered around him and the Kentucky woman. He knocked them aside with a strength born of frenzied panic, then ran like a madman toward the small cabin beyond Lorimer's Store. Pistol in hand, he kicked the door open and flung himself into the room.

For a long instant he stared in wide-eyed silence at the cabin's interior. Susan was kneeling on the edge of the bed, holding her naked daughter to her, her lips pressed tightly against the girl's disheveled hair. She was crooning softly, comfortingly. She turned then, the dark spheres of her eyes finding Chard's and holding them steadily, and had it not been for the tuneless melody that Susan hummed, the dead silence in the small cabin would have been deafening.

With a shudder that racked his entire body, Chard

sagged against the door and emptied himself of the nausea that had plagued him for weeks. Again and again he heaved, until there was nothing left to bring up. But even then, his stomach continued to convulse in a futile attempt to purge itself of all the festering malevolence that he had witnessed since leaving Detroit.

He attempted to speak, but words wouldn't come; he had been emptied of those, too. It took all the strength he could muster to push himself erect and walk the few steps to the bed. But hard as that was, it was nothing when compared to the spiritual strength it took to keep from damning the Lord when he looked at Bitsy. She sat with her legs drawn beneath her, her head resting on her mother's breast.

So small and fragile she seemed, not at all the confident, self-assured young woman who had fought the British to a standstill in Kentucky, not at all the fearless heroine who had won the admiration and respect of the Indians at the gauntlet. Nor, saddest of all, was she the proud, angry beauty who kissed him with such tender passion one moment and kicked him into oblivion the next. No, the person Chard observed was none of those people—it was as though they had never existed.

Chard's gaze traveled down Bitsy's bare back to her tiny waist, then to the gentle flare of her hips. There, spread out on the coverlet beneath the girl's nude buttocks, was a stain of the brightest, reddest blood that he had ever seen.

An anger different from any feeling Chard had ever experienced filled his empty stomach; it was a new form of nourishment—cold, deadly hatred.

Susan saw it all, the sickness, the horror, and finally, the demonical rage that filled the young man's face. And she knew a moment of deep sympathy for Chard, for it was plainly evident that he was responding to her daughter's rape as only a man with great love and respect for a woman could. Susan's heart went out to him.

"Mrs. Patterson," said Chard so softly that Susan could barely hear, "get Bitsy clothed and ready to travel. I'll be back shortly."

Susan shuddered at the look in his eyes as he gazed one last time at her daughter. She had seen that look before

—but where? Then it dawned on her that she had seen that same expression in Morgan Patterson's eyes just before he killed the man who raped Ivy, Judith's handmaiden, twenty-five years before. Susan's reaction to her discovery was pure incredulity. And then, acceptance. She wondered why she had not recognized Chard the moment she first saw him.

"Bitsy," she said gently, taking her daughter's hand and drawing it to her lips, "we've got to get you dressed. You are going home."

That same night, Morgan Patterson lay in the underbrush on the bank of Pickawillany Creek and listened to the night sounds.

He had come far that day in his search for a river crossing, and he liked it not one whit.

Tomorrow, if it killed him, he vowed to find a way to cross the creek. Then heaven help anyone or anything that tried to block his path back to the Miami, for come hell or high water he intended to overtake Bird's army before it reached Detroit. He grimaced. His bold vow, when viewed in the light of his progress thus far, was but a self-deceiving mockery. In that instant, as he looked honestly at his chance of success in his quest to rescue his family, the first seeds of that hero-killer, self-doubt, began to germinate in his heart.

"I'm just a foolish old man who has such a high opinion of himself that he thinks he can do the impossible," murmured Patterson miserably.

Then, remembering the sign Bitsy had left on the Ohio riverbank—the broken branch, the scrape in the mud—he grimaced again, for it was obvious that she, too, believed he was invincible.

"Girl," he said, breaking into a slow grin, "you sure as hell know how to put pressure on a man who was considering giving up."

With renewed confidence, Patterson again contemplated his position. He was aware that Lorimer's trading post was somewhere ahead, not over two days' travel. But Lorimer was known to be a dyed-in-the-wool hater of

Americans who surrounded himself with Indians who were friendly to the British cause.

With that in mind, Patterson carefully weighed his alternatives. In two days' time, he could be at Lorimer's. He needed provisions and might even be able to purchase or steal a canoe. It was an interesting thought—food and a canoe. But by the same token, in two days, he could be back at the main branch of the Miami and once again in pursuit of his quarry.

Patterson shook his head. There was actually no decision to make: the risks at Lorimer's were too great; he would be better off crossing the Pickawillany and returning to the Miami.

He turned his thoughts to his wife. Susan was too smart not to realize that the prisoners had long since been carried too deeply into British territory to expect retaliation from General Clark. He wondered how she felt about that. Had she, as he had done moments before, given up the belief that she would be rescued? In truth, he couldn't blame her if she had, for he was heart-wrenchingly familiar with the tricks of the mind that endless waiting and wondering could generate. He had battled them daily during the two years he had been with Clark's army. He had had to be constantly on guard against the inevitable doubt and despondency, and finally the supreme defeater itself, unwarranted suspicion. That could destroy the stoutest of hearts and make a man so uncertain that he would take the easiest avenue of escape by telling himself that it just didn't matter anymore.

Aye, he admitted gloomily, Susan would have every reason to believe he had forsaken her, for the fact was he should have overtaken Bird's army days before.

"No!" Patterson declared aloud, gripping his rifle so tightly that his knuckles whitened with strain. "I will not belittle Susan's love or loyalty by doubting her strength of will. There is no power on earth strong enough to shake her belief in me or her faith in herself."

Relaxing his grip on the gun, Patterson lay back and closed his eyes, the sound of his own voice and the comforting words of his statement lulling him into a much-needed dreamless sleep.

He would never know that his final sentence was only half right.

Chard marched through the open door of Lorimer's store and glanced quickly at the crowd.

Soldiers, aware that they were leaving in the morning, were trying hard to drink Lorimer dry. Others were purchasing articles with which to cajole last-minute favors from their female Indian companions. But Chard saw none of that as his eyes roved from man to man. They passed over Simon and George Girty who, having brought in another load of meat that day, were heavily into their cups; they passed over McGee and Elliott who were deep in conversation with several fierce-looking Hurons; they passed over the Indian women who were soliciting the soldiers with the shrewdness of professional prostitutes who knew their business was coming to an untimely halt; they passed over them all until they locked on Southhampton and Clarke. The two officers were leaning carelessly on the counter, laughing together, tipping their mugs as if nothing out of the ordinary had occurred, as if they were unaware or insensible to the fact that they had just raped a sixteen-year-old girl.

Clarke caught movement out of the corner of his eye. Smiling broadly, assuming it was one of his fellow officers, he turned just in time to catch the brass butt of Chard's dueling pistol squarely in the mouth. His two front teeth rattled across the bar like a pair of dice cast upon a game board, and blood spewed down the front of his ruffled shirt. He fell hard against the counter, then pitched face first to the floor.

Not losing momentum, Chard continued his swing, cracking the astounded Southhampton across the forehead with a glancing blow that opened a gash a quarter of an inch deep between the man's unbelieving eyes. Southhampton grabbed his face and staggered sideways. Then, sinking to his knees, he raised his eyes to Chard imploringly.

Chard's mouth drew into a thin line as he watched blood trickle between Southhampton's widespread fingers and drip in a steady stream from the end of his aristocratic nose. The sight of it enraged Chard all the more, reminding

338

him of the blood that had spread sickeningly from between Bitsy's thighs, and he fell upon his father with the ferociousness of a man gone berserk with intent to do murder. He was unaware of knocking Southhampton to the floor, had no recollection of winding his fist in the major's hair and pounding the man's face with his free hand. Pounding, pounding, pounding.

Lorimer, along with half a dozen soldiers, fell upon Chard and wrestled him to his feet.

"You'll dance at the gallows for this, m'sieur," promised Lorimer as they stood Chard upright.

Chard grinned crookedly at the man, and a more observant person would have been instantly on guard. But Lorimer was not an observant person and would not remember seeing Chard's fist as it swept up and burst on the point of his chin. But he would hear later that his eyes rolled back into his head and his knees gave way, dropping him heavily across Southhampton.

Everyone in the room—except the Girtys and the Indians, who went on drinking complacently—converged on Chard.

"You better get out of here, Ensign, and keep on going," warned one of Chard's gun crew in his ear. "There'll be bloody hell to pay when Bird hears of this."

Chard could barely hear the man above the roaring of the crowd. And he was baffled by the excitement that was growing more intense by the moment.

"Get out before the guards arrive, Ensign," pleaded the soldier, catching Chard by the arm and propelling him toward the door.

Chard staggered dumbly into the night, still unsure exactly what had taken place. He shook his head to clear his numb mind, and as the mist that shrouded his brain lifted, he glanced quickly toward the mass confusion that was causing havoc in Lorimer's. Running full out, he made straight for Southhampton's cabin where Susan was leaning heavily against the doorframe.

"What did you do in Lorimer's?" she cried as Chard drew near. "It sounded like a war in there."

"Tell you later," he rasped, catching her by the arm and urging her into the yard. "We've got to get the hell out of here."

He rushed inside. Bitsy was fully dressed, but she had backed into a corner where, brandishing one of the major's short swords, she slashed menacingly at Chard. "Don't touch me," she warned, her face white and pinched. "So help me God, I'll kill you if you come near me."

Chard waited until Bitsy raised the blade again. Then he hit her. She went down as though struck by a cannonball. Gathering the girl into his arms, he bolted through the door and pounded his way to his tent. Lowering the semiconscious girl to the ground, he ducked into the shelter and cast off his crimson tunic. Hopping on one leg, he kicked off his boots and snatched on leggings and moccasins. Catching up his deerskin frock, shooting gear, and rifle, he sprang outside.

Men were running toward Lorimer's from all directions, shouting questions, adding confusion to bedlam, and creating a riot of activity that had the whole camp in an uproar. Susan, who had stumbled along in Chard's wake trying valiantly not to cough from the exertion, was on her knees gently slapping Bitsy's cheeks in an attempt to revive the stunned girl.

"We've got to get away from here fast," said Chard, catching Bitsy under her arms and lifting her erect to stand on legs as wobbly as a newborn foal's.

"Can you walk?" He released the girl and stepped back, eyeing her critically.

Bitsy nodded, her green eyes flashing as her senses fully returned. "Chard," she said, holding his gaze, "if you ever lay a hand on me again, I'll cut your throat while you sleep." It was a promise.

"You left me no choice, Bitsy. I didn't enjoy hitting you, if that's what you think." He was deeply relieved by the girl's anger, for he had heard of rape victims who went for days without responding to a living soul. And when they finally did, more times than not, they were permanently despondent and fearful of any man who came near them. Before Bitsy could voice an opinion, Chard ordered her and Susan to follow him and broke into a mad dash toward Judith's tent.

Twenty-five yards from the tent, Chard pushed Susan and Bitsy into the brush that lined the path and put his finger to his lips to indicate silence. Leaving them there, he walked boldly into the small clearing.

"What's going on at Lorimer's, sir?" queried the guard as Chard approached.

"Captain Bird has summoned every able-bodied man to the store immediately. Got trouble up there. Bunch of drunken Indians raising bloody hell."

"Aye, sir," returned the soldier with a grin, glad to be rid of the boring duty of guarding a woman who couldn't escape even if she tried.

Chard watched the man race off into the night, then ducked into the tent and snatched Judith's blanket off the pallet. "Don't ask questions," he said, pushing the baffled woman before him. "There's no time."

Yet, even then, knowing something unusual was taking place, Judith was unprepared for the confrontation when Susan stepped from the brush leading Bitsy by the hand. The two women stared at each other in the darkness. Judith was the first to find her voice, and then she could utter but one word: "Susan?"

"Yes," answered Susan, unsure as to how she should react. "It is me, Judith."

Without hesitation, Judith took her old friend into her arms and kissed her cheek. "I'm so glad to see you again."

Susan, at a loss for words, and wondering at Judith's sincere joy, considering that for weeks she had been mistress to Judith's husband, was more than a little thankful when Chard quickly intervened.

"Ladies," he said, glancing in the direction of the pandemonium that was taking place at Lorimer's, "we've got to get away from here. They are lighting torches, and in a few minutes they will be scouring the countryside."

To their dismay, they could only move at a snail's pace, for trees, vines, logs, and other obstacles seemed to plague their every step. Vision was impossible. But they set their jaws stubbornly and trudged on, putting one foot in front of the other, picking themselves up when they fell, clutching one another for support when they stumbled, and encouraging each other when they faltered. When they finally emerged into a small glade that was bathed in the silver glow of a welcome moon, Susan and Judith touched hands, both remembering a time in the past when three women and a man pushed through the wilderness, afraid and hungry, and wondering if they would live to see the morning sun.

"We will make it," whispered Judith as she squeezed Susan's cold fingers.

Susan smiled bravely, but the burning in her chest was already unbearable. She felt her energy ebb with each step, and she knew with a sinking heart that not even rest and food would revive her. She closed her eyes and prayed that the Lord would grant her just a little while longer to be with her daughter, just a few more days to see Bitsy safely on her way to the country beyond the Ohio.

CHAPTER
· 20 ·

THE SUN WAS UP, but it scarcely illuminated the world beneath the giant trees that encircled the small bubbling spring where the foursome rested from their night-long trek.

They drank thirstily, savoring the coolness of the water, their parched tissues absorbing the liquid with a million greedy little mouths.

"Where are we, Chard?" asked Judith tiredly, swinging her red-rimmed eyes in all directions.

"I have no idea," he returned honestly. "I don't even know which way the river is."

"The river is east of us," said Susan, raising a faltering hand and pointing to her right. "But we can't go that way without passing Lorimer's."

"We'll have to loop around the store and pick up the river below there," agreed Chard, taking a long look to the east and wondering if he had done the right thing for the women. Their escape had been a spur-of-the-moment decision in response to Susan's mistreatment, Bitsy's rape, Judith's impending trial, and his dishonorable reduction in rank. As he turned and let his eyes rove over the haggard women, he felt he had made a colossal mistake.

"Ladies," he said uneasily, "if you so desire, we can return to Lorimer's. I will take full responsibility for our actions last night. Perhaps Bird will be lenient." He gazed questioningly at Susan. "What is your preference, Mrs. Patterson?"

Susan took a deep breath to try and still the persistent

cough that seemed to be getting worse by the minute. "I know it appears impossible that we could survive the wilderness, Chard . . . and we may not," or at least I may not, she thought as a coughing spasm caused her to double over. Straightening, she continued, "But I will not turn back. I'm for going on, regardless of the outcome."

Chard nodded, acknowledging Susan's decision and admiring her for it. He was impressed by her courage and stamina. Although he could only guess at the extent of the pain she was suffering, he knew it must be terrible. "What about you, Bitsy?"

Bitsy looked full into his face, and Chard was dismayed to find that her eyes had aged a hundred years overnight. He was afraid that Southhampton's savage abuse was just beginning to penetrate the girl's stunned mind and body.

He longed to reach out to her, to assure her of something, but for the life of him he didn't know what it was that he could reassure her of. So he said nothing. In fact, his ignorance of the right thing to say or do embarrassed him, and it showed plainly in his face.

The girl's lips drew into a bitter line of self-condemnation and reproof. She hated Chard almost as much as she hated herself; for in her confused and sensitive state, she didn't realize that he was embarrassed for her, not by her, that he suffered with her, not because of her. So when she looked at him, all that her troubled eyes could see was shame behind a false warmth and accusation behind a patronizing smile.

"It matters little to me what we do," she said coldly, turning her face away.

Chard's arms ached to hold Bitsy, to protect her, to show her that it did matter, that everything about her mattered—that she mattered. He was in love with her, and there wasn't enough ugliness in the world to spoil the beauty in that.

"I'm for going on," interrupted Judith quickly. She had read Chard's face like an open book. And she wanted to scream at her son, to tell him that he could not be in love with Bitsy—that she, Judith, would not allow it. Ever.

"Then I guess that's it." Chard frowned at Bitsy, who had turned her back to the group, pushing them farther

344

and farther from her. He sighed. Whether he liked it or not, there were more urgent problems to consider than Bitsy's withdrawal.

"Since we had no time to prepare for our escape," he said, taking inventory of their possessions, "we are in dire straits as far as food, clothing, and firearms are concerned. We have two pistols and Bitsy's rifle . . . and very little else."

"'Tis enough," said Judith, remembering three women and a woodsman who faced the very same obstacles with nothing but a knife, tomahawk, and long-rifle. "Aye, it is enough."

They turned west by south and started their slow march toward the Ohio . . . toward Kentucky.

Lorimer's clearing was a beehive of activity the morning after the escape. Men were everywhere, bustling about in preparation for the immediate evacuation to Detroit.

Captain Bird stood half in and half out of the doorway of Southhampton's cabin so that he could converse with the major while at the same time oversee his command. "The army can't sit here at Lorimer's while you search for the prisoners, Major," he said for the second time in as many minutes.

He frowned gloomily at Southhampton, who sat on the bed, spooning cornmeal mush carefully between his puffed and swollen lips.

"A runner came in at daybreak," Bird continued. "Captain Graves, of the good ship *Hope,* stands off the mouth of the Maumee at Lake Erie this very moment. He urges that we proceed there in good haste."

Southhampton pushed his bowl away and, amid groans and curses, climbed painfully to his feet. He patted his battered mouth gently with a handkerchief. "Cannot the *Hope* wait a day or two longer, Captain? It seems to me that Captain Graves would understand the delay when it concerns the capture of a deserter and a spy."

"Major," sighed Bird, "I appreciate your position in this matter. And I would like nothing better than to bring the culprits back and throw them in irons. But Captain Graves's letter mentioned a direct order from Commandant DePeyster. I have no choice but to follow orders."

Southhampton was furious, but he checked his glib tongue, knowing it was a waste of time to argue with Bird, who would do exactly as the commandant ordered.

Still, he had no intention of going on to Detroit without Judith and Chard. He had meant every word when he told them he would see to it that they paid dearly for their acts of treason and insubordination, and he was not about to let Captain Bird or anyone else cheat him of that satisfaction.

Southhampton's eyes narrowed in thought. "When we leave here, we'll continue up the Pickawillany to its head-waters and portage to the Auglaize, then up the Auglaize to the Maumee, where we are scheduled to meet Captain Graves at its mouth. Is that correct, sir?"

"Aye," said Bird, wondering what Southhampton had in mind. "'Tis close to two hundred bloody miles. Lord, I hate the thought of it. I'll be glad to rest my bones on a real bed in Detroit . . . this damned wilderness is enough to weary one's soul."

"I quite agree," said Southhampton, moving to the door and studying the soldiers who were forming ranks for a last-minute inspection and roll call before setting out.

"Captain," he added hurriedly, "grant me permission to take Lieutenant Clarke and the Girtys and pursue the escapees. We will apprehend them, cut across country, and catch up with the army before Graves can strike anchor."

Bird pursed his lips as was his habit when considering a proposal. He was well aware that the invasion of Kentucky certainly could not be considered a great victory. And while he was gentleman enough not to relish the idea of casting the blame upon the shoulders of a highborn English lady, he was smart enough to realize that she and Ensign Southhampton could very well prove to be his only defense for the many blunders that had jinxed the campaign from the beginning. He remembered vividly DePeyster's words about the escape of the American Major Chapline from Fort Detroit: "I'd give a king's ransom to know the name of the woman who helped Major Chapline escape."

346

Bird scowled. Until last night, he had the party responsible, someone whom they could blame for all their misfortunes and bad timing. Now he had nothing. Only a written report that, no matter how much he praised his own actions in catching Judith and imprisoning her, would be ridiculed to high heaven. Her escape was by far the worst black mark that had yet been struck against an already badly handled military action.

"Very well," he said at last. "Elliott and McGee can replace the Girtys as guides."

He studied Southhampton warningly. "I want Lady Southhampton and the ensign alive, Major."

Southhampton bowed from the waist. He was forced to bite his lip to keep from smiling his triumph. He would do as the captain ordered, up to a point: he would return Judith and Chard to Detroit "alive," but beyond that, he would make no promises.

As the drums rolled and the troops marched down the banks of the Pickawillany to the waiting canoes, Southhampton and Clarke trotted their horses to the cadence of their own heartbeats. Southhampton was well aware that every step the animals took moved them farther and farther from Bird and his army, farther and farther from any pretense of military justice or fair play that might have restricted his elaborate plan of revenge against the fugitives.

Aye, he thought, before I'm through with them, they will curse the ground Bird walks on for his insistence that they be returned to Detroit . . . alive.

By the time the sun had spun off toward the western horizon the third time, Chard knew, without a doubt, that he had made a grave error. They had not eaten since the evening of their escape, and although no one complained, he could not ignore the simple truth: hunger was twisting their insides into aching knots that left their weakened bodies nearly powerless.

As if to punctuate the thought, he turned and studied their backtrail. The path their dragging feet left in the leaves showed as plainly as the King's Highway, and he knew with a sinking heart that if Bird had sent a search party after them, discovery was inevitable. He sighed, dropping the butt of his rifle to the ground and leaning heavily on the muzzle.

Judith walked tiredly to her son's side. "You are thinking of taking us back, aren't you." It was not a question.

"Aye," he said, exhaling his pent-up breath, wondering if his face was that easy to read. "I suppose in the back of my mind, I thought I was man enough to do what Morgan Patterson did when he brought you and Mrs. Patterson out of the wilderness. I know now it was silly, childish bravado. You have my most profound apologies, Mother."

Judith touched his hand. "Don't apologize, Chard. You did what you thought was right. 'Tis all one can do." Squeezing his hand, she continued, "If it will make you feel any better, there were times when Morgan Patterson felt much the same as you do now. He truly did not believe we would ever reach Fort Cumberland alive."

"He did what he set out to do, Mother."

"No, Chard, he didn't," said Judith softly. "He buried a truly wonderful woman in the soil of this wilderness. And while we are speaking of the past, let me point out something you've not taken into consideration. . . ."

Chard looked deep into his mother's eyes and waited. He appreciated her kind attempt to soothe his injured pride, but he was sure that nothing she could say would change the truth: he had failed before he even had a chance to succeed.

"The women whom Morgan Patterson brought out of the wilderness were young, strong, and healthy, not old, tired, and sick. It's not you, son, who was foolish to think we could escape. It was Susan and I. We've not the physical strength to do what we did when we were eighteen."

"I don't know enough about the frontier even to feed you sufficiently to keep up your strength," finished Chard bitterly.

"It's nothing to be ashamed of, Chard," cried Judith, growing impatient with her son's self-condemnation. "Morgan Patterson would not know which way to turn if you set him down in the streets of London. He would be as lost there as you are here."

"So what are we to do," sighed Chard, "give ourselves up?"

"Normally, I would say no. But Susan is getting worse. She's coughing up blood."

"I didn't know." He knitted his brows in concern. "But in truth, it doesn't surprise me. She's hurt internally, Mother, how badly I have no notion."

"'Tis bad, Chard. Unless she receives treatment . . ." Judith's eyes welled with tears. "She's dying, Chard."

Chard frowned. "There's a doctor at Detroit. But that's two hundred miles distant. And Captain Bird sold Susan and Bitsy to Lorimer, so if we went back to the store to get a canoe, Lorimer would claim them as his—"

"Captain Bird *sold* them?" Judith was aghast. "They are not cattle. How could Bird sell them? Has the British hierarchy stooped so low as to take those who have honorably surrendered and sell them as slaves?"

"I asked the same question, Mother. And the answer is yes. Father talked Bird into selling Mrs. Patterson to Lorimer, and then the captain decided to include Bitsy as well."

"Why?" breathed Judith. "Why would James do such a thing?"

"I have no idea," he lied. "I suppose he felt that Bitsy and Mrs. Patterson were more trouble than they were worth to the Crown."

Chard was not about to tell Judith that James Southhampton's sole purpose in disposing of Susan was to enable him to have Bitsy.

"Damn him," Judith breathed, "damn him to hell."

Chard wondered what she would have said if she had known the truth.

The Girty brothers exchanged glances. It irked them, having to plod along with Southhampton and Clarke instead of going on ahead to locate the escapees. But the major had been adamant: the two trackers were not to venture beyond hailing distance.

"We could have caught them by now," complained George Girty, watching the British officers guide their mounts slowly through the dense forest. "'Tis goddamn
349

foolishness for that pompous bastard, Southhampton, to keep us tied to his coattail . . . and them with horses."

"He's afraid he might get lost," said Simon Girty.

"Then why in hell don't he set up camp and let us bring the prisoners to him? You can't get lost in camp."

Simon Girty studied Southhampton through slitted eyes. "He wants to be there when we catch 'em, to see their faces when they realize he tracked 'em down. They call me a renegade, George, a white Indian . . . but even the savage redskins wouldn't waste their spit on a man who sought revenge on his own wife and son."

"You always was squeamish, Simon," said his brother, "like the time you kept the Shawnee from burnin' Simon Kenton. Hell, Kenton would kill you today if he got the chance. What's it matter to us what these Britishers do to one another? It ain't our worry."

Simon Girty looked long at his brother. George was all Indian when it came to dealing with people of his own race. Yet it was Simon whom the Americans most hated.

"Maybe you're right," he admitted with a sigh. He and George walked toward Southhampton and Clarke, who were dismounting from their sweat-soaked horses.

"How far ahead are they?" demanded Southhampton, wiping his perspiring brow with his kerchief.

"Not far," answered Simon Girty.

"The heat in this infernal jungle is stifling," complained Southhampton, stuffing the kerchief into the cuff of his tunic, "and these bloody flies, and mosquitoes—God! This blasted wilderness is fit only for savages."

The Girtys took the reins of the horses and tethered them to a nearby tree. Both brothers' faces remained expressionless, concealing the deep contempt they harbored toward the effeminate British officer.

Fit for savages? thought Simon Girty in disgust. The red man lives in peace with nature. 'Tis the, supposedly, civilized white man who maims or disfigures or enslaves every living creature he touches. Yet 'tis the Indian who is considered a savage.

"We will make camp here," decided Southhampton. "Clarke and I are hot and sticky, and the horses could do with an afternoon of rest."

"*They* won't rest," said Simon Girty pointedly. "They'll push on as long as they can take a step."

"You said yourself we're not far behind them," Southhampton reminded him. "Let them think they have made good their escape. It will make their capture all the more delicious."

Like any Indian, Simon Girty enjoyed a good chase. But Southhampton's contempt for the wilderness and the red man took the excitement out of it. Simon Girty already regretted his agreement to track down the fugitives. And had he not been obliged to go to Detroit to collect the pay owed him for the Kentucky venture, he would have led Southhampton on a goose chase that would have worn the pompous major to a frazzle and allowed Chard and the women to escape.

Morgan Patterson knelt in the edge of the forest that surrounded Lorimer's clearing.

He examined the area, then flicked his eyes to the sky. It had not been a stroke of luck that had brought him to Lorimer's. To the contrary, he had been led there as surely as if the Lord Himself had taken him by the hand, for the very spot where Patterson chose to cross the Pickawillany just happened to be a shoal where the army had been forced to portage. The sign was unmistakable.

Movement drew Patterson's attention back to the clearing. Lorimer had emerged from the trading post and was heading toward the privy.

Patterson watched the man enter the outhouse, then swung his eyes to the store, studying the building carefully. Nothing moved, nor did any sound indicate the trader had company. That suited Patterson fine. He had several questions that needed answering, and he would just as soon talk to Lorimer alone.

Patterson sprinted to the outhouse and kicked open the door.

The startled storekeeper's mouth fell open. "Mother of God—" But that was as far as he got, for the muzzle of the woodsman's long-gun pressed hard against his teeth, neatly shutting off all sound.

351

"Not a word," whispered Patterson, his rock-hard eyes boring into Lorimer's.

The man nodded uncertainly.

"Anyone in the store?"

Lorimer shook his head, no.

Patterson pulled the gun barrel a few inches away from the man's mouth.

"Do you know who I am, m'sieur?" challenged Lorimer belligerently, trying valiantly to redeem a measure of the dignity he had forfeited by being caught in such a position.

"I know you, Lorimer," said Patterson harshly. "You were with the Girty brothers and the Shawnee when they attacked Boonesboro in '77."

"Then you must know, I am not a man to interfere with, m'sieur?"

"How long has Bird been gone?" demanded Patterson, ignoring Lorimer's threat.

The trader sized up the tall frontiersman, taking in his unyielding eyes, his unshaven jaw, his gaunt frame that spoke of having traveled too hard too fast, and finally, the stained, ragged hole in the shoulder of the woodsman's hunting shirt.

A Kentuckian, he thought with contempt, following the army to try to steal his family and friends away from Bird.

"I don't know a thing about any army, m'sieur, and if I did, I would not tell you."

Patterson smiled crookedly, then stepped through the doorway of the privy, casting his shadow across Lorimer and forcing the man to look up at him.

"Lorimer," he said in his soft drawl, "I'm going to stomp you down that hole you're sitting on until all that's showin' is your head. Then, if you don't answer my questions, I'm goin' to make ripples. It's up to you."

Lorimer gulped. He was not afraid of Patterson's threat, but he was in no position to argue the point. That could wait a few more minutes.

"Bird's been gone two, three days, m'sieur," he said, turning his head to stare at the slab-sided wall. He hated Patterson with a venom for taking advantage of him when he had no means of retaliation. Turning again to Patterson, he shouted angrily, "This is no fitting place for a man to talk!"

"I'm not yet sure I'm talking to a man," said Patterson, but he backed out of the building.

Lorimer eased himself off the hole and reached toward a pile of fresh corn cobs lying in a corner.

"Let it go," said Patterson, his voice as hard as nails.

"A man's got to wipe his arse," thundered Lorimer.

"You, Mr. Lorimer, are arse all over. Now, get out here in the fresh air and hook up your breeches."

"Goddamn you," whispered Lorimer, trembling with a rage so intense that Patterson thought sure the man would burst.

"Goddamn you to hell!" cried the storekeeper as he gingerly buttoned his drop-front breeches.

Unimpressed by Lorimer's anger, the woodsman prodded him with his rifle barrel, moving him spraddle-legged toward the trading post.

Just inside the door, Patterson halted Lorimer. His quick gaze took in the unoccupied room. It was no different from a hundred other stores that dotted the fringes of the wilderness.

"I'll have a cup of whiskey," said Patterson, stiff-arming Lorimer toward the bar and making him stagger awkwardly in an attempt to keep his legs apart.

Lorimer lifted a tin cup off a wall peg and dipped it into the barrel. "Where you from, m'sieur?" he asked, playing for time, hoping to catch the Kentuckian off guard.

"You know damn well where I'm from, Lorimer."

The storekeeper studied Patterson from the corner of his eye as he pushed the cup across the counter. He wondered how the man had gotten so far north without being captured or killed by Indians.

Patterson took the cup and sipped slowly, watching Lorimer over the rim. He almost gasped as the fiery liquid burned its way into his empty stomach.

"You got something cooking on the hearth?" he nodded toward the fireplace.

"It'll do if you're hungry enough, m'sieur."

"I am."

Lorimer moved to the hearth and ladled a healthy portion of venison stew into a wooden trencher. He didn't like the way the muzzle of the woodsman's rifle always seemed to be pointing directly at him—an accident? He knew better.

He watched Patterson wolf down the food and hand the trencher back for a refill. I hope you choke, thought Lorimer sullenly as he dipped more food into the plate. Lorimer moved back to the counter and leaned on his elbows. He wondered what the man wanted, but he knew he would have to be careful with his questions. Kentuckians were a watchful and dangerous people who did not take kindly to being interrogated by anyone, much less a Frenchman in the British employ. "Traveling far?" he inquired with a patronizing smile.

"Depends."

Lorimer scowled, liking the woodsman less and less. "On what?" he said, forcing the anger from his voice.

"On how far I have to go before I come up with Bird."

Lorimer studied Patterson carefully, not sure how much information he should reveal. "What's your business with Bird?" he said finally.

"Lorimer," said Patterson, facing the storekeeper, "let's cut the small talk. I've come a long way to catch up with Bird's army, and I'm in a hurry. You tell me how far ahead of me the army is, and I'll be on my way."

Lorimer paled. He was not accustomed to being rebuffed, and he didn't like it one whit.

Still, the man intrigued him; the Kentuckian had followed Bird's army for several hundred miles through an uncharted wilderness swarming with Indians. Very few frontiersmen had ever done that and lived to tell about it.

Lorimer decided to tell the truth and be rid of the man.

"Bird is traveling heavy and slow, m'sieur. He has every Indian in the country following along behind the army, tryin' to get the last of the soldiers' pay. He is just two days ahead of you."

Patterson eyed Lorimer for a long moment. He was amazed that the scoundrel had not tried to lie to him. "I'm obliged, Lorimer," he said, turning to leave.

"You'll never live to see Bird, Kentuckian." Lorimer grinned wolfishly. "The British, they are paying fifty dollars in Detroit for rebel scalps, and every redskin in the country is determined to collect the bounty." Lorimer laughed heartily, pleased with himself as he pulled aside the neck opening of his linsey-woolsey shirt and scratched his armpit, for Patterson's face had drained to a deathly shade of gray.

But it wasn't the fear of losing his hair that had turned Patterson's knees to water and stopped his heart; it was a brief glimpse of the gold chain and locket that hung suspended from Lorimer's beefy neck. Patterson's mouth went dry, and his insides felt as though he would lose the food he had just eaten. "Where did you get that locket?" It was whispered with such intensity that Lorimer looked up in alarm.

Lorimer was not easily frightened, but he was well acquainted with danger, and he knew he had made a terrible mistake when he assumed he had frightened Patterson. Any fool with half an eye could see that the man standing before him was afraid of nothing—not Lorimer, not Bird, not the whole Algonquin nation, not the entire British Army.

Lorimer began to fidget. He didn't like the nervous sweat that dampened his forehead, didn't like the knots that suddenly formed in his stomach.

"It is none of your business, m'sieur," he blustered, not liking the bravado in his voice either. "And just who in hell are you, to come in here and push me around?"

But he already knew the answer to that question. Lorimer was wearing Morgan Patterson's wife's locket, and he cursed himself for being a fool; he should have recognized the man immediately. The brass butt plate of Patterson's rifle smashed into his mouth, and the next thing he saw was the floor as it hurled itself at him and smashed against his face with such impact that he was sure his nose had been driven through the back of his head. Pain crashed through his brain like a white-hot wave, drowning out all instincts save one. Rolling onto his back, he clawed at the knife in his belt.

But Patterson was on him before he could grasp the handle, pinioning his arms to the floor and grabbing his long, greasy hair. "I asked you a question," breathed Patterson, drawing the man's face to within inches of his own. "Where did you get the locket?"

355

Lorimer looked into Patterson's strained features, and the anxiety he saw there gave him heart; he would use Patterson's need for an answer to bargain with.

"Go to hell, m'sieur," he said through mangled lips. "I will say not one word while I lay flat on my back."

The woodsman slammed Lorimer's head against the floor, and before the startled man knew what was happening, Patterson had caught him by the throat and choked off his wind. Then slowly, as Lorimer's eyes bulged in their sockets, Patterson eased the small pearl-handled dagger from his belt and laid the edge of the blade across the bridge of the storekeeper's nose.

"I spent eight years with the Shawnee, Lorimer," he said, "and I learned every trick imaginable to make a man suffer."

He released his grip on Lorimer, and the man made great sucking noises as he inhaled through his open mouth.

"You are a white man, M'sieur Patterson," Lorimer rasped between breaths. "You might kill me, but you have not got the guts to go Indian on me."

"Where did you get the locket, Lorimer?" Patterson caught the gold chain and tore it from the man's neck.

"You have your trinket, m'sieur," sneered the storekeeper. "Now get the hell out of my establishment."

The razor-sharp blade cut through the cartilage of Lorimer's nose and rested against the startled man's lower eyelids. Blood welled up around the steel and streamed off both sides of Lorimer's face, funneling down the indentations below his earlobes and puddling on the floor beneath his head.

Lorimer tried to scream, but blood filled his nostrils and throat, and he made only the gurgling noise of a man strangling on his own gore. He arched his back and tried to fling Patterson from him, but Patterson slammed his head against the floor with such fierce disregard for pain and suffering that Lorimer was sure the man intended to bash his brains out.

"Where did you get the locket?" grated Patterson, drawing the man's head up again.

"I got it from your wife," admitted Lorimer through the blood that clogged his windpipe. "In the name of

God, m'sieur, let me spit out this blood. She is choking me . . ."

Patterson put more pressure on the knife blade, cutting into the man's cheeks. "My wife would never have given you that locket. Where did you get it?" Patterson's eyes were as merciless as an Indian's. "I won't ask again, Lorimer. I'll turn this knife sideways and skin off your face."

"All right," cried Lorimer, afraid of drowning in his own blood. "I found it in the cabin out back. Your wife, she dropped it there."

Patterson slipped the knife from the man's nose and stood up, watching warily as Lorimer rolled onto his side and hacked up large quantities of blood and mucus.

"Damn it, m'sieur," Lorimer whimpered, crawling to his knees, his hands covering his slashed nose, "I think you cut an artery."

"You'll live," said the woodsman dryly. He dragged a dirty rag off a peg by the whiskey barrel and flipped it to Lorimer, who made a compress and pushed it tightly against his bloody face. "Now tell me about my wife and daughter."

Lorimer looked over the bloody cloth at Patterson. He wondered how much of the truth he should relate. Certainly he didn't intend to mention the fact that he had purchased the two women for his own use.

As though Patterson were reading his mind, he said, "If you lie to me, Lorimer, I'll kill you; you'd best pray I find my family."

It was said with such quiet certainty that Lorimer shuddered. "They are not with Bird, m'sieur," he said, hating himself for his cowardice—an emotion he had never before experienced. "They escaped three days ago."

"Which way did they go?"

"West, I think."

"Is anybody after them?"

Lorimer nodded painfully, removing the compress and wringing the blood from it. "Two British officers and the Girty brothers."

Patterson scowled. The two officers didn't bother him, but the Girty brothers could prove dangerous when cornered. And the fact that he and they had hunted together

357

before the war would have little or no bearing on the issue at hand.

"M'sieur," said Lorimer, breaking into the woodsman's thoughts. "If you were smart, you would go back to Kentucky and forget your wife and daughter." He hesitated at the narrowing of Patterson's eyes, wondering if he should chance provoking the man further. But when meanness and common sense clash, nine times out of ten common sense comes out the loser. Such was the case with Lorimer. Grinning triumphantly, he continued, "You will not recognize your ladies when you catch up to them. They have spread their legs for every soldier in Bird's command."

Lorimer didn't regain consciousness for two days.

It was a struggle for the women to hollow out places in the leaves in which to lay their aching bodies. It had been a long, long day, yet because of Susan's illness, they had made hardly any progress at all. Even Bitsy had momentarily come to life and had lent a helping hand when her mother periodically sank to the ground, unable to take another step.

"We are going back," said Chard in defeat. "We tried. Lord knows we did, but there's just too much against us." His shoulders sagged with failure. "Perhaps we can slip into Lorimer's at night and steal a canoe. With luck, we could make the falls of the Ohio in a week, two at the most. They'll have a doctor there."

Susan turned her head so that Chard would not see her face. She did not have the heart to tell him that she would not last two more days, much less two more weeks. And, the truth was, she wished that the end would hurry. The pain had become so intense that even the slightest movement was agony. Even more unbearable was the knowledge that she, whose life was nearly over, was endangering the lives of those who had their entire futures before them.

A tear squeezed from between her lashes. She wanted to live, God knew that, but not at the price of death or enslavement for her daughter. No, Susan decided, gazing lovingly at Bitsy, a few more days on earth were not worth that risk.

Judith sank gratefully into the nest she had prepared.

The leaves felt soft and inviting. She considered Chard's decision to take Susan to the falls of the Ohio. Indeed, it seemed the only route open to them if they wanted to keep her alive. Then she sighed. She knew it was hopeless. And all the wishing or planning in the world wouldn't change that. But she also knew that they must do everything in their power to save Susan or at least make her aware that her life mattered to them.

"I think you are right, Chard," she said. "Lorimer has canoes and horses." Judith sat upright, her face animated. "I wish we had thought of that sooner! If you slipped into Lorimer's and stole a horse, Susan could ride back, she might stand a chance."

Susan cringed at the thought of trying to sit upright on a jarring, bouncing horse. Every step the animal took would be a nightmare of pain for her—and it would be a waste of time. She had gone her last step.

"Mama needs rest and food," said Bitsy. It was the first comment she had made in two days. "We should find someplace to hide."

Chard's eyes slitted in thought. A place to hide . . . food . . . "When Girty and I left Lorimer's to go hunting," he said aloud, "we passed an abandoned Indian hut. There was a cornfield there."

"Do you think you could find it again?" asked Judith, a spark of excitement in her voice.

"I think so," said Chard. "And it's not over five miles from here, if I have my bearings correct."

Bitsy looked hard at him, and he knew what she was thinking: that he had gotten lost once before, not a quarter of a mile from camp.

He held her gaze steadily. "I can find the hut, Bitsy."

The girl turned her head and stared at the gathering darkness. Her silence spoke for itself.

At daylight, Chard looped out a half-mile and circled the camp, foraging for anything edible. He found a few hickory nuts, walnuts, and a vine with several clusters of wild grapes. It wasn't much, but it was better than nothing. The women ate ravenously, cracking the nuts between two stones and carefully picking every morsel of meat from the

359

hulls. The grapes were not yet ripe, but they devoured them appreciatively. The meager fare did little to appease their hunger, but they smiled and said they were full.

Chard drew himself to full height and checked the priming in the rifle. He extended the gun to Bitsy, who looked at him with a blank expression.

"I'm going to try to find that hut," he said. "I shouldn't be gone long, but you'd best have some protection."

"I'm going with you," she announced. "I thought about it last night. When we reach the hut, you can come back for Mama and Mrs. Southhampton. I'll stay there, and if the corn is still standing, I'll have something hot to eat when you return. Also, it will give me a chance to make a soft bed for my mama."

She walked to Judith and placed the rifle in her hands. "There's no need in arguing about it, Mrs. Southhampton," she said, too softly to be overheard. "My mother's life is at stake, and that's more important to me than your concern for your son's virtue. On that score I can relieve your suspicions and your worries. You are perfectly correct in your belief that I am not good enough for Chard . . . or any other decent man. And your son is well aware of it. No, Mrs. Southhampton, you won't have to worry about Chard ever being the least bit interested in someone like me."

Judith stared at the girl, too stunned to comment.

Bitsy turned on her heel and walked to her mother. She knelt beside Susan and hugged her. "We'll find the hut, and I'll make you a fine corn mush," she promised.

"I can taste it already." Susan smiled weakly.

Bitsy's eyes were pathetic as they held her mother's gaze. "I love you, Mama, and I'm proud that I am your daughter."

"And I love you, Bitsy." Susan took her daughter into her arms and held her close, feeling the girl's tears against her cheek.

"Don't cry, baby," she whispered, touching her lips to Bitsy's forehead. "I will be fine. . . . Everything will be fine."

Bitsy wiped her eyes with the back of her hand. "I'll see you soon. I'll have everything ready and waiting . . .

Mama?" She burst into tears and embraced Susan tightly once again. "There's so much I want to say."

"You've said everything I ever wanted to hear, darling. Now, go on, go to Chard. He's waiting for you."

She watched her daughter and Chard disappear into the wilderness. And after they were out of sight, she did what she had been forcing herself not to do for Bitsy's sake: she broke down and cried the tears of a mother who was well aware that she had held her daughter in her arms for the last time.

CHAPTER
· 21 ·

CHARD SCRATCHED HIS head and looked in all directions. Try as he might, he could not recognize a familiar landmark.

Bitsy questioned him about the area around the hut: What was the lay of the land? The kind of trees? Was there a creek or spring nearby?

"There was a creek that ran past the cornfield," he said, frowning in thought. "If we can locate it, we can follow it to the clearing." It seemed to be a revelation to him.

Bitsy shook her head woefully; she didn't know whether to be amused or angered by Chard's ignorance of the frontier, for even a fool had sense enough to know that a stream was one of the best landmarks one could hope for.

She had to admit that he had learned a great deal about the wilderness in the weeks since she had met him. Yet there was so much, so many small things that he didn't know and very probably would never learn. Good woodsmen had the ability to stamp a landmark so indelibly in their minds that, at any time they chose, they could return to that spot with little or no hesitation. Bitsy doubted that Chard would ever master that accomplished science.

They traveled on, neither of them speaking or showing any open consideration for the other. Yet, Bitsy had been badly mistaken when she assured Judith that Chard could not be interested in someone like her, for he was very much aware of her. It was as though her every gesture and look held a special significance; he hurt when she stumbled; he worried when she frowned; he gasped when she was breathless, and he suffered when he looked into her bleak eyes and saw the misery there.

Yet, he did not know how to penetrate the invisible barrier she had raised between herself and the world around her. He didn't know, in fact, even how to talk to her.

They found a small creek and followed it nearly a mile before Chard decided it was not leading in the right direction. Disappointed, they abandoned it.

At noon they rested, ignoring their rumbling stomachs and the aching fatigue that reached to the marrow of their bones. Chard admired Bitsy all the more for her uncomplaining courage. Not once did she indicate, by either voice or gesture, that she blamed him for the time and energy they had wasted exploring the wrong creek. In fact, her silent acceptance of his mistake made him even more determined to locate the hut. As he watched her from the corner of his eye, he made a solemn vow that he would never again let her down.

"You are quite a girl, Bitsy." The softspoken words had slipped out, but he was not sorry; his admiration and respect for Bitsy were very real and powerful emotions, and he was not ashamed of them.

"I am a woman, Chard." She spoke with cool detachment. "Your father left my girlhood soaking into a mattress in Lorimer's cabin."

Chard dropped his head and stared at the ground; he had no answer for that.

Bitsy's lips drew across her teeth in a grimace. "Don't feel sorry for me, damn you. I don't want your pity." Her voice was rising to match her emotions. "I hate you for it, Chard. I don't want your sympathy."

"I don't *feel* sorry for you," he said gently. "I *share* your sorrow. There is a difference, you know." He looked at her imploringly, and a little voice deep down inside him whispered, I love you, Bitsy, can't you see it in my face, my eyes . . . can't you hear it in my heart?

But he left it unsaid. Instead, he climbed to his feet and
363

walked away, leaving Bitsy to stare after him, wishing with all her heart that they could just sit and talk the way they had that night in the forest—just two young people, innocently reaching out to each other to share their dreams and fears and inner selves. It had been the most beautiful night of her life.

It will never be that simple and natural again . . . not for us, she told herself bitterly, watching Chard walk to a small rise and study the forest. For I am no longer innocent, and, as much as you might wish to, Chard, you could never pretend that I was.

Feeling totally isolated, she joined Chard at the top of the incline.

"I believe the creek is over that next rise," he said, pointing ahead.

He hoped that it was not wishful thinking that made the terrain seem familiar, for they could not afford for him to be wrong again. Time and endurance were running out. But something about the lay of the land, the look of the trees, the rise he was standing on, lent support to the feeling that he had been there before. He prayed for all their sakes that he was right.

The creek was there.

Bitsy heard his deep, relieved breath, and she found herself sighing along with him, pleased not only because they were on the right path but because he had led them there. And it was her turn to be embarrassed, for her earlier assumption that he would never have the makings of a woodsman. Their elation, however, soon vanished; they traveled on and on, expecting each time they rounded a bend to find themselves at their destination. As midday swung into late afternoon, Chard's confidence began to waver.

He groaned aloud when he thought of the vow he had made just a few hours before, for with each step he took, he became more afraid that he had indeed let her down again. He was to the point of voicing that opinion when they were forced to crawl under a vine-covered blow-down that had created a tunnel over the narrow stream. When they emerged, they found themselves facing the clearing with head-high cornstalks, beans, squash, and pumpkins intermingled among weed-infested rows.

"Thank God!" whispered Chard, his eyes roving over the field. Then, frowning, he gazed at the sun which was halfway below the horizon. "I'll have to hurry if I intend to make it back to mother's before dark. . . ."

"'Tis already too late," said Bitsy, pushing past Chard to get a view of the clearing. "The sun will be down in less than an hour. . . . It will be better to wait until morning."

Chard blushed. "I can find them, Bitsy . . . even in the dark."

Bitsy didn't answer, her eyes were glued to the haphazard garden. To the starved girl, it looked like a beautiful cornucopia, and her jubilation was so exhilarating that before she thought, she flung her arms around Chard's neck and kissed him on the lips. Chard, equally elated and caught totally off guard by her unexpected expression of joy, responded by slipping his arms around her and returning her kiss with a tenderness that bespoke his very soul.

She stiffened in his embrace, her mouth becoming cold and rigid. But she made no move to pull away. Chard opened his eyes. Their lashes touched, and he realized with a trace of resentment that her eyes had never been closed, that she had not let herself slip into the blissful ecstasy of sharing a kiss with one who loved and adored her. And he knew that in spite of the vow he had made not to let her down he had failed her again—failed to reach the disillusioned young woman who had been so cruelly used that her eyes had the flat stare of the dead as she waited for him to continue his conquest.

Hurt flared in Chard's face. And even though he knew that Bitsy had just lived through an experience that could very easily have turned her against men for the rest of her life, he could not accept her refusal to trust him. Could she not see how very much he loved her? Was she so blind? He wanted to scream at her to give him a chance to prove he wasn't like his father. But he didn't. He simply released her and walked to the far end of the field where the roof of an elm-bark hut was visible. Bitsy stared after him, wishing he had voiced the confusion she had seen in his eyes.

The hut had been deserted since early spring. Inside, delicate cobwebs had been woven by industrious little workmen who scurried to the center of their death traps and drew themselves into small knots, hoping Chard would

365

overlook them. Chard almost laughed aloud as he gazed at their trembling webs. He, too, was caught up in a web of his own making, with nowhere to run to but the center. And he too knew the fear of something bigger and stronger than he that threatened to destroy his delicate little world.

Chard snatched up a stick and slashed and hacked at the fragile netting, venting on the hapless spiders his frustration at having not reached Bitsy.

Bitsy entered the hut and silently observed Chard's frantic destruction of the spiderwebs. She wondered at the savagery of his onslaught, for it was unlike him to find satisfaction in devastation. Yet the look on his face was that of pure pleasure. Bitsy backed out of the building and leaned against the rough bark exterior. It unsettled her that Chard was upset. And she was too honest to pretend that she did not know the reason. She closed her eyes, despair and confusion gnawing at her empty insides. She did not want to tense up every time Chard came near her, but she could not help it. His presence made her ravaged nerves and senses react automatically, leaving her frigid and so desperately frightened that she physically trembled from the shock of it.

She pushed herself away from the hut and stumbled to the garden. The corn was not yet ripe, but she ripped off one of the small ears and stripped back the shucks. She knew better than to wolf down the food, but she didn't care. All she could think about was putting something in her stomach to appease the aching knots that Chard's kiss had created. It was a wasted effort. Unaccustomed to substantial quantities of food, Bitsy retched up all that she had eaten.

Chard walked to the edge of the field and watched her gag and heave and gag again. He went to the creek and slipped off his deerskin hunting frock, then his white ruffled shirt. He soaked the tail of the shirt in the cool stream and headed back to the bent-over girl.

She looked up at him with tear-filled eyes, her face white and beaded with perspiration. Her feeble smile was more a grimace than a grin. "I knew better than to try that on an empty stomach."

Chard nodded. He, too, had considered throwing all

caution to the wind and stuffing himself with the tender corn—and might have, had Bitsy not beaten him to it. Without a word, he blotted her forehead with the dry portion of his shirt, then made a compress of the wet tail and draped it across her brow. He helped her to the creek, where she bathed her face and rinsed her mouth.

Chard left her there and went in search of evergreen boughs with which to fashion a bed for Susan.

He had made several trips and had quite a pile laid in a back corner of the hut when Bitsy entered with an armload of vegetables.

"If you would build a fire, Chard, I'll borrow your knife and skin a tulip poplar."

Chard looked at her questioningly.

"We need something to cook in," she explained.

He nodded, still not understanding what she was talking about.

Bitsy took the knife and disappeared through the small doorway.

Chard gathered a handful of dry twigs and bark from a corner of the hut and fashioned a miniature bird's nest, which he carefully laid in the fire pit. He drove a stick into the touchhole of his pistol so that the sparks could not ignite the powder in the breech and, laying the lock of the weapon over the cup of the nest, pulled the trigger. A shower of sparks shone brightly in the dim room as the hammer fell, and almost immediately Chard had a small flame licking at the dry tinder.

Bitsy was back by the time the fire had gained enough strength to be considered a blaze. She laid out a two-foot-round piece of poplar bark on the floor. In the center, being very careful to cut only halfway through the wood, she drew the point of the knife in an almost perfect circle. Then, again cutting only halfway through the wood, she traced thin lines from the inner circle to the edge of the bark, laying out equal miters. Chard watched with interest as she gently folded the cuts into an awkward bucket of sorts.

"Wrap that piece of hickory bark around the top and tie it," she instructed, nodding toward a thin strip of green hickory that she had laid on the floor. Chard did as he was told, pleased and impressed by the crude cooking pot Bitsy

367

had fashioned. She took the container and disappeared, but was back again in minutes, the vessel half filled with water.

"The fire will burn that thing up," warned Chard, indicating the wooden container.

"No, it won't," she replied, slicing half-ripe vegetables into the water. "I know it sounds ridiculous, but the bark won't burn so long as there's water in it."

She smiled at the disbelief on his face, and Chard smiled in return. It was the first emotion she had shown since he had kissed her, and even that small wisp of a grin was enough to cause his pulse to quicken with hope.

And, indeed, Chard was not imagining Bitsy's faint attempt at cheerfulness. The hut, no matter that it was almost falling down, and the garden, if one could call the weed-ridden patch by that name, and the fire, and the bucket that she had made, all reminded her of Kentucky —of home. And she knew that tomorrow Chard would fetch her mother and Bitsy would nurse Susan back to health, and all would be fine . . . all would be fine . . . Susan had promised.

Those thoughts, mingled together and savored, made Bitsy glad to be alive for the first time since Southhampton had raped her. Again she smiled fleetingly, as though turning up the corners of her lips were something that she wasn't supposed to do, something alien to her.

"Mama will rest easy on the bed you made, Chard. Thank you."

"You don't have to thank me, Bitsy. I admire and respect your mother. I'll gladly help her any way that I can."

Bitsy's eyes misted. "Why are you helping us, Chard? You know what people are saying about my mama . . . and me."

"And you know what those same people say about my mother," he replied crisply. "Only, in her case, it's absolutely true. She did plot against the king and England. She is a spy. And nobody trusts a spy, not even the people she was trying to help."

"Why, Chard? Why did she do that? She's an English lady of noble birth. Why did she throw all that away?"

Chard shook his head. "I have no idea, Bitsy. All she will say is that she had to do it because her conscience wouldn't allow her to let Bird and my father march through Kentucky and wantonly slaughter innocent women and children. I think she's telling the truth—but not all of it. I think the real reason stems from something that happened before I was born."

Bitsy sighed. "Yes, this whole ordeal has been a personal thing between your parents and mine. You and I are victims of something that happened years ago . . . whatever that was."

Chard stared at the small fire that danced between the two flat stones that supported the bucket of stew.

"I wish we knew what happened back then," he murmured. "It would answer a multitude of questions."

"It must have been something really terrible," speculated Bitsy. "My mama won't discuss it, and your mama hates me because of it, and your father—"

"Has gone insane," interrupted Chard quickly, when he saw Bitsy's face drain and her lips tremble at her mention of Southhampton. "But he was probably that way before," Chard added lamely.

They sat in silence then, each preoccupied with identical thoughts of the mysterious past they were caught up in and the horrendous effect it had had on their lives.

The aroma of the cooking food finally prevailed, and Chard looked greedily into the boiling container.

"Do you think I could fish something out of there? I can't stand much more of that smell; it's driving my stomach crazy."

Bitsy speared a chunk of squash with Chard's knife and passed the steaming morsel to him. It was the best-tasting food Chard had ever eaten, and he told her so. Her face flushed with pleasure, which turned to childlike embarrassment.

"Chew slow and easy," she said, attempting to hide her delight at his compliment.

He nibbled the chunk down to bite size, then extended the remainder to her. She eyed Chard curiously; no one had offered to feed her since she was a child. Amusement danced in her eyes as she opened her mouth and he delicately laid the small piece of squash on her tongue. Their eyes held as she matched his rhythm, chewing slowly

369

as he was doing. They both burst out laughing: the small act of innocent consideration, performed with an almost comic solemnity, had triggered a sense of peace that left them smiling happily at each other.

"Do you think you'll be safe here?" blurted Chard, breaking the spell, and leaving Bitsy with a sense of disappointment she did not understand.

"I mean," he explained, "will it be all right for me to leave you here tomorrow when I go for our mothers?"

Bitsy glanced through the open door at the darkening shadows of the forest. A sudden loneliness, mixed with fear, washed over her. She felt secure with Chard—or perhaps it was the combination of him, the hut, the food, and the fire. Whatever the reasons, since arriving at the clearing, she had relaxed her guard, and it felt good. But with him gone? Her face turned ashen. She would be alone again, alone and at the mercy of nightmarish memories.

"I will be fine," she lied, not looking at him. "This is an Indian's or hunter's winter quarters. So whoever planted the garden won't return until the first frost, and hunting parties will be farther south."

"You're sure?"

"Yes."

Chard accepted her answer. It didn't enter his mind that the girl he had admired for her unflinching bravery and perseverance would cower at the thought of being alone with her inner self. And he certainly would not have understood the self-loathing that had plagued her every waking moment since Southhampton had left her lying broken and degraded on Lorimer's bed.

Bitsy took Chard's knife and went again to the forest, returning with an armload of freshly peeled bark strips a foot wide and three feet long. As Chard watched, she cut the strips into one-foot lengths and trimmed the edges until she had a rough, oval trencher that would work well as a plate. Again Chard was impressed by the girl's knowledge of how to make do with what nature provided.

"Bitsy," he said when she filled his plate with half-cooked vegetables, "you are a real wonder."

The girl smiled shyly, thinking to herself that not a week before, she would have been contemptuous of his ignorance of the small things that most frontier folk learned in childhood—but that was a week ago, a whole lifetime ago. They ate slowly, using sticks for spoons, being careful not to overindulge. And although they didn't speak, the silence was not oppressive or uncomfortable. When they had finished, they walked in the darkness to the creek, scrubbed the plates with sand, and rinsed them in the clear, cold water.

A whippoorwill called in the distance, and a hoot owl answered from the ridge beyond the hut. It was a peaceful, serene evening, a perfect evening to forget Bird, Lorimer, the Indians . . . and Southhampton. An evening that was made for the young and innocent, and, although Bitsy would have argued that point, she and Chard were both those things.

He gazed at her silhouette in the moonlight, wishing he could read her expression. But the deep shadows that fell across her face made it impossible to clearly define any of her features, even as she faced him. Throwing caution to the wind, he took one quick step and drew her into his arms. For the briefest moment he felt the warm, soft response of her lips; then it was gone. She trembled at his touch as though standing naked in a blizzard, and her mouth became as hard and unyielding as ice. He had truly believed that she, too, had caught the enchanted mood of the moment and longed to express her tender emotions through touch and taste, to see deeply into one another and hear the beat of each other's heart and soul. Disappointment surged through him. It had all been wishful thinking. Chard released Bitsy and walked into the night.

Bitsy watched him go, making no move to stop him. She wrapped her arms tightly about her abdomen and clenched her teeth against the ache in her stomach. She took several deep breaths in an attempt to relax, but her drawn and taut nerves refused to cooperate. Shaking from the intensity of the constrictions, her mind a whirling agony of hopelessness, she dropped to her knees and doubled over, waiting for the spasms to pass.

Except for the soft glow of the fire pit, the hut was in total darkness when Chard finally returned. He noticed with satisfaction that Bitsy had already banked the coals under the bark vessel; with luck, in the morning they would only have to rake aside the ash and rekindle the fire.

"I'll sleep outside," he said, turning toward the door.

"Don't be angry, Chard" came her small voice.

"I'm not angry, Bitsy. I'll see you in the morning." He heard the evergreen boughs rustle as she sat up.

"Chard?"

"Yes?"

Chard waited hopefully, but when Bitsy didn't continue, he shrugged his shoulders and bent to step through the low door.

"I wanted a cabin . . ." It was said more as a thought than a statement.

Chard frowned over his shoulder into the dark corner where Bitsy sat. What did a cabin have to do with anything?

"I used to dream of a cabin like my mama's . . . and a garden of my own."

Chard peered hard, trying to see her face.

"I wanted to help . . . my husband build that cabin and plant that garden. I wanted to work by his side or, if necessary, fight by his side to protect it. I dreamed of cooking his meals and washing his clothes. I wanted him to be proud to take me as his wife." Bitsy was crying openly. "And I wanted to come to him clean and pure."

Chard took a hesitant step toward her. He had never felt so close to anyone in his life as he did to the beautiful girl who had just ripped off the top layer of her skin to expose her most intimate self.

"But that can never be," she whispered, and Chard, even from where he stood, could feel the hot tears streaming down her cheeks, for his face burned as though her tears were his own.

"No decent man will want me now. How could he ever love me, knowing that I am . . . dirty?"

Chard crossed the room in two strides and sank down beside her. He took her hand, feeling the broken, twisted fingers as they groped desperately to intertwine with his. His heart ached for her, for he realized that the person that she had become was as broken and twisted as her hand, that she was groping in the dark to try and touch something permanent, something she could intertwine with, something she could hang on to.

"Bitsy," he whispered, slipping his free arm around her and laying her head against his shoulder. "A decent man, if he loves you, won't give a damn about something that happened before he met you, something you had no control over."

"No one will believe that," she said bitterly, trying hard to stop crying. "You didn't see the looks I got from the Kentuckians when Bird called me a whore. They knew better, but they believed him anyway."

She cried again, but it was softer and more subdued than before. She wiped her eyes and snuggled her head more tightly against his arm. .

"They're good, God-fearing folk, Chard," she continued between sobs, "yet they believed the worst when I was innocent. How could I expect them to be different now that I am . . ."

"Hush," he said, tightening his arm around her and touching his lips to her hair. "I am a decent man . . . a gentleman." He smiled and kissed her hair again. "I even have papers and a crest to prove it. Yet I have never respected or admired a woman more than I do you."

Bitsy sighed into his shoulder, then tilted her face so that her forehead lay soft against his cheek. "You didn't have to say that, Chard, but it was nice to hear. Thank you."

Chard shifted his position and looked into her upturned face.

The moon, having traveled higher, cast its pale light through the smoke hole in the ceiling, illuminating the small enclosure with a mellow luster that softened the harshness of her eyes and erased the brittle mask of despondency that had aged her beyond her years.

"I love you," he said simply. "I've loved you since the first time I saw you standing on the roof of that cabin at Ruddle's Fort. And nothing has happened to change that; nothing could ever change that."

He bent and kissed her tenderly. Her body convulsed, and she moaned through her clenched teeth. It was evident, even to Chard, that she was fighting hard to overcome the panic that was threatening her very existence.

He relaxed his embrace and stroked her hair and told

her over and over again that it was all right. He felt her tremble, and then she leaned heavily against him as though totally exhausted. They sat like that for a long while, her head against his chest, his arms around her, neither speaking.

"I've never kissed anyone but you, Chard." The words were softly muffled against the fabric of his shirt. "I . . . I liked it."

"You've never kissed me," he corrected, astounded by her revelation. He touched her forehead with his lips. "I've kissed you, but you've never kissed me back . . . but I liked it, too."

"In my dreams, I've kissed you a thousand times," she admitted honestly.

Chard gently raised her face, tracing her eyebrows, her nose, her lips with his fingertips.

"Kiss me, Bitsy," he whispered, tilting her face toward his. But even the soft moonlight couldn't obliterate the fear that suddenly filled her eyes or the cold and clammy texture of her skin under his touch. And a frustrated rage, overpowering because of his inability to shatter the crystal gates that held her captive in the cold, dark dungeon of her own sinless shame, made him drop his head back and cry like a baby.

Bitsy, who had never seen a man weep, and had, in fact, thought such an occurrence an impossibility, was touched to her very soul. She tenderly raised her lips to his. They kissed hesitantly at first, made timid by Bitsy's previous withdrawals. But as they continued to seek and search and explore the simple but glorious pleasure of touching mouths, they became more natural and less guarded. As their fears and constraints slowly dissolved, a pair of young, healthy male and female animals emerged, a couple so mentally thrilled and physically excited by the intensity of their newly discovered attraction for each other that they sank panting and breathless into the sweet evergreen boughs and stared with wonder into each other's eyes.

Very slowly, Chard drew Bitsy's tattered dress up over her knees. His fingertips barely touched the rounded softness of the calf of her leg, but even that brief encounter petrified her muscles into rigid, unyielding flesh that was cold to his touch. He saw fear widen her eyes, and he wanted to scream at her not to retreat back into herself, not to withdraw into that safe, sterile sanctuary that he couldn't enter.

She shuddered violently, then slowly relaxed against him.

Chard's hand shook as though suddenly struck with palsy as he gently rested his moist palm on her knee. Bitsy shuddered again, and again Chard could sense the terrible battle that raged within her. He was nearly wild with desire for the beautiful woman who lay trembling in his arms, yet an emotion far stronger than lust granted him the strength to master his need to satisfy his own desires. So, even though Chard's every fiber screamed for release, he fought for self-control, telling himself that he would rather take a vow of celibacy than spoil forever the chance he might have to free Bitsy from the hellish prison of abject self-hatred in which his father's brutal rape had entombed her.

He forced himself to be calm, to go slow, take one step at a time. It was a long while before he felt her tension ease and finally subside, and then his heart soared; for although he could only guess at the degree of courage it took for her to overcome the fear of being touched, he knew that she had won the first battle in a conflict that was destroying her as a normal, healthy woman.

Chard tilted her face to his and kissed her warmly, smiling with pride and appreciation as he slowly withdrew his lips. He longed to cry out his joy to the old man in the moon, who, as songsters said, governed such phenomena, but he was afraid that a spoken word, even such a heartfelt endearment, might shatter the fragile enchantment of the moment.

For a long while, they lay in each other's arms, her forehead against the hollow of his throat, his fingers gently stroking her body.

And Bitsy, being blessed with a normal, healthy sixteen-year-old's physical sensibilities, could not help, finally, responding to Chard's caresses. Without realizing it, she began to undulate her hips to the rhythm of his touch, while her lips eagerly sought his in the first kiss of passion that she had ever bequeathed on a living soul.

Bitsy's kiss opened a floodgate of pent-up emotions that she wasn't even aware existed. Her breasts tingled; her breathing grew irregular; her heart fluttered against her ribs like a caged bird that must stretch its wings or die.

And suddenly, the dress that Chard was awkwardly wadding up around her waist and attempting to draw over her head became a suffocating shroud that hampered her ability even to breathe. She moaned for him to hurry.

Her hands flew to his shirt, nervous, unpracticed, and fumbling, as she drew it over his head and then wondered what she should do with it. He took it from her and cast it into a corner. She watched in breathless anticipation, blushing prettily because of her wanton desire to see him completely naked as he kicked off his leggings and breeches.

As if they moved of their own volition, her fingers touched his well-formed chest, explored the muscles of his rippling belly, and before Chard could stop her, trailed lightly down his abdomen and wound themselves around his most private part. Chard's body convulsed under her touch. And although he tried gallantly to check his impatience, her fondling pushed his self-control beyond any restraining limits he might have possessed.

Bitsy's careful upbringing in the sheltered wilderness of Kentucky had left her naive about the intricacies of the male anatomy. So when she felt Chard's sperm splash across her bare thigh, she quickly put her hand over him in an honest effort to stop the pulsating flow.

Bitsy looked at Chard apologetically. "I'm sorry, Chard," she whispered, confused and embarrassed. "I didn't know it would do that. I thought a man had to be inside a woman before that could happen."

Chard dropped his head back, and his laughter rang gloriously. Bitsy smiled, wondering what he found so amusing.

"Chard?" she whispered, on the verge of tears. "Please don't make fun of my ignorance."

"Bitsy," he chided, taking her into his arms and rocking her, "you are the most precious person I have ever met." And it came as something of a shock to find that it was true; of all the girls he had known, some very intimately, Bitsy was the only one who had managed to touch his heart, to enslave his soul. He had been waiting all his life for her. It was as though he had never experienced another

376

woman, had never felt the excitement of touching a female body, had never known the true meaning of desire . . . or love.

So, with those thoughts racing through his mind, combined with a young man's natural ability to rekindle a romance in a heartbeat, Chard eased Bitsy down into their bed of sweet-smelling evergreen boughs and covered her body with his. Anyone watching the old man in the moon as he cast his soft rays through the smoke hole in the roof of the hut would have sworn that his mouth turned down at the corners. For, out of nowhere, a small dark cloud scurried across his craggy face and hovered there, casting the hut into total darkness and obscuring the beautiful mating of a young man and woman, a mating that had been destined since before they were born.

CHAPTER
· 22 ·

MORGAN PATTERSON SCOWLED at the sky. A dark cloud had crossed the moon, throwing the forest into a pitch-black void that neatly erased the hoofprints of the two horses he had been following. He had made good time since leaving Lorimer's, for a child could have followed the trail left by the two British officers.

Patterson glanced again at the sky. His normal reservoir of patience had run bone-dry now that his family was only hours ahead of him, instead of the days that had previously kept them out of reach.

He took a deep breath and tried to relax. He needed to listen to the night sounds, watch the forest for movement, and pay attention to his surroundings. Even if he was momentarily halted by the darkness, he could not afford to relax his vigil—not now, now that he was so close.

Patterson strained his eyes, trying to penetrate the veil of night that shrouded him. But he could see nothing. He thought about what lay ahead. It would not be easy, slipping up on Simon and George Girty, but it could be done.

If, for some reason, he could not take them unawares, he would simply kill them from afar. Either way, the Girtys were going down first. He didn't bother to consider the British officers, for without the Girtys they would be completely at his disposal. Patterson smiled thinly. Aye, the British were in for a surprise. Being in their own friendly territory, with allies all around them, they no doubt considered themselves safe.

378

He glanced again at the sky and frowned; as long as that cloud insisted on hiding the moon, the British were safe. He hunkered down and waited.

Judith was bent over Susan, delicately blotting her friend's perspiring brow, when the moon winked out. Susan had taken a turn for the worse shortly after Chard and Bitsy's departure.

Intermittent chills and burning fever had set in, and Judith had torn a strip from the bottom of her dress and made trip after trip to the spring in an effort to ease Susan's suffering. But to her dismay, the wet compresses were of little help, and Susan tossed and turned in delirium, forcing upon Judith the strenuous task of physically holding the thrashing woman still until the spasms subsided. Judith was exhausted. She frowned when it became so dark under the tall trees that she could not even see the woman she was trying so desperately to help. She laid her palm against Susan's brow. The skin was like dry parchment with a flame burning deep beneath it. A moment before, it had been wringing wet with sweat.

Judith bent down and pressed her cool cheek to Susan's flushed forehead. "There are so many questions I wanted to ask you," she whispered to the unconscious woman. "So many answers I need to know . . . years and years of answers."

Her eyes misted; she closed them and breathed deeply. "I have envied you for so long. Did you know that, Susan? I lay awake at night and wished that I were you. 'Tis amusing—I in my castle and you in your cabin, and yet I envied you.

"I've wondered what your life was like after the French and Indian War, how many children you had. And I wondered about Morgan . . . Has age changed him, Susan? Is he still the handsome, heroic man I remember? Or was he just an illusion of a silly eighteen-year-old girl?"

Judith hugged Susan close with an intimacy unblemished by jealousy or malice. For even though she was still very much in love with the husband of the woman she

379

nursed, her devotion to Susan Spencer was almost as strong as her adoration for Morgan Patterson.

"Have you been happy, living in Kentucky?" she went on in her soothing voice, allowing years of unsatisfied curiosity to pour from her lips in an uncontrollable flow of conversation that neither expected nor required answers, for she knew in her heart that Susan Patterson was beyond hearing. Judith babbled on, asking question after question, talking of Bitsy, wondering what it was like to raise a daughter in the backwoods, inquiring about the social life at the fortified settlements scattered across the Kentucky frontier, until she realized she was prattling just to hear her own voice.

She also discovered that she had been clinging to Susan like a child who was afraid of the dark, afraid of the invisible predators that seemed to be all around her, closing in, stifling her every breath. She could hear them plainly —reptiles slithering in the leaves, the whisper of hairy and hooved feet as the nocturnal animals prowled the shadows, the pounding of heavy wings as the night birds searched for prey, the rustle of underbrush and the snapping of twigs that could very well be savages creeping through the forest, the screaming of the crickets and tree frogs. All those terrifying noises that under normal circumstances would not have bothered her at all suddenly joined together to create a roaring in Judith's ears that threatened her sanity.

Shaking like a leaf, she hugged Bitsy's long-rifle tightly to her breast and rested her cheek against the barrel. The cool steel had a lethal feel that soothed her strained nerves, and all at once the forest seemed to draw back. The sounds that had terrified her the moment before became no more threatening than the quiet rustle of a breeze, the scurry of a small rodent, the flutter of a songbird roused from its roost—just normal night noises that were not at all frightening.

Judith laughed nervously and tightened her grip on the rifle; she had almost let her imagination run wild.

Settling herself more comfortably against Susan, she wondered whether Chard and Bitsy had found the hut. Chard and Bitsy. The two of them were alone; he fancied
380

himself in love; she had nothing left to lose—a dangerous situation to say the least.

Judith had fought with the problem of Chard and Bitsy for weeks. At first she had been uneasy about their emerging friendship, and then she had begun to worry that they might have an affair. Finally, she had awakened one night drenched in sweat; she had dreamed that Bitsy was pregnant with Chard's child.

"It would be the ruin of you both!" she cried aloud, shattering the silent wilderness with her outburst as she envisioned Chard and Bitsy alone at the hut. "For even if something happened to me, if I died tonight and you never learned the truth, it would be your destruction. My sins will surface in your children, and in your children's children . . . Oh, God! Why didn't I tell them? Why didn't I tell them?"

But she hadn't, and now it was probably too late. She recalled Bitsy's parting words: "No, Mrs. Southhampton, you won't have to worry about Chard ever being interested in someone like me." Judith laughed bitterly at the memory, for she knew her son better than that; she knew that if he truly loved Bitsy, nothing on earth would change his feelings toward her, not hardships, not suffering, certainly not the fact that she had been raped by James Southhampton, for when it came to loyalty, he was just like his father.

Judith buried her face in her hands and wept.

When the moon disappeared, plunging the forest into an inky void, Southhampton quickly turned his eyes to the reassuring light of the fire. He hated total darkness. It represented death and the unknown, and he was afraid of both.

He shuddered, forcing his thoughts to something more pleasant—the escapees. Tomorrow he would overtake them, and the chase would come to an end. He frowned in disappointment. He was enjoying his cat-and-mouse game —especially since the mice had no idea the cat was even on their trail.

Southhampton was looking forward to that part of it:

the shock on their faces when they realized they had been stalked and trapped like wild animals and had actually never been free at all.

He grinned, pleased by his own cunning. He, Major James Southhampton, represented the authority, strength, and superiority of the British Crown. Nay, he corrected himself with pride, I represent the whole British nation. Then he sneered, thinking of Judith, Chard, Susan, and Bitsy who considered themselves independent of British rule, even going so far as to actually sympathize with the stupid, self-sacrificing Americans who fought with Washington. He shook his head, wondering how they could seriously believe they stood any chance of success in their ridiculous quest for independence. Britain would crush the American forces, as Major James Southhampton would smash his enemies.

His mouth formed a sardonic smile. "Sometimes," he mused aloud, spitting contemptuously into the fire, "a little taste of independence makes the ultimate confinement all the more intolerable."

Bitsy lay in quiet wonder, her body pressed warmly against Chard, his arm cradling her head. She studied his face in the pale moonlight that once again filtered through the smoke hole. He was the most beautiful man she had ever seen. She felt his chest rise and fall, brushing her nipples with the slow, easy rhythm of his breathing. He looked so young and vulnerable when he was asleep.

She snuggled closer against him, contentment dragging a long sigh through her slightly parted lips. She felt gloriously alive and fulfilled; nothing in her whole life had prepared her for the tranquillity and the blissful gratification she was experiencing. In short, she was deeply in love.

She wished the night would never end, for the filtered light of the moonbeams cast softening shadows on the harshness of reality that daylight seemed to accent. And sure enough, as the first lessening of darkness, that pale dimness they call false dawn illuminated the hut, Bitsy rolled away from Chard and studied him in the new light. The peace and complacency that had enlightened her soul, that had caused her face to take on a delicate radiance that made her more beautiful than ever, suddenly wavered.

She took her lower lip between her teeth and chewed it nervously. What would Chard think of her when he awakened? Would he still respect her? Would he still love her? Her face grew grave as question after question fought its way to the surface of her shallow self-confidence and cast doubt on the endearments Chard had whispered. Wishing he would awaken, while at the same time terrified of what awareness might bring, she pushed herself away from Chard and watched him as though he were a stranger.

And that's the first thing Chard saw when he opened his eyes: Bitsy, sitting fully clothed with her chin resting on her knees, her eyes big with uncertainty.

"Good morning." He smiled, raising himself to his elbows.

She waited. One reassuring word would have sent her flying into his arms, but in his youth and inexperience, Chard had never been faced with the complexities of a woman's mind after she had given her body and soul to a man for the first time, so he had absolutely no understanding of her seeming aloofness. As insecure in the wonders they had shared as she, he took her silence for accusation. Suddenly embarrassed by his nakedness, he snatched on his trousers.

"Look here, Bitsy," he said, avoiding her eyes by slipping his shirt over his head, "if I took advantage of you last night, I humbly apologize . . ."

It was the worst thing he could have said. Bitsy flinched as though she had been struck, her great, unblinking eyes turning to stare at the wall. "You didn't take advantage of me," she murmured.

Chard glanced angrily at her. She had wanted him as much as he had wanted her. She had made that plain—yet now, this morning, she acted insulted, or hurt.

"Damn," he said softly as he donned his moccasins. "And I thought I was in love with you. All you enjoy doing, Bitsy, is making me feel like a failure—at everything."

He caught up his dueling pistols and shoved them through his belt. "Damn you," he repeated, stepping through the doorway, "why did I ever get involved with you?"

"And why couldn't your love have been real?" she whispered after he was gone. "Why did you go to all that trouble just to bed a piece of used baggage? Why didn't you just rape me, as your father did?"

Chard took long strides to the creek and bathed his face in the cool water. He was fully angry by the time he returned to the hut. Without a word he took the trencher of food Bitsy offered and fell to eating, stuffing his mouth and swallowing before it was half chewed. He watched Bitsy through his lashes, wondering what made her tick. When she looked at him, there was a great sadness in her eyes that had not been there yesterday—not bitterness or depression, as before, just a great sadness. He finished his stew and laid the trencher aside.

"I'll be going for them now," he said, rising.

She nodded.

"We'll be back as soon as we can," he added expectantly.

Again she nodded.

Chard stood at the door for a long moment. He prayed for a sign from Bitsy, some indication that what had passed between them the night before had not been wanton lust; it had to have meant more to her than that.

But there was no sign. Instead, Bitsy turned her back to him and began stirring the contents of the pot. Taking one last look, Chard ducked through the doorway and walked angrily toward the forest.

Bitsy ran to the opening and stared after him. She felt cheap and used—he was Southhampton's son after all.

Judith watched the wilderness come alive. Even before the first rays of sunlight penetrated the layers of overhead branches, the birds were twittering, the insects buzzing, and a woodpecker had begun its hollow rat-a-tat, sounding loud in the distance.

She rose stiffly to her feet and stretched her cramped muscles.

Susan was sleeping peacefully, a welcome relief that Judith had not expected. Catching up the rifle, she walked to the spring and bathed her face and hands.

Absently, she wondered when Chard would return. She had halfheartedly expected him to arrive at daylight. Her eyes traveled across the expanse of wilderness as far as she could see, examining the open lanes between the tree trunks, but nothing moved. She sighed and turned toward the camp. A scream rose in her throat, but she clamped her teeth together so quickly that only a whimper escaped; Southhampton, with Clarke and the Girtys flanking him, was standing not twenty feet away.

"Good morning, my dear," he said mockingly. Then, laughing sarcastically at the shock on her face, he strode arrogantly toward her.

Judith watched him come. She told herself she shouldn't have been surprised, that she should have known he would not give up easily. But she was surprised, then defeated, and then angered.

But Southhampton, never observant, saw only her astonishment, and it filled him with a grand sense of triumph. So his surprise was even greater than hers when Judith snatched Bitsy's long-rifle from the tree where it had been leaning and raised it quickly to her shoulder.

Southhampton froze, his eyes gone wide with fear. He took a step backwards, then another.

The muzzle of Judith's rifle yawned big as a cannon as she sighted on a spot between his eyes.

Southhampton screamed in terror as Judith's finger tightened on the trigger. And as the pan flashed its puff of blue-white smoke that was normally the predecessor to the muzzle blast, he clutched his forehead and crumpled into the ferns. Then, as everyone stared in open-mouthed amazement, wondering what had happened, the damp, slow-burning powder in the flash pan ignited the breech, and the rifle erupted.

"A goddamn hangfire," said George Girty to Simon. "And the son of a bitch swooned. I wish to bloody hell she had killed him, the gutless bastard."

Simon Girty walked to Judith and calmly took the rifle from her shaking hands.

385

"'Tis a shame, Mrs. Southhampton," he said. "I thought for a minute you had him."

"So did I," she returned coolly, staring at her unconscious husband.

Clarke moved to Southhampton and knelt beside him. He cuffed the major's face several times before Southhampton's eyelids fluttered open.

"Where am I shot? Will I live?" came the major's feeble voice.

"You fainted," lisped Clarke through the space where his front teeth should have been.

"But I saw her pull the trigger—saw the smoke . . ."

"A flash in the pan, Major, that's all."

Southhampton's face flushed. He sprang to his feet, his rage so great that the veins on his forehead pulsed and throbbed as though they would surely burst through his delicate skin. Berserk, he flung himself on Judith, beating her face with his fists, then kicking her savagely after she had fallen.

He stood over her, panting.

"You made a fool of me. You made a goddamn fool of me."

Judith raised herself to one elbow and grinned up at him, her small, even teeth stained pink with blood from her split lips. "You have always been a fool, James. Until now, however, no one knew you were also a coward."

His face mottling with rage, Southhampton lashed out with his foot, catching her savagely in her side.

Judith gasped and burst into tears, and Southhampton's lips drew into a pleased smile. He had tried to stave in her ribs, and he gloried in the fact that he had obviously succeeded.

He squared his shoulders and strode to where Susan lay.

"She's unconscious," said Simon Girty, eyeing Southhampton with distaste as the major bent over Susan's lax body.

"Wake her up. I want her to know she's been captured."

Girty dropped to one knee and caught Susan by the shoulders. He shook her gently.

She moaned and tossed her head, but her eyes remained closed.

"Leave her alone," cried Judith, her arms wrapped tightly around her midsection, her face white with pain. She staggered to her feet and, still clutching her sides, stumbled to Susan.

"Let her die in peace," she sobbed angrily. "Have you no common decency at all?"

Girty looked up at Southhampton, awaiting instructions.

"Leave her be . . . for the present, anyway." Southhampton looked around the campsite. "Where are Chard and the girl?"

"Gone," said Judith.

"Don't attempt cleverness with me, Judith. You are not nearly intelligent enough." Southhampton doubled up his fist. "Where are they?"

"Gone," she repeated, flinching as he drew back his arm threateningly.

"Better tell him, ma'am," said Simon Girty. "We'll track 'em down anyhow." She was well aware that Girty was pleading with her to tell Southhampton the truth, to save herself another beating or possibly even death.

Judith's shoulders slumped, and great tears of surrender streamed down her cheeks. She opened her mouth to speak, hating herself for what she was about to do. But she knew she could not stand another beating, and as Girty had said, they would locate Chard and Bitsy anyway.

"Go straight to hell, James." She was as shocked as they by her soft statement.

Girty dropped his eyes, but not before Judith saw the first emotion she had ever witnessed there. For a split instant, admiration had flashed from his dark pupils, and then it was gone, as though a veil had been drawn across them.

Southhampton trembled with suppressed rage. He had been sure Judith would crumble under his threat, admitting to the world, after years of haughty aloofness, that he was indeed her superior.

"I'll kill you," he said flatly, drawing his pistol with slow deliberation and pointing it at her head.

Judith closed her eyes in expectation of the blast that would end her life. She told herself it would be over in an instant; it would happen so quickly that she would not even realize when she stepped from one life into another. Then the irony of the situation hit her, and she opened her eyes and laughed in his face; for she was in exactly the same position he had been in only moments before, and she would be damned if she would react as he had.

Southhampton stared at her over the gun barrel.

"She's insane," he whispered in awe. "Fear of dying has snapped her mind."

Through her nearly hysterical laughter, Judith heard Southhampton's words. And be it nerves or fear or courage, or whatever it is that prompts a human being who is facing death to do the unexpected, she walked slowly toward Southhampton, cursing him with every foul adjective she had ever heard that described a coward.

Southhampton could not believe what was happening. For years he had harbored a secret desire to kill Judith, had dreamed of it, planned it, schemed for it, but in his imagination she had always begged and pleaded for her life, never openly advocated her death. He felt cheated, and the feeling left him enraged. By God, he would kill her just to show her he could.

"Major!" cried Clarke, flinging himself at South-hampton in an attempt to push aside the pistol that was aimed at Judith's head. But in his haste, he stumbled and fell. Pushing himself quickly to his knees, he pointed an accusing finger at Southhampton. "Captain Bird ordered us to return the prisoners alive. Think, man! Our future is at stake, not to mention our necks. If word of this gets out, we will stand court-martial for murder."

Southhampton's eyes wavered as Clarke's words penetrated his fuming brain. His every instinct screamed for him to end her life, yet the thought that he might also die threw him into a quandary.

He stood there, undecided, fighting an internal battle. Was his desire to see her dead strong enough to chance losing his own life?

"They'll hang you, James," said Judith, smiling pretti-ly. "You'll kick and scream and beg for your life just like

388

that man at Fort Cumberland. Remember, James, the man you hired to kill Morgan Patterson? Remember how they had to grab his dangling legs and throw their weight on them in order to break his neck? Remember how his face turned black and his tongue swelled out of his mouth?" Her smile turned to contempt. "Kill me, you cowardly son of a bitch. It would be worth dying just to know that you would hang. Go on, kill me!"

Southhampton paled. He remembered the man, Baylor, remembered him shooting Morgan Patterson. He remembered the crowd at Fort Cumberland when they captured Baylor and raised his struggling body over their heads, waiting for the acting commandant, Lieutenant James Southhampton, to grant permission to hang the man. And he remembered nodding his head, yes, then watching with excitement as they put the noose around Baylor's neck. And as the memory became even more vivid, Southhampton's hand flew to his own throat.

"Very well," he said, turning his back on Judith. "I'll not hang for killing the likes of you. Why should I? They'll hang you in Detroit anyway."

He strode to Susan and pointed his cocked pistol at her head. "But unless you tell me where Chard went, I will gladly hurry Mrs. Patterson's trip to hell."

"She's been in hell ever since you invaded Kentucky," said Judith. "I expect that she would welcome any help you might give her to speed her soul to heaven."

"So be it." Southhampton sighted carefully down the barrel.

"Wait." Judith's shoulders sagged in defeat. She would never have divulged the information to save her own life, but she could not stand idly by and let Southhampton murder Susan, not as long as she had the means to stop it. "Chard and Bitsy went in search of an Indian hut near a cornfield. Chard said that Girty showed it to him when they were hunting."

"I know the place," said Girty, "about eight miles from here as the crow flies."

Southhampton shoved the pistol through his belt. "We're wasting time, Mr. Girty. Bring up the horses. We've a half day's ride ahead of us yet."

Southhampton turned to Clarke. "You take Judith up behind you. I want her where I can watch her."

"What about the other one?" Clarke pointed at Susan. Southhampton didn't answer.

George Girty led Southhampton's horse into the camp and handed him the reins.

"Which way are we going?" inquired the major as Girty gave him a hand up.

"North," returned the renegade. "It's quicker that way."

Clarke fetched his own horse and climbed into the saddle. Then, catching Judith by the wrist, he drew her up behind him.

She clutched Clarke's waist for support, her head reeling from the pain in her side.

"Go as slowly as possible, Lieutenant," she grated through her teeth. "I think my ribs are broken."

"'Tis your own bloody fault," he said over his shoulder. "You tried to kill your husband. I'll have no sympathy for one such as you, madam."

"Then ride on, you bloody bastard," she said, kicking Clarke's horse in the flank, causing it to lunge unexpectedly, nearly unseating its master.

"Lead off, George," said Southhampton dryly as Clarke worked at the bits to try and bring his skittish mount under control. "Or else the lieutenant will be there hours before us." He chuckled at his attempt at humor.

"What about Mrs. Patterson?" inquired Simon Girty, who had moved to Susan's side, and was trying hard to awaken her.

"Kill her." Southhampton spun his horse toward the trail Clarke had taken.

CHAPTER
· 23 ·

MORGAN PATTERSON COCKED his head, turning his ear toward what could have been the sound of a distant shot. He stood poised, listening, but the noise was not repeated. Still, he did not move. He surveyed the forest around him as far as his eyes could see. Nothing moved.

Like a shadow, he crept to the trunk of a gigantic maple and squatted at its roots. He stayed like that for several minutes, watching, listening.

He had covered a lot of ground after the moon came from behind the cloud the night before, and he knew by the fresh droppings of the horses that he was close to his adversaries—maybe an hour behind—so he was cautious . . . very cautious.

He hunkered beneath the tree for thirty minutes, but not a sound broke the eerie silence. Something inside him began to gnaw at his nerves; and a voice in his heart whispered, Go to her now before it is too late . . . before it is too late . . .

Patterson began to sweat. He fought down the almost overwhelming impulse to throw all caution to the wind and bolt headlong toward the distant gunshot that he was not even certain had been anything more than a product of his imagination.

Again the voice rustled: Go now, Morgan Patterson, go now . . .

Patterson's leg muscles twitched, begging for action, and his fingers tightened on the silken smoothness of his gunstock. But he had too long been a woodsman to lay aside hard knowledge and succumb to instinct. Men who grew careless in the wilderness died violent deaths.

A dead tree, not ten feet from where he squatted, cracked and groaned. Then, with an earsplitting crash, it measured its length in the decayed leaves and ferns of the age-old forest. It quivered and moaned, settling into its final resting place, its long, gnarled, lifeless branches extending imploringly toward Patterson.

I have been here from the beginning of time, it seemed to say, and, like you, Patterson, I have stood tall and strong among my brothers. I had no wish to die, and I fought against it with all my strength, but my time is here. You heard me scream in fear as my body gave way and sped me toward the earth that has nourished me since birth; you heard me moan as my old limbs snapped and splintered on impact, but everything dies, Morgan Patterson, nothing lives forever. You cannot cheat destiny. Had you chosen to hide under me, instead of my brother, the maple, you would be dead now. If it is your time to die, Patterson, hiding and waiting will not save you.

Patterson heard no more, for he was off and running. Fleet as a panther, he jumped on the huge trunk of the tree just fallen. He touched it lightly with his moccasined foot for the added leverage he needed to speed him on as he lunged through the mayapple and ferns that littered the forest floor in the direction of that far-off shot.

Chard moved steadily over the same trail he and Bitsy had used the previous day. He was well aware that it was a roundabout way, and he hated the extra time it would take to return to Judith and Susan, but he was afraid to strike out in search of a shorter route that might, in the end, prove more time-consuming than the known trail he was following.

Even though he was certain he had heard a rifle crack some fifteen minutes previous, and even though he was equally sure it had come from the direction of Judith and Susan's camp, Chard did not succumb to the impulse to dash ahead and see what had taken place. He took a deep breath and grew more wary, then crept stealthily on, surveying the forest closely before venturing through that section and spying out the next. Bitsy had taught him that: keep your wits and vigilance about you, no matter what.

Because Chard hesitated, Southhampton's party, following Girty's short route, passed undetected through the forest not over a half-mile away, a half-mile of trees, bushes, and leaves that obliterated any chance of his having heard them, any chance he might have had to beat them to the cabin where Bitsy waited alone.

Simon Girty slipped his tomahawk from his belt and tested its weight by gently slapping the side of the razor-sharp blade against his palm.

He did not like what he was about to do. But, in a way, Southhampton was right; Susan was close to death. It would be an act of mercy.

Still, he was reluctant. He had taken food at Susan's table in Kentucky; he had shared the warmth of her fireside in the winter; he had hunted with her husband—but that had been years ago, when she was little older than Bitsy.

He stared at the thin shell of the woman he had once known.

"It will be a favor to you," he told the unconscious woman. "You have suffered enough."

He tested the razor edge of the hatchet with his thumb. One quick blow, and it would be over.

"End it, Simon," came her shallow voice. "For old times' sake, do me that service."

The unexpected response startled Girty. He had been unaware that she had wakened; in truth, he would have wagered that she was beyond ever regaining consciousness. He studied her through unblinking eyes, undecided about his next move.

Susan saw his indecision, and it angered her. "You have killed Kentuckians without conscience, Simon Girty. One more will make little difference in God's eyes."

"God can be damned for all I care," said Girty. "I'll not kill the only woman who ever showed me kindness." With that, he jammed his tomahawk through his belt and trotted into the forest.

"But you would be returning that kindness," she whispered to his retreating back. "A kindness . . ."

She watched him a moment longer before her strength ebbed and her cheek dropped gently against the pungent, decaying leaves that pillowed her head.

She could smell the scent of the forest around her, hear the wilderness sounds, the whispering leaves, the insects, the birds, the bubbling of the nearby spring, and she smiled. She loved the wilderness almost as much as she loved Morgan Patterson, and she could think of no better place to die than where she lay. It would be perfect if only Morgan were there to hold her hand.

That was how Morgan Patterson found her, her cheek pillowed softly against the leaves, a gentle smile on her bloodless lips. He gathered her to him and buried his face in her heavy silver-streaked hair.

Somewhere deep down inside her being, Susan felt his arms tighten around her, felt his lips against her hair, felt his heart against hers. And she fought hard to retrace her steps from that peaceful wilderness of the unknown where she had begun her final trek, fought hard to find her way back to Morgan Patterson.

Her eyelids fluttered open, and she smiled serenely into his haggard face.

I knew you would come, she whispered, her fingertips touching his lips, his cheeks, his eyes, pushing his hair off his forehead as she had done a thousand times in the past when he held her.

I tried to tell myself that I did not want you to find me, she continued falteringly, *but that wasn't true. I searched for you every day and prayed for you every night.* She looked longingly into his face. *I have done things, Morgan, worse things than you could ever imagine, and the only way I could keep my sanity . . . was to close my eyes and pretend I was doing those things with you.*

I tried to kill myself rather than submit, Morgan. But God intervened . . . so he must have meant it to be. Please don't hate me, my darling . . . please. Her large obsidian eyes sparkled with tears. *I've never deserved a husband as fine as you, Morgan . . . and I always wondered why the Lord saw fit to pair us together. But he did, and I've been grateful . . . and happy. My life with you was perfect, Mor-*

gan. I would have changed nothing . . . except that I never gave you a son. I have regretted that, my love, but only that.

The tears spilled down her cheeks and dripped on his arm where he cradled her head. *I love you, Morgan. I never stopped loving you . . . and I never will, not even in heaven.*

Seeing her tears, Patterson trembled with emotion. Using the tail of his hunting frock, he gently dabbed at the corners of her eyes.

I've got so much to say, she went on, smiling through the pain in her chest, trying hard not to let him see her suffering. *So much you need to know . . . and so little time.*

She talked earnestly and passionately as she gazed into his eyes, warning him of Southhampton and Clarke and the Girty brothers, telling him of Judith and how beautiful she still was; and finally about Chard—his son—and Bitsy. *Chard loves Bitsy, Morgan,* she said, smiling into his face. *It is as though God meant all this to happen just so they would discover each other . . . Oh, Morgan, I'm so happy for them . . . and for you.* Susan's eyes misted. *Judith had the son I could never give you . . . and he is a fine man, my love. You will like him.*

Susan felt herself drifting and fought hard to stay the moment. *Would you . . . kiss me, Morgan?* she asked. *Just once? It would mean so much to know that I am forgiven.* She gazed hopefully into her husband's face, but he remained motionless. *Please, Morgan.* Her eyes were imploring, begging. Still he hesitated, and a great agony sent tears streaming down her cheeks.

And Morgan Patterson, seeing her anguish, gently touched his lips to hers in an expression of so much love and tenderness that Susan thought her heart would surely break.

I never stopped loving you, Morgan, she whispered when they drew apart. *Remember that always.*

Patterson smiled down at her, his face aglow with more love than she had ever seen there, and she was happier than she had ever been in her life. She sighed with contentment. It was the last sound she ever made. "I love you, Susan," he whispered softly, as the joyous light in her eyes dimmed forever.

He gently closed the blackest, most beautiful eyes that had ever gazed on the earth, the warmest eyes that had ever smiled into a man's face, the most heartbroken eyes that had ever cried when a man suffered. Patterson dropped his cheek to her breast, comforted by the act of laying his head against her body as he had done so many times over the years. But unlike those times, there was no flurry of heartbeats, no rise and fall of her breasts, no warmth.

He drew back and gazed into a serene face so thin and drawn he hardly recognized it, and he wondered what she had been trying so desperately to tell him. He bent and kissed her cold lips again, lips that had moved in earnest speech yet had uttered not one single syllable.

Patterson sighed heavily. There was one thing he had understood, she had said it with her eyes: I love you, Morgan Patterson. I always have. I always will. And he had kissed her for it.

Patterson gathered Susan into his arms and rose solemnly to his feet. She weighed nothing; her body was no more than skin and bones, and Patterson could not help comparing her to the girl he had carried over the threshold of their cabin so many years before. She had been young and beautiful then, her body supple and seductive, and she had maintained that youthful figure throughout all the years of their marriage.

A great ache filled his heart. And when he looked at the shadow of the woman he remembered, he saw her as she once had been: lovely and alluring. She was his wife, a part of his very heart and soul.

He laid her gently beneath a great dogwood, knowing that in the spring when the tree blossomed, she would rest easy beneath its spreading branches. "Christ's trees," she had called them, showing him the mark of the nails on their petals. "These trees are blessed by the Lord."

Aye, he thought as he gazed down at her. This tree is truly blessed . . . truly blessed.

He withdrew his tomahawk and began hacking out the soil. The grave would not be as deep as he would have liked, but it would keep the predators away until he could return and bury her properly.

Patterson had finished the grave and gathered Susan into his arms for the final time when Chard appeared on the knoll above him. He didn't look at Chard, but he knew he was there. And he knew the man was sighting down the barrel of his gun at him.

Drawing Susan's body protectively against his chest, Patterson steeled his shoulders and stepped toward the newly turned earth.

"Don't make another move, mister." Chard's soft threat was emphasized by the sound of his pistol snapping into full cock.

Patterson hesitated, then cut his eyes to Chard and held the young man unwaveringly, waiting.

"What have you done with my mother?" demanded Chard.

The question caught Patterson by surprise, and for a flickering instant it showed on his face.

"Don't act as though you know nothing about her. She was here! I left her with Mrs. Patterson." Chard's voice was edged with fear.

"The British have her," returned Patterson uninterestedly. Then, ignoring the menace of Chard's pistols, he turned again toward the dogwood tree.

Chard's knees sagged. He had failed them all: Bitsy, Susan, and finally, his mother. He braced himself for the nausea that he fully expected to rise up in his throat, but it didn't come. Instead, a quiet steadiness spread throughout him, calming even the shaking of his hands under the weight of the pistols. He saw the woodsman anew, registering for the first time the man's torn and dirty buckskins, his long, matted hair and stubbled beard, his bronzed, weathered features and thin frame, and the way he unconsciously shielded Susan's body with his own. Chard felt foolish for not having understood immediately what was transpiring.

"I humbly apologize, Mr. Patterson," he said with sincere regret. "I would consider it an honor if you would permit me the privilege of assisting you with Mrs. Patterson's burial. She was a fine lady, sir."

Without answering, Patterson carried Susan to the shallow pit and laid her lovingly beneath the tree. He crossed her arms over her chest and carefully brushed aside a lock of hair that had fallen across her brow. Slipping his ragged hunting frock over his head, he used the pearl-

397

handled dagger to split the worn buckskin down the front. He smoothed out the wrinkles and carefully laid the frock over her.

Almost as an afterthought, he removed the small porcelain locket from around his neck and placed it on the buckskin just above her heart. "I don't want her to enter heaven with nothing," he said, raising his face to the skies, "so please accept this token of my appreciation, Lord. She was the finest woman that ever drew breath." And that was the closest that Morgan Patterson ever came to verbally thanking the Lord for anything.

He was aware that Chard had moved up beside him, but he didn't care. Without looking up, he began to push the newly turned earth back into the pit. Chard bent to help Patterson fill the grave. He was totally unprepared for the elbow that caught him in the face, propelling him backward with such force that he crashed heavily into the trunk of the dogwood before sliding in stunned surprise to the ground.

Patterson stood over him on widespread legs, his face unreadable, his eyes deadly. "If you so much as touch that gravesite, I'll kill you."

Chard blinked at the man above him. Then a quiet anger surged through him. "Mr. Patterson," he said, his jaw forming a hard line, "I am taking into consideration that you are grieving over the loss of a loved one, but don't ever strike me again, sir, for any reason."

Patterson eyed the young man harshly. "I meant what I said."

Angry and grief-stricken and disappointed, Chard watched Patterson fill in the grave. He had expected Morgan Patterson to be bigger than life. Susan and Bitsy had said he was. Yet the man who was spreading leaves and brush over the freshly turned earth was no different from the Girty brothers or a hundred other frontiersmen he had encountered.

Chard pushed himself to his feet and stalked angrily to the woodsman. "I'll have that pearl-handled knife," he demanded, extending his palm. "It belongs to me."

"I took it off a dead Wyandot," said Patterson, ignoring Chard. "It belongs to me."

Chard's eyes narrowed threateningly. "Mr. Patterson," he said, "that knife has special meaning for me. I never expected to see it again, but now that I have, I want it back."

He considered telling Patterson the truth, that he had given the knife to the Indian in exchange for Bitsy's life. But something new to him, something powerful and real, rose up within him and sealed his lips. And for the first time in his life, Chard experienced a sensation that was not an artificial product of his birthright: an earned pride.

"This knife," said Patterson, touching the handle, "belongs to Judith Cornwallace."

"And she gave it to me," interrupted Chard coolly.

Patterson studied the young man. Aye, he decided, he has the look of Judith about him: fine skin, straight nose, haughty attitude.

Silently he passed the knife to Chard. Then, without further ado, he snatched up his rifle and trotted down the path the horses had taken.

CHAPTER
· *24* ·

SOUTHHAMPTON DIDN'T CATCH Bitsy unawares. Morgan Patterson had taught her early in life to keep a constant vigil. And even though the Girtys had halted the horses long before they were in sight of the hut, Bitsy had heard them.

She glanced quickly around the interior of the cabin for a weapon, but there was neither staff nor stone, save the ones the pot was resting on, and they were too hot to touch.

She ran to the door and peered into the forest. Her heart stopped. Then her knees turned to water, and she was forced to lean against the post for support. Abdominal pains shot through her, bending her at the waist, her hands clutching her stomach. For a moment she was sure she was going to be sick: Major James Southhampton was standing at the edge of the trees watching the hut.

"Chard!" he called, his voice high pitched and commanding. "You and Bitsy surrender yourselves immediately."

Bitsy quickly pushed herself away from the door and backed farther into the darkness. Obviously Chard had not been captured. And as long as he was free, there remained a chance for escape. Again she looked for a weapon. Again her efforts ended in frustration.

"Chard!" came Southhampton's angry voice. "We have your mother out here."

Bitsy slipped to the edge of the door and peered out. She could see Clarke and the Girtys and Judith, but Susan was not visible. A great foreboding engulfed her, and she tried to push it aside; her mother could be resting in the shade—it could be as simple as that. Her eyes moved involuntarily to the shadows at the base of the trees, taking in every detail. Susan was not there.

"Where's my mama?" she cried, unable to fight down the panic rising in her chest.

"She died," called Southhampton.

"No, she didn't, Bitsy," shouted Judith. "They left her back at the camp, but she's alive."

Southhampton spun on his heel and stared at Judith. "You're wrong, my dear. I left Simon Girty behind. He tomahawked her."

"You son of a bitch," breathed Judith, her fingers drawing into talons. "You monstrous son of a bitch," she screamed, throwing herself on Southhampton furiously. She raked his face with her fingernails and clawed at his throat, searching for the jugular vein. She scratched at his eyes in an attempt to blind him, and had it not been for the Girtys and Clarke she would have succeeded.

They fell on Judith from all sides and wrestled her to the ground, pinioning her securely under their knees until Clarke knocked her senseless with the butt of his pistol.

Southhampton cupped his bloody face in his hands. "Kill her!" he screamed through his sticky fingers. "For Christ's sake, kill her before she kills one of us."

The Girtys climbed to their feet and brushed leaves and twigs from their leggings.

"Kill her your own self," said Simon Girty. "If you got the guts. Me and George has done our job. We tracked 'em down. From here on they belong to you."

"I'll have you hanged for this," shouted Southhampton. "I'll see you swing from the gallows for disobeying orders."

"Major Southhampton," replied George Girty, laying the barrel of his rifle across his forearm so that it was pointing at Southhampton's chest, "me and Simon has had a bellyful of you."

"All right, all right," said Southhampton hastily. "I spoke out of turn. I apologize." He pulled a lace kerchief from his sleeve and dabbed delicately at his lacerated face. "But your job is not complete until you deliver Clarke and myself and our prisoners safely to the ship where we are to

401

rendezvous with Captain Bird. Those are Captain Bird's orders, Girty, and you'd better obey them."

Simon Girty's mouth drew into a thin line. "Be careful how you talk to us, Major. We won't be pushed no more, you understand?"

"Aye," said Southhampton affably. "I was a bit distraught, that's all. Let's forget about it, shall we?"

Simon Girty grunted noncommittally and stepped to the edge of the brush, surveying the hut. He wished he could assure Bitsy that he had not killed Susan. But he did not want Southhampton to know that he had disobeyed his orders.

Southhampton watched the man through slitted eyes. Once before, he had vowed to see the Girty brothers suffer for their insolence and insubordination. This time he would see to it that they hanged. Aye, he decided, the minute you get me safely aboard the *Hope*, I'll demand that Captain Graves swing the pair of you from the yardarm.

Smiling smugly to himself, he turned to Clarke. "Fire a round through the wall of that hut, Lieutenant. That'll bloody well shake Chard up."

Clarke raised Bitsy's rifle and sent a ball splintering through the building. Bitsy heard the slap of the lead as it tore through the slab and lodged in the rear wall. She stared vacantly at the thin shaft of sunlight left by the projectile. But it didn't mean a thing—her mother was dead.

Another boom sounded, and a ball clipped a piece of fabric from Bitsy's sleeve. Then two more shots followed in the path of the previous one, the bullets buzzing through the hut like angry bees.

Bitsy moved as though in a trance. Slowly she crossed the room and with a cry of anguish destroyed the evergreen bed she had so neatly laid for Susan. Next she grabbed up the pot of vegetable stew and smashed the container against the wall, flinging its contents over the room. Then she fell to her knees and laid her forehead against the floor and cried her heart out.

"Fire again," said Southhampton to the three marksmen. He anxiously watched the door of the hut for signs of

Chard. Perhaps they had already killed him? Nay, he decided, I wouldn't be so lucky. Chard will make a fight of it.

The thought made Southhampton cringe. He was afraid of Chard, and had been since Chard was a small lad. The boy had thought for himself even then, had never been easy to sway when he felt he was right. And that independence had grated on Southhampton from the beginning. It still did. And Southhampton was well aware that Chard would have killed him at Lorimer's had the soldiers not intervened.

Southhampton sweated, studying the hut nervously. Given the opportunity Chard might try to kill him again. The major had not considered that before, and he found the possibility unnerving. At that moment, Southhampton truly regretted having raped Bitsy—but his remorse was, as usual, for all the wrong reasons.

"Shoot into that building again!" he cried. "I want them dead, both of them."

Clarke frowned at Southhampton. The major's fanatical attitude was beginning to unnerve him. Still, he was a professional soldier who knew better than to disobey an order. He nodded at the Girtys, and together they sent another volley through the hut.

Morgan Patterson was running with the wind at his heels. And Chard, who was in his prime, was hard pressed to keep up.

Patterson paused for breath only when he topped a rise that gave view to a long range of forest. At those brief moments, he would study the terrain as carefully as his far-searching eyes could reach. Then he would be off again, leaving Chard to wonder where the man found the strength to continue such a pace.

Finally Patterson drew to a halt beside a small spring and dropped to his haunches. He scooped water into his cupped palm and drank, his eyes endlessly searching the forest ahead. Chard puffed up beside him and fell to his knees. He dropped his face into the pool and drank deeply. Patterson watched without interest. If the young man

403

continued to be so careless, he would not last a month in the wilderness before his hair decorated some Indian's willow hoop.

When Chard finished and sat up, Patterson spoke. It was abrupt and to the point: "Is my daughter alive and well?"

Chard looked at the man, then quickly gazed into the forest. "She's not the girl you remember, Mr. Patterson."

Patterson's eyes flashed in anger. "Answer my question, mister."

Chard took a deep breath. "Mr. Patterson, she's alive and healthy, but to be truthful, sir, the campaign wasn't at all what Captain Bird intended. It got completely out of hand almost before it got started. Bird lost control of his Indians . . . and also several of his senior officers." Chard hesitated, searching for the correct words. "Many of the Kentuckians suffered greatly because of it. Mrs. Patterson and Bitsy were among them."

"How bad were they mistreated?" Patterson's voice was hard as stone.

Chard met his gaze. "Bad, Mr. Patterson. Bitsy and Mrs. Patterson were treated worse than most."

"Why?" Patterson's eyes bored into Chard like a lance.

Chard shifted uneasily, but his gaze held steady. "I've asked myself that question for five hundred miles, and I still don't know the answer."

Patterson nodded, appreciating the young man's honesty. He did not press Chard for details. It was done. He could not change what had happened. But he vowed to himself that it would never happen again—so long as he lived.

Chard exhaled with relief. He did not want to be the one to reveal his father's criminal mistreatment of the prisoners, particularly of Susan and Bitsy, to anyone— much less to Morgan Patterson. For even though he despised everything Southhampton represented, the man was still his father, and Judith had raised Chard from infancy to respect and honor the family name and, no matter the circumstances, never to join an outsider against a family member. So although Chard had not hesitated to beat his father to a pulp and, given the opportunity, would gladly have done it again, he was honor bound to stand with him against his antagonists.

"What of your mother?" said Patterson after a long interval.

Chard's mouth drew into a grim line. "If they return her to Fort Detroit, she'll hang."

Patterson had been surveying the forest, but his eyes swung to Chard. "For what?"

"Because her sympathies lie with the Americans," said Chard simply. "She threw her birthright away trying to stop the invasion of Kentucky. She almost succeeded."

"How could a lone woman do that?" said Patterson skeptically.

"She helped the American, Major Chapline, escape so he could warn the settlements. She poisoned Captain Bird, not enough to kill him, just enough to lay him up for a couple of weeks. She started a rumor that you and General Clark were waiting for us at the falls of the Ohio, so the Indians refused to go there. And she tried to spike Bird's cannon, because she knew that, without them, he could never take even one small Kentucky station. She was captured spiking the cannon."

Patterson was incredulous. He remembered Judith from the French and Indian War. And the woman just described was not the spoiled, arrogant, self-centered young brat he had spent months with in the wilderness. He ran his hand through his month-old beard. People changed in twenty-five years. . . . Then he thought of Southhampton. Some people don't.

"Where were you trying to escape to?" he asked abruptly.

"I took the women and ran. I thought I could do what you did years ago. Well, I couldn't. We finally decided to slip back to Lorimer's and steal a canoe." Chard hesitated, watching Patterson with sincere regret. "We were hoping to get your wife to the falls of the Ohio . . . to a doctor."

Patterson nodded slowly. "I'm obliged for what you've done."

Chard dropped his head. "I'm afraid it wasn't enough. I'm sorry, Mr. Patterson."

405

Patterson rose to his feet, his face sad and lonely as he gazed down the trail. "You did your best. A man can't ask for more than that."

Bitsy, her cheek still pressed against the earthen floor, raised her eyes to the bullet holes in the wall; the place was beginning to resemble a sieve. Most of the holes, however, were above head height, so she guessed that the gunmen —probably the Girtys—were firing high on purpose.

The knowledge did little to comfort her, for in truth, she almost wished they would drop the muzzles of their rifles a foot or so.

What did she have to live for? Her mother was dead, murdered by a man she had never harmed, a man she had forgotten ever existed, until he came to Kentucky in search of her. No, she corrected herself, he came in search of Morgan Patterson, but he found his wife instead.

Tears turned the earth to mud under Bitsy's cheek. "Oh, Mama," she whispered, "I love you so much, so very much . . . and I need you, Mama. I need you to talk to, now more than ever."

At intervals, bullets whipped through the building, but Bitsy didn't hear them. "Mama," she continued, crying softly, "I gave myself to Chard last night; I gave him my heart and soul, everything that is me. I held back nothing. I love him, Mama, and it seemed so right, so beautiful." Bitsy could feel the damp, cool soil of the floor beneath her skin, and it was soothing, as her mother's cool cheek had been when Bitsy was a child. "But it wasn't beautiful, Mama," she sobbed. "It was dirty and vulgar. He lied to me, and I accepted his lies as truth, because I cared so much . . . because I needed his love and understanding so desperately. He made me feel so special, Mama." Bitsy's voice broke. "He knew exactly what to say and do to a girl who had lost her pride and honor, and he preyed upon that, Mama. It was naught but a cruel game he played so he could have his way with me.

"Are all men that way, Mama? Are they all cold and indifferent once they acquire the most precious thing a girl can give? I have let you and Papa down, Mama. You always trusted me so much. Oh, Mama," the girl cried inconsolably, "I'm so sorry . . . but I love him."

Southhampton paced back and forth. Nothing was going as he had planned. "Chard, damn you!" he cried. "Come out of there this minute, or we're coming in after you—and when we do, you and Bitsy will regret the day you were born."

He watched the hut expectantly. Nothing moved.

"Do you think we got him?" he asked the three riflemen.

"Why don't you walk in there and find out?" suggested Simon Girty.

Southhampton sneered arrogantly at the man, then turned to Clarke. "Lieutenant," he commanded, "walk up there and see if they're dead."

Clarke dropped the butt of Bitsy's rifle to the ground and leaned on the barrel. "Major," he lisped, "your son killed a bear with a dueling pistol. With all due respect to your rank, I don't think I'll be taking such a chance with my life, sir."

"Cowards!" shouted Southhampton. "The three of you are nothing but cowards!"

George Girty's hand fell to the handle of his tomahawk, but Simon's eyes held his brother's, stopping the action as surely as if he had caught George by the arm.

"Major," said Clarke, "we could slip up behind the hut and listen for movement."

Southhampton smiled narrowly. "Do it, Lieutenant."

Clarke frowned. "The Girtys are trained skulkers, Major. They can slip up on an Indian. I think, sir, that they should be the ones—"

"It's not our job," interrupted Simon Girty with a finality that left no room for argument.

"Damn your job!" cried Southhampton. "I'm sick of hearing what is and is not your job. You're being paid to return these prisoners to Detroit, and by God, you will do whatever it takes to get your job done."

Simon Girty's hand flashed out and wound itself in the lace at the throat of Southhampton's shirt. "Major," he whispered, "I'm about a half a step from killing you here and now. If you blink at me wrong, you're a dead man."

George Girty grinned ruefully. He was well aware that his brother had had enough of Clarke and Southhampton, and he knew beyond a doubt that Simon would do exactly as he had said. Southhampton's gaze grew wide. Gnats buzzed into the corners of his eyes and lighted there, driving the major nearly mad as they crawled across the pupils.

Judith, who had heard the exchange, quickly pushed herself to her elbows. "Blink, damn you!" she cried. "If you ever blinked in your life, do it now!"

George Girty laughed contemptuously as Southhampton's bulging eyes swung to Judith, then quickly back to Girty. Not once did he blink. Simon Girty pushed Southhampton from him, then ambled over to a huge maple and leaned languidly against the trunk.

Southhampton clawed at his eyes, blinking rapidly to free himself of the gnats. But the tears that streamed down his face were not from the irritation caused by the insects. He was so humiliated by his own cowardice that he wept with frustration and rage. And he blamed it all on Chard for putting him in the position of having to rely on scum like the Girtys.

"Clarke," he hissed with a rush of pent-up breath. "Get your arse up to that hut and see what's happening, and that's an order."

If Clarke had ever wished that he had never joined the army, that was the moment. Although he had ordered hundreds of men to cross the open plain of battle where death was imminent, he had never been called on to perform that particular task himself. Officers were not supposed to expose themselves to unnecessary danger —everyone understood that. It was a part of the unwritten code of military conduct.

He stared hard at Southhampton, but the years of service in His Majesty's Royal Army, of never questioning an order from a higher-ranking officer, finally prevailed. He spun on his heel and raced through the edge of the woods until he could approach the hut from the rear.

Sweat stained the armpits of his scarlet tunic as he stepped into the open and walked slowly toward the small building. Each step he took was agony, and every twig that snapped under his highly polished riding boots sounded loud as a musket shot to his sensitive ears.

It was said that cowards died many times. Clarke, had he told the truth, would have admitted that his heart stopped a thousand times as he crossed the open ground between the forest and the hut. He slipped up beside the cabin and pressed his ear against the bark covering. For several seconds he heard nothing, and he wondered if indeed the occupants had been killed.

He moved to a bullet hole and tried to peer inside, but he could see nothing. He pressed his ear against the hole. Soft sobs came from within. He listened a moment longer. Then, determining that Chard was either wounded or dead, he drew his pistol and walked bravely through the door.

Bitsy, her eyes red and swollen, looked up in surprise as Clarke's form filled the opening. She rose slowly to her feet and backed to the far corner of the room.

"Murderer," she breathed. "Cowardly murderers, all of you."

"Where's the ensign?" demanded Clarke, glancing at the empty cabin.

"He abandoned me," she lied. "He ran off and left me."

"Tell me the truth, or I'll beat the bloody hell out of you." he cried, bracing himself on widespread legs.

Clarke charged across the room and drew back his fist. Bitsy cringed against the wall, hiding her face protectively behind her raised arm. Then, faster than Clarke could have imagined, Bitsy spun on her heel, throwing her weight into her movement. Her bare, callused foot caught the unsuspecting lieutenant in the groin. Clarke's face burst into a mask of hideous pain as he dropped the pistol and sank to his knees, clutching his testicles with both hands.

Seizing the opportunity, Bitsy snatched up Clarke's pistol and sprinted out the door—straight into the arms of Simon Girty. Girty wrenched the gun from her and cuffed her savagely across the face. She careened off the outside wall of the hut, then sprawled headlong into the weeds. She lay there, panting for breath, a thousand shooting stars bursting in her head, and wondered why nothing she did ever turned out right.

409

Girty caught her by the arm and hauled her to her feet. Bitsy's knees buckled, but Girty's strong hand held her erect. He waited for her head to clear.

Clarke—bent from the waist, his face the color of wood ash—staggered through the door. "Kicked my balls up into my belly," he gasped painfully. "Probably ruined me."

Girty ignored the man. He had no use for whiners. "You should have kept runnin' while you had the chance," he told Bitsy.

Bitsy blinked, her head still spinning. "I couldn't leave my mama," she said, dazed.

"Your mother was a dead woman even before she left Lorimer's. 'Twas folly to think you could save her." Then, moving his mouth close to her ear, he whispered, "She's alive, lass. I didn't kill her like Southhampton said."

Bitsy almost collapsed with relief. Her eyes thanked Simon Girty, even as she said aloud for Clarke's benefit, "I'd rather die knowing that I tried to save her than live knowing I thought only of saving myself, Mr. Girty."

"You may get your druthers, missy," whispered Girty, pushing Bitsy before him toward the waiting major.

Bitsy walked with a light step. Susan was alive, and Chard was free. It would work out. She knew it would.

"What about Chard?" asked Southhampton as the trio drew near. "Did we kill him?"

"He isn't here," said Clarke, still humped over. "The girl was alone."

Southhampton glanced nervously around him as though afraid Chard might come charging out of the nearby brush.

Seeing the major's alarmed glance, Simon Girty's lips drew into a disgusted line. "If he was still here, you would be dead by now, Major."

"You're wrong, Girty," sneered Southhampton. "He hasn't got the guts. When we took Ruddle's Fort, he never fired a shot. He even tried to stop the Indians from coming inside. He's a coward, a bloody goddamn coward."

Southhampton walked purposefully to Bitsy. "Where is he?" When she did not respond, he backhanded her hard

410

across the mouth. "I won't ask you again, Bitsy. Where is he?"

Bitsy eyed him murderously. Then she smiled. "You enjoy beating women, don't you? It's the only way you can feel like a man. Well, let me tell you something! Chard doesn't have to hurt people to be a man."

Southhampton hit her again, dropping her to her knees. "Silence!" he cried, glaring down at her. "Chard will never be the man I am, never!"

He placed his boot against Bitsy's shoulder and sent her sprawling in the leaves.

"On second thought," he said as the disheveled girl attempted to push herself to her elbows, "we don't need to know where Chard is. He's just stupid enough to come back for you."

Southhampton walked to George Girty. "Take both those sluts into the woods and keep them company." He turned to Simon. "Tie the horses outside the hut. We'll wait for Chard inside."

"You think he'll be crazy enough to just walk right in there?" asked Simon Girty cynically. "Your son's smarter than that, Major."

"Chard has always had a noble streak in him, Girty. He won't think twice about his own safety if he thinks the women are in danger. And you, George," he said, turning to the other brother, who had not moved, "I told you to get those women out of here."

George Girty caught Judith's arm and snatched her to her knees.

"On your feet!" he ordered. "And you, too," he said to Bitsy, who still lay where Southhampton had left her.

Pushing the women before him, he headed toward a small rise two hundred yards distant.

Standing on the hill, he squinted at the hut where the horses were tethered. The field of vision was fine; the range was a long shot even for a rifle—but it could be done. "Get down on your bellies, and keep your mouths shut," he said, turning to the women. "If you even breathe loud, it'll be the last breath you ever take."

Judith and Bitsy did as they were told, dropping to their stomachs and peering over the rim of the hill, their eyes fastened to the small building where capture, and possibly death, awaited Chard.

Morgan Patterson slowed his pace and became more watchful. For the past five minutes he had been smelling the faint odor of wood smoke. He trotted to a fallen log and hunkered down behind it, waiting for Chard to catch up.

"Describe the clearing and the hut to me," he said as the young man joined him.

Chard squatted, and wasted no time raking away the leaves and twigs. With the point of the pearl-handled dagger, he cut an X in the dirt. "The hut," he said in explanation. He made several slashes, telling Patterson they represented the garden. Then he made a wavering line that was the creek. "The whole clearing, from creek to tree line, isn't over three, four acres at the most."

Patterson nodded; he was familiar with such plots.

He studied Chard's diagram one last time, burning the hut, the cornfield, and the stream indelibly in his mind.

Glancing up at Chard, he said, "They'll be expecting you to come down this trail, so likely as not they'll be watching it."

"Aye," said Chard, wondering what Patterson was getting at.

"Don't disappoint them."

"And you?"

Patterson gauged Chard for a long moment, making the young man shift uncomfortably under his penetrating stare. He considered telling Chard the simple truth: that while the British were engaged with Chard, Patterson intended to kill every last one of them, including the Girtys. But, true to form, he said nothing at all. Instead, he pushed himself erect and thumbed the frizzen of his lock forward, checked the priming, and snapped the pan shut.

His hand, from sheer habit, dropped to his knife and loosened it in its sheath, then repeated the gesture with the hatchet thrust through his belt.

Patterson's movements were the unconscious preparations of one thoroughly practiced in the art of battle—not the drums-and-fife "honorable" warfare that Chard had learned but the blood-and-guts kind where the only honor was the the simple determination to be the one left standing when the smoke cleared.

In spite of himself, Chard shivered. All at once he knew that he was facing the most dangerous man he had ever met. All the legends he had ever heard about Morgan Patterson and Boone and Kenton suddenly became real. They were men who protected their own—or avenged them. They were men who expected no quarter, nor did they give any.

Chard wondered if his father had really understood the nature of the man he would someday have to face when he forced Morgan Patterson's wife into prostitution and raped his only daughter . . . Bitsy . . . Bitsy. Her name rang in Chard's mind; Bitsy, who, in the midst of a world filled with pain, torture, and ugliness, had emerged so splendidly pure and beautiful, that like the chimes of a bell, she made a man stop and listen, glad he had passed her way. Then Chard's mouth hardened. The very thought of the precious night she had given—then taken away—left him with the overwhelming desire to snatch her up and shake her until her teeth rattled, for no matter how clear her tone, it always seemed to end on a sour note. Sour note? He had said something similar to her the night they had gone into the forest to talk. Chard groaned inside. It wasn't Bitsy who was striking discord. It never had been.

"You sure you want to do this?" asked Patterson, bothered by Chard's fluctuating expressions and wondering if he was having second thoughts about facing his countrymen. "There's two British officers down there."

"Mr. Patterson," said Chard, following Patterson's example and checking the priming of his pistols, "if I live through whatever it is that we encounter down there, I am going to marry your daughter, and if I don't live through it, you tell her to settle for nothing less than that cabin with a garden nearby."

Patterson's head snapped up. "Marry Bitsy? What in hell are you talking about? She's just a child!"

413

"She's no child, Mr. Patterson. Bitsy grew up while you were gone. And so have I."

"She didn't grow up that much," said Patterson harshly.

She's a woman, Mr. Patterson, thought Chard as he started down the path toward the cabin. My woman. But all he said was, "You tell her, Mr. Patterson, word for word what I said."

CHAPTER

· 25 ·

SIMON GIRTY, HIS long-gun resting casually in the crook of his arm, relaxed against the inside back wall of the hut. His expressionless eyes revealed none of the contempt he harbored for the two men who nervously watched the doorway. Both Southhampton and Clarke had their pistols drawn and cocked. Had Girty not known better, he would have sworn they were expecting a Shawnee war party instead of one lone young Englishman who, Southhampton said, had never even engaged in battle.

They'll kill him the minute he steps through that door, Girty mused. Regardless of Bird's orders, they'll blow him to hell. He idly wondered what lie they would fabricate to cover the murder, but he didn't dwell on it. It was not his affair.

Actually, all Girty wanted was to get it over and done with, to deliver Southhampton to Captain Graves and, with any luck, never see the man again. He asked nothing more than to be allowed to collect his pay and disappear into the wilderness. He had decided to winter with his adopted tribe, the Delaware . . . and Catharine Malott. Furthermore, working with Bird, Clarke, and Southhampton had convinced him that any future fighting he might do in this revolution would be done beside his red brothers. He felt sure that George, too, had had his fill of the British Army.

Simon's eyes narrowed as he heard footsteps outside the hut, and a moment later Chard's voice penetrated the stillness: "Hello, the hut? This is Richard Morgan Southhampton. I am surrendering peaceably."

Southhampton and Clarke exchanged glances. Chard's surrender was an unexpected twist that complicated matters.

Clarke was the first to speak. "Come in with your hands raised."

"No," said Chard. "I will surrender out here."

Clarke eyed Southhampton.

"We've got to get him in here," whispered the major. "I want no witnesses."

"But, sir," said Clarke, "he's surrendering peaceably."

Southhampton ignored Clarke. "We make no deals," he called through the doorway. "You either surrender under our terms or not at all. It's your choice. You have ten seconds, Chard."

Chard studied the forest. No sign of Patterson. "And if I don't?" he said, playing for time.

"We have your mother and the girl in here," lied Southhampton. "We will shoot Bitsy in five seconds . . . four . . . three . . ."

"I'm coming in," said Chard, moving quickly to the door.

Judith clutched Bitsy's hand, her face a mask of fear as she watched Chard approach the hut.

George Girty's knife blade pricked her throat. "One word from either of you and you're dead."

Judith buried her face in the crook of her arm. She would gladly have taken her chances with Girty, but she was not even sure her voice would be strong enough to carry to the hut—and if it did, would Chard heed her warning? She thought not. So she hid her eyes, afraid to watch the drama in the clearing, deciding that if Chard was harmed, she would kill Southhampton before the day was done—or die trying.

Bitsy, no less terrified, saw Chard hesitate outside the hut.

He's not going in, she thought with relief as he gazed toward the forest while speaking to someone in the hut. She strained her ears, but the distance was too great to make out what was being said.

Don't go in, Chard, she prayed, her eyes glued to him, hoping he would feel her presence and look in her direction. Please don't—go—in.

Her prayer locked in her throat as Chard ducked his head and stepped through the opening.

Tears blurred Bitsy's vision. She wiped her eyes with the back of her hand. She, too, realized something: if they killed Chard, they might as well tomahawk her because she would not want to live without him.

On entering the hut, Chard was careful to keep his hands raised and in plain sight, aware that he was at the mercy of the men who had tracked him down, and also aware that they were probably looking down their gunsights at him.

Surprise raised his brows when his eyes adjusted to the dim light.

Southhampton chuckled with appreciation. "Did you really believe I would allow you to escape, Chard?"

Chard shrugged, trying hard not to show his apprehension at not finding his mother and Bitsy in the hut.

"I didn't think we mattered that much to you, Father, but I would be less than honest if I said I had not guessed who it was that followed us."

"You don't matter at all, Chard," said Southhampton, raising his pistol and pointing it at Chard's chest. "It's your mother we need. Without her, it will be difficult to explain why an expedition the size of ours was such a disaster in Kentucky."

"You're going to try to lay it all in her lap," said Chard, fighting hard to control his anger. "It won't work, Father. I'll testify at her trial, you know. And when I finish revealing the neat little pact you made with the Girtys to massacre the Kentuckians—and the very fact that you yourself opened the gates and allowed the Indians to enter the fort after it had honorably surrendered . . ." He eyed his father defiantly. "All my mother was attempting to do when she committed her so-called treason was to prevent a bloodbath that will someday prove to be a stigma that will shame the decent people of Britain forever."

"While you're so busy defending your precious mother," cried Southhampton, "there is something I've wanted to tell you since the day you were born."

The major smiled callously at Chard, purposely delaying his narrative. He had waited twenty-five years for that precise moment, twenty-five years of harboring such an intense hatred for the young man that the release was almost sexual in its gratification. "Your mother and I were betrothed," he screamed, his eyes wild and glazed with passion. "We had been engaged for more than a year! A year! And I never *once* tried to seduce her. I was a gentleman. Even though I wanted her, I always honored her wish to remain a virgin until we were wed."

Southhampton eyed Chard speculatively, before going on, "And while I was being so careful to protect your mother's reputation and family name, she ran off into the wilderness with Morgan Patterson. Oh, she tried to lie her way out of it when she returned, said Patterson rescued her after Braddock's defeat at the Battle of the Wilderness. She swore he saved her life."

"What's the point of this, Father?"

"The point is," said Southhampton through his teeth, "that your mother, who was so careful not to let me touch her, wasted no time spreading her legs for that base-born scum, Morgan Patterson. Your mother came back to me pregnant—pregnant! You are a bastard, Chard! Nothing but an illegitimate bastard. And the fact that I married your mother changes that not one whit."

Chard's eyes narrowed as he slowly absorbed Southhampton's revelation. Then, bowing from the waist, he said with a slow, one-sided grin that looked very much like Morgan Patterson's, "Thank you, Major Southhampton. You just brought my whole life into perspective."

Chard didn't hear the blast that lifted him off his feet and slammed him against the wall beside the door. He didn't feel the ball that tore through his chest and erupted out his back, leaving an exit hole twice the size of the entry wound.

He clawed at the rough-hewn slabs with numb fingers but could not muster the strength to hold himself erect. And knowing a moment of abject pity for his mother, for Bitsy, for himself, and for Morgan Patterson, he slid slowly

418

down the wall, a streak of his own life's blood trailing him to the floor.

Moments before Southhampton shot Chard, Morgan Patterson arrived at the clearing. He crouched in the heavy shadows, his eyes narrowing as he studied the cornfield, the forest, and the horses tied before the hut. Chard had to be inside, which complicated matters. Patterson had hoped to catch the group in the open and use the Indian's philosophy of scattering his enemies and then picking them off one at a time. Scowling, he settled down on his haunches. Sooner or later the British would be forced to evacuate the premises —and Patterson would be waiting.

Then a new thought hit him: he wasn't sure Chard could be trusted.

Moments later, however, that uncertainty was answered for all time. The cabin reverberated with the muffled boom of a discharged weapon, and before the echoes had reached the range of timbered hills surrounding the clearing, Patterson was up and running.

The shot snapped Judith's head up as though it were on a string. "Oh, God, no!" she moaned, her lips drawn tight across her teeth in an involuntary grimace.

Despite Girty's threat to kill either of them should they move, Bitsy clambered to her knees. She didn't care about Girty, she didn't care about herself, only about Chard. He was dying . . . or dead. Then she stiffened: a buckskin-clad woodsman had raced out of the forest and was dashing toward the cabin.

She grasped Judith's hand and wrung it tightly. "It's my papa," she breathed. Then, her excitement growing, "It's my papa!"

She was so engrossed in watching her father that she didn't see George Girty drop to one knee, steady the barrel of his rifle against a tree limb, and sight on the man bolting toward the hut. But Judith did. And as Girty reached for the trigger, she lashed out with her foot, catching his thigh and sending him sprawling into the grass. He was up immediately, trying to resight on Patterson. But it was too late. The woodsman had reached the hut and, without slowing his pace, had flung himself through the door.

Girty's eyes narrowed to angry slits. "I'm goin' to kill you," he said in a voice that held so much malice that Judith shuddered. She watched with mounting horror as he slipped his long-bladed scalping knife from its sheath. And her mind screamed out at Girty that he couldn't kill her—not now, with Morgan Patterson so close . . . so very close.

Patterson sprang through the door like an enraged panther —and twice as deadly.

Even before his eyes could adjust to the dimness, he swung the barrel of his rifle toward a movement in the shadows and touched the trigger. The ball took Clarke in his right eye, blowing away the back of his skull, splattering his brains over Simon Girty who still lounged against the back wall. It happened so fast that both Girty and Southhampton were stupefied. In the time it took for them to collect their wits, Patterson had flung his rifle aside and drawn his razor-sharp Damascus hunter's knife.

His eyes darted around the room, taking in Girty against the rear wall, Southhampton standing horrified beside the quivering body of Clarke, and Chard, sitting against the wall by the door, his chin on his blood-soaked chest.

"Kill him," cried Southhampton, cringing away from Clarke's lifeless form. "Kill him, Girty!"

Dropping into a crouch, his knife held low, cutting edge up, Patterson's eyes pierced Girty's.

"Hello, Morgan," said Simon Girty softly. For a long moment neither man moved; then Girty leaned his rifle against the wall and crossed his arms. "Fancy seein' you here." He smiled without mirth.

"You in this or out of it, Simon?" demanded Patterson in his easy drawl, watching Southhampton out of the corner of his eye.

"If you'll let me, I'll walk out of here, Morgan. I got me a woman with the Delaware. Reckon I'll be headed that direction. This, my friend," he finished casually, "is a family affair. I'm out of it."

420

"Don't leave me, Girty," cried Southhampton, flinging aside the pistol he had discharged into Chard and dropping to his knees as though to plead for his life.

Girty ignored the major, his eyes holding the woodsman's. Patterson flicked his head toward the door. "I'll see you in the tall timber, Simon."

Girty nodded his understanding. He and Morgan Patterson were finally true enemies. He regretted that, for he had always admired Patterson, had even considered him a friend of sorts. . . .

The renegade caught up his rifle and stepped carefully over Clarke's body. Then, without a word, he ducked through the door and into the sunlight. He raised his rifle over his head and, with a sweeping motion, pointed toward the forest beyond the creek.

The sound of a shot from Patterson's rifle had stopped George Girty cold in his attempt to kill Judith. He was as puzzled as the women when Simon stepped from the hut and made his signal. But he and Simon had been together too long for him to question his brother's judgment. So, without a word or a glance at Bitsy or Judith, he sheathed his knife and dropped off the hill, running easily toward the distant wilderness.

The two women climbed slowly to their feet and stood unmoving, staring at the small hut below.

"I'm going down there," said Bitsy, gathering her skirts and starting down the hillside.

Judith caught the girl's arm. "No, Bitsy. We will be better off here."

Bitsy attempted to shake free of Judith, but the older woman was stronger than she appeared. "Let me go," she demanded, pushing Judith to arm's length. "The only two men I love in this whole world are down there."

"The only two men *I've* ever loved in this whole world are down there," returned Judith, gripping Bitsy's shoulders tightly.

"And you're going to listen to me," she commanded, shaking the girl with a strength born of desperation, snapping Bitsy's head back and forth like a rag doll's, "because there's something I should have told you long ago . . . about Chard."

When Morgan Patterson stepped aside to allow Simon Girty access to the door, Southhampton made his move. In one sweep of his hand, he snatched up the cocked pistol that Clarke had dropped and pointed it at Patterson's heart. He pushed himself unsteadily to his feet, giddy that he, Major James Southhampton, had at last reached the pinnacle of his existence: he held in his hand the instrument that would snuff out the life of the one human being he hated more than anything else on earth. And he held in his heart an even more lethal weapon—knowledge that would completely destroy Patterson's soul.

"I've waited a long time, Patterson, but this is worth every moment I've suffered because of you," laughed Southhampton victoriously. "I've never had a wife, thanks to you," he went on. "Oh, I've been married to Judith all these years, but she was never a wife. So I traded her for your wife, Patterson, your beautiful, holier-than-thou Susan . . . , and I laid with her so many times I bloody well got sick of her. Then I gave her to my command. Think about it. . . . All those men and your wife. And she pleasured them in every way imaginable, ways you wouldn't believe. But it was your daughter that I enjoyed the most. I took her virginity, just like you took Judith's. I held Bitsy down, and I raped her. And I did it in front of your wife, Patterson."

Southhampton's smile faltered. For twenty-five years he had looked forward to getting even with Patterson, had dreamed of it, had painted a mental portrait of Patterson's reaction. But Southhampton was sadly disappointed. For Patterson's stony countenance did not reveal the emptiness that spread through his entire being, the ache that filled his chest, and the lacerating pain of the sure knowledge that his wife and daughter had suffered cruelty far greater than anything he had imagined. Nor did his face reveal the murderous rage that was building in his heart—a fury so great that his own life held little significance or meaning.

"Did you hear me, Patterson?" shouted Southhampton, furious with disappointment. He felt cheated and swindled. His revelation should have crushed Patterson and reduced him to a sniveling ruin. Had it not been that way in his dreams? Had that not been his own reaction when Judith bluntly informed him that she had carried Patterson's child? Aye, he, James Southhampton, had been destroyed—so why wasn't Patterson?

As Southhampton watched the woodsman advance quietly toward him, he wondered what had gone wrong, why all his conquests were without triumph or victory. His eyes gleamed into narrow slits, and his finger tightened on the trigger; he would finish it. He would have this long-awaited victory, and he would not be cheated. This was the one triumph that he would cherish until his dying day.

"You can't be in love with my son!" cried Judith. "He's your half brother, Bitsy. Morgan Patterson is Chard's father."

Bitsy's mouth fell open. All she could do was gape at Judith.

Tears formed in Judith's eyes. "That's why I tried to keep you apart. I even sent you back to your people so you wouldn't be near him . . . and I forbade Chard from searching you out."

"Damn you!" shouted Bitsy, pushing Judith from her with such force that the woman stumbled and fell. Bitsy stood over her like a warrior, fierce, commanding.

"Why didn't you tell me weeks ago that Chard was Morgan's son? Or better yet, why didn't you tell Chard years ago? Do you have any idea how much suffering your silence has caused? Do you even care? I doubt it. You are so wrapped up in yourself that you would destroy Chard, rather than have your secret exposed. You are the most selfish, cowardly person I have ever met, Mrs. Southhampton."

Bitsy was so angry that she began to cry. Raking the back of her hand across her eyes, she continued, "Chard and I wondered what all this mystery was about. We nearly drove ourselves crazy trying to figure out what was wrong with *us.*"

Judith stared up at the girl, awed by the intensity of her outbreak.

Bitsy caught her breath then continued. "I can understand how a woman might find herself with child out of wedlock, Mrs. Southhampton, yes, I can understand that very well, but for the life of me, I can't understand how a mother could allow her son to pay the price for that misfortune. You are despicable, madam. And I'll tell you something else. If Chard is dead down there in that hut . . . and the good Lord should bless me with his child, you can rest assured that baby will grow up knowing who its father was!"

Judith's eyes widened with horror. "Chard made love to you last night?"

"Yes, and now that I know he is Morgan Patterson's son, I pray to God he made me pregnant!"

"You don't mean that, Bitsy. It would be incest!"

"I mean every word of it," cried Bitsy. "I would do anything in my power to see to it that Morgan Patterson's blood does not die when they lay him to rest. I would have slept with Chard weeks ago if I had known who he was, for I would stop at nothing to ensure that the Patterson lineage lives on in me, that I might honor Morgan Patterson by producing future generations of men like him."

Bitsy's accusing eyes searched Judith's face.

"Why couldn't you have trusted Chard's common sense and good judgment enough to tell him who his father was. . . ."

"I couldn't tell him that I became pregnant out of wedlock," sighed Judith. "What would he have thought of me?" Her voice pleaded for understanding. "I needed his respect, Bitsy."

"Respect!" countered the girl angrily. "You had more than that, Mrs. Southhampton, you had his love. And nothing you, or Southhampton, or anybody in the whole world said could have changed that . . . but you didn't believe in him enough to give him the benefit of the doubt!"

"That's not true, Bitsy," said Judith, dropping her head. "I wanted to tell him yesterday, before you and he went in search of the cabin. But how do you explain to a child that the girl he has fallen in love with is . . . Oh, Bitsy, how could I have ever made Chard understand how very much I loved Morgan Patterson?"

"Chard is no child, Mrs. Southhampton," came Bitsy's

infuriated reply. "You should have told him the truth. Because if you had, you would have learned from your son whom I told several nights ago." Bitsy was crying openly, anger and hurt making her words slow and stilted. "If you had confided in Chard," she repeated, "or me, my mother, or any of the Kentuckians, you would have learned that Morgan Patterson is not my father. It is no secret, my real parents were killed by Indians in the Yadkin River Valley in North Carolina. Everyone knows it. It's an old story that happens nearly every day on the frontier. Why, half the folks in Kentucky have taken orphans to raise . . ."

"Oh, Bitsy," said Judith. "I never—"

"Look at me, Mrs. Southhampton. I don't resemble Morgan or Susan at all. Did you not wonder at my green eyes and auburn hair? All you had to do was ask. Unlike you, I would have set this monstrous misunderstanding straight. The truth is, madam"—Bitsy eyed Judith bitterly—"I was cut from my mother's belly after they killed her. I was born to no living woman, Mrs. Southhampton. Indians are experts at cutting an unborn child from a woman's womb. Did you know that? They can do it with such expertise that the child doesn't die immediately, so the savages can claim one more life . . . one more scalp. But Morgan Patterson killed the Indian who birthed me before the man had a chance to bash my brains out.

"Morgan cut the cord and tied it himself. He wrapped me in his hunting shirt and put me in his haversack. He kept me alive, God knows how, all the way to Williamsburg, Virginia. He gave me to my mama . . . to Susan Patterson. That's how I got my name, Bitsy. When Morgan took me from the haversack, Mama said, 'Why, Morgan, she's just a little bit of a thing.' They called me Bitsy from then on."

"Do you have any idea who you really are?" breathed Judith, climbing to her feet, fascinated by the girl's story.

"I know exactly who I am, Mrs. Southhampton," returned the girl unfalteringly. "My mama told me many times that when my papa rode out of Kentucky after choosing our homesite, God turned him toward the Yadkin Valley, sent him out of his way to find me. Mama said that God had it all planned, that He sent me to her through the body of another woman. Susan believed that, and so do I.

425

Yes, madam, I know who I am: I am Morgan and Susan Patterson's daughter. I always was . . . I always will be."

Bitsy's head snapped toward the hut, her throat constricting. Another blast had shaken the small building.

Morgan Patterson peered through the dense gun smoke that all but hid Southhampton in its enveloping haze. Flagging his hand in an effort to clear a breathing space, Patterson made his way to where the major lay in a crumpled heap against the back wall of the cabin.

Patterson knelt and looked into the man's eyes. They were already beginning to glaze in death, but surprise was still visible in the pale irises.

Patterson frowned, perplexed and disoriented. He still didn't quite understand what had happened. From the magnitude of the blast, he had thought Southhampton's gun had exploded. But the unfired weapon was still clutched tightly in the major's stiffening fingers.

Patterson's frown deepened, his eyes drawn to the major's chest; Southhampton's crimson tunic was pierced by two tattered holes, so close together that the palm of a man's hand would cover them. And they were both less than an inch below the major's heart.

"I had them both, Patterson," Southhampton whispered, blood trickling from his nostrils and mouth. "Everything that was yours was finally mine . . . your wife . . . our daughter . . . I even killed your . . ." He coughed. It was a rattling, hollow sound.

Patterson caught Southhampton by his lapels and snatched him close. "Where is my daughter? Quick, man, before you die! Where is Bitsy?"

"Dead by now . . . and Judith too. They're all dead . . . all of them, Patterson. Every human being who loved you." Southhampton gazed long at Patterson as if he were imprinting the woodsman's image in his mind. Then he laughed weakly. It was the last sound the man ever made. He died with a sardonic smile on his arrogant face. His final conquest was triumphant. Patterson released Southhampton, and the lifeless body sighed back against the wall.

Then it penetrated the woodsman's numb brain: the two bullets had been fired from within the hut. Chard.

426

Patterson spun on his heel. Chard, a dueling pistol hanging limp in each hand, blinked up at him.

"I thought you would never move enough so I could get a shot, Mr. Patterson," he said with great effort. "These pistols were so heavy . . . so very heavy . . . I was afraid I couldn't hold them up much longer."

Patterson knelt and took the weapons from Chard's flaccid fingers. "You did fine," he said gently. "Just fine."

Chard smiled feebly. "I finally did something right, Mr. Patterson . . ." Then his eyes closed, and his head slowly dropped to his chest. Patterson caught Chard by the shoulders and shook him viciously. "Where is Bitsy? Damn you, boy, do you know where my daughter is?"

When Chard failed to respond, Patterson's white face blushed crimson with guilt. He owed the young man his life, yet he had been prepared to shake the answer out of him, though he was beyond answering. Patterson climbed to his feet and ran his hand wearily through his hair.

He gazed at the bodies sprawled haphazardly around the room, and the stench of blood and death filled his nostrils.

"Dead by now," Southhampton had said. Patterson studied the major's face, the open sightless eyes, the insolent smile.

"She's not dead!" He flung the words at the lifeless officer, as though by shouting he could make them true.

Judith and Bitsy had already left the hilltop when Patterson, Chard hanging limply in his arms, stepped out the cabin door.

Patterson watched them come, their dresses riding high above their knees, their bare legs flashing in the sunlight as they fled down the incline, and across the open ground before the hut. Patterson studied Bitsy openly as she ran toward him. Chard had been right, Bitsy had changed. The person coming to meet him was not the gangling little girl he remembered from two years ago. She was a woman full grown—one any father would have been proud to call daughter.

Judith stopped several yards out, but Bitsy sped on,

and her embrace when she flung her arms around Patterson's neck nearly staggered him. "I knew you would come!" she cried.

"Easy, lass," he laughed, as she smothered his face with kisses. "You'll make me drop the lad for sure."

Bitsy pushed herself away from Patterson. Then, heedless of the spectacle she made, she caught Chard's pale face between her hands, and kissed his bloodless lips long and passionately.

"You are wasting your kisses, girl," said Patterson. "He's shot clear through and can't feel a thing."

"Yes, he can, Papa," disputed Bitsy, laughing and crying at the same time. "I just know he can," and she bent and kissed Chard again.

Judith felt her knees go weak. She stared into Morgan Patterson's eyes, and her heart raced back through the years to a night in the wilderness when a great golden moon hung so low that, had she tried, she was sure she could have reached up and touched it, a night when she had been lost and alone in the endless wilderness, certain that she would never see friends or family again. But Morgan Patterson had tracked her through the forest and rescued her. And later that same night, she had whispered over and over, "I love you, damn you . . . I love you," as she gave him the most beautiful gifts she possessed—her virginity . . . and her heart.

And as she stood there before the hut and studied his lined and haggard face, she knew that, although life had moved on, time had stood absolutely still; the only difference was that he was carrying their son, the fruit of those gifts, in his arms as he slowly walked toward her.

Patterson's mind had also receded to twenty-five years earlier, but it was not the memory of a great golden moon that filled his thoughts; it was the delicate silver scar that ran from Judith's hairline to her eyebrow.

His gaze fell to the young man in his arms, taking in his white, pinched face and blood-covered chest, and Patterson vividly recalled how Judith had been disfigured. He remembered, too, the terrible aftereffect—her insanity. So with mixed feelings and bated breath, he raised his eyes to Judith's face as she gazed long at Chard's bloody form.

Patterson had almost panicked by the time Judith

finally raised her eyes to his, for he was sure he would see again that eighteen-year-old girl plunged into madness. But he was wrong: Judith's eyes were clear, soft . . . and thankful.

Patterson sighed with relief. "I give you your son, Judith," he said in his slow drawl, holding Chard out to her as though the boy were an offering—which indeed he was.

Judith's eyes misted, but they didn't waver as she slipped her arms under Chard and grasped Morgan's hands. "And I give you . . . your son, Morgan," she whispered softly.

EPILOGUE

Two weeks dragged by before Chard had recovered enough to make even the short trip required to bury Susan properly.

It wasn't until they had laid Susan in her final resting place that Bitsy finally acknowledged her death, and the sight of her grief was pitiful to behold. She clung to Chard and wept her heart out for the woman who had given so much of her life to a girl who was not even her own flesh and blood.

Morgan Patterson, his face and his thoughts unreadable, had never felt so alone in his life.

Judith moved to Bitsy and softly stroked the girl's long, tangled hair. "Take Bitsy back to the cabin, Chard. Morgan and I will finish hiding the grave."

Leaning heavily on a hickory staff, Chard urged Bitsy toward the tethered horses, but she broke away and flung herself into Patterson's arms. He held her to him, his and Susan's daughter, and the lump in his throat almost stopped his breath.

"We will come back someday, Papa," she whispered between sobs, "and we will uncover her headstone for all the world to see."

Patterson dropped his eyes to the partially covered marker he had so painstakingly engraved. The stone would have to remain hidden until the Indian threat was over for all time. His arms closed tightly around Bitsy—it was a promise.

Years later, when the nation was at rest, people would

430

wonder about the epitaph on the lonely marker in the middle of the quiet forest:

SUSAN PATTERSON
Born Sept. 26, 1737
Died 1780
She was born a lady.
She never changed.

It was four trail-worn people who paddled their canoe across the wide Ohio River toward Louisville, Kentucky, on October 10, 1780.

Nearly four months had elapsed since the fall of Ruddle's and Martin's forts, four long months when every day seemed like a year and every night was filled with memories that would plague the survivors for the rest of their lives.

Their bodies bore the scars of their trek beyond the Ohio: Morgan Patterson carried a blue, puckered bullet wound in his shoulder that would eventually render the arm nearly useless with rheumatism; Judith Southhampton was forever ashamed to show her bare back, crisscrossed with thin, narrow scars left by the cat-o'-nine-tails; Chard's neck would always be ringed with an angry red line etched by the leather thong of the Wyandot leash; and Bitsy would have only limited use of a gnarled, drawn hand that her grandchildren would laugh at and call her "claw." But those were obvious scars for all the world to see—the invisible ones were the most damaging.

Morgan Patterson reported immediately to General Clark, only to find his friend, the hero of the Illinois country, desolate and bitter.

Although Clark and his thousand Kentuckians had burned and looted many Indian villages, including Piqua-town and Chillicothe, two major Indian strongholds, Clark was disappointed and resentful. His dream of taking Detroit and freeing Kentucky once and for all from the threat of Indian massacre was gone forever. The sad truth was that General George Rogers Clark had peaked in his military career.

Bitsy and Chard were wed on October 15, 1780, at Louisville. Both Morgan and Judith were pleased by the union, and Morgan felt sure, somehow, that Susan smiled her approval, too. Shortly after the wedding, the four left Louisville and made their way to Williamsburg, Virginia, where Chard and Judith, along with Bitsy and Morgan, were welcomed with gracious hospitality into the home of Vernon and Rebecca Rothchild, mother and stepfather of Susan Spencer Patterson.

Patterson didn't tarry. He made his apologies to his mother- and father-in-law; said farewell to Chard, Bitsy, and Judith; and rode north to offer his services to General George Washington. Judith watched him go, knowing he was grieving over Susan's death far more than anyone but she realized.

He will be back, she told herself, as his horse trotted around a bend in the road and was hidden by the dreary, leafless branches of the winter forest. "You may never want me, Morgan," she whispered, "but if you ever do, I will be waiting . . . I love you."

On the banks of the Hudson in New York, General George Washington commissioned Morgan Patterson a colonel in the Continental Army of the United States of America. He ordered Patterson to join the Marquis de Lafayette at his headquarters in Richmond, Virginia.

Patterson was with Lafayette and Mad Anthony Wayne when the Americans engaged Judith's cousin, British General Lord Charles Cornwallis, in a bloody battle just outside Jamestown, Virginia, July 6, 1781. And he was with Lafayette and Washington on September 28, 1781, when the Continental Army marched on Yorktown, Virginia, to begin the battle that broke Britain's back.

And on October 19, 1781, he stood beside Henry Knox, Anthony Wayne, Baron von Steuben, Benjamin Lincoln, Moses Hazen, John Laurens, Stephen Mazlan, David Bushnell, Tench Tilghman, Peter Muhlenberg, and scores of other fine officers and enlisted men, heroes each and every one, and watched with pride as Washington, on his fine white charger, oversaw the British surrender at Yorktown.

Patterson returned with Washington to Newburgh, New York, in March 1782. Chard joined him there in June of the same year and was immediately commissioned a major under Patterson's command. Chard was mustered out of the service shortly after April 19, 1783, when it was announced to the world that a "cessation of hostilities" had been called between the United States of America and the King of Great Britain. He had not seen a military engagement of any kind, but somehow his former ambition to prove himself in battle no longer seemed important.

On December 23, 1783, Morgan Patterson shook the hand of his lifelong friend, George Washington, for the last time. They sat their horses and looked into each other's eyes. No words were spoken. None were necessary. Washington turned his horse toward Mt. Vernon, and Patterson headed toward Williamsburg. They were free citizens of what would become the greatest nation on earth.

Morgan Patterson and Judith Ann Cornwallace Southhampton were married on New Year's Day 1784 in a quiet ceremony at the home of Rebecca and Vernon Rothchild.

Judith finally got an answer to the question she had once asked Susan: she found out exactly what it was like to live in a frontier cabin instead of an elegant castle. For she and Morgan, along with Chard and Bitsy, returned to Kentucky and built new homes on the Licking River. And she never regretted it for one moment.

Bitsy's lifelong dream of a cabin of her own, a garden, and a husband who loved, honored, and respected her came true, even the detail of standing beside her man and defending what they had built together, for Kentucky remained "the dark and bloody ground" for years to come. But that was all right, too. The Pattersons had come home to stay.

ABOUT THE PATTERSONS

INDEED, THE PATTERSONS had come to Kentucky to stay, and Bitsy's prayer, "I would do anything in my power to see to it that Morgan Patterson's blood does not die with him when they lay him to rest," was overwhelmingly fulfilled. The Pattersons and their descendants have gone on to help make Kentucky and America the great state and country they are today.

Kentucky and South Carolina proudly boast governors of Patterson heritage. And when Kentucky became a tame and civilized country, Patterson descendants went farther west to homestead Texas during its wild and dangerous days just after the Civil War, when more timid folk feared to venture beyond their front gate. Pattersons have served their country heroically in every war since the French and Indian War of the mid-1700s.

In later years, it is interesting to note, the Patterson descendants intermarried with the Boones and the Clarks. It is only fitting, to my way of thinking, that the blood of three such fine frontiersmen should finally mingle. Also, to my knowledge there have been six generations of Morgan Pattersons, the latest born to Duane and Roseann Patterson on February 12, 1984. He was christened Zachary Morgan Patterson.

When Morgan Patterson died, they took his body to the cemetery on a sled pulled by six white horses. He is buried on a hill overlooking the small town of Olaton, Kentucky, in Ohio County.

About the knife that was passed down through the generations?

When my uncle by marriage, Walter Hacker Patterson, was a boy, he accidentally dropped the knife in the well at the old Patterson homeplace. The knife stayed underwater for sixteen years, until Hacker and my grandfather, Van Owen House, cleaned out the well and recovered the knife, which was passed on to Hacker's grandson, Zachary Morgan Patterson, in 1984. Surprisingly, the knife is still in excellent condition.

D.K.W.

FROM THE AUTHOR

HISTORY HAS RECORDED events that are far more interesting than any fiction I might dream up. In this novel, I have made use of those events, weaving them into a story that may sound like something straight from the imagination.

But the story you have just read is true. Through the use of letters, diaries, ledgers, and eyewitness accounts as told to Lyman Draper, who recorded them in the *Draper Manuscripts,* I have tried to re-create the story before, during, and after the fall of Ruddle's and Martin's Stations. I used authorial license to change the names of a few of the people who actually suffered the terrible ordeals and used my characters' names instead. I sincerely pray that I have portrayed those frontier folk, through my characters, as strong, courageous, heroic, and human as they actually were.

By the same token, if I characterized the British as less than honorable in this engagement, the history of Bird's invasion speaks for itself.

1. Major Chapline did indeed escape from the British and Indians and warn the Kentucky settlements of Bird's intended assault, and his warning did go unheeded.
2. Captain Bird did, for some unexplained reason, take over two weeks to transport his army and supplies across the portage from Auglaize River to the Great Miami. It should not have taken over two or three days at the most.
3. Captain Bird's original intention to attack Clark's

Fort at the falls of the Ohio (Louisville) changed abruptly when his Indian allies believed the untrue rumor that Clark had returned from the Illinois country—thus losing Bird the opportunity to capture Kentucky and bring it under British rule.

4. The capitulation and massacre at Ruddle's and Martin's Stations were almost exactly as I described them; they were so atrocious there was little need to embellish them.

5. Captain Bird suffered one soldier killed (McCarty) and one Indian wounded in the attack on Ruddle's.

6. An Indian did manage to crawl under the puncheon floor of Mrs. McFall's cabin. Boiling liquid was poured through the cracks, routing him in a hurry.

7. George Rogers Clark's return from the Illinois country (Fort Jefferson) was as I described, even to the events at Harrodsburg.

8. An English spy named Clarke did steal a horse and ride to the Ohio to warn Bird that Clark was at Louisville raising an army.

9. Two Kentucky women, Mrs. Easton and Mrs. Christian Spears, did drown while crossing the Licking River.

10. Captain Bird did lose a cannon while crossing a makeshift bridge that spanned the south fork of the Licking River. History has it that for fifty years afterwards it was the ambition of the neighborhood boys to dive into the river and "touch the cannon."

11. A young woman in her late teens did run the gauntlet. She was so fleet of foot that the Indians were forced to chase her for half a mile before she was "knocked down by an Indian club."

12. As Bitsy stated, Simon Kenton did run the gauntlet on nine different occasions. He suffered a fractured skull, a broken arm, and a broken collarbone.

13. During the long march to Lorimer's Store, there was no meat, save that which George Girty provided. The male captives subsisted on one cup of moldy flour a day, the women and children a half-cup per day. George Girty was irate. He was quoted as having cursed Captain Bird for dividing the deer meat he

brought in between himself and his officers. Girty said to Bird, "You are meaner than any Indian, having plenty of rations and carrying your captives back to starve without them."

14. A young British officer did take pity on the Kentuckians, allowing the elderly to ride his horse, until he was ordered to "cease such actions."

15. A man was forced to run the gauntlet, which he did successfully. The Indians then decided to burn him at the stake, but a hard rain set in, thus saving his life. He was traded to an Indian for twenty buckskins, then sold to a trader (Lorimer?) for five pounds.

16. It was said of Ravencraft, who was burned at the stake, "If this is a man, then a man is a strange-looking thing." Ravencraft returned to Kentucky and, years later, died of old age in Harrison County.

17. British Colonel Banastre "Bloody Ban" Tarleton, who terrorized the southern frontier in 1780, made the statement that he had "killed more men and ravished more women than any man in America." Quite a statement for a British officer and gentleman!

18. Captain Bird was court-martialed at Detroit for his conduct in the Kentucky invasion, especially the inhuman treatment of his prisoners, but he was acquitted.

19. Simon Girty did marry Catharine Malott, but the wedding took place four years after he accompanied Bird's invasion of Kentucky. Girty died in 1816 in Canada, blinded by old age, and still bitter toward Americans.

20. Benjamin Logan, under orders from George Rogers Clark, attacked and destroyed Lorimer's Trading Store in November 1782. Lorimer barely escaped with his life.

21. Lorimer did go with the Girtys and the Shawnee to attack Boonesborough in 1777.

22. The majority of the captives who were taken beyond the Ohio became slaves to the British and Indians. Those who survived did not see Kentucky again until the signing of Mad Anthony Wayne's treaty on August 3, 1795. They had been captives for over fifteen years.

These are but a *few* of the actual happenings I uncovered and used in this story, while researching Ruddle's and Martin's Stations.

My brother David and I spent several days traveling the route taken by Bird when he drove the Kentuckians north to Lorimer's Store. We stood in the rain in a field beside the south branch of the Licking River that had been the site of Ruddle's Station two hundred years ago, and tried to envision the scene the Kentuckians faced that stormy morning in 1780.

Although it is on private property—and I thank the owners for granting David and me the privilege of trespass—there is, lying on its side and covered by honeysuckle, a stone monument erected over fifty years ago, commemorating the fort. Other than that, one would never know a massacre had happened there, so peaceful is the Kentucky countryside today.

Dave and I followed the Licking River to the Ohio, then traveled up the Ohio to the Big Miami River. We followed the Big Miami to the Pickawillany (Lorimer's) Creek, and up that creek to Lorimer's Fort, where the local librarian made a special effort to aid us in our search for the truth.

To fully appreciate what the Kentuckians underwent, one should follow in their footsteps. It is a marvel to me that any of them survived the trip, much less, as Morgan Patterson said, that they "stood up to be counted."

Don Wright